M000086144

Past Suspicion

Therese Heckenkamp

Ivory Tower Press

www.ivorytowerpress.com

© 2003, 2012 by Therese Heckenkamp

www.thereseheckenkamp.com

All rights reserved.

ISBN-10: 0615719325
ISBN-13: 978-0615719320

This is a work of fiction. All the characters, organizations, places, and events portrayed in this novel are either products of the author's imagination or are used fictitiously. Any resemblance to actual persons, living or dead, is entirely coincidental.

Scripture verses taken from the Douay-Rheims Holy Bible.

No part of this book may be reproduced, stored in a retrieval system or transmitted in any form or by any means without the prior written permission of the author, except by a reviewer who may quote brief passages in a review.

Cover design by Robin Ludwig Design Inc.
www.gobookcoverdesign.com
Cover photos: Ancient building under night sky © Rbv, Dreamstime.com; Portrait of a beautiful girl in the park in autumn © aleshin, Fotolia.com; Summer sunset © suerob, Fotolia.com; Lilac © saras66, Fotolia.com

Published by
Ivory Tower Press
www.ivorytowerpress.com

Printed in the United States of America

Past Suspicion

Awarded the

Catholic Writers Guild Seal of Approval 2012

Also by Therese Heckenkamp:

Frozen Footprints

www.frozen-footprints.com

To my sisters, Monica and Cassandra,
my very first readers.
And my mother,
who opened the wondrous world of books to me.

Living the past is a dull and lonely business;
looking back strains the neck muscles,
and causes you to bump into people
not going your way.

— Edna Ferber

Prologue

Lilacs . . . their sweet scent drifted into my nostrils, twirled through my mind, and disturbed my sleep. No matter. It had not been a sleep of rest anyway.

Images of spring, butterflies and blossoms bloomed in my mind, prodding at my memory. Thoughts came slowly. It occurred to me that my eyes were closed and that I should open them. But I didn't want to. It would take too much effort. And besides, I felt safe under the cover of my eyelids, seeing only what I wanted to see, and I had a foreboding that if I opened my eyes, I would regret it. But something was pulling at me, a sort of fear of the unknown, urging me to open them, and it was even stronger than the smell of lilacs. Too strong to resist.

So I gave in and opened my eyes.

Since then, I have not known peace.

My surroundings brightened, revealing that I was in a small white room, not unlike a hospital room. In fact—a wave of fear swept through me—it *was* a hospital room. My heart pounded against my chest as my brain asked, *What am I doing here?*

It was a question I could not answer. My mind refused to try.

I realized then that there were people in my room. But who were they? I didn't recognize their faces. My fear swelled. I tried to get ahold of myself, to understand what was going on, but my head hurt, felt disoriented. And I was hot. I could feel the sweat trickling down my forehead. My

9

body ached, and I couldn't distinguish one limb from another. Panic added to my fear.

The strangers were talking, but I couldn't make sense of their words; the syllables blended together into an undecipherable hum. I yearned for these people to be silent so I could ask what I so needed to know.

"Why—am I here?"

No answer.

Struggling up from my warm, moist pillow, I took a deep breath and spoke as loudly as I could.

"What's going on—why am I here?"

This time they heard me. "She's awake!" someone cried. Instantly, people were swarming over me, suffocating me. I wanted to push them away, but I didn't have the strength. I wished I hadn't said anything—wished I hadn't woken up. Dizziness and exhaustion overtook me, and forgetting my frustration, I fell back and closed my eyes.

~

A man's round face peered down at me through a halo of haziness. He spoke in a voice that, though gentle, held a note of urgency.

"Tiffany, how do you feel?"

I blinked to clear the haze. The face shimmered in and out of focus, but I could see he needed a shave and that his glasses were slipping off his nose. There was something oddly familiar about the man, but even though I knew I should know him, I couldn't identify the face. He knew me, but I didn't know him. That's when it hit me: I didn't know who I was.

"Am I . . . Tiffany?"

"Tiffany!" Behind the round glasses, alarm reflected in the man's eyes. "You don't remember?" For an awful second, I thought he was going to cry. Even though I couldn't remember who he was, I knew I didn't want to hurt him.

Still, I had to ask . . .
"Who am I?"

~

"It will come back. Just don't try so hard. Give it time."
That's what the doctor told me repeatedly over the next few
days. "You've had a bad accident. You need time to heal.
You have serious bruises and a broken leg, but you're a
lucky young lady to be alive."

I didn't feel lucky.

They told me about the accident, but since I was alone
when it happened, no one knew the details. They'd hoped I
would be able to fill them in. I tried to remember, but the
threads of memory were tangled in my mind, and the more I
tried to untangle them, the more tangled they became.

Was it a castle or a mansion? A bridge or a balcony? A
push or a fall?

Most disconcerting of all, when I began to remember, I
wasn't sure if I was actually remembering, or simply
recreating from the things they told me . . .

From the mansion's balcony I had a view of a lush lawn,
green as emeralds and sprinkled with brilliant flowers,
stretching to the horizon. Shrubs and trees encircled a rock
garden far below me. I leaned over for a better look. That's
when the vision changed to a nightmare. I heard a cracking
like the sound of splintering bone. The balcony's wooden
railing suddenly gave way, and I was falling, falling to those
rocks below.

While this memory meshed with what they told me about
the accident, I knew it wasn't complete. I felt as if I were
looking through a carefully focused lens. Outside the lens
was what I needed to see, but I didn't know how to take the
necessary step back to view my surroundings as they really
were.

People came to visit me. I was supposed to know them;
they said they were my friends. Everyone tried to cram my

head with memories I was supposed to have but didn't. A woman who owned a garden nursery brought me a pot of chrysanthemums tied in a yellow bow, claiming we were great friends and that I used to visit her after school. Mr. Stafford, editor of the local newspaper, said I worked at the paper as an intern. Now he wanted to interview me. Teachers, neighbors, friends . . . these people were hidden in the shadows of my past, and I struggled to bring them into the light.

Maybe I was trying too hard. Some things did come back, but gradually—in jumbled, disconnected pieces that floated about in my head, and I wasn't strong enough or fast enough to catch all the pieces and fit them together.

The round-faced man was my older brother—ten years older—and my only living relative. Our parents were dead, and had been for a long time. My father had died first: 1966, in the Vietnam War. I'd hardly known him because I was only five when he died. Seven years later my mother died, and my brother came home from college to look after me. Now he was twenty-eight and I was eighteen. These were the kinds of simple facts of my life that returned a little each day.

I began to recover, and I was looking forward to returning home and to school and to a normal life.

Then *he* came to see me.

He was a tall, dark young man with dark eyes. He was the one who had brought me the lilacs. He was handsome, but for some reason this frightened me. Something about his face, his chiseled features and deep eyes, was too intense. When our eyes met, I had to catch my breath. He told me he was my boyfriend; everyone else said he was my hero. For all I remembered of him, he certainly could be.

But I didn't want to believe it. My memory of him did not return and grow as it did with the others.

The young man tried earnestly to make me remember. But it was as if something in me did not want to remember. I dreaded seeing him, though I didn't know why. Since I couldn't justify these feelings to myself, I couldn't tell anyone else; I didn't know how to explain and didn't want anyone thinking I might be crazy on top of all my other worries.

I made the nurse take the lilacs away. I didn't want them in the room to remind me of him. I suddenly found myself praying more than I ever had in my life.

He came to see me as often as he could, always asking questions, his dark eyes probing, scrutinizing any response. He said he understood what I was going through, and he was gentle and patient with me, whispering words of encouragement.

But it didn't last. One night he accused me of only pretending not to know him.

Then he threatened me. He demanded something from me that I could not give him. I didn't know whether or not to believe the things he told me, and I didn't know what to do —I had nowhere to turn—because I feared what he might do. I was scared to believe him; I was scared not to believe him. All I wanted was for him to leave me alone.

But he wouldn't.

Things got worse. They got so bad that I could stand it no longer. So I made up my mind: no matter what it took, I was going to escape.

Chapter One

I know now why my mother kept her past a secret from me: she loved me. Keeping it secret was her way of protecting me. She must have thought what I didn't know couldn't hurt me. Too bad she didn't realize that what I didn't know just might end up hurting me the most . . .

My mind was as cluttered and disorganized as the people boarding the plane, cramming luggage into overhead compartments and stuffing it under seats. Since I didn't feel like talking, it was just my luck to get stuck sitting next to a man who began telling me his life story before we even left the gate. As if it wasn't going to be a long enough flight, I had to hear how he had been raised in a bubble (with only two other people) for some kind of seclusion-environment observation project, and you'd think he'd be shy, but—go figure—he just couldn't stop talking.

"So," he said amiably, "what about you? You look like a nice little girl. How old? Fourteen? Fifteen?"

"Eighteen," I said, to shock him. *It's almost the truth,* I reasoned, since my birthday was in less than three weeks.

He wasn't shocked, though. I wasn't even sure he'd heard me. "Visiting relatives in Wisconsin?" he asked.

Not feeling up to tackling that subject, I gave him a weak smile and mumbled an incoherent reply. In my head, I heard my mother's shrill voice reminding me to never talk to strangers, and I stared out the window to hide the moisture in my eyes.

Not that I saw anything out that window. My mind had no room for scenery. Thoughts which I'd wadded up like unwanted notes over the course of the past week began uncrumpling in my mind. Thoughts like, *My mother's too young to die. This can't be happening. It's too unexpected.* But meningitis, the doctor told me, happens like that. Unexpected. And it didn't matter how old you were or how much you had to live for.

Clattering and rattling, the drink cart rolled by. "Want anything, little lady?" asked Mr. Bubble. I shook my head.

What I wanted was to be left alone. That's what I'd told Mrs. Gills, my mother's lawyer, shortly after she informed me my mother had left instructions for me to go live with my uncle in Lorens, Wisconsin.

"What uncle?" I demanded. "I don't have an uncle."

"Oh yes, you do," said Mrs. Gills, giving me a patient, lipstick-laden smile, as if I were a child and of course she did not expect me to understand such complicated matters. "He's your mother's brother. The instructions are quite clear. As your only living relative, this uncle is now your guardian."

That's how I ended up on this plane, sitting next to Mr. Bubble and zooming away from my life in California to live under the control of a stranger—my mother had left "instructions."

She's gone, I thought, swallowing hard, *but she's still running my life.* All I wanted was to stay in California until I could figure out my future. Sure, I'd always wanted to travel, but I had in mind places like Paris, Egypt, South America, or Australia. Exotic places. Not a place called Lorens. *The town's probably so tiny,* I thought, *even a speck on a map would be an exaggeration.*

I turned to Mr. Bubble, who was entertaining himself by floating crushed pretzel pieces in a cup of tomato juice. "Have you ever heard of Lorens?"

"What's that? A town? A person?" Using his finger, he began stirring the pretzel juice mixture. "Nope, never heard of it."

I nodded, my suspicions confirmed. I was headed for the middle of nowhere.

After somehow swallowing his concoction, Mr. Bubble fell asleep and began snoring, an erratic *snort-snort* sound that almost made wonder if he needed some assistance from the oxygen mask.

To add to the noise, a baby started crying two seats ahead of me. Even from a mere back view of the mother's head, it was easy to tell she was stressed. Her hair looked as if she hadn't combed it in weeks, and not only that, it was in desperate need of a dye job.

I listened to the wailing while my heart hung heavy, feeling betrayed by my mother for forcing me on this lonely journey. I went over my plan, which I'd formed the day Mrs. Gills told me I had no choice in this matter because I was a minor. *I'll be eighteen soon, and when I get enough money, I'm going straight back to California.* Until then, I'd simply view my time in Lorens as something to be endured, like a sore throat or bad vacation. When it was over, I would forget all about it.

The baby stopped crying, and even Mr. Bubble's snoring subsided to a level that I could tune out, so I settled back against my seat and closed my eyes.

It seemed only a moment later that a voice over the loudspeaker announced we were landing at Mitchell International Airport. I roused myself and peered out over Milwaukee. Against my will, I was intrigued by the city's thousands of lights piercing the night, like stars below me instead of above.

We landed all too soon. I waited until Mr. Bubble pushed his way into line, then let several people pass me before I stood up, hoisting my carry-on bag, and joined them in filing out of the plane.

I'd expected my uncle to march up to me the instant I left the terminal, so I was surprised when, after the crowd of hugging people dispersed, I was left standing alone. I searched all the unfamiliar faces, but no eyes met mine. *So this is how it feels to be invisible,* I thought.

After a moment of waiting like this, I walked to a row of vacant seats and plopped down, even though my feet wanted to walk me right out of the airport and into the city, where my uncle would never find me. The idea was tempting, but since I'd never had a chance to do anything crazy like that before, I wasn't sure I had the nerve to pull it off.

As the minutes ticked away on my mother's watch—now my watch—I found it increasingly difficult to be patient. I studied the watch, the fading gold casement, the worn leather band, until my eyes became bored. Then I studied my wrist, the light golden hairs, the thin white scar running up the inside of my arm. Still my uncle did not come.

Did he even get the news? I wondered, running a hand through my blond hair. Maybe I'd end up waiting here all night. My heartbeat accelerated. I would give my uncle his chance, and if he didn't show up by morning—why, I *would* leave the airport—I'd find a job somewhere in Milwaukee and fend for myself. At least that would be exciting, much better than vegetating in Lorens. The more time passed, the more my hopes rose. Maybe this uncle really didn't exist.

"Robin?"

I looked up to see a short, middle-aged man hurrying toward me, and all my plans evaporated.

Yes, it's me—how did you guess? I thought wearily. *Maybe because I'm the only person waiting here?*

"I'm sorry I'm late. It took me longer to get here than I figured," he explained. His eyes shone behind the round glasses, and he smiled a big smile, making his face look very round. "I knew it was you right away. You look so much like your mother."

You can't be serious, I thought, raising an eyebrow. I knew I didn't look like my mother. Her hair was dark brown, for a start. We were different in a lot of other ways, too. But

17

I figured my uncle would discover that soon enough.

"I'm sorry about your mother," he said. "I know it's a hard time for you right now, but I'm glad you could come . . . I think you'll like Lorens."

At least one of us does. "It's nice to finally meet you," I said, trying to be polite despite my negative feelings. Then I stood up, shouldering my bag. My foot had fallen asleep, and I tried not to wince. As we walked, my mind moved on to my plan. I began wondering how I was going to get the money to return to California.

"Is there any place I can get a job in Lorens?" I asked. My mind flashed my stock vision of a tiny hick town with a gas station and maybe one McDonald's.

My uncle paused in retrieving my luggage. "There's no reason for you to get a job, Robin. You should just relax and have fun, make some friends, not be stuck indoors all summer—"

"I really want to work," I persisted. I had no intention of staying in Lorens all summer and certainly no desire to form ties to the place by making friends. "I need the money."

I followed my uncle through the poorly lit parking structure. With his back to me, I couldn't see his face. His words echoed when he spoke. "Well, if you want to work that bad, I've been planning on hiring someone to help me in my bookstore. You can have that job if you like."

Interested, but wary, I began weighing his offer in my mind, wanting to make sure this was a genuine deal. I climbed into his Oldsmobile and fished around for a seatbelt. I noticed a car freshener, the kind shaped like a pine tree, hanging from the rearview mirror, as well as a rosary. It reminded me of all the times my mother and I had prayed the Rosary together, almost every day. Lately, though, I hadn't been keeping up with that . . . I wondered if my uncle would have a set prayer time that he would expect me to keep.

But back to the business at hand. "What kind of work would I do?"

"A lot of different things," my uncle said, easing the car out of its parking place. "But I'm warning you, the work can get tedious." He glanced over his shoulder. "I buy and sell used books. There's a lot of material to keep track of, boxes to sort through, books to shelve, customers to take care of . . . That sort of thing. The store is open six days a week, nine to five."

It sounded like an easy job—better than flipping greasy burgers—but I still had to consider the most important detail. I darted a glance at my uncle, who appeared to be intent on driving. "How much would you pay me?"

"I'll start you at five an hour."

Considering the type of work, that sounded reasonable. And considering five dollars was probably worth a lot more in Wisconsin than in California, I figured I wouldn't get a better offer. This might be my only chance. Finding another job would take time, valuable time, and other teenagers were probably already staking out summer jobs—of which I didn't expect there to be an abundance in Lorens.

"You don't have to work every day," my uncle continued. "You can pick your own schedule. You'll want some time to have fun, too."

"Mm-hmm." Quickly calculating in my head, I realized that if I accepted the job and worked steadily, I could be back in California in less than a month.

"I'll take it," I said. "I want to start as soon as possible and I want to work every day."

"Except Sundays," my uncle added.

Yes, Sundays. Of course. *Keep holy the Lord's day,* I almost heard my mother whisper.

Our conversation ended there. I settled back for the ride, closing my eyes, and that made the silence more comfortable. The air freshener fragrance and the drone of the car soon put me to sleep, so that when we arrived in Lorens I had no idea how long it had taken us to get there.

I shivered when I stepped out of the car, and I was still

shivering two minutes later, inside the house. I was too groggy to see my surroundings. All I wanted to do was snuggle up in bed. My uncle, apparently concerned I might be hungry, offered me some cold leftover pizza.

"Uh—no thanks. Not hungry." I asked where my room was, and he told me it was upstairs, first door on the right.

"Let me take your luggage and I'll show you to it."

"That's okay." I had an intense need to be by myself. "I'll find it, but thanks."

Heaving two suitcases, I climbed the flight of creaky stairs alone. Somehow managing to trip on the edge of the carpet at the entrance to my room, I almost dropped the suitcases on my toes. But when I spotted the bed, I forgot to be annoyed. It stood against the wall, spread with a bright patchwork quilt and looking ridiculously cozy, like something out of *Little House on the Prairie*. I went over to it. Heat from a floor register wafted into the room, and I took my sandals off and let the warmth caress my feet. The rest of my body shivered as I got ready for bed.

Catching sight of a crucifix on the wall, I knelt beside the bed and managed an awkward prayer, finishing with, *Help me, dear Lord, to get back home.*

Moments later, I pulled the crisp sheets over my head and snuggled into a cocoon. As I drifted off to sleep, a clean, fresh scent filtered into my nostrils. *The detergent . . . clean sheets,* I thought, my mind relaxing. *Mmmm . . . smells like flowers, like lilacs . . . lilacs . . . ?*

~

I awoke the next morning to loud knocking on my door.

"Go away," I moaned. It couldn't be morning already; I'd only just fallen asleep.

"Robin? Are you awake? It's seven-thirty. Birds are singing. Time to get up for work."

Suddenly I remembered where I was. I moaned again, and this time I smacked my pillow. I hadn't realized I would have to work so soon. But then, I was the one who had insisted on starting right away.

"Are you sure you want to work?" my uncle called through the door, apparently reading my thoughts. "There's no reason you have to start today. You can sleep in if you want to."

Yeah, but you've already woken me up, I grumbled silently. Not a morning person, I had to force myself to sit up and open my eyes. "I'm up, I'm up," I called, disentangling myself from the sheets and trying not to sound nasty. "I'll be ready."

How dreary these next few weeks are going to be, I thought, shivering as I pulled on my socks. But I was determined to stick it out so as soon as I turned eighteen I could go home.

Ten o'clock that morning found me reminding myself of my resolution as I sat cross-legged among ragged cardboard boxes and piles of dusty books. Why had I assumed this would be an easy job? I'd been trying to sort and divide books into categorized piles for the last hour, and I wasn't getting anywhere. Besides that, I felt as if I were coated in dust. Every so often, I let out a good sneeze just to let my uncle know how I felt about being stuck away in this dingy corner with tall dark shelves surrounding me. I felt like a prisoner.

A familiar feeling. Something squeezed at my heart, and I knew what was coming. Closing my eyes, I blew the dust off another book. Memories came, overpowering me as I recalled times when my friends went places by themselves, and I couldn't go because my mother wouldn't let me out of her sight.

"Robin can't go anywhere without her mommy," the other kids would jeer before heading off to a friend's house, the park, or the mall.

It got harder as I got older. It's difficult to keep friends— let alone make new ones—when your mother is so

21

protective, needing to know exactly where you are, what you're doing, and who you're with, every second. I'm sure she would have homeschooled me if she hadn't had to work. At times I thought I would go crazy.

When I turned thirteen, my mother had made "the rule": no dating until I was eighteen. As much as I resented this rule, she needn't have bothered making it. No one wanted to date me.

I used to wonder if it was my looks. But my teeth were even and straight (and after enduring braces for three long years, they'd better be), so there was nothing wrong with my smile. My nose was sprinkled lightly with freckles, but you could hardly notice them unless I'd been out in the sun too long. And I'd heard my eyes called hazel, so that's what I'll say they are, even though they're just brown.

I knew I was nothing special to look at, but I'd seen plenty of guys going with girls no better looking than me. It didn't take me long to figure out what the matter was, and I didn't blame the guys. I blamed my mother. She scared them off. I wasn't just tied to her apron strings, I was strangled by them. My mother was gone now, and I knew I should forgive her, but it wasn't easy.

A jingling noise brought me back to the present, to my dreary corner, and it took me a moment to realize someone had entered the store. The first customer of the day. I crept out from my corner, curious as to what kind of person would bother to stop here. I figured it might be an old lady with time on her hands.

Book still in hand, I settled myself in front of the shelves. From here I had a view of my uncle. He had been bent over the front desk doing paperwork, but now he looked up as the customer entered.

I couldn't see the customer yet, so I watched my uncle's face. At first I thought he was going to smile, but his lips didn't follow through. Instead he stared, his eyes seeming to dilate into saucers behind his glasses. I heard the customer's footsteps coming closer, making a deliberate *slap, slap* sound on the wooden floor.

With surprise I saw the person was a man, not a woman; and he was young, not old (so my guess couldn't have been more wrong). I wondered why he was here. I could tell my uncle was wondering the same thing.

The man stopped at my uncle's desk and stood sideways to me. My uncle finally spoke. "Can I help you with something?" His voice was so low I could hardly make out his words.

Reaching into his back pocket, the man drew out his wallet and produced some sort of card. When he spoke, I could easily hear his words. "I'd like to introduce myself. I'm Justin Landers, a reporter for the *Lorens Daily Journal*."

Feeling secure in the knowledge that neither of the men noticed me in the shadows, I continued listening.

"I'm searching for a local interest story, and I wanted to know if you'd be willing to let me do a feature on your bookstore. Something on the history of the place and that sort of thing—"

"No," my uncle cut in.

The reporter continued talking. "Folks are always interested in stories with a local flavor, and my job's to give them what they want. But there's something in it for you, too. It'll bring your store to people's attention. That means more customers and—"

"I said no." My uncle did not raise his voice, but though I hardly knew him, I detected a warning note. I sucked in my breath.

The reporter glanced my way. He didn't seem surprised to see me, just lifted his eyebrows in an amused sort of way. I attempted a smile, and he returned it. Then for some reason, I looked down at the book in my hands.

In my mind, I could still see his face. It wasn't handsome —at least not like you would find in some teen magazine—

but there was something about it—some quality that made my heart skip a beat—something about the angular profile, dark hair and eyebrows and bold eyes, that made me look again. I found myself wishing I could see what color his eyes were, but the lighting in the bookstore wasn't bright enough. Besides, he was too far away. And no longer looking at me.

The men continued talking, and I returned to the book in my hands, pretending to read it, though I was really listening to every word they said.

"It's my decision to make, correct?" my uncle asked. Then, without waiting for an answer, "I've decided I'm not interested."

"I'm sorry to hear that, sir, and I'm sorry to have bothered you." I felt the reporter glance my way again, but I kept my eyes glued to the book. To this day, I don't know what the book was about.

"I should have called first, but I guess I was so sure you'd jump at a chance like this. Most people do."

"I'm not most people," my uncle said calmly, tapping a pen against his desk, "and I'm quite happy with the business I have."

I frowned. What business? I knew it wasn't my place to say anything, but I didn't understand my uncle's attitude. His store was about as desperate for business as I was for a ticket home.

"I wish I knew why you're so against the idea," the reporter said.

There was an uncomfortable pause, and I got the strange feeling that if I weren't there listening, my uncle would have had a lot more to say. As it was, he only glanced at me before returning his attention to the reporter. "Odd that you should come here today. I've had this bookstore for ages."

"Well, the older the better," the reporter replied, a lift to his voice. "More of a history to the place."

"That's not what I meant."

The discussion sounded innocent enough on the surface,

but I sensed an undercurrent of hostility. I was half hoping for an argument to break out when my uncle walked to the door. The reporter followed him, yet I got the impression he wasn't admitting defeat. When he spoke, there was confidence—almost defiance—in his voice. "If you're sure you won't change your mind—"

"Quite sure." My uncle opened the door.

"Here's my card—"

"Quite sure," my uncle repeated, not taking the card.

"Then I guess I'm going to have to search elsewhere for a story." The reporter glanced at me again, and this time I met his eyes. They were asking me something. But I couldn't reply. I didn't understand what they were asking, or why a sense of urgency swept over me. "So long," he said, and I wanted to call, "Wait!"—but he was already gone.

My uncle remained by the closed door, a somber expression clouding his face. Eventually he turned, and his eyes met mine. I sensed a challenge.

I don't know what came over me. I leapt to my feet, dust flying and the book falling from my hands, and marched to the front of the store.

"Why wouldn't you let him do the story?" Something warned me I was using this outburst unfairly to take my accumulated anger and grief from the past stressful week out on someone—anyone—but I couldn't stop myself. "I'd think if you cared anything at all about this store you—you'd jump at the chance he just offered you!" I realized too late that I'd stumbled into the same trite phrase the reporter had used.

"It's not the story he's after," my uncle said quietly.

I opened my mouth, ready to make a curt reply, then shut it. How could I reply to something I didn't understand?

My uncle didn't offer to elaborate, however, and suddenly I didn't care what he meant; I was sick of trying to understand people. No one ever gave me answers to anything. At that moment, I felt about as insignificant as an ant on the floor, and all I wanted was to get away, out from under people's big trampling feet.

The door was right in front of me. I took one glance at my uncle—now back at his desk, scratching away with pen on paper—then sent the bells jingling madly as I yanked open the door and made my escape.

Chapter Two

$\mathcal{I}$ took a deep breath of fresh air and, contrary to popular belief, this did not help to calm me. I spotted a diner across the street and found myself thinking how hungry I was.

Thinking about food when I was upset made me feel ridiculous, but I couldn't help myself—I hadn't eaten since yesterday afternoon. And since that was airline food, I wasn't sure it counted.

As I moved to step off the sidewalk, I caught sight of a man leaning comfortably against the next building, looking as if he didn't have a thing to do. It was the reporter.

I bit my lip. Obviously, he'd been standing there ever since he left the bookstore. I paused with one foot on the sidewalk, one foot on the road. Could he have overheard my outburst? I hoped not, because suddenly I realized how childish it would have sounded.

At that moment, he turned and caught my eyes on him. His eyes worked like a magnet, pulling me in his direction. When he smiled, I got the feeling he'd been expecting me.

"Hi there," he said.

"Hi." Attempting to avoid an awkward silence, I said the first thing that came to mind. "I thought you'd be after another story by now."

I wished I had kept my mouth shut. The statement sounded terribly lame, like a line out of a corny detective movie. Then I wondered if he'd even heard me. I waited for him to speak, but he just stood there looking at me. Strangely. I became conscious of my beating heart as I tried to avoid his eyes. Maybe he sensed my uneasiness, because he finally shifted his gaze and answered.

"It's difficult to find anything interesting going on in a small town like this." He squinted across the street. "But it's my job to dig something up. Something hot but local—you can probably see why I've got problems." He turned to face me again. "But don't get me wrong—I like a challenge."

I scanned the quiet streets. A few cars were parked beside a cumbersome row of mismatched apartments. Not many people were outside. Across the street, a mother pushed a stroller past The Perfect Petal Florist Shop. One car drove by. A bearded man stepped into a comic shop. I realized that all the kids would be at school this time of day. I thought of the high schoolers, who probably had a prom coming up. Back home, my high school prom would be in a few days, then graduation. I was going to miss them both. Sure, I'd finished school, but in a very rushed, informal way; there would be no commencement ceremony for me. I sighed.

"Something wrong?"

I practically jumped. Then I wanted to disappear. I couldn't believe I'd done that—drifted off into my thoughts, forgetting he was standing there. This time I didn't blame him for looking at me strangely.

It took all my composure to answer without tripping over my words. "No—" I took a deep breath, thinking, *Change the subject*—"I don't know why my uncle is so set against letting you write your story."

The reporter wasn't staring anymore. Relieved, I told myself to stop being paranoid, that it's perfectly normal for people to look at each other when they talk. I moved a little closer to where he stood so that my uncle wouldn't see me if he happened to look out the front window.

"So he's your uncle, huh?" As the reporter leaned against the brick wall in that relaxed way of his, I could almost imagine him with a cigarette between his lips. It would suit him somehow.

"That's right," I replied, wondering if he cared or if he was just trying to be polite. I darted a look over my shoulder at the bookstore, almost expecting my uncle to emerge and drag me back inside, as my mother surely would have done if she'd caught me talking to a stranger. "I just started working for him. I used to live with my mother, but she died . . . I'm new in Lorens. I just got here last night—" I stopped, shocked to see he had pulled out a pocket notebook and was recording my words. And why had I been flooding my life story out to him anyway?

"What are you doing?" I cried. "Why are you writing down what I'm saying?"

"Don't be alarmed," he said, glancing at me and almost laughing. "You sound like Eliza Doolittle—"

"What?" I took a step backward, beginning to think my mother's rule about talking to strangers was a good one.

"You know—in *Pygmalion?* By Shaw?"

"Who?"

"George Bernard Shaw. He wrote *Pygmalion.* Doesn't register, huh? You've never read the play? Not even in school?" He frowned. "I'm surprised. It's a good story . . . *My Fair Lady* is based on it—surely you've seen that? Well, anyway, there's this guy standing on a street corner recording what everyone's saying and—" He stopped. "Heck, your uncle's got a bookstore—go find a copy and read it."

Pygmalion. How typically Wisconsin sounding. Probably about a pig farm. The subject wasn't worth pursuing, but he still hadn't answered my question. I hesitated, not sure what to think. "So why were you writing down what I was saying?"

"What makes you think I was? Ever heard of a thing called a grocery list? But, come to think of it, maybe I could use you for a story." He held his pencil poised. "You say you're new here? All right, first give me the facts: name, age, where you're from, and what you think of our little town."

The thought of anyone wanting to read my boring life story struck me as so ludicrous I had to laugh. My tension melted. "I'm not telling you anything—not until you put that notebook away."

"All right, all right." He stuffed the notebook into his front shirt pocket and tucked the pencil behind his ear. "If you're not going to take this seriously, I guess I won't either. But I'm warning you—" he held up his finger, ink stained, I noticed—"you just passed up a chance to be front-page news."

"Someone new arrives in town . . . that's front-page news? Wow," I said, shaking my head, "this town must really be boring."

"Don't let it fool you, though," the reporter said. "Every town's got something to make it unique. Local legends. Buried history. Something in its past that you wouldn't expect."

He was watching me. Were his eyes narrowed in contemplation or merely squinting against the sun? Our eyes met, and I felt again as if he were trying to ask me something . . . without words. Uncomfortable, I moved my eyes. "Like what?"

As if he hadn't heard me—or maybe because he had—he looked across the street. An unsettling silence followed. I shifted on my feet.

"It's getting hot standing here." The reporter straightened. "Were you headed anywhere special?"

My heartbeat quickened. "I was maybe going to get some lunch."

"Sounds like a good idea to me. Mind if I join you?"

I knew I should say, "Yes, I do mind." I sensed something not quite right about this guy. Something "shady," as my mother would say. Yet part of me was attracted to him. And part of me argued that, after all, he wasn't a complete stranger. We'd been talking together for the past ten or fifteen minutes. I also couldn't help being flattered that this guy, who must be at least twenty-two, was even bothering to talk to me. Could it be that he was just the tiniest bit interested? I hoped so. And I didn't want to brush him off because I was sure I wouldn't get another offer.

I could almost hear my mother saying, *Don't you dare go with him!* But I told myself, *Lighten up.* I couldn't go around being like my mother, suspicious of everyone I met. This was my decision to make, and my mother couldn't interfere. Not anymore . . .

"All right," I agreed, my tone subdued.

So we crossed the street together, and I hoped my uncle *was* looking out the window. I wanted him to understand that I intended to make my own decisions here in Lorens, and I held my head slightly higher than was necessary.

"By the way, my name's Justin Landers."

"I know. I mean—I heard—" I dropped into silence, feeling awkward.

"And you are?" he urged.

Stupid. I felt my ears grow warm. *I don't even have the sense to introduce myself.* "Robin Finley."

"Robin, as in Wisconsin's state bird?"

Lighthearted as the question was, it set me thinking. My real name was Roberta, but if anyone called me that, I probably wouldn't answer. Robert was my father's name, and the nickname Robin had come from him . . .

I blushed, realizing how long it was taking me to answer. "No," was all I could say.

"Well, nice to meet you, Robin. Just call me Justin."

I smiled. "Okay."

Justin held open the door of a place called Mary Anne's Diner. "I eat here a lot," he said. "I think you'll like it."

From the outside it didn't look like much. Kind of like a trailer home without wheels. The windows were trimmed in gaudy purple. But I was happy to be here. Maybe because it was new to me.

No. The truth was, I was happy because I was here with Justin. I'd been waiting so long for this kind of freedom that I'd almost given up hoping. Here at last was my chance to relax and hang out like a normal teenager, with someone who didn't know my mother and couldn't be scared away by her nunnery rules.

Inside, the diner was empty except for an old couple and a large, greasy looking man sitting on a stool at the front counter. I didn't care where we sat as long as it wasn't next to him. An old jukebox stood in a corner, but it didn't fool me; the music played from a boombox hidden behind the counter.

We sat in a corner booth near a window. The whole front of the diner was lined with windows. When Justin took off his black leather jacket and draped it over the seat before sitting down, I was surprised at how tan his arms were, as tan as his face. I imagined him as an outdoors kind of person. Someone who does something outdoors, who doesn't just lie on a beach all day.

I picked up a worn menu and made myself focus on the prices, meaning I searched for the cheapest. I could get something called a Bitty Burger for seventy-five cents, but it didn't sound very dignified.

I'd just decided to spring two dollars for a chicken sandwich when a waitress ambled up to us, her hair coming loose from her ponytail.

"All right," she said, pulling a notepad out of her coffee-stained apron, "what can I get you folks?"

Justin looked at me. "What do you think? The Diner Special sounds good, doesn't it?" I had no idea because I hadn't looked at it, but Justin didn't wait for my reply. "We'll have two Diner Specials and a pitcher of lemonade," he said with confidence. Too much confidence.

"You don't even know if I like lemonade," I said as soon as the waitress left.

"If you don't, you should learn to," Justin replied. "It's

the only drink they serve that's any good." He leaned closer to me. "I know, I've tried them all. The coffee's like mud, the milk's usually warm, the soda's flat, and the water's boring. I'm telling you—I'm surprised they actually remember to add sugar to their lemonade."

I caught the twinkle in his eyes—brown eyes—and picked up the game. "I thought you said this was a good place to eat. If the drinks are that bad, who knows what they'll serve us to eat?"

As we waited for our food, I couldn't help noticing that though Justin's nose was kind of big, it suited his face. I also noticed the pencil was gone from behind his ear, and I wondered where it went. Then I realized I was staring. Glad Justin couldn't read my thoughts, I turned away to study a picture that was hanging, slightly crooked, on the wall beside us. It was a watercolor painting of a flower. A bright, garish thing, and I almost cringed. That was not the way to use watercolors, which are a gentle, translucent medium. Of course, I was no expert, but I'd done enough watercolor painting in California to feel like I knew a thing or two.

Drawing was my real passion though. When I could get away from my mother, which wasn't often, I liked to head out to the dunes on the beach—just me and my pencils and sketchpad.

And I don't mean the crowded, public beaches but the hidden, secluded ones. The ones where the gulls aren't used to people, and they fly away when you approach. That's the way I liked them. Wild. The way they're meant to be. Not like the gulls on the public beaches, where the tourists turn them into greedy, snack-craving creatures.

On those dunes, it was just me and nature. My mother would have had a fit if she knew. Sometimes I'd just sit and do nothing. Only . . . it wasn't nothing, because it was times like this that I felt I was really doing something. When the moment was right, I would pick up my pencil and draw. Lost in the process, I would feel free, happy. I could almost feel that sea breeze now, tousling my hair.

"That must be some picture," Justin said, breaking into my thoughts. "Personally, I think it's ugly."

I smiled and turned back to him. "It is."

After the waitress brought us our pitcher of lemonade, she returned with two plates heaped high with food. Fearing my stomach was about to growl, I said a quick silent blessing and dug in hungrily.

"So, Robin," Justin began, "forgive me if I'm applying the five W's: who, what, when, why, and where? But I am a reporter. That's what I do." I looked up from my meal as he asked, "How old are you?"

"That's a 'how,' not a five W's question."

"True. You're perceptive," he said, "but humor me."

"Eighteen." I hesitated. It wasn't a lie and yet it wasn't the truth, and for some reason I felt compelled to tell those dark brown eyes the truth. Justin was no Mr. Bubble. "In two weeks," I added.

"So you have a birthday coming up, huh?" There was a slight pause before he asked, "What do you want?"

There was only one thing I wanted and, surprisingly, I told him.

"To go home."

"Home? I thought you live here now. With your uncle."

"Only temporarily. That doesn't make it my home." I felt suddenly let down, disappointed that he'd jumped to conclusions like everyone else, assuming I was going to stay wherever I was sent, like a child, and spend the rest of my life in a dinky little town that had dinky diners and served such a thing as a Bitty Burger. How depressing.

"I guess not . . . but then where is home?"

"California."

"Really? You'd want to live in a huge crazy place like California all by yourself?"

"What's wrong with that?"

"I just thought—since your parents are dead—you'd

need a relative to live with."

I tilted my head slightly. "How do you know both my parents are dead? I only told you my mother is."

Justin didn't answer right away. "You've got me there," he admitted. "I suppose I just assumed. Or it was a good guess. Something about you . . ." He ran a hand through his hair. "I don't know . . . made me think you're used to being pretty much on your own. And you said you lived with your mother. You never mentioned a father."

"You're right," I said, feeling defeated. "He's dead."

"I'm sorry."

I managed a smile. "That's okay." *May they both rest in peace,* my mind whispered. I poked a fork at my potato salad. "I never really knew my father . . . he died a long time ago." My mother had told me about the accident, but never in detail. I didn't want details. They wouldn't change anything.

There was silence, until I realized something else Justin had said. "And I don't need to live with a relative. At least not once I turn eighteen. I'm only staying here now because I don't have a choice. But once I save enough money, I'm going back to California." The words came out sharper than I'd intended.

"I see." But the slight degree of coolness in his voice told me he didn't.

I hurried on, trying to make him see things my way, because suddenly it mattered. "I don't even know my uncle —my mother never told me she had a brother. Why should I stay here when I grew up in California? That's my home!"

My face felt hot, and I took a quick gulp of lemonade, only to succeed in choking on it. When I'd finished coughing, Justin spoke as if he hadn't noticed what a fool I'd made of myself. I wasn't sure whether to be grateful to him or not.

"So how are you going to get the money to go back?"

"I told you, I work at my uncle's bookstore." I shrugged.

"I'll earn enough eventually."

"And your uncle doesn't care if you go back?"

"Why should he?"

"He's your uncle."

"So?" Quietly, I continued. "I don't know him, and he doesn't know me."

"Couldn't you get to know each other?"

"Sure, but I'm leaving as soon as I can—probably in less than three weeks—so what's the point?" I knew it sounded heartless, but I'd gotten by quite well for seventeen years not knowing my uncle existed. Why should I need him now?

"I guess I just don't understand your reasons. At least here you have an uncle. Who do you have in California?"

No one. My mother had seen to that. But I didn't need anyone. I could take care of myself. Why was that so difficult to comprehend?

"My home's in California. That's where I grew up, and that's where I want to live." Why couldn't Justin agree with me, or at least see my point of view? I had a feeling he liked arguing.

"You were born in California?" Justin leaned back and waited—smugly, I thought—as if he already knew the answer.

"No." I felt the heat rushing to my cheeks again. I was born in Colorado. My mother and I had moved to California after my father died. But that was none of Justin's business. "A home is a place where you live—a place you love," I defended myself. "It doesn't have to be the place where you were born."

"Well said."

Apparently, the debate was over. I tried to relax, but there was no retrieving the comfortable atmosphere. The food no longer appetized me, and I was relieved when the waitress came to deliver the bill. I reached for it, but Justin was quicker; he snatched it from under my fingers and pulled away when I leaned over to see.

"I need to know how much I owe."

"No you don't," Justin replied. "It's my treat."

But the novelty of this outing had worn off. I was weary of Justin's questions and his arguments. Why should he even want to pay for me? It wasn't as if we'd been on a date. If I let him pay, I would feel as if I owed him, and I certainly didn't want to be in his debt.

"I can pay for myself," I insisted.

"You're stubborn," he said, grinning, "but so am I." He pulled out his wallet. "Besides, you have to save every penny if you want to get back to California. The sooner the better. Hey, I *should* use you for a story; it would make a great headline: 'Robin can't wait to leave Wisconsin and fly back to California.'"

I didn't smile. Now I knew why he was paying for me: I was his entertainment. A quick laugh, then goodbye. *Fine,* I thought, *but I'm not taking the bait. I'm not playing your game.* With great effort, I bit back a reply as he laid down some bills and stood up.

Outside, I blinked against the sunlight, a blinding white reflecting off the sidewalk. I wished I had my sunglasses.

"You know," Justin said, "this town isn't bad. In fact, there are a lot of good things about it; but you need to see it to appreciate it. Better yet, you need to live here. I know. I've lived in big cities, and I'd take Lorens any day."

"That's your choice." I squinted across the street at the bookstore.

"What would you say if I asked you to let me show you around town? If you just got here last night, you couldn't have seen much of it."

I turned back to Justin in surprise. He was acting as if we were good friends, but despite the meal, we were still only casual acquaintances. And what was it I saw in his eyes? It was something normal people don't have: a look of speculation, but more than that. Not a carefree sparkle or shine, but a hungry glint.

"I would say no." I spoke without a hint of expression. I was too confused to know how I should sound. I began to edge away. "Look, it was great meeting you and everything and I enjoyed the lunch, and thank you for paying, but I really have to get back to work now."

"Good answer." He looked normal again, almost made me wonder if I'd imagined the glint in his eyes. "Do you realize you don't really know me? It's not a good idea to go anywhere with a stranger. You can't trust strangers . . . Keep that in mind."

Even outside in the bright sunlight, his words started something cold creeping up my spine. I couldn't figure him out—and I wasn't sure I wanted to. But it was like he wasn't on his own side all the time, like he switched back and forth inside himself, almost like two people.

"Goodbye," I said.

To my immense relief, Justin began to walk away. "See you later, Robin," he called, lifting his hand in a wave, "and remember what I said."

I didn't reply. I turned quickly and crossed the street, forgetting to check for traffic. My mind was murky with his strange words; there was no danger of my forgetting them.

And he had said, "See you later."

I hoped he wasn't serious.

Chapter Three

I slipped back into the bookstore as if nothing had happened. My uncle, still at his desk, barely looked up when I entered. "Finally ready to get back to work?" he asked.

I waited for him to say more.

When he didn't, I returned to my box of books, confused. Whatever reaction I'd expected from him, this wasn't it. I guess I'd been prepared for some kind of battle, and now without one, the bookstore's silence felt like an anticlimax. Obviously, my uncle hadn't seen me with Justin.

I hung around in the back of the bookstore feeling like a shadow. I didn't understand how my uncle could claim he needed me here, because I didn't think I was doing anything very useful. I sorted through boxes, stacked books into categorized piles, shelved some, and even dusted the bookcases. But these tasks were nothing my uncle couldn't have managed. It wasn't as if the store was overrun with customers.

By three o'clock, only two more people had stopped in. One was a flustered looking woman who had been cleaning her attic and wanted to get rid of an old box of books; the other was an elderly lady who called me "sweetie."

Time passed slowly. I found myself looking at my watch every ten minutes. Then, sorting through the donated box, I discovered a Victoria Holt novel. The memory came back to me of lonely Friday nights—nights when other teens were out on dates—when I'd curl up in bed with one of these Gothic suspense novels, telling myself I didn't care that I wasn't out too. And once I started reading, I didn't care.

With its yellow, tattered pages, the book I held in my hands looked as if it had been read many times. I opened it carefully but the spine still crackled. I read the first chapter. Then I was hooked, as I'd known I would be. A good book was just what I needed to divert my mind from my disturbing morning. I shouldn't have talked to Justin; I knew that now. Settling in a back corner, I shoved all thoughts of him to the most remote section of my mind. Dim light filtering through a dirty slice of window created the ideal reading atmosphere, and I was soon absorbed in another world.

About halfway through the second chapter, bells jingled into my consciousness, breaking the book's spell by announcing another customer's arrival. I grumbled to myself and moved farther back in the corner, although my cobweb-laden hair and clothes later proved what a mistake *that* was.

Because my uncle was still at his desk, and therefore technically "busy," I knew I should go see if the customer wanted help. But I stayed where I was. A moment later, I wasn't surprised to hear my uncle call, "Robin, we have a customer," which I figured was his polite way of saying, "Get out here and help."

I closed my book, committing the page number to memory, and set it on the windowsill. If this customer turned out to be half as fussy as the one who'd come in earlier, I wouldn't get a chance to return to the book for quite some time.

Now, the way I saw it, the chances of meeting two good-looking guys in one day in the same obscure bookstore were virtually nonexistent, so I was genuinely startled to discover this customer was a tall, blond-haired young man.

I couldn't help wondering if he had perhaps wandered into the wrong store. Maybe it was just the effect of his dashing bandit's mustache (honest, on him it looked awesome), but I found it impossible to picture him reading a book—at least not for pleasure. What was he doing here?

When he smiled at me, I had to reach out and take hold

of the edge of the closest bookshelf. "Hi," I said, slightly breathless, "can I help you?"

"Sure can," he replied, and for some crazy reason, I blushed. My eyes darted to my uncle, but he was once again absorbed in his papers. Gladly, I returned my gaze to the customer and found myself thinking how odd that I, who'd almost never spoken to a guy for more than two minutes—let alone without swarms of people around—had spent the morning with a good-looking guy, and now I was meeting another. This guy was more handsome than Justin, I noted, and bound to be less weird.

I broke out of my thoughts to realize he was speaking. "I was thinking of picking up a mystery book. Something that'll keep me awake at night. Got anything that would qualify?"

"Of course." I turned to lead the way. "They're here in back." I led him to the last aisle, glad that I had dusted the shelves. "Are you looking for any title in particular?"

"No, I think I'll browse."

So there was no reason for me to hang around. "Just tell me if you need any help," I said, thinking, *At least I have my book to keep me company.* As I picked it up, the young man turned to face me.

"What do you have there?"

I held it out for him to see. "I just started reading it," I said, not knowing why I was telling him this.

His eyes skimmed the jacket. "Romantic suspense . . ." His eyes met mine with bold directness. "That's what you like to read?"

I tightened my hold on the book. "Maybe," I said. "I like it so far." This guy was making conversation, and I told myself his attention should make me happy, but instead, a strange weariness swept over me. I was tired of answering questions that were no one else's business.

The man was still talking. ". . . adventure and treasure and far away places . . . Those things are great in books, but they're even better in real life." A knowing smile spread across his face. "Some people sit around and dream about those things." He paused, looking me straight in the eye. "Other people go out and find them."

I blinked. What a strange thing to say. I was about to ask him what he meant, but suddenly I didn't need to. The words slid together and made sense, perhaps simply because he had spoken them.

It must have been the mustache. I'd seen handsome heroes wearing mustaches like that in old movies. It made me imagine this guy as some kind of an adventurer, almost like someone out of a book himself. A buccaneer. Maybe even a prince. He had a look about him that suited the past, the time of pirates and treasure and treasure maps.

"Oh, any old book will do, I guess." He pulled a leather-bound volume from the shelf and gave me an amused smile, in which his lip lifted slightly and one corner of his mouth turned up. On anyone else it would have looked like a sneer. "You don't talk much, do you?"

I raised my chin. "That depends on whether I have anything to say." I saw he was holding a copy of Daphne du Maurier's *Jamaica Inn*, a book I had read and enjoyed very much. I nodded toward it. "Do you want to buy that?"

"Is it any good?"

"I liked it."

"Will I?" His gray eyes glinted teasingly.

"How should I know? I don't know you."

"You could get to know me."

I ignored his words, though I knew my face, growing warmer every second, gave me away. "You won't know whether you like it until you read it."

"You're so serious," he said, "but very logical." Was that supposed to be a compliment? "I'll probably never read this." He tossed the book into the air and made an impressive catch. "I never read books for pleasure."

I raised my eyebrows, but I'd caught the humor in his

eyes and couldn't help smiling. I wondered if my uncle had seen the book sailing through the air. "Then why in the world did you waste your time coming here?"

"Ah, but it wasn't a waste of time," he said solemnly. "I met you, didn't I?"

The meaning of his words was unmistakable. Unfortunately, I had no idea how to answer, no skill in this sort of situation as I knew some girls did. I'd hear them flirting in the halls and in the lunchroom, and I always wondered how the girls knew exactly what to say. If they learned it in high school, it was in a class I never took. Again, I ignored his words.

But I was attracted to him. He'd already proven himself friendly and funny, not to mention handsome, and I wanted him to like me. *Don't get carried away,* I warned myself. *You don't even know him.* Now I wasn't thinking logically . . . all friends start off as strangers. *All people are strangers until you get to know them. If I never give anyone a chance, I'll never have any friends,* I thought, completely forgetting my resolution to remain friendless in this town.

"I saw you come in here this morning. I rent one of those shacks across the street," he explained. For a moment I was confused. My mind didn't flash a picture of any shacks across the street. Surely I would have noticed—

All at once, I realized he was exaggerating.

"I usually see the old guy come in by himself. But today you were with him, and I thought to myself, 'Hey, there's a pretty girl I'd like to meet.'"

"He's my uncle," I explained, ignoring the fact that I was blushing again.

With a little prompting, he got me to tell him the whole story of why I was here in Lorens and what I was doing working in this bookstore. I glanced around our dim surroundings and attempted a laugh. "This sure wasn't my choice, coming here."

"Kinda like a dungeon, isn't it?"

"Yes. Exactly." *At least he understands me,* I thought, *and doesn't challenge my every word. Unlike a certain reporter.*

He told me his name was Philip Barnstrum, and that he was new in town, too. Why was he here? Simply because he'd never been here before. I liked that.

"But I don't know how long I'll be staying," he said. "Depends on when I get the urge to move. I never stay in one place very long if I can help it. There are too many places to go, things to do and see . . . if you know what I mean."

I knew exactly what he meant.

It was amazing, the strong response Philip evoked in me. He knew just what to say. Listening to him talk about places he'd been, I couldn't help envying him his freedom. But I'd be eighteen soon. I just had to keep reminding myself that. Soon I'd be free to do whatever I pleased. Though just what I wanted to do, I wasn't sure yet. My dreams did not lie in the direction of math or science or other cataloged disciplines. But I did love my art.

"A waste of time," my mother had insisted, but I knew it wasn't. Now, the full reality of my impending freedom sent my blood surging with new force.

I forgot to be defensive and actually enjoyed talking to Philip; he made it easy by asking most of the questions. Not questions like he was drilling me, but conversational questions, asked by someone who had a natural, friendly interest in me. Relaxing, I leaned against a bookshelf and even made some of the books fall. Both scrambling to pick them up, Philip and I knocked heads. After the stars cleared, we laughed.

By the time I realized the narrow shaft of sunlight on the floor had shifted into oblivion, I felt as if I'd known Philip for years.

"So, do you want to buy the book?" I finally asked, reluctant to end the conversation and see Philip go. But I was aware of my uncle at the front desk, and though he couldn't see me, he probably knew I hadn't been talking books all this time. I was afraid my uncle might not pay me for my time if I didn't start working. And anyway, if the vibes I was getting were correct, this wouldn't be the last time I'd see Philip.

"I sure do. Like I said, I'll probably never read it, but if I want to, it'll be there."

"That's what I like about books," I said, walking to the front of the store to ring up the sale. "They're reliable. Not like people."

Philip smiled, showing perfect teeth. "Well, here's something you can rely on: I'll be seeing you again soon, and that's a promise." He took the book, flashed me one last worthy-of-treasuring smile, and left.

From where I stood at the cash register, I watched him through the front window as he disappeared down the street. I was sorry he hadn't asked for my phone number. Then I smiled, realizing I didn't even know my number. No matter. Philip would find me again if he wanted to. Of that I had no doubt.

"You know that young man?" my uncle asked, looking up from his desk across the room. His tone sounded impartial enough, but it didn't fool me. The question still resembled the start of one of my mother's cross-examinations.

"I do now," I said.

Chapter Four

*P*hilip Barnstrum. Throughout the day I thought of his name, and it never failed to set my pulse quickening. I didn't even try to tell myself I wasn't eager to see him again.

Now that I'd found someone to relate to, I no longer felt like a prisoner, and the self-pity I'd felt earlier vanished. As the day wore on, I even began to feel like being nicer to my uncle. The truth was, I felt ashamed of the way I'd treated him. He didn't deserve the grudge I was holding against him; it wasn't my uncle's fault that I'd had to come to Lorens. Since he was my only living relative, I guess he hadn't had a choice in the matter, either. Maybe he hated my being here as much as I did.

But he didn't seem to.

As my uncle and I walked homeward that evening after locking the store at exactly five o'clock, I had my chance to start a conversation and set things right between us. Only problem was, I didn't know what to say. So we walked on without speaking, our footsteps making a dull rhythm on the sidewalk.

I turned my attention to the scenery, the quaint homes and yards. I saw a veranda that looked set up for company with charming white wicker furniture and a wooden porch swing. The house itself reminded me of an overgrown dollhouse. Little colored glass bottles stood lined up in the front window, glimmering. On her knees, a woman whistled a merry tune while working in her front garden. Most lawns were sprinkled with bright dandelions, and blossoming trees and bushes grew everywhere. Palm trees were the only thing missing.

When we passed a blooming wall of lilacs, my eyes were drawn to the purple clusters of little star-shaped flowers. Their fragrance floated into my nostrils and stirred my memory. It was what had touched me last night when I had smelled the clean sheets. But I had fallen asleep too quickly to grasp it, this something that had been lingering in the back of my mind for more than a week . . .

I had been with my mother that last evening when a nurse entered the hospital room with a bunch of lilacs. Someone had sent them to my mother as a gift. The card read: *From an old friend*. That was all. It had puzzled me for a moment, and then I had forgotten about it. Greater worries were on my mind. My mother had grown worse. The doctor had done all he could, and I knew my mother was dying. I called our priest, and he came to give her the Last Rites.

I stayed by my mother's side all that night, praying desperately as she wandered in and out of consciousness, mumbling strange things. Sitting beside her, listening, I wondered where she was. It sounded like she was far away, in another place and time, but every once in a while her mind floated back to me.

"Robin?" she'd say, and I would take her icy hand, as if by doing this I could keep her thoughts with me. "I'm sorry —so sorry. I tried . . ." And she'd be gone again.

I stroked the damp, dark hair back from her forehead, the way she used to stroke my hair when I was little.

"Christopher?" my mother called out desperately. "Robert?"

Robert was my father. Who was Christopher?

"Please . . . just away, away . . . "

She didn't speak again for so long that when she did, I had no idea whether or not she was on the same train of thought.

"No—I don't—stop!—you're scaring me!"

I drew my hand away from her forehead. She was scaring *me*.

47

Lord, help her.

At one point, I must have been dozing. My heart jumped when she grabbed my hand and whispered, "Don't trust anyone . . . He wants it . . . won't ever give up . . ."

I could hardly be human if I said her words didn't frighten me, there in the dead of night with medical machines blinking red lights in the blackness of the room.

". . . take care of you . . . let him . . ." Her words dissolved into a sigh. In the darkness, I saw the whites of her eyes, saw them glaze over before closing.

"Peter, I know it's growing like a weed . . . rhubarb always does . . ."

The name Peter meant nothing to me. It meant as much as all her other delirious rambling. Christopher and Peter— were they the names of people from her past? I had no way of knowing. Was she reliving some part of her past? I'd heard people do that sometimes when they're nearing the end.

It chilled my insides, but it also frustrated me, the fact that if my mother was reliving her past, it was a past I knew nothing about. Somehow my mother had always managed to avoid the subject. I'd never realized it until this night, when it struck me and set me wondering, wondering about my mother's life before I was born. I wanted my mother to answer my questions, but it was too late to ask.

"Rhubarb pie . . . your favorite, Peter." I think she smiled. I strained to hear more. "I'll bake one . . . tomorrow . . . "

She didn't, though.

Three o'clock that morning, my mother died.

Now tears prickled my eyes, and I detested myself for remembering all this and bringing back the suffering of that night. I wondered if I would ever be able to forget.

I blamed the lilacs for starting these disturbing thoughts, and that card that had read: *From an old friend.* My mother didn't have any friends. I bit my lip. Well, she knew a few people from church and maybe from her housekeeping job, but an old friend? My mind drew a blank. I knew nothing about any old friend.

Because I knew nothing about my mother's past—it always came back to that.

Guilt washed over me in a sudden, overwhelming wave. I gulped for air while my mind floundered for excuses, but the guilt only grew stronger. I didn't know anything about my mother's past, but I *should.* Here I was in her hometown, living in her old home with her brother—it made me feel obligated, somehow, to find out what I could.

I told myself I should be eager to do this, yet something stirred uneasily, deep inside me at the thought.

My uncle and I had long since passed the lilacs, but they had done their damage. The evening air slid over my skin like a clammy hand, making me shiver.

I glanced sideways at my uncle. *Ask him,* I commanded myself. *He's my mother's brother. He'll be able to answer my questions.*

But my tongue wouldn't move.

My uncle and I had an employer-employee relationship at most, and I had my own cool behavior to thank for that. As we walked, I kept peeking at him from the corner of my eye, trying to determine what kind of person he was. He was an excessively ordinary-looking man, somewhat short, a little overweight, hair brushed with gray. He could be anywhere from early forties to late fifties—I couldn't tell. And I couldn't read his eyes behind the little round glasses.

When it came down to it, I guess the only thing I did know about my uncle was his name: Peter Hutch. Mrs. Gills had told me that much. With a start, I only now connected the name. *Peter—my uncle must be the Peter of my mother's memories.*

I was about to speak when my uncle finally decided he had something to say. "What would you like for dinner? I have pizza in the freezer. It won't take long to bake. Do you like pepperoni, or do you prefer sausage? I have cheese or vegetable if you don't like meat."

Whatever I had been about to ask was lost. "I—I don't care. It doesn't matter . . ." I was still sorting out my thoughts when we reached the driveway.

But my thoughts went on hold when I got my first real look at the house. When we'd left that morning, my mind still fogged with sleep, I hadn't even glanced at it. Now I stopped in my tracks to stare. The house was Victorian style, trimmed with what looked like wooden lace. Two round turret rooms pointed skyward like the peaks of a fairy tale castle. One of those rooms was mine, I realized. The one on the left.

Large as it was, the house was set far off from the road, looking comfortably settled in among numerous trees and shrubs, as if they had all grown up together. The lawn sprawled wide and vibrant green, the grass long and brushy, probably from recent spring rains. The evening sunlight showed off the house paint, a creamy white of age, and shadows hung back along the house's sides, tangled among tree branches. Full-blooming lilacs brushed one corner of the house and a flourishing vine clung to the other.

There was an enchanting quality about it all—something I'd never encountered in California. I don't think you can find it in new houses . . . it's the dignity of age, perhaps. Yet I'd seen plenty of old houses in California. Just none quite like this. I had a sudden desire to sketch the scene.

Leaving my uncle to get the mail, I crossed the lawn to the left side of the house, where the lilacs grew. I looked at them only a moment before passing them by.

My eyes skipped over a large stump, momentarily wondering why a tree had been cut down. My gaze fell on an unkempt garden bordered with rocks and half bursting with some large, fan-like plant. "Is this rhubarb?" I heard myself ask aloud. I was surprised to receive a reply.

"It is. Rhubarb is a persistent plant. It comes back year

after year, even if you ignore it." I turned to see my uncle retreating to the front of the house. "I should get the pizza on."

"Uncle Peter!" I caught up with him as he mounted the front steps. Inspiration had struck me, and I didn't even realize this was the first time I'd bothered to address him. "If you don't mind, I'd like to make dinner tonight—a homemade meal. If you don't mind eating late, that is."

My uncle nodded without turning. "That would be fine." He paused with his key in the door. "There are a lot of old cookbooks in a cabinet in the kitchen. Feel free to look through them. Make anything you'd like."

He disappeared inside, leaving me to find my own way to the kitchen. With all its doors and halls, the house reminded me of the inside of a carnival funhouse—without the fun. It must have taken me five minutes to find the kitchen as I wandered from room to room, pausing to admire paintings and porcelain figures filmed with dust. I was surprised my uncle hadn't asked whether I'd ever made a meal before, or if I even knew how to cook, for that matter. He'd just assumed I knew what I was getting myself into.

And I do, I thought.

The lilacs had made me realize it was time to find out more about my mother, and the rhubarb had provided me with the means to do it. I would make a fabulous homemade dinner—dessert too—and set the ideal opportunity to ask my uncle to tell me everything he could. There was so much to find out, because I knew almost nothing. It hadn't really mattered to me before, but now that I was here in Lorens, if only for a little while, I felt compelled.

I located the ragged, food-spattered cookbooks. Most of them were made up of pasted-in or hand-written recipes, compiled over many years, I supposed. Some recipes were so old and faded that I couldn't read them. It didn't matter, because I had more than enough recipes to choose from.

Of course, I already knew what I would make for dessert.

I found a rhubarb pie recipe on a dog-eared page, proving its frequent use. The recipe was written in spidery handwriting, and I had to concentrate to decipher it. I wondered if my mother's mother—my grandmother—had written the recipe. Or maybe it went back even farther, to my great-grandmother.

"Grandmother." I said the word quietly, almost reverently. My tongue liked the way it felt. I wasn't used to thinking about relatives. Long ago, I think when I was in third grade, and all the kids were supposed to write letters to their grandparents for grandparents' day, I'd asked my mother about mine and she'd told me we didn't have any. "It's just you and me, baby," she'd said. "We have each other." But my grandparents had been alive at one time, had lived in this house—had baked and eaten this pie.

Shaking myself free of such thoughts, I took out a mixing bowl. Following the recipe carefully, I cut butter into flour and mixed in water to make the crust. I ran outside to pluck five thick stalks of rhubarb, then wasted time trying to find my way back to the kitchen. I was relieved to finally put the pie in the oven.

I was surprised to see that it was a modern oven with electronic buttons. Smooth looking, but I didn't think it suited the old-fashioned style of the kitchen. Checkered curtains, wooden utensils displayed in a ceramic cream pitcher, and copper pans hanging from the ceiling all seemed to oppose such technology.

While the pie baked, I searched through the cupboards, pantry, and refrigerator to see what ingredients were on hand for making dinner. The kitchen turned out to be fairly well-stocked with cans and boxed foods, but there weren't many fresh ones. A package of ground beef sat lonely on a fridge shelf, an unappetizing pool of red juice collecting around its base. The freezer was crammed with pizzas. My lips twitched with a smile. Unless I made dinner, it was clear what I'd be eating every night.

When the meal was ready, I set the dishes on the table, called my uncle, and after a brief prayer of thanks we began. Everything tasted as good as it looked, and though I was weary from the effort, I couldn't help feeling proud of the results. I knew I wouldn't mind making more meals in the future. True, I wasn't going to be here much longer, but while I was, I might as well enjoy the freedom of the kitchen and taste some of my new-found family's heirloom recipes. Maybe I would even copy some of the recipes before I left. It would be something unique of my mother's—and grandmother's—to keep with me and carry on.

During the meal, my uncle didn't say much, but I could tell he was pleased with the food. After all, you don't eat three helpings of Layered Beef Bake if you don't like it.

As the meal progressed, I was conscious of time slipping away. I knew I should bring up the subject of my mother, ask my questions, but for some reason I kept stalling. I promised myself I would ask when I served the rhubarb pie.

I was more proud of that pie than anything else. I waited tensely for my uncle's reaction. After the first few bites, he spoke.

"Your mother used to make a good rhubarb pie."

Of course, I knew this already.

"This is good, too," my uncle said. "Maybe with a little more practice, you'll be able to match hers. It was my favorite."

I stuffed a forkful of pie into my mouth and chewed rapidly. *Now is not the time to be sensitive,* I warned myself.

"There's a lot I don't know about my mother." This was even harder for me than I had anticipated. *Lord, give me the words I need.* "I was wondering if you could . . . fill me in."

My uncle waited till he was completely done chewing, then he took a long drink of milk before answering. "I wondered what this was leading up to."

While I considered that remark, he cleared his throat.

"I gather there is a lot she never told you. But first, why

don't you tell me what you do know. Then I'll have somewhere to start from."

I pushed the pie about with my fork, making a gooey, pink-green trail on the ceramic plate. "She didn't talk about her past much, and I guess I just never brought it up because—" I searched for an explanation—"because there was never any reason to." I took a deep breath. "I know that almost twenty years ago my mother married my father, a doctor, in Colorado. That's where I was born. My father died in a car crash when I was a baby. Then my mother and I moved to California, and that's where I grew up. That's where my home is."

My uncle took off his glasses and began polishing the lenses with a corner of his napkin. "But she told you nothing about before her marriage?"

"No." My heart rate sped up. "So what is there to tell, and why didn't she tell me?"

"I believe your mother had her reasons. She wanted to put it behind her. That's why she left and didn't keep in contact. She never told you she had a brother, did she?"

The question surprised me. Surely he knew the answer. That's when I realized my uncle must have a lot of his own unanswered questions, though his were of the years since my mother had left Lorens. I wondered if this hurt him. If it did, he didn't show it.

"No. But she talked about you that last night." It suddenly sounded awful to me, as if my mother hadn't cared enough about her brother to keep in touch. Then she died and dumped me on him—after all these years when she hadn't had anything to do with him. I felt embarrassed for her. "I'm sure she thought about you a lot."

"Do you know about your grandparents?" he asked.

"I know that they're all dead," I answered softly.

"Yes. Both your mother's and your father's parents died before your mother and father married—"

"You knew my father? I thought they met in Colorado."

My uncle shook his head. "They married in Colorado, but they met here. I'll start from the beginning. Your grandfather, Steven Hutch, died in 1966 in the Vietnam War. Your mother was five at the time; I was fifteen. Our mother had a bad heart. She died seven years later. Your mother and I lived on here, and we made out all right. I got a job, and your mother was an excellent student with a very promising future."

When he paused, the silence that came was emphasized by the steady ticking of a clock coming from somewhere in the house, a ticking I hadn't noticed until now. I waited, almost not wanting to hear what would follow.

"But something happened in her senior year. An accident." He cleared his throat. "She was working on an article at the time, a local history story. You see, she was interested in journalism, and she had a part time job as an intern at the paper. She came up with an innovative idea and somehow convinced the editor to let her write a feature story. If it was good enough, he agreed he would run it. Tiffany had a way of convincing people." My uncle smiled, but it was nothing like the beaming smile he had greeted me with at the airport.

"She was very ambitious, very enthusiastic about the story. In fact, I'd never seen her more serious about anything in her life before. She put her all into the story, taking great efforts with her research—"

"But what was it *about*?" What did any of this have to do with an accident?

"Her story focused on the history of the Ingerman Mansion, an old mansion on the outskirts of town. Understandably, since it was one of the first places built here, over the years many rumors have developed about it. But Tiffany set out to get the facts. At the time, the mansion was owned by Anthony Ingerman—his family built the mansion in the eighteen hundreds and it had always been owned by one of them—he was the last of the line. He didn't live in the mansion because it was too large, too run-down. And though he needed the money, he wouldn't sell it. Tiffany, being Tiffany, managed to get his permission to explore the house. But only on the condition that she be extremely careful. Unfortunately, the house was more run-down than anyone realized." My uncle shook his head. "She shouldn't have even been on the balcony. She should have known it wasn't safe. The railing broke, and she fell . . . twenty feet to a rocky garden below."

I gasped, but my uncle continued.

"She was lucky to survive. She'd hit her head and was unconscious, and she broke her leg. If she hadn't been found when she was . . ." My uncle's voice trailed off. Then, suddenly, he found it. "She was rushed to the hospital. They did all they could, but the fall affected her mind—her memory. She regained consciousness, but had amnesia. For a while, it looked as if she wouldn't remember anything. Then, gradually, things started to come back . . ."

My uncle paused, as if searching for words. "But the accident affected her in a more complex way. Of course, she was behind in all her schoolwork—her friends had graduated and were ready for college by the time she could have even begun making up the work—but she could have overcome that. Only . . ." my uncle frowned, forming deep creases in his brow, "she said she didn't find it easy anymore. But it was as if she wouldn't try. She'd lost all her enthusiasm. She changed. Tiffany had never been a nervous person, but after the accident she often became anxious for no reason at all. She avoided her friends and stayed home as much as possible."

From the way he kept referring to her as Tiffany, I knew he still thought of her as his sister, not my mother.

"I don't know . . . there was more to it than I could possibly understand. The doctors said she was still suffering aftereffects. She saw a lot of different doctors and specialists. I did everything I could for her, but it wasn't enough. Or maybe it was too much. She wanted to get away. She didn't want college anymore, or anything she had wanted before. She married one of her doctors—your father—and he took her away. I never heard from her again."

My uncle replaced his glasses.

I shook my head, bewildered. This person he was talking about . . . was my mother? Incredible. I'd expected my uncle to tell me something simple. Something like my mother had lived such a boring life that she'd had no reason to talk about it.

"But why?" I asked. "Why didn't she tell me?"

"She wanted to forget," he repeated. "She couldn't adjust after what happened here. The best thing was to start over, leave it all behind, and everyone and everything that would remind her."

Including you, I realized. I looked at my uncle's eyes, but saw only his glasses reflecting blankly back at me. Suddenly I felt sorry for him. I wished I hadn't been so self-centered. If I'd only known what he'd been through, what my mother had been through . . .

"Tell me," my uncle said suddenly, "do you think she was happy?"

I opened my mouth to say, "Yes, of course," but I couldn't say it. Because I didn't know. All seventeen years I'd lived with my mother, I'd never really known her. Couldn't have. Not if she'd kept secrets like this from me. I was already overwhelmed by what my uncle had revealed, and now my heart ached terribly, throbbing with remorse for the mother I had never known. I'd wanted my uncle to answer my questions, but all he'd done was give me more.

Had she been happy? I fumbled through my memories. There had been times when she seemed happy, but other times—more frequently—I had sensed her uneasiness, her worry. But it would come and go. She prayed frequently, and that seemed to help.

"We did a lot together in California," I finally answered.

"We laughed a lot. She seemed happy."

I rubbed my forehead, trying to slow my whirling mind. I was the one who should be asking questions. There was so much I didn't understand, so many questions to ask that it seemed impossible to focus.

"The mansion," I said, grasping the one fact that emerged in my mind, "the mansion where she had the accident—is it still around?"

My uncle nodded. "It stands just outside of town. More dilapidated than ever. It's closed up and has been ever since Ingerman died. No one goes there now."

He looked at me a long moment before he spoke again. "Robin, I told you all this because . . . it's right that you should know. But it's in the past, and I want you to realize there are some things that happen that we don't understand— questions we'll never be able to answer—and it's best we leave them in the past." I thought he was finished, but he added, "Trust in God to take care of the future."

In the silence that followed, I realized we were both sitting at the table in the dark and that my pie still sat, half eaten, before me on my plate. I knew I was not going to finish it.

Pushing back my chair, I stood up. My voice broke the eerie silence. "When my mother lived here, which room was hers?" I don't know where the question came from. But the answer did not surprise me.

"Your room. It only made sense to give it to you. It was all ready . . . only needed a good cleaning. I dusted the furniture, vacuumed and shampooed the carpet. I thought perhaps you might want to look through some of your mother's things. They're all yours now, you know. She didn't take much when she went, and I left everything the same. Just in case."

So I'm living in my mother's old room, in her old house, in her hometown, I thought, and shuddered.

It's as if I'm taking her place.

Chapter Five

I was drawn upstairs and down the hall to my room—my mother's room. As I pushed open the door, I realized that my mother must have been about my age the last time she'd passed through this doorway. The hairs prickled up on the back of my neck.

I switched on the light, and it was like I was seeing the room for the first time. Last night didn't count, because I hadn't known then that this was my mother's room. I hadn't realized that the carpet was not just "a kind of purple color," but a faded lavender. A nightstand stood beside the bed, and I ran my hand over the smooth, dark wood, felt the little nicks and scratches embedded in the surface and wondered what had caused them.

In the drawer of the nightstand lay a black Bible. I lifted the book reverently and the substantial heaviness felt reassuring, somehow. The pages fell open to a yellow ribbon marking chapter forty-two of Ecclesiasticus. My eyes landed on verse nineteen: "For the Lord knoweth all knowledge and hath beheld the signs of the world. He declareth the things that are past and the things that are to come, and revealeth the traces of hidden things."

My eyes read a few more verses. Then, swallowing an untold sadness, I nestled the Bible back in the drawer. *Later,* I promised, though I wasn't sure if I was promising myself or God.

Turning my attention back to my mother's room, my gaze drifted past the bed, the dresser, and a collection of framed cat and horse pictures. I saw a desk. One side was lined with drawers. Above this desk were rows of shelves packed tightly with books. But for some reason, what my eyes finally focused on was the closet.

I crossed the room, ignoring my suitcases, which still leaned against the foot of the bed waiting to be unpacked, and opened the door. On a metal bar, bare wire hangers hung in a forlorn row. My gaze moved to the back of the closet, where shapes protruded from the dark. This was where I needed to start.

My fingers trembled as I reached into the shadowy depths. The back of the closet was cold, and the smell reminded me of locker room showers, musty and dank. Holding my breath, I dragged out three boxes. Behind them, in the farthest corner, sat a wooden chest—my fingers told me this before my eyes did. Not being able to bring myself to pull the chest out into the light just yet, I decided to save it till last.

I blew dust off the three boxes, realizing too late what a mistake that was. After my day in the bookstore, I did not need more dust. Coughing, I went to the window and swept aside the lacy curtains. I opened the window and leaned my head out, taking a deep breath of the cool evening air. The scent of lilacs drifted up from the blooming bush below.

That was enough fresh air for me.

I pulled my head inside and returned to the boxes, ready to unpack my mother's past.

I was disappointed to find the first box full of old clothes. They were pieces that had once been out of style but, in the circular way of fashion, were now coming back in: embroidered frilly blouses, bell-bottom pants, long flowery skirts—things sold in unique little California beach-side shops . . . things I could not imagine my mother wearing. Of course, she had not been my mother when she'd worn these. She'd been Tiffany Hutch. There, I was coming to realize, quite a difference.

The next two boxes contained odds and ends such as games, stuffed animals, and a mood ring. The cardboard sides of the games were broken off, and the pieces came sliding out. I found a pet rock still sitting in its original box; a Rubik's cube, stickers peeling; and two Chicago records protected in cloudy plastic slipcovers. Having no use for these things, I packed them away. The mood ring, however, I kept. Its deep midnight-blue color intrigued me, and I slipped the ring on my finger. A perfect fit.

Now to unpack the chest. Getting down on my hands and knees, I dragged it out, my heart thumping heavily. I'd saved the chest for last because, somehow, I sensed it contained something important. It had to. I wanted it to. I ran my fingers over the tarnished hinges and smooth grooves of wood, speculating. For a moment I felt like Pandora, about to open a forbidden box of secrets. Or Eve, about to bite into the forbidden fruit. Once I lifted this lid, there could be no turning back.

Why do I always think such strange things? I wondered. Maybe it came from reading too much. I smiled, but my stomach fluttered as I lifted the lid.

Creak . . .

A light, flowery scent floated up to meet me. I caught my breath, completely unprepared for the ugly thing I saw lying on top of a spread out handkerchief. I didn't dare touch it. Until, upon closer scrutiny, I realized it was only a shriveled branch of withered flowers. They were brown and crinkly, breaking into coarse fragments at my touch. Not knowing what to make of it, I carefully rolled the branch up in the yellowed handkerchief and set it aside.

By removing the handkerchief, which had probably been white when my mother first placed it there, I uncovered a blue book. I picked it up and read the gold lettering: *Lorens High School Yearbook, 1978-79.* I paged through it slowly, seeing the usual rows of teacher photos, sports teams, and award recipients, as well as collages of black and white photographs showing mismatched bodies and heads.

Several pages were devoted to poems and artwork.

Skimming the names of the contributors, *Tiffany Hutch, senior*, caught my eye. Her drawing was of a river with a wooden bridge arching over it. A weeping willow stood on the riverbank, its leafy tendrils trailing serenely in the water. I studied the drawing for a long time, admiring the way my mother had used just the right quality of line and shading to capture the scene in subtle beauty. But more than the skill of the artist, I was taken by the fact that the artist was my mother. I'd never known she could draw like this.

The remaining yearbook pages were devoted to class photos. Skipping to the seniors, my eyes were drawn to a hauntingly familiar face. *Tiffany Hutch* was printed beneath the square photo.

Even in a black and white photograph, it was obvious this girl's hair was blond.

I blinked. For as long as I could remember, my mother had been a brunette. So what did this mean—that she had dyed her hair all these years? Was she really a natural blond, like myself? I shook my head. How could I have never realized the truth? Surely I would have been able to notice something like that. Holding the book, my hands trembled. But had I ever really looked at my mother's hair? Close enough to discover brown was not her natural hair color? Apparently not. I wondered how I could have been so blind.

It was another thing my mother had kept from me, and I wanted to be angry at her for this. I told myself I had every right to be angry. But instead I felt guilt; if I had been closer to my mother, maybe there would not have been any secrets; maybe she would have felt she could confide in me, whatever her reasons had been for those secrets.

Then I felt fear. What other things had she kept from me?

I stared at her photo even longer than I had at her drawing. I'd never seen such a lovely picture of my mother. She looked so young! I did have my parents' wedding photo, taken in September of 1979, and since my mother was eighteen in that, she was not even a year older than in this picture. Yet she looked so different in the wedding photo. And not just because her hair was brown. There were subtle differences in her face, a tightness around her eyes and lips that made her look so much older than a mere several months should have.

I frowned. In this school photo she wore her hair long, loose and wavy. I liked it that way. It suited her face and was much more becoming than the short, prim style I'd always seen her wearing. And her smile was unlike any smile I'd ever seen. Her eyes shone with a radiating joy. Her soft face, with its smooth skin and high cheekbones, could easily be called beautiful. *If only I looked a little more like her,* I thought ruefully.

When at last I turned the page, I saw a final group photo. *Class of '79* was printed boldly at the top. I searched, but this time I could not find my mother. At the bottom of the page, after the long list of students' names, I read: *Not pictured, Tiffany Hutch.*

I closed the book softly. I knew why my mother had missed that picture. She had probably been in the hospital about that time. That young, beautiful girl . . . I couldn't believe something so awful had really happened to her.

I laid the book aside. Part of me did not want to go on with this unraveling of the past, yet I couldn't bring myself to stop. My hand returned to the chest, and this time it drew out a small velvet box.

As I'd expected, the box contained a piece of jewelry. It was a small, heart-shaped locket that glinted golden against the box's black velvet surface. I used my fingernail to pry the locket open, but the heart pieces separated to reveal only empty space where a photo should have been. My disappointment was displaced by the mesmerizing sense of mystery that came from wondering whose photo had once occupied the locket, and why it no longer did.

Putting the locket aside, I moved on to the next item and lifted out a kind of portfolio. My mother's name was sprawled in black ink across the cover. Opening it, I discovered a thick sheaf of drawings. I paged through them, fascinated and impressed by my mother's talent. I'd never known my passion for drawing ran in the family.

Her collection was remarkable; the drawings captured a wide range of subjects, including nature scenes, houses, animals, and portraits. I wondered why my mother hadn't continued with her art. Because, like my uncle said, it was part of her past? But what painful memories could be connected with these beautiful pictures? Curiosity made me impatient, and I tucked the stack of drawings back into the portfolio, promising myself I'd look through it more closely later.

Two items remained in the chest. One was a thick binder, stuffed to overflowing with loose paper. I tried to sort through the pages, tried my best to read the sprawled handwriting, but the papers were a jumble of notes. Only after some tedious deciphering did I begin to get an idea of what this was: my mother's research work on the Ingerman Mansion. As I sat there holding that confusion of papers, I felt that this was the most significant find of all.

The notes were difficult to follow, but I gradually pieced together some of the facts of the mansion's history. The Ingerman Mansion had been built in the early eighteen forties, not long before Wisconsin became a state. About this same time, the town of Lorens began to form. I hadn't realized Lorens was such an old town.

The notes went on to explain that the Ingermans, as one of the first families in the area, had always been important town citizens. They were very rich, and this set them not only slightly above but also apart from the other people. At one time, an Ingerman had been mayor of the town.

At about this point I began to yawn. I was stacking away the disarray of papers when I came across a page that made me sit up straight.

It is a fact that Connie Ingerman, in 1851, fell to her death from a balcony of the Ingerman Mansion, although there is much speculation over the circumstances surrounding her fall.

It is known that Connie fell in love with a common townsman by the name of John Kurselli, whom her father refused to let her marry. As a result, John went off to California in the Gold Rush of 1849 in hopes of striking it rich and proving his worth. Apparently, luck was with him, because about a year later Connie received a letter from him informing her he had found a fortune. He buried the gold for safekeeping somewhere in California and, it was rumored, sent her a copy of his map as a kind of trust until he returned to fetch her.

But his luck ran out. John was killed on the journey back. And shortly after Connie received the news, she was discovered dead on the ground beneath her bedroom balcony, her neck broken from the fall.

Thus the story everyone tells of the mansion is a tragic one: a tale of love lost, resulting in suicide. Not surprisingly, the Ingerman Mansion is rumored to be haunted. Some say Connie's sorrowful soul can't rest, and she roams the mansion, guarding the treasure map and waiting for her love to return.

And what of the map? No one knows. Some say Connie destroyed it; some say she hid it, and that it remains hidden to this day, a curse hanging over it. Still others say the map never even existed . . .

I sat on the carpet, shivering. My uncle hadn't told me any of this, but it struck me as uncanny that both Connie and my mother had fallen from the same mansion, perhaps even the same balcony. I read on, convinced my mother's story would have been published if she had ever completed it. But she hadn't. She had locked all her notes away to be forgotten.

My head was soon spinning with such a clutter of thoughts that I didn't think I could contain any more information. Reluctantly, I gathered the papers back into the binder and moved on to the last item in the chest, a brown book with a scrollwork pattern on the cover. I read the spine and discovered, with surprised delight, that it was a Victoria Holt novel.

When I glanced up at the shelves above the desk, I discovered an entire collection of Victoria Holt novels. Other books were familiar, too, and I felt a thrill go through me. Novels by Phyllis A. Whitney, Lois Duncan, Betty Cavanna. Not contemporary novels, of course, but I recognized them anyway. In the libraries, I had read as many of these authors' books as I could find. But I'd never known my mother had shared my interest.

I looked at the novel in my hands. How odd, I thought, that my mother should single out this one book to hide in the chest. I turned it over. Only then did I realize the title was identical to the one I'd been reading today. I opened the book about a quarter through, trying to find the place where I'd left off reading. I smiled, remembering the interruption, and for a moment my eyes didn't see the page. Instead, I saw Philip's eyes gazing into mine. Had he really meant it when he said he'd see me again? Oh, I hoped so.

With my spirits lifted back to life in the present, I didn't feel like brooding anymore on the past. Besides, my head hurt from thinking so much, and I was tired.

I intended to go to bed so that I could get up easily for work; I didn't mean to read more than one chapter of the novel, but it was so easy to lose myself in the fictional world, in someone else's problems as I followed fascinating characters and experienced the heightening suspense. Only when my eyelids became too heavy to hold open and the words dissolved on the page did I realize, with a start, how late it was.

My legs had fallen asleep beneath me. Awkwardly, I stood, returned my mother's things to the chest, and closed the lid. Because my room was too small to keep it in the middle of the floor, I pushed the chest back into the closet. The novel I set on the nightstand beside the bed, just before I collapsed into sleep.

~

I lay alone in the peaceful darkness, sleeping, when suddenly the quiet was shattered by alarming noises, voices, screaming—something was terribly wrong. Someone grabbed me, crushed me against them so hard I could barely breathe.

I didn't know where I was, but I was suddenly alone, cold and afraid. I needed my mother, my father; I needed to feel safe. Everything rushed by so fast in the darkness . . . I didn't know what was happening. All I knew was fear. Terror.

Screeching, crashing—cutting pain in my arm. I screamed. Gravity disappeared and I was flying up, up through the darkness. Up to the moon. Then, just as suddenly, the world flipped and I was falling—

I woke up gasping for air, my forehead pouring hot sweat onto my pillow. I smelled the sour smell of fear.

Just a dream, just a dream, I told myself. But this didn't convince me. I kept my eyes closed, too scared to move, yet not knowing what I was afraid of. I was frozen with the ultimate fear: fear of the unknown.

It seemed to take forever for my heartbeat to slow— seemed hours, in which time my mind roared with the dream I didn't want to remember.

I hadn't had the dream for at least four years. I'd thought I'd conquered it. I'd thought it would never return.

But it had, with a terror more intense than ever.

And now there was no one here to comfort me, no one to rely on but myself. With a burst of courage, I lunged for the bedside lamp, nearly knocking it over in my desperate attempt to turn it on.

Then I sat trembling on the bed in a tangle of sheets, blinking in the sudden light, trying in vain to calm myself. I was being foolish, I told myself. It was only a nightmare.

Or was it?

Instinctively, I reached out to feel along the inside of my left arm, running my fingertips gently over the familiar scar.

I took a deep breath. What was it my mother had told me? When I was a baby I had knocked over a vase and cut my arm badly on the glass. It was that simple. But after all I had discovered today, how could I believe anything my mother had told me? Why was it that when I had this nightmare, I always clutched my arm?

I wanted my mother to explain and, in her convincing way, reassure me. Back when she was alive and I awoke with this nightmare, I would call for her and she would come swiftly as an angel. I ached for her now, yearned so strongly for her comforting presence that I could almost hear her words. "It's all right," she would say, holding me close. "You're safe now. I've got you, nothing's going to hurt you."

My fear would begin to subdue, and I'd stop sniffling; but I never understood why then, when my mother hugged me again, so tightly, she would begin to cry. She would stay in my bed with me for the rest of the night, and I would feel safe in the smothering thickness of the warm quilt, aware of her protecting presence beside me.

Now, I sat alone on my bed—my mother's bed, actually —but I wasn't comforted. Without my mother to reassure me —even if it was only false reassurance—the nightmare was

68

still too horribly vivid to forget.

So I sat up all night with the light burning as intensely as my fear and didn't attempt to go back to sleep. For I was afraid that if I did, I would re-encounter the nightmare. And that was a risk I could not take.

Chapter Six

All night long I fought my heavy eyelids. When dark thoughts crept into my mind, I read some of my mother's Bible. But when dawn finally came, with its gray light seeping through the edge of my window shade, I gave in to exhaustion and slept.

It was a dreamless sleep, in which I abandoned all my tensions. I slept so soundly that when I awoke, I instantly knew I had been in bed too long. Sure enough, the clock radio on the nightstand glowed ten-thirty.

I tossed back the sheets and scrambled to get dressed, reproaching myself for wasting the chance to put in a full day's work. Silence told me my uncle had already left for the bookstore. *Why didn't he wake me?* I wondered as I galloped down the carpeted stairs.

I ran the sidewalk like a racetrack into town, until the heavy warmth of the sun forced me to slow to a walk. Above, a polished blue sky promised a day too beautiful to spend cooped up in a dusty bookstore. My spirits sagged. The closer I got to the store, the more my feet dragged. I wiped the damp hair off my forehead, wishing I could escape to the beach. *Except there is no beach in Lorens,* I reminded myself.

My thoughts shifted to the terror of last night's dream, but it seemed ridiculous now in the context of this bright morning. Yesterday had been a long, strange day. I had been stressed-out by my encounter with Justin, excited by meeting Philip, intrigued by the discovery of my mother's past, and wrapped in the suspense of a Victoria Holt novel. Surely it wasn't surprising that these things should mingle together in my unconsciousness and trigger the dream.

Sometime during this reasoning, I noticed a figure in the distance, walking up the sidewalk in my direction. I wondered absently why more people weren't out taking advantage of the weather. I'd be outside all day long if I could. I squinted at the approaching figure, who increased in size and clarity the nearer he came. My heart leapt. I recognized the face, but most of all the hair, shining gold in the sun. It was Philip.

"So we meet again," he said, smiling, as he reached me. He didn't sound at all surprised. I smiled back, not wanting to say anything quite yet, not wanting to betray my delight. Philip swung around to walk beside me.

"Mind if I walk with you?"

"You are," I replied as our footsteps fell into rhythm.

"Going to work, I suppose," Philip said with a sigh. "What a waste of a beautiful day."

"It is," I agreed. But I was thinking I didn't have to step into the bookstore if I didn't want to. It wouldn't take much to make me drop my resolve.

"Why don't you take the day off, then?" Philip stopped walking and I paused, turning to face him. My steps lingered, part of me wanting to stay, the other part urging me to work. "I know," Philip continued, his face lighting up, his words growing with enthusiasm. "I'll show you around Lorens. How about it? My car's just across the street. We can cruise the town—anywhere you want to go—just name it. What do you say?"

He stood there waiting with eyes bright, daring me to refuse. I forced myself to catch my breath. I was flattered by his offer, which was more than enticing, but . . . "I'd love to," I said, taking a small step backward, "but I really shouldn't. I have to work."

"Oh, come on," he scoffed, "do you really think your uncle can't get along for one afternoon without you? You only just got here. What do you think he did all the years before you came?"

"It's not that—I know he can get along without me—but I need the money." I took another step back.

"One day won't make a difference." Philip's eyes never left mine. *Wow,* I thought, *does he ever blink?* "Besides, work can't compare with what I'm offering you: a chance to enjoy the day, get to know me, have some fun . . ."

He crossed his arms, and the way he looked at me made me feel as if he could see right into my thoughts. "When was the last time you did something just for the heck of it?"

My silence was his answer.

"Too long," he said quietly. And before I knew it, he'd covered the steps between us and had my hand in his.

Suddenly, there was nothing I wanted more than to spend the day with Philip. As for work, I'd already missed half the day—why not miss it all? Today I would break away from all the pressures, worries, and responsibilities that had suddenly appeared in my life—things I had not asked for and did not want—pressures that had made the nightmare return.

"Let's go," I said.

"I knew you had spirit." Philip flashed a sparkling smile before catching me by the arm and leading me off the sidewalk and onto the street.

"Run!" he yelled, and we tore across as if a semitruck was bearing down on us. I could feel the blood coursing through my veins, and I thought, *This is the feeling of exhilaration!* Philip opened the door of a shiny red convertible, and my eyes widened.

"She's a beauty, isn't she?"

I could only nod agreement.

"A BMW," Philip said proudly.

He gunned the engine and we sped away from the curb. The wind ripped through my hair. This was my first ride in a convertible, and I expected to feel thrilled.

Instead, my heart dropped inside me. I froze. Then I started shaking. I didn't know what was wrong. Only, I was going too fast, flying out of control—couldn't take it. I fought for air. My heart pounding against my chest, I fumbled for the seatbelt and somehow managed to yank it on.

Slight as it was, I think the restraint of the belt helped. In a few moments I began to get used to the speed, and my hands unclenched themselves. I couldn't understand why I had reacted so strangely. Only . . . it had felt like the dream. I shuddered. I glanced at Philip, but he simply looked at me and smiled. Good. He hadn't noticed.

I pressed my back against the seat, determined to enjoy the ride. *This is a convertible,* I told myself sternly. *Enjoy the ride while you can. Everyone is envying you.* I looked around. *Well, that is, they would be if we weren't the only ones on the road.*

I lifted my head, purposely turning into the wind. My heartbeat accelerated as the air rushed past my face. I took gulping breaths and thought, *This is freedom!*

"No pressures, no worries, nowhere special to go—you can't beat this!" Philip called above the roar of the wind. When he pressed harder on the accelerator, I smiled harder. I knew he was showing off, but I also knew he was doing it for me, and that made me feel more special than I could ever remember feeling.

Eventually he slowed down enough so I could actually see some of the town. But there was nothing much to see: a little library, a post office, a bank. I counted three rummage sale signs. We drove past a red brick school, where kids were running wild outside; and a park, which would surely be swarmed by kids once school let out, but right now it looked peaceful. We bumped over a railroad track and the next moment I gazed out at a lake.

"The grand beach," Phillip announced.

But I was looking beyond the scanty stretch of sand to an island not far from shore. "It's like an overgrown potted plant." I imagined rowing out to have a picnic on it.

Phillip nodded. "They light fireworks from there, and people crowd the beach and pier and hills to watch. One year it caught on fire."

"What did everyone do?"

"Don't know. I wasn't living here then. Just my luck to miss all the excitement."

Leaving the lake behind, we passed a garden nursery, then took a rambling road past more quaint buildings and out of town. Houses became less frequent and the land rolled into country farms with red barns and black and white cows grazing lazily behind fences. *It's a cute little place,* I thought, *but nothing compared to California.*

Philip turned to me. "Had enough?" He didn't wait for an answer. "Then how about lunch? There's a great little restaurant not far from here. You'll love it." I was sure I would because in my haste to leave the house, I hadn't eaten breakfast.

Settling back, I let my cares sail away with the wind. I was aware that this was temporary, that this contentment couldn't last. But right now, with Philip behind the wheel, I didn't care. I closed my eyes, thinking I could ride beside Philip forever, content in the moment and feeling young and alive, enjoying all I had been missing for far too long.

The car stopped with a jolt, making me bounce against the seatbelt. My eyes snapped open to see a low, dark building with blinds drawn. "This is it?" I asked.

"It's even nicer inside," Philip replied.

It was dark inside. I stayed close to Philip, but my eyes shifted nervously through the restaurant. Smoke hung thick in the air of an adjoining room, from where I could hear loud voices, laughter, and clinking glasses. As we passed, a tall man with slits for eyes smiled at me, and, feeling ashamed and not knowing why, I moved my eyes away. They fell on a waxy-looking plant near an unlit window. Surrounded by swirling smoke, the plant didn't look too perky. I knew how it felt. I tried not to breathe, but smoke still entered my nostrils; it mingled with a faintly odd, exotic aroma that might have been from food or perfume.

I tried to keep my head high, but my ears were burning with self-consciousness. Only Philip, so tall and confident beside me, gave me the courage to keep walking.

In a dim corner near the back, we were seated at a table for two and given menus. At least I couldn't see the bar from here. But those crazy smells stayed in my nostrils. With a pang of alarm, I felt I was going to be sick, but I turned to the menu and my nose forgot the odors.

The prices were ridiculous. And I didn't want Steak *au Poivre* for lunch anyway. Soon I wasn't seeing the menu, but recalling yesterday, comparing Justin and the dinky diner to today and Philip. Then, realizing what I was doing, I frowned. Justin had no right to force himself into my memories. Especially when I was trying to enjoy myself with Philip. But the more I tried to push Justin out of my mind, the more I remembered him and his notebook and pencil and strange questions. Typical that he would be as stubborn in my thoughts as he had been in reality.

"Something wrong?"

I looked up to see Philip regarding me quizzically. I flushed and looked down at my folded linen napkin.

"No," I fingered the soft material, "everything's fine. I was just thinking that—this is a very fancy place."

Philip's eyes crinkled at the corners as he smiled. "Don't worry about it."

"I'm not. It's just that—"

A waitress swooped in to take our order, and I bit my tongue. Nothing on the menu enticed me. I ordered a small salad.

There was silence when the waitress left. And, of course, darkness. I continued fiddling with my napkin. *What kind of people eat lunch at a place like this?* I was tempted to stand and open the blinds. What was the point of having windows if you couldn't see out of them? Maybe it hadn't been such a good idea to come here after all. Wouldn't my uncle be wondering where I was? A thought struck me. What if he called the house and no one answered? Would he go looking for me?

"Robin," Philip reached across the table and covered my hand with his, "relax. Enjoy yourself."

But it wasn't as easy for me to be reassured in these gloomy surroundings as it had been outside in the bright sunlight. I was flustered that my uneasiness was so obvious. Now Philip probably knew I wasn't used to dating. Suddenly, I had no desire to continue this facade; all I wanted was to escape.

"This is very nice of you—" I began.

"I know it is."

"But maybe . . . a fast-food restaurant might have been a better idea."

Philip glanced around, and I hoped he was seeing our surroundings for what they really were. "Fast food? That's boring." His eyes focused on mine, making me shift in my seat. "I'm sorry if you don't like this place. Maybe I'm trying too hard to impress you—but I wanted to give you a new experience, a chance to see something different." He squeezed my hand. "Isn't that what you wanted?"

"Yes, but . . ." Underneath Philip's hand, I twisted the napkin. "But this wasn't what I meant. I don't think I should be here."

Philip's mouth, and his mustache, turned strangely. "Oh? Your uncle wouldn't approve?"

My chin shot up. "That's not what I meant." My blood began to churn hot inside my veins. "But at the moment, I *am* dependent on him. Until I can get back to California."

"California," Philip repeated, "now there's one of the few places I've never been. But I'd like to go there someday. Tell me about it."

"You'd love it," I said. I even attempted a smile. "The way you drive, you'd fit right in." But I didn't want to get sidetracked. I glanced over my shoulder. "You know," I said hopefully, "they're taking an awfully long time to get our food. Why don't we just leave? I'm not that hungry anyway."

Philip frowned. "Now look, Robin, what's really the matter?" He eyed me closely. "Is it me?" He withdrew his hand. "That's it, isn't it? You don't trust me."

I didn't want to admit it, but my hesitance to answer gave me away. Philip set his jaw. "Our food's coming."

I wanted to say something, but decided I'd be better off if I kept my mouth shut. I always managed to say the wrong thing. It was true I didn't feel comfortable here with Philip, but the truth was I wouldn't feel comfortable with anyone in a place like this. At least, not with someone whom I'd only just met.

For Philip's sake I pretended to enjoy my salad, even though the lettuce tasted like paper and the carrots crunched like wood. I got through it somehow. Then I sat waiting, the food sitting like lead in my stomach, while Philip took his time cutting his steak into tiny chunks and chewing each piece a million times.

I wondered why I couldn't relax like any other normal person out on a date. *That's the problem,* I told myself miserably. *I'm not a normal person.* Living with all my mother's paranoid precautions, she'd affected me with her suspicious nature until now I couldn't trust anyone. Was this how I would be for the rest of my life?

I let Philip pay the bill. After all, this had been a true date. My first real date. Too bad I'd ruined it.

Outside, sunshine flooded over me, bringing with it a sense of relief, and things no longer appeared so threatening. I realized I could still make things right between Philip and me if I really wanted to.

I caught his arm as he opened the car door. When he turned, I looked into his eyes, being careful to keep my own eyes steady. He had to know I was sincere. "Philip, I do trust you." It took all my courage to go on, but I knew he needed to hear it. "And the more I get to know you, the more I like you."

For an awful moment I thought he was going to laugh. But when he spoke, his voice was serious. "I'm glad you feel that way, because I feel the same." Our eyes held, and for an alarming second I thought he was going to kiss me.

But he didn't. Maybe it had just been my imagination. I hoped so, and hopped into the car. Things were fine just the way they were. I didn't want them moving too fast.

"Look at that." I pointed at a parked car with the license plate LV LRNS. "'Love Lorens'? Someone actually paid for that?"

Philip drove out of the lot. "People do funny things in the name of love."

I couldn't help wondering if this day was a dream, and I was almost afraid to let myself enjoy it for fear it would disappear and I would wake up to find I had an eight-hour shift awaiting me at the bookstore.

As we sped along, Philip turned to me. "Well, where to now? It's your call. I said I'd show you around Lorens, but I've done that already. It doesn't take long. Anywhere special you want to go?"

I almost shouted, "Keep your eyes on the road!" Horrified at how prudish that would sound, I quickly answered, "Yes!" And suddenly I had an idea. "Do you know where the Ingerman Mansion is? It's supposed to be on the outskirts of town."

Philip's eyes darted to mine and I was afraid I'd said something stupid. But he only nodded and said, "Sure thing."

I felt the car surge forward with a burst of power. It took my breath away. No doubt about it, Philip was exciting to be with. He was just what I needed. The romance of the situation intrigued me, and I felt like a heroine in a book, being swept away by a dashing buccaneer.

We rounded a bend and bumped along a rutted dirt road.

Trees tightened in around us and sunlight filtered through the leaves, sprinkling us with shreds of light. Little white puffs floated through the air—seeds of some sort—and I was fascinated as we sailed through them.

"Is this what snow's like?" I asked.

"Ha! I wish."

Then there it stood before us: the Ingerman Mansion, set off alone on a vast expanse of shaggy lawn, surrounded by trees and scraggly bushes. I thought the mansion, old as it was, looked grand in a forgotten sort of way. Once upon a time, it must have shone vibrant and new with crystal clear windows; but now it stood broodingly, a dull gray and brown, its windows cloudy and dark. I sat unmoving in the car, my eyes riveted to the immense structure, until I realized *I* was being stared at. By Philip.

I scrambled out of the car, but I could still feel Philip's eyes on me.

"How did you know about this place?" he asked, joining my side. "I thought you were new in town."

"I am." My eyes returned to the mansion. "But my uncle told me about it . . ." I let my voice trail off. I was so intent on the mansion, I hardly heard my own words. I was listening to the wind stirring the leaves of the trees, making a sound like rushing water. "This place is just like I imagined it would be," I said, almost in a whisper.

Philip laughed and sprinted ahead. "Come on, let's get a better look!"

I ran to catch up, tearing through the long, tangled grass and dandelions. Dandelions everywhere . . . some were fluffy white, but most were still yellow, covering the lawn like a thousand gold coins.

"There's no one else around, is there?" I called. The thought struck me that we were trespassing. "It doesn't really matter if we're here, does it?" I wanted to be reassured that we weren't doing anything wrong.

"Not as long as no one catches us!"

Philip smiled at my alarm. "It's not as bad as all that. But surely you don't think this is an open park? A place for just anyone to come? No—if you want to get technical, we are trespassing. But no one cares. The Ingermans are all dead and this place is abandoned. There's no one around for miles. Don't worry so much. Where's your sense of adventure?"

I glanced about me uneasily but said, "I'm not worried." And to prove it, I bounded up the stone steps, past a formidable looking statue of a hawk, its beak broken, to the massive front door. I felt tempted to use the tarnished, old-fashioned knocker, but I shook my head and put my hand on the door handle. If Philip was willing to take a risk, so was I.

"Not that way. It's locked, of course. But if you want to check out the inside, there's a way through a window in the back. Come on."

I turned, then halted on the steps. "How do you know? You've been here before?"

Philip grinned. "I've been any place that's worth checking out in this town. That's why I'm the guy to show you around. The first thing I do when I get to a new place is find out what's hot and what's not. For Lorens, this mansion is about the hottest it gets. You know—haunted house, ghosts, and all that fun stuff."

I nodded slowly, following Philip to a large window, from which a weathered board hung by a rusty nail.

"I read about Connie Ingerman in my mother's papers."

"In what?" Philip paused with the window half open.

I realized he didn't know what I was talking about, so I explained how my mother had been writing the mansion's story for the newspaper and how I'd discovered her work.

"Sounds intriguing," Philip said. Then he helped me through the window and into the mansion.

Chapter Seven

When my eyes adjusted to the dimness, I saw what looked like large white bodies bulging out of the walls. Catching my breath, I realized they were merely pieces of furniture covered in dustsheets.

When I spoke, my voice automatically came out as a whisper. "It's creepy in here, isn't it?"

Philip's eyes sparkled silver. "That's what makes it exciting."

Maybe so, but I knew I wouldn't want to be here alone. Shadows draped the room like black cobwebs and the air hung thick with dust. I jumped at a sudden whistling noise. "What was that?"

"You're a bunch of nerves." Philip laughed. "Don't worry—it's not ghosts—just the wind."

That really made me feel foolish. My thoughts drifted back to the tragic story of Connie Ingerman and how her ghost was supposed to haunt the mansion. I began wondering about the map. Was it a legend, or did it exist? And if so, could it be hidden somewhere in this mansion? As Philip and I crept across the carpet, its thickness muffling our footsteps, I asked, "Have you heard the story of the treasure map?"

"Of course. That's what led me here in the first place." He turned to face me. "How did you find out about it so quickly?"

"In my mother's papers."

"Ah, that's right." Philip sounded disappointed. "Too bad. I thought I was going to have the fun of telling you all about this place. Now you probably know more than I do."

We drifted into a solemn, silent tour of the mansion,

which had clearly been a place of elegance at one time. Its past grandeur was preserved in opulent paintings, lush carpets, and thick draperies. Were they velvet? I touched them gently, felt the soft coating of dust. A crystal chandelier hung high above us, dim with its own film of dust, and I imagined how magical the room would appear if lit. I could almost see dancers spinning across the dazzling room and hear the waltzing music.

I felt the influence of this bygone age so strongly that, instead of bringing the present with us into the rooms, it was as if Philip and I were transported into the past. *This is how it feels to be inside a haunted house,* I thought. Haunted not with spirits, but with things from long ago. Almost as if by remaining undisturbed, the mansion's interior cast a self-fulfilling spell, preserving itself by preserving the atmosphere. Its decrepit exterior acted merely as a disguise.

Having the uncomfortable feeling that I was an intruder in the mansion, I followed Philip into a large room lined with bookcases so tall, a ladder was propped against the wall. The center of the room was dominated by a large oak desk, beside which stood a globe of the world. A leather chair sat before an immense fireplace, and I wondered briefly why these things weren't covered in dustsheets.

Walking into the room, my footsteps resounding loudly on the wooden floor, I caught sight of a huge portrait hanging above the fireplace mantel. I had never seen such a stern looking man. Though his face was draped with cobwebs, which blended with his white hair and beard, I could see his eyes burning through. *How could anyone read a book in this room,* I wondered, *with that man glaring down at them?*

Philip came to stand by my side. "Feels like he's watching us, doesn't it? Old man Ingerman, still guarding his realm . . . Wonder what he'd do to us if he was alive right now and knew we were here searching for the treasure map."

"Philip, don't say that!" Deciding I'd had enough of this

room, I turned to leave. Philip's laughter echoed behind me.

"It's true," Philip said, catching up to me. "The Ingermans can't stop the curious—not even their ghosts can. What's to stop us from finding that map?"

I paused. Was he serious? His question was like a joke, yet not quite, and he seemed to be waiting for an answer. I tried to laugh. "It's just a legend. We don't even know if there is a map."

Philip took my hand and drew me toward a massive, curving staircase. "Well, I think there is. These rumors have to start from something. Think about it. After Connie died, the other Ingermans ignored the rumors because they didn't want to tear this place apart looking for the map. They didn't need the gold, so they chose to forget about it. But that doesn't mean we have to." Philip's voice took on an unnatural rush of enthusiasm. "We could find it if we tried."

Pure speculation, but for a moment, I think I believed him. I felt caught in a net of mystery. The thought of finding the map held such alluring possibilities. I followed closely at Philip's heels as he climbed the stairs.

"What about the curse?" I asked.

"Do you believe in curses?"

God wouldn't allow such things, would He? "No."

"Well, there you go."

The conversation ended, and the idea, fascinating as it was, slipped to the back of my mind as Philip and I toured the top floor, which consisted of a long hall with many rooms branching off from it. And I had thought my uncle's house was large!

I was glad for Philip, not only because I could easily get lost in a place like this, but also for his solid presence, which helped to keep my imagination in check. I found myself wondering what this place had been like when my mother explored it. Not abandoned, I knew, yet not lived in, either. So it had probably been very similar to this, and I wondered at my mother's courage to roam through here alone.

The upstairs rooms were as lavishly furnished and ornamented as the downstairs. The master bedroom looked the way I would expect a palace room to look. I gaped at the ornate tables and chairs, the heavy canopy above the bed, and dared not touch anything for fear I might disturb it from its ancient sleep.

Apparently, Philip had no such qualms. In the corner of the room, I found him poking his finger into a spider web. Watching the spider scurry away, he said, "That's what most people do when something scares them. Run away and hide."

"But it will start spinning a new web as soon as it feels safe."

"It shouldn't wait. It should conquer its fear and start spinning now."

"Then you'd get tangled in the web, wouldn't you?"

"I guess so," and he laughed, as if this thought were appealing.

At the end of the hall was a room—small compared to the master bedroom, but small by no other means—laid with faded, rose-colored carpet. Intricately carved antique furniture stood powdered with dust, and rambling roses, painted on yellowed wallpaper, bordered the room. Silken draperies, tied back with braided cords, matched the pink canopy over the bed.

Ridiculing all this beauty was a terrible musty smell, which I somehow didn't mind because I knew it belonged here . . . another testimony to the mansion's age.

The mansion was like a fairy tale castle—asleep for more than a hundred years. Thinking this, I was suddenly overcome by how exactly like Sleeping Beauty's room this was. Or at least, how I imagined it to be. My mother used to tell me the princess story every night before bed. "Don't you want to hear about Cinderella or Snow White?" she'd sometimes ask.

My answer was always the same: "No—Sleeping Beauty!" This was my favorite bedtime story because I would fall asleep imagining I was Sleeping Beauty, hoping that when I awoke, I would find my own prince waiting to take me to a castle in the clouds.

Now I felt a tingly sensation along my spine as I crossed the carpet and passed a fireplace to stand before a large, gilded mirror. I could not resist running my finger over the cloudy surface. It left a silver streak of reflection, and that's how I noticed Philip was no longer with me.

I whirled around. Where had he gone? I told myself to remain calm, but I felt the blood draining from my face.

"Philip?"

No answer.

"Philip?" I crossed the carpet to a pair of etched glass doors through which weak sunlight filtered. Perhaps Philip had gone through those.

"Philip?" I put my hand on the cold latch, ready to lift it, when a dark shape lunged up from the other side. I stepped back and stifled a scream as the door swung open.

Philip stood there, his face illuminated. He had no idea how badly he had just scared me.

"Take a look at this view!" he exclaimed, dragging me out onto the balcony. To keep myself from tripping, I pulled my arm away, wishing he didn't have to do everything at such an alarming rate. I was still trying to catch my breath.

But I lost it again when I looked off the balcony at the fertile expanse of land which rambled down into a distant valley, and I was suddenly imagining how enchanting a sunset would look from here. But at the moment it was only early afternoon, and the sky was baby blue, dabbed with powder-puff clouds. Birds twittered carefree songs into the wind, wind that was still rustling the leaves of the trees . . . Among all this, an unpleasant thought slithered into my mind. "You don't think this is the balcony that—that Connie fell from, do you?"

"Could be," Philip replied.

Then the rose room is hers, whispered my mind.

I rested my hand on the white wooden rail and looked directly down, far, far below to a rocky garden overgrown with grass and dandelions. Some kind of pink flowers mingled with the weeds and rocks.

Suddenly the world—which had seemed so bright and real a moment ago—transformed into a mirage. Still looking down, my head swelled with dizziness as yellow, pink, and green swam before my eyes. My hand tightened on the rail until wooden slivers pierced my palm. The rail seemed to give way, and—feeling a sensation similar to when you're just drifting off to sleep and something subconsciously alarms you, reflexes react, lurching you awake—I jumped back.

Philip stared at me, probably wondering if I'd gone crazy. Maybe I had.

"Robin? Are you all right?"

I nodded. I didn't know how to explain the fear; I didn't understand it myself. "Let's go back inside." My voice seemed to come from very far away. I could barely hear it for the ringing in my ears. I realized I was about to faint.

I battled it, but my head felt as if it were floating off into the air like a balloon. I even flailed my arms, trying to retrieve it. Blackness flickered before my eyes. I shook it away, but in doing so, lost my balance. I fell, my eyes seeing nothing.

Someone caught me. Held me tightly. But for some reason this increased my fear, and I fought against the restraining grip, fought to push the arms away—

"Robin!" The voice broke through my terror, and I felt someone shaking me. "What's the matter?" I opened my eyes and saw Philip.

My swirling mind gradually subsided. Even so, Philip's hold on me was painfully tight, and I pulled away.

Philip stared at me, his brows furrowed. Extremely embarrassed, now that I had my wits back, I fumbled to explain. "I—I don't know what came over me. But the balcony and—and the height—" we were inside now, my fear dissolving fast, and the more I spoke, the more foolish I sounded—"it just scared me, I guess."

Philip's eyes searched mine. "But you're all right now? You're sure that's all it was?"

"Yes, yes, of course." But I was thinking how I'd ruined everything. Philip would never want to see me again. "Look, I'm sorry, Philip." I rubbed my head. "It's just—" but I still couldn't explain—"thinking about Connie and her fall . . . I guess it just got to me."

To my relief, Philip grinned. "Sure, I understand. But don't let it. You don't even know if this was her room or if that's the same balcony."

True. But that didn't change how I felt. And I *felt* that this was Connie's room. The air hung so thick with tragedy, I wondered how Philip could fail to feel it. He seemed satisfied with his conclusion, though. As much as I wanted to be, I wasn't. I wanted to get out of this place. I'd had enough. This expedition had lost all its charm; there was nothing fascinating about the mansion anymore. Only morbid. My mother's life had been ruined here!

Before I knew what I was doing, I was slumped against the wall, overcome with emotion. I didn't know what Philip's reaction was; I couldn't see through my tears. But I felt him near me, though he didn't try to touch me. I heard him say, "It's okay. Let it all out."

But I wanted to give him some sort of explanation so he wouldn't think I was a weak, emotional, blubbering fool. "There's something I didn't tell you—my mother . . ." and it came pouring out between shuddering sobs, all that my uncle had told me about the accident, until, by the time I was finished, my tears were used up and I felt sick. Why had I ever wanted to come here?

All I knew was I needed to go back to my uncle's house and think things out. By myself. I wiped away the remains of my tears and asked Philip to take me home, and he agreed, reaching for my arm.

Automatically, I pulled away.

I flushed under the hurt, almost accusing look in Philip's eyes. But this time I didn't try to explain. I didn't have the energy.

On our way down the stairs, I noticed a portrait on the wall, one of a young woman. *Connie Ingerman?* I wondered. Her light hair was swept up in an old-fashioned style, quite becoming to her fine-featured face, a face so smooth that I got the impression it was a mask. Perhaps it was just my current state of mind, but I thought I could detect something hidden behind her face, and that's why I thought of a mask. The individual features did nothing to suggest this—lovely eyes, full lips with just a hint of a smile—yet her countenance as a whole appeared tragic. I decided it was definitely a portrait of Connie Ingerman.

The moment I thought this, it was as if her eyes moved and met mine. And those lips—they looked as if they were about to separate and speak. I found myself pausing on the stairs, waiting to hear her impart some vital message.

"Robin? Are you coming?"

I started, and ran down the stairs to catch up with Philip.

What a relief to be outside. I breathed the clear air and exhaled strongly, hoping to expel all the dust that had accumulated in my lungs.

Cleansing my mind was another matter. Even as we drove away, my uneasiness told me that I had started something back there at the Ingerman Mansion, something that would eventually come back to haunt me . . . and no matter how far away I ran, I would not be able to escape it.

Chapter Eight

Four o'clock that afternoon, I had to get out of the house; the ticking clock was driving me crazy. So I walked into town, picked up some groceries, then kept myself busy making dinner. Over the meal, I told my uncle I would have come to work that morning if I hadn't overslept. "Why didn't you wake me?"

"You have an alarm clock."

So I started using it, even though I hated alarm clocks. This one was especially obnoxious, because I couldn't even set it to wake me with music. I detested the beeping noise which jarred me awake so violently I needed another night's sleep to recover.

The mansion remained in my thoughts. Or, more precisely, the balcony room and the young woman's portrait. I was convinced that the room belonged to Connie Ingerman, and equally convinced that the portrait was of her. The mansion followed me into my dreams, where I walked alone through the vast rooms, yet not alone. The darkness echoed with laughter. Ghostly laughter. I ran, searching for a way out, and came to a glass door. Instead of pausing to open it, I broke through. Glass splintered around me, piercing my skin. In my haste to escape, I realized too late that the door was not a way out. It led to the balcony, and suddenly I was falling.

I was thankful for the alarm clock when it woke me from that dream.

During the day, uneasiness hovered near, like a shadow ready to cast its coldness on me at the slightest fading of sunny thoughts. I was afraid I would be haunted by these feelings as long as I remained in Lorens. So I made sure I worked, putting in eight-hour shifts, earning the money that would take me back to California.

As the days passed, I was disturbed by my contrasting feelings, which were pulling at me from two sides: the yearning to find out more about my mother's past and how it was connected to the mansion, and the part of me that resisted, not wanting to know. I stayed away from the chest in the closet. Yet I told myself I would go back to it when I was ready.

For now, I worked. At night, I read my mother's Bible. And when I woke up early on Sunday morning, I walked by myself to church, arriving just in time for the first Mass. My uncle went to the second.

By Monday, after only one day off, I was finding it difficult to get back into the dreary work routine. Most of the morning I spent gazing out the narrow bookstore windows, longing for sunlight. I did my best to subdue my restlessness, but by noon I could stand it no longer. Hoping my uncle would not ask questions, I told him I was going to take the afternoon off and spend it in the park. This was the truth, but I wondered if my uncle believed me. I could never tell what he was thinking.

"Go ahead," he said. "You can have as many days off as you want."

Clutching my sketchpad and pencils, I left the store and headed for the park. Heat from the sun radiated from the sidewalk onto my legs, and I felt warm with the prospect of a whole afternoon to myself. I wasn't sure how many days had passed since I'd last drawn, but I remembered where I'd been: in California—sitting atop the sand dunes, drawing the seashore, the palm trees, and the gulls. That was the night I'd gotten home late, the night my mother was rushed to the hospital. Taking a deep, tremulous breath, I closed my eyes tightly and then opened them, trying to clear my mind.

I had been away from my drawing for much too long.

Maybe that was why I felt so lost lately. Drawing was a part of me, a God-given gift, and I needed to keep it alive if I wanted to feel satisfied. My fingers weren't used to going for such a long time without creative release—I could almost feel them tingling to begin. And from what I'd glimpsed of the park, I knew they wouldn't be disappointed. Like all of Lorens, the land was a luscious green, speckled with dandelions and endowed with trees blooming pink or white blossoms. This place was such a tiny yet significant piece of God's beautiful creation. There was a pond in the park, maybe even a river—but I wasn't sure about that because I hadn't had time to see everything when Philip drove me past.

Philip. I smiled. He always drove too fast. But that was just his way. I liked him like that—all alive and enthusiastic. He had so much excess energy that when I was with him, I couldn't help catching some of it.

I was thankful for Philip. After my strange experience at the mansion, he hadn't abandoned me as I was afraid he would. He'd called me the next day, just to say hi and ask how I was. I told him I was fine. He told me he'd like to see me again.

Tonight we had a dinner date set at an Italian restaurant, a little place that Philip had assured me I would like. He'd described it as "a friendly family place."

Now, reminded of food, I stopped in at a Food Mart and bought myself a sandwich for lunch. By the time I reached the park, I was humming to myself. Picnic tables dotted the landscape, residing near bushes, in the shade of trees, and in the open sunlight.

I sat down at one of the sun-drenched tables near the pond and stretched out my feet for the rays to soak into. I gazed out dreamily over the placid, gray-green water, and slowly, I smiled. Nothing like the ocean, but it would do. There were no gulls, but a pair of ducks came floating toward me, trailing lazy ripples of water behind them.

I didn't unwrap my sandwich right away. Kids were in

school, so the park was peaceful . . . almost too peaceful. I was aware of what was coming, but I couldn't prevent it. My thoughts returned to my mother—Tiffany Hutch—the girl who had grown up in this town. Surely she'd come to this park many times.

I shivered and unwrapped my sandwich, the plastic crinkling rudely in the quiet. Acutely aware of my surroundings, I felt like an actor trapped on a set, playing a part I didn't want to play. This wasn't why I had come here, to be immersed in the past and think such weird thoughts. I bit into the sandwich, not tasting it. Why wouldn't the past stay in the past where it belonged? Why did the memory of my mother have to invade me everywhere I went in Lorens?

Because this was her home, her town; it was where she had grown up; in a way, she was still here. This answer came to me from nowhere, yet somewhere. It came to me on a flower-scented breeze, soft as a whisper. The sun beamed down on me as strongly as ever, but I suddenly felt cold. My fingers touched the dark wood of the tabletop, the fragile peeling paint. Once upon a time, Tiffany might have sat at this very table. Perhaps, like me, she had eaten her lunch here while watching ducks on the pond. But *her* mind had not been troubled as mine was. She had had no ghosts of the past floating in to haunt her. Why was God letting them haunt me?

I studied the old surface of the table, the collage of scratched-in initials. My eyes searched for *T.H.* . . .

Stop! Don't do this to yourself!

I lifted my head and gazed at the deserted sandbox, slides, and swings. Long ago, Tiffany must have laughed and played with her friends in this park. For a moment I believed I heard their voices and laughter drifting in from far away, echoes defying time. Perhaps if I listened hard enough, they would give me answers.

Why had my mother gone away all those years ago and never come back? Because of the accident? But that was over and done with—nothing she could change by leaving. There was so much I didn't understand. Tiffany Hutch had married and become another person—Tiffany Finley—by changing her name. But inside, she had to be the same person. Tiffany Hutch had not vanished. She was still here in Lorens; I could feel her. Why had my mother made me come here? Could she have known how it would affect me? Did she really think she had no choice?

I tore a few scraps of crust from what was left of my sandwich and tossed them to the ducks. So much for a relaxing afternoon in the park. Why couldn't life be simple? I watched the ducks snap up the soggy morsels and paddle around in circles, waiting for more.

Life had been simple, once. Back when I was little. I remembered what happiness and security felt like: my father, the man with a shadowy face, tossing me high into the air. "Look at little Robin fly!" And my mother would laugh.

All that had changed when my father died. My mother had loved him, that much I knew. Once I caught her sitting on her bed holding their wedding photo, just staring at it. I heard her say softly, "You were the most self-sacrificing man." Then, even softer, "I miss you so." And she kissed his picture. My ears burning, I'd crept away from the door before she could see me.

As I grew older I began to sense the unrest, even fear, that my mother carried with her. It was clearer to me now, thinking back. One moment she'd be smiling, the next she'd be blinking back tears, and I didn't know why; I never asked questions. I never knew what would set her off. Unstable was what some might call her. Yet I'd never thought of her as that. After all, she had been the strong one, the one who had looked out for me and fed me and loved me all those years. By herself. It couldn't have been easy for her. Something choked me. Had I ever thanked her for all she'd done?

I blinked rapidly and looked down at my sketchpad. Such

thoughts would do me no good now; thinking them would only drive me insane with regret. I opened the sketchpad. If I started drawing, my mind would focus and I could stop dwelling on such sad thoughts.

For a moment I felt panic. What was wrong with me? How could I sit here on this cloudless day, a breeze murmuring through the trees, birds singing in the branches, the sun and blue sky reflecting off the water, and feel depressed?

Help me, Lord.

I looked down at my last drawing, a picture of the shoreline with a lone gull sailing above. It reminded me of one of the verses I had read last night in the book of Matthew. Something about birds . . . "Are not two sparrows sold for a farthing? And not one of them shall fall on the ground without your Father . . . Fear not therefore: better are you than many sparrows."

Thinking on this, I flipped the page in my sketchpad and the sight of the fresh white paper worked like a deep, calming sigh. I picked up my pencil, and it felt natural in my hand. As I stroked in some soft lines, I found release, striving to catch not just the ducks on the water, but the whole mood of serenity that went with them. My hand and the pencil melted into one, and I became oblivious to everything beyond my drawing.

Until the shadow.

My hand froze on my pencil. The shadow lay over me and my paper, and I knew someone was standing behind, watching me. A breath of wind stirred my hair and goose bumps rose on my arms. *Get a grip,* I ordered myself. Then I swung around.

Justin Landers, reporter, smiled down at me.

"Not bad," he said, referring to my drawing. "In fact, it's very good."

I stiffened. Our last encounter was still clear enough in my mind so that I didn't feel comfortable in his presence.

"Mind if I join you?" He strolled around to the other side of the picnic table, plopped down a brown paper bag, swung his long legs over the bench, and sat directly across from me. "This is a nice spot, isn't it?" He glanced over his shoulder at the pond. "When I work, I always come here to eat lunch, unless it's raining. Then I eat at Mary Anne's. But you know all about that place." He smiled at me and I could see the laughter in his eyes.

"So I see my friends are waiting for me," he went on, "but they don't look too hungry." He frowned. "Were you feeding my ducks?"

Just my luck, I thought. *Out of all the picnic tables in this park, I* would *choose the one Justin Landers thinks he owns.* "Yes," I said, hoping it sounded like a challenge. *His* ducks, indeed.

"Oh, well." He shrugged and pulled out a sandwich. "The greedy little things are just having a lucky day, I guess." He took a big bite of his sandwich and began chewing.

Obviously, Justin did not intend to leave anytime soon. I closed my sketchpad.

"No, don't do that. You can keep drawing. I don't mind."

"Well, I do."

Justin arched his dark eyebrows. "Do I detect a note of animosity in your voice? I don't know how exactly I offended Your Majesty, but it's not very comfortable eating lunch with an enemy."

"That's okay. I can move," I said, standing up.

"Go ahead, but it won't do you much good. I can move anywhere you do."

Exasperated, I sat back down. "What is it you want?"

"Are you always this hostile?" Justin shivered. "You make it feel like January instead of May."

I can't believe that made me smile.

"That's more like it," Justin said. "Now maybe your mood ring will change to a nicer color."

I looked down at my right hand, where I wore my mother's ring. Sure enough, the stone shone murky black.

I shook my head, a mixture of amusement and aversion confusing my feelings. I could leave and go back to the bookstore, but curiosity got the better of me. I stayed.

"Now tell me," Justin said, tearing off a crust and throwing it over his shoulder to the ducks, "how are you finding our little town so far?"

"It's all right." I twirled my pencil between my fingers. "I've had the 'grand tour,' and I guess it's like any other small town."

"Maybe. But every small town has its unique qualities. Even Lorens."

"I know." I paused before adding, "I've seen the Ingerman Mansion."

Justin's eyes shot up to meet mine. At first I thought I saw alarm, but I must have been mistaken, for when he spoke, his eyes were as calm as his voice. "Already? I'm surprised your uncle let you—"

"He didn't. He didn't know," I admitted. "A friend took me. He's the one who gave me the tour of town."

"Oh? What's his name? Maybe I know him."

I doubted it. Yet this was a small town, and I'd heard everyone knows everyone in a small town.

"Philip Barnstrum."

"Hmm . . . can't say it rings a bell." He crumpled his lunch bag and went on. "So I'm guessing you already know the story behind the mansion—the rumors about ghosts, a curse, and a treasure map?"

"Sure," and in an attempt to impress him, I told him about my mother's ambitious undertaking to write the mansion's story.

"Sounds like your mother would have made a good reporter."

My eyes wavered from his.

"Sorry," Justin said, apparently realizing the tactlessness

96

of his comment. Unexpectedly, I felt my heart warm at the way he said it—so much like he meant it. He wasn't making fun of me now.

He stood up and suggested we take a walk.

"Don't you have to get back to work?" I asked.

"Nah, I'm important enough that I can afford to make my own schedule."

We walked in silence for a while along the bank of the pond, the ducks trailing hopefully beside us. I was thinking how nice this was, and how absurd that I should feel comfortable walking with Justin; I never would have imagined it after our last encounter. The reason must be that this time he wasn't barraging me with questions or provoking me with strange comments. Consequently, I didn't feel intimidated. I looked up at the sky, clear except for a few chalky-white jet trails. *I'll be on one of those jets soon,* I promised myself.

But for now I enjoyed walking along the river, pausing now and then to pick scattered violets or buttercups, and I asked Justin if he really came here every day to eat lunch. "I think you just made that up about the ducks."

"Now why should I do that? Don't you trust me?"

"Truthfully? No. Besides, you're the one who told me not to trust strangers."

"That's right, and I meant it. It's good advice. But it doesn't apply to me anymore. I'm not a stranger."

"Oh, don't be too sure of that," I began, a playfulness rising inside me. "You never answered the five W's for me yet."

"You're not a reporter." There was a sudden lack of humor in his voice, but I went on anyway.

"Doesn't matter. I've just as much right to ask questions as you. How's this for starters?" I fired off questions as fast as I could think them. "Where did you grow up? Who were your parents? What made you decide to become a reporter? When did you leave home? Why did you come to Lorens?"

An unusually long silence followed, during which my cheeks grew warm, waiting for Justin to speak. Suddenly, my questions seemed childish and rude, and I wanted to take them back.

Finally, he said, "It would take me a long time to answer all those questions."

"I have time—"

"Not enough."

Startled by the bitterness in his voice, I stopped walking.

Justin turned to face me. "Sorry." He tried to smile. "Look, how about we drop the questions? They'll probably just get us into an argument. Besides, I don't think I know the answer to all those things myself. And if I did, I can guarantee you wouldn't want to hear them."

I didn't know what to say. But Justin took my hand and I found myself walking over a wooden bridge. It creaked with every step we took. I wanted him to say more.

"Robin," he hesitated, "once you get to know me . . . you'll realize that I sometimes say things . . . without thinking, things that don't make a whole lot of sense, so don't try to make sense out of them—or me—and you'll be a lot better off."

This strange speech was probably a good example of what he was trying to say. I laughed and let it go.

There were other things to think about. Like how peaceful the river ran under the bridge and ambled its way downstream, the enchanting way the weeping willow dipped its new green leaves into the water.

I believe it was a full minute before I realized.

Chapter Nine

"Oh," I said, feeling slightly dizzy as I took in our surroundings, "I recognize—I know this place."

"You've been here before?"

"Yes. No." The picture in the yearbook flashed before my eyes. "I mean—my mother drew this scene. Years and years ago, but it looks—exactly the same." I lifted my hand to my forehead, feeling the blood swirling in my head like the water over the rocks in the river below.

"That makes sense," came Justin's voice, gently, through the confusion. "You said your mother grew up in Lorens. Of course she's been here, and it's not surprising she'd want to draw it. This is one of the most scenic places in the park." He knew what I meant, and I didn't even have to explain. "A place like this doesn't change much in twenty years." The logic of his words helped to calm me.

"You're right." I let my hand fall. "I don't know why I reacted like that. It almost felt like . . . like I jumped back in time. I'm not usually so sensitive. Only lately," I fumbled with my words, "I can't seem to shake these weird feelings." I sighed. "Maybe if the past weren't so—so unreachable, I wouldn't feel this way. Like something is missing."

"Maybe," Justin said quietly. "But remember, that's what makes it the past. No one can ever go back."

I lifted my head and tried to look into Justin's eyes, searching for something hidden behind his words, trying to discover what he was feeling. Because it was as if he understood—understood even more than I did—and I felt a sudden need to connect with him. But now when I wanted them to, his eyes wouldn't meet mine.

We left the bridge and returned to the picnic table, where I gathered up my sketchpad and pencil, still feeling disturbed. For days I'd been trying to avoid my feelings, but all that got me was fear and insecurity. I couldn't take it anymore; it was time to do something. Time to quiet these ghosts of the past so that they, and I, could rest in peace.

The only way to settle my uneasiness was to find the answers to my questions about my mother, about her life here in Lorens. About her accident. I ventured to speak, breaking the solemn mood. And yet somehow I didn't break it; when I spoke, my voice blended in as if it belonged.

"I wish I *could* go back. There's so much I want to know." I clutched my sketchpad to my chest. "Connie Ingerman wasn't the only one who fell from the mansion's balcony." I took a deep breath. "My mother did, too. When she was my age. When she was there researching her story."

Justin didn't speak. His eyes still told me nothing. Yet I felt he was listening seriously, so I went on.

"How could it happen? I don't understand—but I need to." I clapped a hand to my throat as all the emotion I'd been building up and holding back surged over me. "She never told me about the accident or where she grew up. How could she keep so much from me? It's horrible. I know nothing about my mother. Not really—all I've ever known or thought I knew—none of it is real. I've been living in a dream."

Even now, I felt as if I were in a dream, and I wondered if I would ever wake up. Justin put a steady hand on my shoulder, and I thought numbly, *He probably thinks I've lost my mind.*

Instead, he surprised me by saying, "If you really want to find out more—about what happened to your mother—there are ways." He paused. "But only if you really need to know."

"I do."

"Something like this isn't a game. Once you start, you can't quit."

"I wouldn't want to quit."

"What if you don't like what you find?"

"At least I'd have the truth."

"But is it that important to you—important enough to risk the pain it could cause? It might end up being worse . . . sometimes it's better not to know. You can't change the past, and that can be a hard fact to face."

"You sound as if you know."

"I know," he said, taking his arm off my shoulder. "If what you want is peace of mind, the best thing you can do for yourself is to forget the past and move on."

I fought to keep my voice steady. "My mother's dead, and I know nothing will bring her back. But coming here to Lorens . . . has made me feel like I never really knew her. If I could only find out who she was—it—it would help me." I faltered at what I could not speak aloud, at what I had only just begun to realize: maybe it would help me understand myself.

Justin ran a hand through his already disheveled hair. "All right." His words, grimly decisive, left no room for doubt. I felt immense relief, as if simply by his consent, everything would work out. "I'll tell you where to start. It's a place even reporters turn to for doing research. Maybe you've heard of it—it's called a library."

Our laughter broke the tension.

We walked along the sidewalk for about a block before reaching the public library. When we stepped inside, the air conditioning hit me like a bucket of cold water, waking me from my dreamlike state and dunking me back in reality. This was no dream, and I wasn't going to accomplish anything by simply drifting along. I was glad I'd made my decision.

"You can start by looking through the old newspapers," Justin said. "There's sure to be an article on the accident. Probably more than one, because something like that would have made big news in a small town." After a pause, he added, "It's obvious why people aren't supposed to go inside the mansion anymore."

Prickling at his tone, I replied, "I wasn't alone."

"I know. You had Phillip what's-his-name to protect you."

"Barnstrum."

"Sure. Anyway, they keep old local newspapers on microfilm." Justin, apparently very familiar with all this, led me to a small room in the back of the library. The walls were lined with dated film cartridges standing neatly on shelves.

"You work the machines like this." I watched carefully as Justin demonstrated, but it turned out to be a simple enough process, nothing I couldn't have figured out on my own. "I've got to get back to work now," Justin said, moving away from the table. "They're probably afraid I've left for good this time."

I smiled. "Thanks for all your help." I meant it, and as eager as I was to get started, I found myself wishing Justin didn't have to leave.

"You know," he said, and I looked up expectantly, "we could go out for pizza tonight or something when I get done with work."

My heart jumped. Then I remembered Philip.

"Sorry." I looked down at the machine. "I already have plans for tonight. I'm going for Italian with Philip." *Besides,* I told myself, *living with my uncle, pizza is the last thing I want.*

Justin shrugged. "Have a good time then. I just thought maybe you'd like to talk over what you find—if you do find anything."

You could at least sound disappointed.

"Whatever it is you're looking for, good luck. Oh, and about your question—come and see for yourself."

"Huh?" I looked up. "What question?"

"You asked if I really do eat lunch at the park every day." He grinned. "Stop by one of these days and see for yourself."

With a smile, I rolled my eyes and turned back to the projection machine.

~

Cartridges of film stood stacked in a precarious tower beside me on the table. Whatever I was looking for, I wasn't finding it.

I rubbed my temples and sighed, but I was determined to go through however many rolls of film it took to find something relating to my mother's accident. What I wanted was an official account. All the facts.

Because hearing it told wasn't enough. Though I was going on nothing but instinct, I felt that the story my uncle had told me was incomplete. I wanted something concrete to help me pinpoint what was missing.

Once I had the exact circumstances of the accident set before me in the clear black and white perspective of newspaper type, maybe that would also help them become clear in my mind.

I put in the last microfilm roll dated 1979 and cranked slowly through the pages. I couldn't afford to miss anything, not even the tiniest article, because it might be just the one I wanted. The word "Ingerman" flashed before my eyes in giant letters, and suddenly there was the headline I'd been looking for: ***Ingerman Mansion claims another victim***.

How awful the way newspaper people had to make everything sound as dramatic as possible; all they cared about was selling their papers. Reading that bold headline, I almost didn't want to go on.

But I couldn't stop my eyes from running down the article.

> *Tiffany Hutch, an 18-year-old senior at Lorens*
> *High School and an intern of this newspaper,*
> *was rushed to a hospital late the afternoon of*

103

May 3 after falling 20 feet from a balcony of the Ingerman Mansion.

I cringed as a vision of the rocky ground beneath the balcony flashed before my eyes.

After questioning Anthony Ingerman, 63, owner of the mansion, it has been established that Hutch, who had been given his permission to go through the dilapidated structure, was there gathering research for a story she was writing. Ingerman had entrusted Hutch with a key to the mansion, enabling her to enter.

Examination of the broken railing shows that the old wood had been decaying for quite some time. Therefore it would not have taken much force to break it. It is believed that Hutch, unaware of the danger, leaned against the rail, causing it to break.

Ironically, it was from this very same balcony that Connie Ingerman—a great-aunt of Anthony Ingerman—is believed to have thrown herself to her tragic death in 1851. In a further twist of fate, it is this incident that constituted a large part of Hutch's research.

Fortunately for Hutch, she was found by a friend, Christopher Renton, 22, with whom she had a date to meet that afternoon at her home. Upon finding her absent and after being informed by Hutch's brother, Peter Hutch, of her whereabouts, Renton told investigators that he decided to drive to the mansion.

"I wasn't really worried," Renton said, "I thought she'd probably just lost track of time or something." Upon discovering Hutch's unconscious form, however, Renton saw this

was not the case and immediately went for help. "I was afraid she was dead," Renton said.

Authorities say it is very likely Renton saved Hutch's life by finding her when he did. A half an hour more could have been too late. At the time of this printing, Hutch is still unconscious and listed in critical condition. Peter Hutch offered no comment. The incident is still under investigation.

The "incident." So that's what they called it. I shuddered. The report gave the facts in such a cold, unfeeling way. Everything fit with what my uncle had told me, but he hadn't gone into such detail. I turned the projector handle, searching for more, hoping for a follow-up article. Several editions of the paper later, I found one.

Hutch unable to remember accident

Tiffany Hutch, 18, is now listed in stable condition after her fall from a balcony of the Ingerman Mansion on the afternoon of May 3. Her injuries include numerous scratches and bruises, a broken leg, and a head injury resulting in memory loss.

As yet, Hutch cannot recognize friends, let alone recall the accident. However, it is believed by officials that with time and care, Hutch will gradually recover from this state of amnesia. "How much time it will take we have no way of knowing," stated Dr. Kimberling. "It really depends on the individual."

As of this time, no new information pertaining to Hutch's accident has been found.

My heart was thumping so loudly, I expected a librarian to appear and order me to silence. I tried forcing my tense muscles to relax, which of course did no good. Wondering if there could be another article, I rolled madly through the film, half hoping—half fearing—there would be.

There was.

Injured girl's memory returns—
but not completely

Tiffany Hutch, 18, is still suffering aftereffects from her traumatic experience: a 20-foot fall from a balcony of the Ingerman Mansion on May 3. Yet while much of her memory has returned, Hutch can recall no particulars of the accident, and further questioning by investigators proves futile.

"Of course, in an incident such as this, nothing is ruled out immediately," explained Detective Bankwell. "With no witnesses to the accident, we have to consider the possibility of foul play. Yet with no new developments, we have no reason to believe foul play was involved, and at this point I think we must conclude that Miss Hutch was merely the victim of unfortunate circumstances."

When I looked up from the projection machine, it took me a moment to realize where I was. Except for my beating heart, the library was unearthly quiet, making me feel more than a little ill at ease, sitting alone in that tiny microfilm room.

I found no more related articles. The three I had found, I reread so many times that I felt I had them memorized. There were the facts, all cut and dry as I'd wanted. Now I should be satisfied.

But I wasn't. Perhaps I'd known all along I wouldn't be. What was it Justin had said? "This isn't a game. Once you start, you can't quit." I hadn't reached the end yet, and though I had no idea where the end lay, I knew I hadn't gone as far as I could go. And that's why I couldn't be satisfied.

I continued turning through the last pages of the paper, and paused to read the page devoted to the 1979 graduating class of Lorens High School. My mother's name was not listed. Of course, I'd known it wouldn't be.

You were so close, Mom, I almost whispered. *Why did you throw it all away? It wouldn't have been so difficult to catch up.*

It was as if she didn't care.

There was nothing more for me to learn here, so I put everything away and left the room, absorbed in thought. I felt let down that I hadn't made any great discovery. But, I consoled myself, I had found something new. Something my uncle hadn't mentioned. Someone named Christopher Renton had found my mother, and by doing so, probably saved her life. I wondered why my uncle hadn't told me this.

I stopped right in the middle of the library entrance while the name was fresh in my mind and jotted it in my sketchpad. Then, as I was writing it, I realized there was something significant about the name. I felt a spark of excitement. Yes! That last night by my mother's side, I had heard her mention Christopher. Possibilities began rushing through my mind.

Christopher Renton was probably still alive. He'd only be forty-two. Maybe he still lived around Lorens. My thoughts skipped ahead eagerly. Maybe I could locate him.

I turned around and fairly ran to the information desk, where I asked for a telephone book. I skimmed down the list of names. *Rent . . . Rentil . . .* No Renton. I closed the book and caught the librarian's attention.

"Excuse me, does the library keep old phone books?"

The librarian nodded. "Over there against that wall." She

pointed to a low shelf. "But we only keep books going back five years."

I looked through those books, but wasn't surprised when I didn't find Renton listed. These books were too new. What I needed was a book from when I knew Christopher had lived here, twenty years ago. Because if he didn't live here now, at least his old address might give me some place to start looking for him. I was about to return to the desk to ask where else I might go to find old phone books, when I noticed the clock on the wall. Four-thirty. Philip would be picking me up in less than an hour. I had to get home and get ready.

Hurrying out of the library, I managed a smile as I passed a young mother leading a little boy and girl inside. The kids were dressed in matching outfits, and I wondered briefly if they were twins. On the street corner, I passed a few teenaged girls huddled in a group, talking and laughing so loudly, I couldn't help catching strands of their conversation.

" . . . and everyone was laughing at her. I mean, she's seventeen and she's never even been kissed! Can you believe it?"

More laughter.

"But can you blame her? I mean, who'd want to kiss that girl? She's got a face like a—"

I purposely quickened my steps and passed out of hearing range, feeling repulsed and suddenly very much alone.

I'm not sure why their words had such an impact on me, why they made me want to turn and declare: "I'm almost eighteen, and I've never been kissed. I'm not ashamed of it. Why should I be? I'm not going to kiss someone just to prove something—I have more respect for myself than that. If I ever do kiss someone it will be out of love, nothing else. So maybe I'll live to be a hundred without kissing a guy. So what? At least I'll have been true to myself."

The only thing stopping me from proclaiming this was

that I knew the girls would go off into gales of laughter. These were no mild-mannered milkmaids. California or Wisconsin, teenagers were the same.

Sometimes, it made me ashamed to be one.

Chapter Ten

By the time I saw Philip's sleek red car pull into the drive, I'd managed to work myself into a better frame of mind. I was determined to enjoy the date that I had been so looking forward to earlier.

My uncle had only recently arrived home. On my way to the front door, I passed through the kitchen, announcing, "I won't be here for dinner. I'm going out with Philip."

My uncle looked up from the pizza he was unwrapping. "I assume this is the same young man that you went out with the other day?"

"His name is Philip. And yes, he's the same." At that moment the doorbell rang.

"I'd like to be introduced," my uncle said.

When I made the introductions, Philip was his usual charming self, and he even complimented my uncle on his well-kept front lawn.

So that should satisfy him, I thought as we drove away. *I bet he'll be sitting up all night waiting for me, though.* Philip turned up the radio then, and the blaring music drowned out my thoughts.

A short time later, Philip swung into a gravel lot and pulled up to the front of a rather simple, boxy building hung with a banner striped in red, green, and white—the colors of the Italian flag. "Here we are. Little Italy, the only Italian restaurant within thirty miles." He opened the car door. "Hope you like it."

The moment we swept inside, I knew I would. It was a simple yet appealing place, and the windows actually let in light, a welcome contrast to that other restaurant. We were led to a cozy table near the back wall. Italian music floated through the room in soft romantic strains, creating a pleasant foreign atmosphere.

A young waitress, her flushed cheeks suggesting she was very busy but her smile implying she enjoyed the activity, came to take our order. Raven hair framed her face in a soft, careless way that was very becoming. Her eyes sparkled as she spoke. I noticed Philip's eyes lingered on her a little too long, and I felt a twinge of jealousy at the way he smiled at her.

"Working hard tonight?" he asked.

The waitress's eyes got even brighter, if that was possible. "Yes. Every time I step out of the kitchen, someone flags me down."

"Maybe because you're the loveliest waitress they've ever seen."

I bit my tongue and stared at the menu. *Don't let it get to you. That's just how Philip is,* I told myself. *He's friendly with everyone.* But I knew this was more than friendliness; this was flirting.

"But she's not nearly as lovely as you," Philip clarified as soon as the waitress left.

I merely mumbled an incoherent response while nibbling on a breadstick.

"Enjoy your meal," the waitress told us after delivering our plates.

I will now, I thought as she flitted away. I had already forgotten the name of the dish, but it tasted delicious. Recalling Justin's offer to take me out, I smiled, thinking I could very well be at the dinky diner and eating pizza for the umpteenth time this week, if I hadn't been careful.

"What's so funny?" Philip asked, twirling spaghetti around his fork.

"Oh, nothing." Then, in a mischievous mood, I added, "I was just thinking how much nicer this place is than that little diner—Mary Anne's, I think it's called—and I'm glad you asked me out, because I had an offer from someone else."

"Oh?" Philip's mouth smiled, but his eyes probed mine, and I suddenly wished I hadn't said anything. "I'm glad you realized the better offer. Who is this guy? What's he doing moving almost as fast as me?"

"You wouldn't know him."

"Try me."

I shifted in my seat. "Justin Landers, some reporter for the *Lorens Daily Journal*."

"How'd you meet him?"

Let's see . . . I was not going to go into detail here. "He was just helping me with some . . . research. At the library. That's all." I put a forkful of fettuccine in my mouth and began chewing. A few strands escaped my teeth and slithered down my throat. I didn't want to talk about Justin. For some absurd reason, it made me feel guilty. As if I was betraying him or something.

"You don't need his help, Robin. You've got me. I'd be glad to help you with anything, anytime at all. Remember that. What sort of research?"

I took a sip of water before replying. "I was trying to find out about my mother." My voice grew quiet. "About her accident. I found three old newspaper articles."

"And what did they tell you? Anything you didn't already know?"

"That's just the problem. I mean, the articles reported the accident . . . but that's about it."

"The problem is?"

"I was looking for something more."

"Like what?"

"Something to indicate—that maybe it wasn't an accident." The words came out on their own, startling me. Then I realized this suspicion had been in my mind, fermenting steadily ever since reading that detective's statement about considering the possibility of foul play. Now I was considering it, and my words caused a tense silence that even the sweet strains of dinner music could not fill.

"Robin," Philip said, taking my hand, "how'd you ever get an idea like that? Surely not from the articles."

"They did mention the possibility of foul play."

"Mentioned? Possibility? That doesn't sound like much." Philip frowned. "Robin, don't do this to yourself, don't search for more heartache. You've got to let this go."

"What do you mean by that?"

When Philip spoke, he sounded more serious than I'd ever heard him. "I'm afraid you might be latching onto this because you don't want to face the truth—"

"But that's just it." I almost pulled my hand away. "No one knows the truth. No one knows what really happened. No one but my mother—and she couldn't remember. So the newspapers just published what they assumed happened, and that was the end of it."

"I see." Philip picked up his glass as if to drink from it, rotated it while staring at it, then set it back down with a *clunk*. "And you, Robin—you don't think that's the end of it?"

"No. Yes. I don't know." I stood up, shaking my head. "I'm sorry, Philip, but this is all very confusing."

Philip pushed out his chair and hurried around the table to my side.

"Of course it is, Robin, and I understand." Did he? I searched his eyes as we stood together under a dim, multicolored-glass hanging lamp and was touched to see just how serious they were. He really cared. In the midst of my disordered feelings, I felt as if I was being given a rare insight into Philip's character.

"The way it happened is too suspicious," I tried to explain, not only to Philip but also to myself. "How could my mother just fall? She wouldn't be that careless. She wasn't a careless person."

"It could happen."

"Then why didn't people think that when Connie

Ingerman fell?" I didn't wait for an answer. "Because everyone had already formed their conclusions. They knew she'd lost her love, so they decided that was a reason for her to commit suicide."

"Are you saying you think your mother tried to commit suicide?"

"Of course not!"

"Sorry, it kinda sounded like—"

"What I mean is, it's as if people just make their own conclusions, whatever suits their fancy at the time, and then it sticks—like fact—when it isn't fact at all. What if the answer isn't always the obvious one?" My voice had grown loud and my face, hot. People turned to stare.

Philip ignored everyone else and concentrated on me. "Well, if you want to look at things in a different way," he said, his voice lowering, "have you asked yourself why your mother kept her accident a secret from you all these years?"

"Of course I've asked myself that . . ." I let the sharp words fade into silence.

"See, I don't quite understand." Philip hesitated. "To me, above anything else you've told me, that's what strikes me as the strangest. Why did she keep all this from you? What else was she hiding?"

I studied his face before answering. "Philip, what are you getting at?"

"Well, if she didn't tell you the truth—what's to say she told anyone the truth? What's to say your mother really had amnesia? What's to stop her from lying about that, too?"

"Don't say that!"

"I'm sorry."

I sat back down. "I'm sorry, too." My voice was quiet. I didn't want to be angry at Philip, but I didn't like the new suspicion he'd planted in my mind. I didn't want to add more complications to an already confusing situation. "Why would my mother fake something like that?"

"I'm not saying she did. Only, people can be funny. You

can't know what motives they might have hidden. They can seem perfectly normal, and you'd never suspect—"

I dropped my head into my hands.

"Maybe I'm going about this the wrong way. I want to help you, Robin." I felt gentle fingers run over my hair in a soothing motion. "I'm not trying to hurt you. Understand that. I'll help you in any way I can. And if you're looking for answers, probably the best place to start is already at your fingertips."

I lifted my head.

"Your mother's papers," Philip continued, "the ones you told me about, her research papers."

"But I've already gone through them."

"I know. But how thoroughly? You said there were a lot."

"An overwhelming mess," I admitted.

"Then you might have missed something important." Philip paused. "Tell you what. How about I help you search through them?"

I pretended to study my fingernails. It was true I didn't want to go through the papers by myself. That's why I hadn't touched them since that first evening. Having someone to go through them with me would keep me from becoming submerged in sadness. And it was such a considerate offer. I wasn't quite sure what we would be looking for, but Philip seemed confident this was the right thing to do, and that was good enough for me. "All right," I finally agreed.

"Great. How about I take you out for dinner again tomorrow night? I'll come over early—say five?—and we can go through the papers first."

I almost said yes, but for some reason I thought of my uncle. I didn't want to push things with him. "Let's make it Thursday."

"Why?" Philip looked disappointed.

"I—just need some time."

"I understand." I was grateful he didn't press the issue.

"Now, how about a movie?" Philip asked, reverting to his carefree self.

"As long as it's something light and humorous. I've had enough drama for one evening."

Driving out of the parking lot, Philip cut a sharp turn past a parked Jeep. Spraying gravel, he barely missed making contact with the bumper.

I let out my breath.

"You weren't worried, Robin, were you? You know me better than that." Philip accelerated with a burst of speed. "I know how to handle this baby. You don't think I'd be careless with her, do you? Heck, I probably had a whole two inches to spare."

~

Not a single light lit the windows of the house when we pulled into the driveway, meaning my uncle had already gone to bed. This surprised me. I guess I was so accustomed to being under my mother's constant watch that it was difficult for me to get used to the idea that no one was going to watch out for me like that anymore.

That's fine, I told myself. *That's what I want.*

The moment Philip's car stopped, I jumped out. Forcing my voice to sound cheerful, I called, "See you Thursday!" Then I let myself into the dark house and shut the door.

~

When Philip picked me up from the bookstore Thursday afternoon, I couldn't wait to go through my mother's papers. All day long my enthusiasm had been mounting until now I stood at the peak of optimism. Of course I had missed something important among all those papers, and whatever it was, Philip would help me find it.

Leading Philip into the living room, I told him I'd bring the papers down, but he followed me upstairs. "We might find something else important in your mother's room," he

116

explained.

I gladly handed him the overflowing binder. He sat back in the desk chair to read. I sat on the bed, watching. Minutes ticked away as he sat silent, absorbed in the papers.

"Listen to this," he said finally, tapping a page. "Your mother really argues in favor of the treasure map. 'No one has ever found the supposed map to John Kurselli's buried gold, but that doesn't mean it doesn't exist. On the contrary, Connie Ingerman had no reason to make up the story; her heart was for John, not his gold. Even the fact that no one ever saw the map is of little importance. If Connie's sweetheart asked her to hide it, devoted as she was to him, of course that is what she would do.'"

"Makes sense," I said, tracing a quilt square with my finger. I began thinking about the possibility of the map still being hidden somewhere in the mansion. Then I caught Philip looking at me, his eyes alight.

"The map exists."

"What?"

"It's just like she said—just like I told you. The map exists." He waited for me to say something.

"It sounds very likely," I began, warily. We were speculating again about the map, and this wasn't what we had started searching for. "But its existence doesn't really change anything. I mean, if no one's ever found it, what are the chances—"

"Don't you see, Robin? It's like I told you before. If no one's ever found it, that means it's still where Connie hid it, which makes it all the more likely that we *can* find it. Someone will eventually. It might as well be us." Philip spoke so fast, my thoughts could hardly keep up. "Isn't this what you've always wanted, Robin? To search for a treasure? What an adventure, what a chance of a lifetime!"

I could feel Philip's enthusiasm infecting me, running through my veins, intoxicating me until the thrill threatened to force all other thoughts from my mind.

"You'd know a treasure map if you saw one, wouldn't you?" Philip asked.

"Why—of course." I faltered. True, I'd never actually seen one before, but why shouldn't I recognize one if I saw one? I looked at Philip quizzically.

"Good," he said, returning to the papers.

It seemed only a minute later that he said, "Robin." I looked up, startled by his tone, to see him grasping a piece of loose-leaf paper. I leapt off the bed and joined him, reading over his shoulder a scribbled paragraph headed: "A Rumor No More."

> *In my investigation, I discovered a letter between the pages of a novel in the mansion's library. This letter is important not only for its historical value, but also for the information it contains. The map exists! This letter, written by Connie Ingerman, proves it. And it hints at the map's location.*

That was all.

Philip broke the silence. "This is what we've been waiting for." His voice lowered. "Now we have the chance that no one else has. This letter Connie wrote—it's the key to it all."

"But we don't have the letter."

Philip began fumbling madly through the papers, scattering them, mumbling, "It's got to be here . . ." Suddenly he threw the papers to the ground. "Why doesn't she have the letter?"

I dropped to my knees and began shuffling the papers back together. "Maybe she left it where she found it—"

"Why would she do that?"

"I don't know. I'm not my mother! Maybe she couldn't take anything out of the mansion, maybe—"

"All right, all right, it's okay." Philip took the papers

from me and continued reading. I dropped back onto the bed.

Philip's head jerked up. "What was that? It sounded like a door—"

"It's just my uncle," I said. "He's home from the bookstore. I guess I should run down and let him know what I'm doing tonight." I got up reluctantly.

"You do that." He lifted the papers. "I'll just finish looking through these."

I was back in about two minutes, stinging from my uncle's suggestion that "you should bring your young man downstairs now that he's had his tour of the house."

I flushed when I saw Philip had my sketchpad in hand. He must have found it in the desk. But he didn't appear in the least concerned at having been caught with it.

"These are real good," he said, paging through. "You have talent."

"Thank you." Apparently, he'd lost interest in my mother's papers. They lay strewn across the carpet.

He turned a page and came to my last drawing, the one of the ducks, and was about to close the pad when something stopped him.

"What's this?" he asked, pointing to the top of the page.

"Oh," I craned my neck and saw it was the name I had jotted down, Christopher Renton, "I almost forgot to tell you. That's the name of the guy who found my mother after her fall."

Chapter Eleven

At work the next day, I could not focus. I ended up shelving horror books with cookbooks and children's books with romance. My mind was preoccupied with the previous evening. Philip and I had gone out to dinner, but I hadn't enjoyed it much. All he wanted to talk about was the letter.

"It's sure to lead us to the map. We need to find it."

"How? We have no idea where it is."

"Yes, we do. Since your mother didn't have it—and I don't know why she didn't just take it—"

"Maybe because it didn't belong to her—"

Philip gave me an exasperated look, then continued as if I hadn't spoken. "It must still be in a book in the mansion's library."

"But you don't know which book it's in, and there must be hundreds."

Philip smiled, but I saw the determination in his eyes.

"You don't mean you're going to look through them all!"

"Whatever it takes. And you can help me."

In my mind appeared a bleak image of the mansion's interior, the shadowy library and the stern portrait glaring down from the fireplace, and I didn't answer.

Philip hadn't thought much of my Christopher Renton theory.

"But he's the one who found my mother after her fall," I tried to explain. "If I could locate him and talk to him—"

Philip shrugged. "You could try."

But since he didn't offer any suggestions on how to go about doing this, I was left on my own. As I said, Philip's thoughts were all for the map.

My own thoughts turned to Justin. I couldn't help remembering how he'd said he would help me, and how he'd helped me already. Would he help again? There was only one way to find out, and by noon Friday I found myself wondering if he'd be at the park having lunch as he'd claimed. Even as I made up my mind to find out, I wished there was some other way of going about this, because the idea of asking Justin Landers for help made my stomach flip.

But since I couldn't think of any other way, I said a quick prayer and went.

He was there, sitting at "his" table, and before I came within ten feet, he turned to grin at me. "I was wondering when you'd show up."

Groaning silently at his cocky attitude, I suppressed the urge to walk right past him. I reminded myself that I'd come here strictly on business and should act accordingly. Without a word, I drew a slip of paper from my pocket and held it out to him.

"Nice to see you, too," Justin said.

I continued holding the piece of paper on which I'd written the name Christopher Renton. "This is the guy who found my mother after her—accident," I began. "The article said he was her friend. I want to—"

"So you think the next step is to trace this guy?"

"Yes—"

"How do you know if he still lives here? Or if he's even alive? More importantly—what if he refuses to talk to you?"

I thought Justin's curtness was completely unnecessary. "I *don't* know whether he's alive or not. That's what I need to find out. And he *doesn't* live here—at least, he's not listed in the phone book—and I *won't* know whether he's willing to talk to me or not until I locate him."

A smile spread across Justin's face. "And you'd probably find a way to make him talk, even if he didn't want to." While I wondered what to make of that comment, Justin glanced back down at the piece of paper and his smile faded.

"Since you're a reporter, I thought you'd know how to go about this sort of thing . . ." I waited for Justin to pick up the sentence. When he didn't, I went on. "So I thought maybe you'd know where to go from here. Maybe you could—"

"I'll see what I can do, but I can't promise anything." Justin stood up, frowning at his watch. "I have to go."

"Oh." I'd assumed he'd have plenty of time to talk. But, as usual, things weren't going as expected. "Okay. When do you think you—"

"Don't worry about it," he said, already walking away. "I'll find you when I have something to tell you."

"Oh. Okay . . ." I faltered, wondering how he could be so sure. "Wait!" I yelled after him, suddenly realizing he hadn't taken the piece of paper. I waved it in the air. "You don't have the name—it's Christopher Renton!"

"I'll remember," he called over his shoulder.

~

On my way back to the bookstore, I nibbled on a sandwich, wondering whether I'd done the right thing. Could I rely on Justin? *He might not bother to do anything,* I thought. He certainly hadn't seemed eager to help. I brushed my fingers off on my jeans before entering the bookstore and returning to work.

Who was I kidding, anyway—why should Justin make time to help me? Reporters were busy people, with deadlines to meet. Of course he wouldn't want to get himself involved in my problems. Then I felt disappointed in him for leading me on. Last time, he'd acted as if he cared.

Neither Philip nor Justin seemed to realize the importance of my find, and it became clear that if I was going to find out anything at all about this Christopher guy, I'd have to do it myself. With this in mind, I stopped in at the library at four-thirty (my uncle let me leave work early, thanks to my mention of a headache, which wasn't a lie), and found a librarian.

"I understand you only keep phone books going back five years. Can you tell me where to find books going back as far as, say . . . twenty years?" Waiting for her answer, I held my breath.

"Oh, that's easy," the librarian said with a big smile, and I let out my breath. "We send them on down to the historical society. Do you know how to get there?"

"No. Is it far?"

"Oh, no. It's only a block away. I'll give you the address." She wrote it down on a slip of paper and handed it to me.

"You'll have to hurry if you plan to go today," she added. "It closes at five."

"Thanks," I said, almost breaking into a run.

Once outside, I did run, and I was panting by the time I reached the colonial style building that served as the Lorens Historical Society. It looked old and weathered and in need of repairs, and yet something about it was strangely welcoming, despite the fact that on the lawn, a cannon stood aimed at me. Perhaps because the historical building had been a part of this town so long, it felt its duty was to be friendly to everyone. I shook my head. *Buildings don't have feelings,* I told myself as I pushed open the door.

When my eyes adjusted to the dim interior, I saw a tall woman advancing in my direction. My first impulse was to turn and run. The woman's rapid approach reminded me of a hawk swooping down on its prey.

"Old telephone books?" she asked in response to my stuttered question, and her voice was sweet and gentle, a startling contrast to her appearance. "Yes, we keep them here. They're in the back room on the far right. I'm afraid they aren't used much, so we keep them wrapped in plastic for protection. You're quite welcome to the books. Just make sure you wrap them up again when you're finished. Give me a call if you need anything, but keep in mind we close in ten minutes."

And suddenly she was gone, swallowed up by the dark hall. *Almost like a ghost.*

My footsteps echoed through the lonely hall. Something told me I was the only visitor. I felt a twinge of pity as I passed rooms arranged in an intriguing old-fashioned manner, with antiques and other outdated items on display, and I wished I had time to stop and look at everything more closely. Maybe I'd come back another time, but today I couldn't let myself stray from my purpose.

Locating the phone books, I hurriedly paged through the thick book of 1978-79, conscious of the precious minutes ticking by.

This time I found him: *Renton, Christopher . . . 5218 Far Street.* A telephone number was also listed, but the address was what I wanted. I uncrumpled the paper containing the historical society's address, and on the back I jotted Christopher Renton's address using a pencil stub I found in my pocket. Thanks to my habit of drawing, I always wore clothes with pockets and I was usually never without some kind of pencil.

After rewrapping the books, I stood, ready to leave, when a thought made me pause. These books gave me access to the last twenty years. Why not look up my mother? I glanced at my watch. Five minutes to five. Plenty of time.

Tiffany Hutch and her brother were listed together until 1980. From that year on, it was Peter Hutch alone. Which made sense, because my mother had moved away in September of 1979 to get married. But I knew all this already. I'm not sure why I looked her up—it was almost like I did it to assure myself she had really existed.

On an impulse, I flipped to Renton. In 1980, Christopher was no longer listed. *Just like my mother.* I pressed the pencil eraser against my chin thoughtfully. I knew my last name was Finley. My mother had married Dr. Robert Finley, so it was senseless even to speculate . . .

Yet I did. This Christopher Renton and my mother had been friends. *Just how good of friends?* I wondered. They had disappeared from the Lorens phone listings the same year, the year my mother had moved and married. But it wasn't Christopher Renton she had married.

Unless—unless he'd changed his name. I shook my head, battling the uneasiness inside me. Why would he do that? It was absurd for me to even think such a thing. *I have to find out more about this Christopher,* I thought. *Now more than ever.*

I couldn't remember my father very well, other than those times he'd tossed me up into the air. Sure, I had my parents' wedding photo, so I knew what he looked like. But just knowing a man's face doesn't tell you who he is. Now I became flooded with doubts. Crazy doubts. Because I knew nothing about my father—nothing other than what little my mother had told me.

And from what I'd discovered lately, this was not reassuring.

~

That evening after a dinner of pizza (surprise, surprise) I made up my mind. Philip and I hadn't made any plans for tonight, and I was glad. This was something I had to do on my own. I told my uncle that I was going for a walk and I wasn't sure when I'd be back.

The truth was, I intended to take a stroll past 5218 Far Street. It was as if now that I had information, I couldn't rest until I did something with it, couldn't pass up the chance of discovering something new. I had to find out if 5218 Far Street still existed.

My insides fluttered like a flock of seagulls as I walked down the sidewalk. Not much goes on in a small town on a weeknight, and the silence made me feel extremely self-conscious. Once in a while a car drove by, and I imagined it slowing, the driver staring at me . . . and I quickened my pace.

I paid close attention to the green street signs. High Street. Lake Street. My tour with Philip had given me some idea of the street layout, but not enough to keep me from wondering why I hadn't looked at a map before setting out. Searching on foot was time consuming and tiring. I left the business district behind and, relying mostly on instinct and after retracing my steps several times, I eventually found Far Street.

Here the houses seemed to shrink in width and grow in height as I walked, giving me such an Alice-in-Wonderland sensation that I had to pause and take a few deep breaths before going on. Many of the houses, especially the ones surrounded by hostile metal fences, were in need of repairs. I thought a few of them should be torn down. I shivered under violently shifting shadows. Trees waved their branches as threateningly as if they had read my thoughts and felt they now had to guard the houses.

When I finally located number 5218, it was to discover that it was not a house at all, but part of a duplex. Gathering all my courage but still feeling cowardly, I marched past an especially menacing tree, mounted cracked concrete steps, and rang the bell.

At first I thought no one would answer. I was suddenly relieved. What would I say if someone *did* answer? I was about to turn away when the door handle moved. Panic seized me, and any strategy I might have formed deserted me. The door creaked open and I found myself staring blankly down at the face of a child. Her hair hung long and stringy and the corners of her mouth were stained purple from grape juice or a Popsicle. She regarded me curiously for a moment, then smiled.

"I've got a new doll," she said, holding up a plastic doll with tangled curls.

Before I could answer, a voice shrilled from the dark interior, "Janie, who is it?" A woman appeared and pulled the child back from the doorway so she could fill it herself. She was an incredibly large woman, making me feel incredibly small.

"Well, what do you want?" she asked. "If you've come for those old bottles, I've already—"

"No," I broke in hastily, finding my voice. "I'm sorry to bother you." I forced down the lump in my throat. "My name is Robin Finley. I was just wondering—I just wanted to know if maybe you could give me some information—about someone who lived here before you. His name was Christopher Renton—"

"Honey." The woman put a hand on her hip. I could see the little girl peering out from behind, eyes bright with interest. "I can hardly keep track of my own family, let alone someone else's. People come and go here all the time. If they're lucky, they find somewhere better to live. Anyhow, I don't recall that name. It wasn't the name of the one who had this place before us, that much I know."

"Well, this guy—he lived here twenty years ago—"

"Twenty years ago!" A dark look crossed the woman's face. "Honey, I think you need to find yourself a better hobby than wasting people's time with nonsense like this. Twenty years ago! What you need is a time machine—"

"I'm sorry to have bothered you." I turned away, blushing fiercely. When I heard the door slam shut behind me, I flinched. I was so grateful to get back on the sidewalk that I wasn't even annoyed with myself for giving up so easily. My confidence was shaken to an extreme. How could I have thought I could just ring a doorbell and start firing questions at a stranger? And how could I have expected answers? Christopher Renton hadn't lived at 5218 Far Street for decades.

I sighed. The woman was right; what I needed was a time machine.

I jumped at the sudden honk of a horn. I spun around to see Justin waving to me from a green Jeep. "Hop in!" he called, and I was so relieved at not having to walk home alone in the settling darkness, that I did.

"Well, well, look who's playing reporter," was the first thing to escape his lips. I immediately wished I'd stayed on the sidewalk. "I should have known you'd do something like this."

I couldn't tell whether he was angry or not. And I didn't care. "Something like what?" I whirled in my seat to face him. "What business is it of yours if I choose to—"

"Hey, simmer down—and buckle up."

I did, clicking the buckle as loudly as possible. *Philip wouldn't act like this,* I thought indignantly.

"Now tell me," Justin said, leaving Far Street behind, "what did you expect to accomplish by bursting in on strangers and barraging them with questions?"

"I—"

"That's very unprofessional." Justin switched on his blinker to turn right. My ears focused on the ticking sound, trying to avoid hearing his harsh words. "This isn't television. This is real life. You have to use common sense—"

"Where are we going?" I broke in, realizing this wasn't the way back to my uncle's.

"You have a special time you have to be home? A bedtime, perhaps? With all the late nights you've been spending, I wouldn't think one slight detour would make a difference."

The sarcasm in his voice cut me, and whatever friendly feelings for Justin I might have gradually been accumulating vanished. "What business is it of yours? And how would *you* know how late I—"

"For one thing, you told me yourself that you've been going out with that Philip guy. Or have you forgotten? Seems like you only remember me when I can help you with something."

I opened my mouth, ready to make a retort, then closed

it. Was it true what he was implying? Was I a selfish person who used others only for what I could get out of them? Lately, maybe I had been. But I didn't mean to be. I didn't mean to hurt anyone.

"I'm sorry." Mentally, I made a note to go to confession one of these days real soon. As soon as I could sort out my long list of sins.

"Anyway," Justin went on, his voice becoming husky, "I did a search and I didn't come up with much. This Renton fellow lived in that duplex, which you apparently already know, and he worked at a hardware store until he moved in September of 1979. After that—he disappeared—there's nothing more to report."

I settled back, feeling deflated and emotionally drained. There was silence but for the hum of the motor and the tires on the road.

"You think I should give up, don't you?" My eyes wandered over the gray dashboard. "You think I should forget all this—this pointless searching—"

"Do you think it's pointless?"

"No."

"Then it's not. Only—you have to be able to draw the line between the past and the present," I turned my head to look at Justin, waited for him to go on, "the relevant and the irrelevant. The changeable and the unchangeable. In short, you have to know when you've done all you can, then leave the past behind. Where it belongs." Justin frowned over the steering wheel. "I think Edna Ferber said it best: 'Living the past is a dull and lonely business; looking back strains the neck muscles, and causes you to bump into people not going your way.'"

The impact of those strange words kept me silent for a full minute. I didn't even think to ask who Edna Ferber was. Quietly, I said, "I'm not living the past."

"Maybe not, but it's still something to think about."

But I didn't want to think about it. It was too weird. We

129

bumped along the road, wrapped in the fading evening, and I still didn't know where we were headed. I was about to ask when I realized this passage between the crowded trees looked familiar. Justin swung the Jeep through a tangle of brush and cut the engine.

"The Ingerman Mansion," I murmured. I turned to face Justin. "Why did you bring me here?" He didn't say anything right away. I found myself listening to the silence—a silence so strong that I wanted to reach out and touch it, but it remained just out of reach, making it all the more enticing.

"You've been here already, I know," Justin said finally, not answering my question.

We stared up at the mansion's imposing form. Shrouded in dusk, it looked unreal, a mere outline wavering in the shadows, as if it were a ghost itself. Or a mirage that might vanish at any moment.

"Yes, and it's creepy in there," I said. A vision of the rose room and the balcony floated before my eyes. I hugged myself. "I'm never going inside there again. Ever." Somewhere in the distance, an owl hooted.

"Do you think it's haunted?" Justin asked. I glance at him in time to see a soft shadow cross his face. Then he answered his own question. "I don't believe it's haunted. But it's best to leave it alone . . . for other reasons."

My eyes were drawn to the mansion's empty black windows, half expecting a white form to appear. I shivered. Without a word, Justin slipped off his jacket and draped it over my shoulders.

"Have you ever been inside?" I asked, fingering the soft leather and bringing it closer to my skin.

"People aren't supposed to go inside. But I guess most folks around here have, at one time or another. Me included."

I only half heard him now. I knew the sun was setting, but I couldn't see it because the mansion blocked my view. But I could see part of the sky, pastel colors spreading out from behind the mansion like a watercolor wash, making a background so bright that it enhanced the mansion's darkness and turned it into a sharp silhouette. The perfect picture of a haunted house.

"See that?" Justin's voice was low. "That's the one thing that makes me wish I were on that balcony right now."

I knew which balcony he meant, though we couldn't see it from here. Despite the jacket, I shivered and looked away. "It would take more than a beautiful sunset to get me on that balcony again," I said, almost in a whisper.

Justin's face took on a distant look. "You haven't seen a sunset till you've watched one from there." His hand was still on the wheel, but I saw his fingers relax. When he suddenly cleared his throat, the look disappeared and his fingers tightened. "I guess I'd better get you home." The engine burst to life.

We drove without speaking. The mansion, so eerie in the twilight, remained in my mind long after it was out of sight.

It wasn't until after Justin had dropped me off and I was staring out my bedroom window at the glowing moon, unaware I was still wearing his jacket, that I realized I still didn't know why he had brought me to the mansion.

Chapter Twelve

I stood in the mansion, in front of the etched glass doors leading to the balcony. Only, I wasn't me. I felt weighed down by my long dress, tightly bound, poised and feminine under the hair piled atop my head. I felt faint.

Fresh air was what I needed. I opened the glass doors and stepped onto the balcony, where a stray wind teased out a few tendrils of hair and whispered against my face and neck, tickling me.

Oh, the sunset! I had the perfect view from this balcony, facing west. I stood watching the vibrant blend of rainbow colors, gold melting into orange into pink . . . I could watch them forever. The sight brought joy and comfort to my heart; and I needed that terribly tonight because my heart ached with emptiness, as it had for days, ever since . . .

But I must not think of that. This sunset helped sooth the pain and fill the emptiness, if only for a little while.

I felt no fear, standing high up on the balcony. Rather, I found exhilaration from being above the rest of the world. I could almost believe I was floating, if those railings weren't in the way, marring my view.

Tonight I needed to get closer. Closer than I ever had before. My head light and dreamy, I moved nearer and leaned against the rail with a sigh. So caught up in my fancy was I that when the rail gave way, I didn't act immediately, in that split second that might have saved me.

At first I thought I was flying. But when I saw the ground rushing up to meet me, the spell broke, and I knew the truth.

I was falling.

Gasping, I sat up in bed, my body bathed in sweat. It had been such a beautiful dream, then suddenly—what a nightmare! I had been so foolish to lean against the rail.

"It was just a dream," I whispered. "Forget it." But that was impossible; the vision was too vivid, and as I stared into the darkness of my room, the scene played itself over and over before my eyes.

My visit to the Ingerman Mansion must have set it off, I realized. And I was ashamed at my vulnerability, ashamed that I could be so easily affected.

I hadn't been myself in the dream. That much I knew. Unconsciously, my mind had played me into the role of Connie Ingerman, twisting my own confused thoughts and fears into a tangled nightmare, suggesting that Connie's fall had been an accident.

What was the matter with me? I was becoming obsessed, so caught up in the past that I was losing my hold on reality. My hands trembled. Was it as Justin had implied, and before long I would be completely lost, living in the past?

No. That wouldn't happen. I gripped the sheets. I wouldn't let it happen. I would go back to California and leave all this behind. What was I doing here, getting myself involved in other people's lives, putting them before my own, forfeiting my sanity in the process? It wasn't right. Whatever I was trying to uncover here in Lorens, the quest I was undertaking—it had to stop. As long as I remained in Lorens I knew I wouldn't be strong enough to resist; the only answer was to go away and leave these things behind.

But wouldn't that be running away?

I remembered my mother. *She* had tried to run away, and where had it gotten her? Had she ever really escaped?

I knew the answer was no.

So how could I escape?

Yet how could I remain here to be tormented by fantastic illusions, out of a past that was not even my own? I hated feeling this way. I wanted to feel in control, not . . . not . . .

Hopeless, whispered my mind, and the word sounded sinister. I shook myself, trying to control my imagination. I could not remain like this, working myself into a frenzy. I reached out and switched on the bedside lamp, closing my eyes and reopening them, trying to adjust to the glare.

After a minute of staring unseeingly, I finally noticed the book on the nightstand. It had been lying there for days. So engrossed had I been in my own concerns that I'd forgotten about the Victoria Holt novel. Now, with a great sense of relief, I picked it up. Here, in these pages, I knew I could escape, turn myself over to someone else's world, and with this temporary release, stabilize myself. Then, with my mind clear, maybe I would be able to think my own problems through.

Or I could read the Bible, my conscience prodded.

But my hands were already opening the novel, and my eyes caught on an inscription, which I had overlooked when I first found the book in my mother's chest. The words were written in bold black ink on the inside title page:

April 13, 1979

To my Tiffany on her eighteenth birthday,

May your own life be filled with romantic adventure, and may you follow your dreams always, wherever they may lead you.

Love,

Christopher

Christopher. Christopher Renton.
And it was signed *love.*
I knew I would not sleep anymore tonight.

~

How thankful I was that the next day was Saturday. I'd had an unrestful night, to say the least, and was relieved to be able to lie in bed for as long as I wanted. True, the bookstore was open on Saturdays, but my uncle had stressed from the beginning that I could have Saturdays off for a free weekend whenever I wanted.

I wanted.

The truth was, I didn't feel like getting up and facing the day. In fact, I didn't feel like getting up ever again. I pulled the sheets over my head, but even as I lay there under the blankets, I had no peace. Thoughts churned through my mind, scraping and grinding like malfunctioning gears.

I finally figured I'd be better off if I got up and did something—anything—so long as it would distract my overactive mind. Dragging myself out of bed, I dressed, plodded downstairs, and ate a bowl of cereal. Stale as could be. No wonder I usually skipped breakfast. I returned to my room and stood at the window, feeling out of place in the big, silent, empty house. I noticed the lilacs below my window were starting to shrivel up, turning brown and ugly. "Good," I said out loud.

I turned to face my room. The unmade bed and clothes scattered across the floor told me it needed cleaning. On the desk, I noticed that the wedding photo of my parents was askew in its frame. For that matter, I realized, so were most of the pictures on the walls. Even the crucifix. I frowned, wondering if my uncle had been sneaking around my room, touching things.

No. I had to be honest with myself. Though I didn't know much about my uncle, I knew he wouldn't do that. He minded his own business. So much so that I hardly knew he existed.

I straightened the photograph, then the pictures and crucifix, remembering how back home, Saturday had always been cleaning day. Recalling layers of dust on tables and shelves, I decided this whole house could use a good cleaning. It would be something nice I could do for my uncle. From the looks of things, he probably cleaned once a year at the most. And, as this was May, apparently he did not do it during spring-cleaning time.

I went downstairs and turned on the living room stereo, tuned in to the only station I could find that was playing anything familiar, and turned up the volume. *There,* I told myself. *That should keep me company* and *block out my thoughts.*

Once I began cleaning, I became ambitious, exterminating every speck of dust I could find, polishing the woodwork from the tables to the stairway banister, vacuuming the carpets, and sweeping the hardwood floors. Periodically, a familiar song played on the stereo, and I sang along.

I felt more normal than I had in days.

Finally, I surveyed my work with pride. This house most likely hadn't looked so good in years. Probably twenty years.

Tired, I sank into a worn, overstuffed living room chair and let my hands dangle over the sides. That was when I realized there was one thing I hadn't done. It was silly, really —yet I couldn't resist—it had always been my favorite part of cleaning. I used to look forward to it when I was little because I never knew what treasures I might find. My mother would tell me to reach my hand down the sides of the furniture to search for any small objects that had sunken in, and it always delighted me to find loose change, which my mother let me keep, or a long-lost toy, such as a doll's comb or a little book.

I wondered when the last time these pieces of furniture had been searched, if ever. The sofa and chairs looked old enough to have been in the house forever. I slid my hand into the depths of the first armchair. Ugh. My fingers recoiled at the touch of dry dust and matted hair. (I'd forgotten about this part of the job, and no wonder.) I felt carefully for any solid objects. Nothing. I felt along the other side.

Aha! I came up with two coins: one, a very dull penny, the other, a 1975 dime. Pocketing the money (after all the work I'd done, I figured I'd at least earned eleven cents), I moved on to the sofa. Here, I found a pen and two more pennies. (So make that thirteen cents.) I searched down the side of the last armchair, which scratched me with its coarse brown cloth. My fingers brushed something cool and metallic, probably another coin.

But no, it was the wrong shape. My fingers grasped and pulled up a small tarnished key. I turned it over in my hand, intrigued, wondering what it was meant to unlock. I'd begun imagining all sorts of possibilities when a loud pounding on the front door startled me, and I froze. Until I realized I had nothing to be scared of. Why was I so paranoid? I crept forward, parted a curtain, and peeked through the front window to see who was standing on the porch.

"Philip!" Pocketing the key, I opened the door and tried to act natural—I didn't want him to know how alarmed I'd been just because someone knocked on the door when I was home alone.

He stepped right in and gave me a quick hug. "Hi, Robin. I hoped you'd be here. I just wanted to stop in to see you—and give you these." A bouquet of red roses appeared like magic from behind his back. He held them in my face, waiting for me to take them.

"Oh!" was all I could say. No one had ever given me roses before. If they had, my mother probably would have sent them to a lab to be tested before she'd even let me smell them.

The beauty of the roses choked me. "This is so sweet of you, Philip," I finally managed, and I forgot any resentment I'd felt towards him for not helping me look for Christopher Renton. "Thank you. They're absolutely gorgeous!"

"Maybe," and he gave me a wide smile, "but if you want

gorgeous, look in a mirror."

I felt my face turn the color of the roses. Fumbling with the bouquet, I turned away. "I need to put these in water. Make yourself comfortable." I led him into the living room, grateful I'd cleaned the house.

When I returned, I set the vase of flowers on a little table beside a Virgin Mary statue. Philip leaned forward in the scratchy brown chair, facing me. I noticed the stereo was turned off. Now I could hear my thumping heart.

"Brace yourself, Robin. I have something fascinating to tell you."

I waited, my heart pounding harder.

Philip glanced over his shoulder. "The old geezer's not around, is he?"

I shook my head, assuming he meant my uncle and feeling a bit offended by his word choice.

"Good." Philip paused before saying, "I found it."

I stared blankly into his eager eyes. Eyes that looked as if I should know instantly what he was referring to. "You found it?" I repeated.

"Yes. The letter—the letter that tells where the map is hidden—the map that shows where the gold is buried."

"But—how—"

"I just kept thinking about your mother's note, couldn't get it out of my mind." Philip's eyes blazed; I'd never seen him so excited.

"So yesterday," he continued, "I went back to the mansion—"

"You were at the mansion yesterday? When?"

"Does it matter?"

I was thinking of my visit to the mansion with Justin. But Philip couldn't have been there then—we would have seen his car. "No, I was just curious. Why didn't you wait for me to help you search?" I was relieved he hadn't. I wouldn't have wanted to go with him. I had no intention of ever setting foot in that mansion again.

Philip shrugged. "You worked yesterday. I couldn't wait."

"So you searched through all those books—by yourself?" I asked, incredulous.

Philip smiled. "I was lucky. I only had to go through three shelves before I found it. All it took was a little common sense." He tapped his head. "How did the letter get in a book in the first place? I figured Connie left the letter in a novel she was reading. Then the book was found in her room, probably after she died, and simply returned to the library—maybe by a maid—and no one ever knew there was a letter between the pages.

"So I asked myself what kind of novel Connie Ingerman would be interested in. Well—tastes don't change that much —I thought of the kind you like to read. So I went through some romance novels. And I found the letter, still in its envelope."

"Amazing," I whispered. "It sounds almost too easy."

Philip lifted an envelope and carefully drew out and unfolded a crinkled paper, which looked brittle enough to break at his touch. I knelt down beside the chair to get a closer look. The paper was so yellowed, the small curly writing so faded, I could hardly make out the words.

"Don't try to read it all," Philip said. "It'll take forever." He pointed two-thirds of the way down the page. "Start here —this is where it gets interesting."

They ask me where the map is, but I shall never tell. I have hidden it, as John asked, and my promise to him means more than anything else. I loved him, and now I have lost him. All because of gold and greed—evil things. I care not for money. John's gold is not worth what it cost both him and me, and I want no more to do with it. We did not need gold for our happiness; it was the gold that destroyed our happiness.

Joyfully would I forfeit all I have if it would bring my John back.

Alas, that can never be. As for the map, I hate it. I wanted to destroy it, but could not bring myself to do so, because that would mean breaking my promise to John, who asked me to keep it for him until he came back. He is never coming back, I know. Each morning when I awaken to a new day, I have to remind myself of this.

Thus while I have kept my promise to John —hiding the map where it is close and secure—I have put it in a lowly place, where I will never have to look upon it again, where every day it will be treated as it deserves, trodden upon, forgotten . . . But I am rambling. Forgive me; I shall say no more of the map.

Dear Stephanie, I know I can trust you. You care no more for gold than I, for you have found something worth far more: true love—as I, too, had . . . though for far too short a time.

I wish you all the best for the future,

Connie Ingerman

"She practically spells out the map's location," Philip broke in, apparently figuring I'd finished reading the clue by now. He started folding the letter. "She hid the map under the floor."

I blinked a few times. My throat felt strangely tight, and my voice sounded unnatural when I spoke. "I wonder why she never mailed this—"

"So I got down on my hands and knees on the floor of her room, the rose room, and I came to an edge where the carpet wasn't secured. I slid my hand under the carpet, and

140

do you know what I found?"

"Why, the map—"

"No."

I frowned, confused.

"Hear me out," Philip said, obviously delighting in stretching out the climax. "The map wasn't there. But it used to be. What I *did* find is this—"

He lifted his arm and dangled a silver bracelet before my eyes. It shifted and caught the light, winking at me.

"It's your mother's. See the initials? T.H."

I practically snatched the bracelet from him. I turned it over affectionately, then let it rest in my palm as I stroked the smooth, slender chain, thinking, *This was my mother's. She wore it when she was my age . . .*

"Robin," Philip's voice shattered my tender thoughts, "your mother already found the map."

Chapter Thirteen

$\mathcal{P}$hilip's words didn't sink in right away. I sat on the carpet at his feet, staring at the bracelet curled in my palm. A coldness spread over me, but I didn't shiver. It came like a slow freeze, spreading through my bones, my blood, my skin. When I spoke, I couldn't feel my lips.

"But that's impossible." I tried to laugh, but all that came out was a dry rasp. "My mother couldn't find a treasure map. She couldn't even find her own sunglasses on top of her head—"

Philip didn't laugh.

"The map was there, Robin. And now it's not. Face facts. Your mother read the letter. It doesn't take a genius to figure out where the map was hidden. Since she had a key to the mansion, it would have been easy for her to get inside and search for the map. It only makes sense that she'd look for it. Heck, we should have realized that right away. But the bracelet's the final proof—it proves she reached under the carpet—"

"But she would notice if her bracelet came off—"

"Why should she? She found a treasure map! I would imagine she'd be rather preoccupied."

"You don't have to be sarcastic. It's easy for you to surmise all this, but it doesn't mean that's what happened."

Philip's voice remained calm. "Don't try to deny it, Robin, it won't do you any good. The map is gone. That's your mother's bracelet you're holding. Put two and two together and the outcome is obvious."

But no matter how obvious it looked to him, I couldn't believe it—didn't *want* to believe it. Perhaps because I knew what it meant. More secrets, more lies.

"I know this is a shock. But it's also a great discovery. Think of what it means . . . for us." Philip leaned forward, his voice almost a whisper. "We're closer to the treasure map than anyone."

"But it's gone!" I cried, exasperated. "You said yourself that my mother took it."

"*Think*, Robin, *think!*" Philip's eyes drilled into mine. "What do you think happened after your mother found the map? What did she do with it? We know about her accident, but what did she do with the map? There was never anything in the newspapers about finding a treasure map on her, and that would have been big news. So if she didn't have it on her, she must have put it somewhere—hidden it—between the time she found it and the accident. Then when she fell, she got amnesia—"

"And didn't remember!" I broke in, suddenly enlightened.

"Which means the map is still where she hid it."

I groaned. "But this is no better than when Connie hid the map. It could be anywhere."

Philip grabbed my hand.

"No," he said adamantly. "No. This is a million times better, because now we're certain there *is* a map. And you—you're your mother's daughter." His voice lowered to an unrecognizable level. "You can find it."

I blinked.

"You can," Philip repeated. "Say you will."

"I—I can't promise anything . . . "

"But you'll try?" His hands tightened on mine.

"Of course I will—"

"And you *will* tell me if you find anything? Right away?"

"Yes."

Philip smiled at me, his eyes sparkling wildly. "This is real excitement, Robin. Could you ask for a better adventure? And we're in it together—don't forget." He pulled me up from the floor so that we stood only inches apart, facing each other, looking deep into each other's eyes. "Do you know what this could mean—for both of us?" He didn't wait for an answer. "You'll be eighteen soon. You'll be free to do what you want with your life. Thousands of dollars could give us a good start, take us anywhere we want to go, California included. Think about it!" With that, he released my hands and headed for the door. "I've gotta go now, but I'll be sure to call you tonight."

I stood breathless on the front steps, my brain pounding as he zoomed away. He had just described all that I had told myself I wanted: freedom, California, adventure and romance. So why did I feel so confused?

Because it was too much, too fast.

Inside the house, I could not stand the quiet. Silence overwhelmed me, clogging my brain so I couldn't think. And there was so much to think about. About my mother and her past, about myself and my future.

Philip had hinted at a future—a future with him. I turned this thought over tentatively in my mind. Philip and me . . . together forever.

I decided to take a walk and clear my head with fresh air.

But the air was damp and heavy, and before long my hair was clinging in sticky strands to my face and neck. Uncomfortable as this was, I soon forgot about it.

My mother found the map. I repeated this to myself over and over. I hadn't wanted to believe the words when Philip first said them—still didn't want to—but deep down, I knew my denial only confirmed my belief.

My mother had found the hiding place and the map was gone. There was no doubt in my mind that the bracelet, which I still held in my hand, was hers. I fingered the slender silver, slid my fingertips over the engraved letters. Then I put the bracelet on.

Philip thought he had everything figured out, but one question remained. Where was the map now? What had my mother done with it? It was a question Philip expected me to answer. But how could I? I tried to think like my mother but realized I didn't know how.

Instead I wondered what I would do if I were the one who had found the map. But it would depend on the circumstances, and I didn't know the circumstances. I'd never felt such utter frustration. *Compared to this,* I thought wryly, *physics class would be a pleasure.*

Since I couldn't know what the circumstances were when my mother found the map, I could only speculate. But I didn't want to speculate; that was all anyone ever did, and it didn't satisfy me.

But if I had *discovered the map,* I thought, giving in and returning to my previous theory, *I'd be careful—I'd need time to think what to do next. I'd take the map home and— taking no chances—not mention it to anyone, but hide it away somewhere safe, most likely in my room.*

I pushed aside the damp hair plastered to my forehead. Yes, the only logical conclusion was to hide the map. Temporarily, of course. And then what?

I frowned. It had all seemed to make sense the way Philip explained it, but there were other ways of looking at it. Too many. I couldn't help wondering if there was still something I was missing.

"She must have put it somewhere—hidden it—between the time she found it and the accident." Philip had said this so confidently, but he didn't know when my mother had found the map. What if she had found it the same day as her accident? For that matter, she could have found it *after* her accident. Philip hadn't even considered that.

My mind played with the idea of my mother finding the map the same day as her accident. The map might never have left the mansion. Maybe my mother merely transferred its hiding place. I didn't know why she would do that, but it was a possibility. Because if she hadn't transferred the map to another hiding place, the map would have been discovered in her possession at the scene of the accident.

But it wasn't.

Was it?

For a brief moment I became conscious of the sweat trickling down my forehead, but my mind, refusing to be distracted, moved on to its conclusion. *Maybe the person who found my mother also found the map.*

But I knew who that person was: Christopher Renton.

I need to find him! screamed my brain.

My head ached under the hot sun, but I continued aimlessly down the sidewalk, which sent shimmering waves of heat to my face. When I finally looked at my surroundings, I saw I was passing a long, plastic-roofed tunnel. Curious, I slowed my steps and squinted. Rows of flowers and green plants standing on tables came into focus underneath the curved roof. Adjacent to this stood a building of crumbly gray stone, above which hung a sign, Sunroof Nursery.

I became aware of the faint, spritzy sound of a revolving sprinkler coming from somewhere in the greenhouse, and I began imagining how refreshing the water would feel on my skin. I stepped off the sidewalk, crossed a gravel path, and passed through the archway. Almost immediately, a gentle mist descended upon me. I closed my eyes, savoring the coolness while the smell of sun-soaked plants filled my nostrils.

I heard a door open from the adjacent building. I hurried away from the sprinkler and tried to compose myself and act as if I knew what I was doing. Catching sight of a rack of seed packets, I hastened over to them and screwed up my forehead, pretending to be absorbed in reading the planting instructions, while out of the corner of my eye I caught a glimpse of yellow.

"Hello there, dear," chimed a voice at my side. "Are you finding everything you need?"

"Yes, thank you," I answered, not turning to face her. I

could feel water droplets clinging to the hairs on my arms, and I wished they would hurry and evaporate.

"Good, good," the woman said, pumping more enthusiasm into those two words than I'd ever heard anyone use. "Just call out if you need anything, anything at all. That's what I'm here for. Are you looking for anything special?"

"No. I was just—"

"What sort of garden do you have? Vegetable or flower? Both, perhaps?"

"Actually," I reluctantly turned to face her, as I was beginning to feel ridiculous talking to seed packets, "neither."

"Oh, I see. You want to *start* a garden." The woman clasped her hands in anticipation. "What kind do you want?"

"Um—" my eyes focused on the bright yellow ribbon in the woman's gray hair—"a vegetable garden." Where had those words come from? I did not want a garden.

The woman's wide face grew wider with her smile. "Then you don't want seeds, my dear. Oh, no—they'll take too long to get started—and here it is practically June! What you need are plants. Big healthy plants! I have some that would do nicely for you, I think, though most have been picked over already—by the ones who come bright and early, you know. But don't worry; it's not too late. We'll find something. What do you think you'd like? Zucchinis? Peppers? Cucumbers? Those always produce nicely . . ."

She had been rambling eagerly, and I wondered why she let the sentence fade. She regarded me with her head slightly tilted, and I could tell her focus had drifted. I shifted on my feet self-consciously, wondering what was wrong. Were my arms and hair still glistening with water? Did she somehow know the truth, that I had not come here to buy plants? I was struck with fear that she could read my mind.

"Forgive me, my dear," she said, "I'm getting old, I know, but—I never do forget a face. Tell me, what is your name?"

I told her.

"But you are related to Tiffany Hutch, aren't you?" She said it in such a matter-of-fact way, I could only give her a blank stare.

"Yes, you are! I can't believe I didn't see it sooner. You look so much like her!" The woman clapped her hands together like a happy child. "A little shorter, perhaps, but yes —yes—you must be her daughter!"

How could she possibly know?

"Oh, my dear, my dear, you must tell me all about her. My, it's been so long! She used to buy all her gardening things from me. Tiffany loved to garden, and she had quite a green thumb, too. But I'm babbling. Please, tell me how she is."

Finally finding my voice, I grappled to steady it over the frantic beating of my heart. "Y—you're right," I said stupidly, for the woman obviously needed no reassurance of this. "My mother was Tiffany Hutch." I told myself to stop overreacting, that it was not unusual that someone should remember my mother, who had lived in Lorens for eighteen years. Still, my heartbeat refused to slow. "She's dead." I hadn't meant it to come out so abruptly, but then I'd never been a tactful speaker.

"Oh, dear." A pause. "I'm sorry." The woman sounded it, and I braced myself for a dramatic display of this sorrow. Instead, she crossed herself and I imagined her offering up a prayer for my mother, and the simple act moved me profoundly.

"I have such fond memories of Tiffany." She smoothed her hands over her sky blue pants and spoke slowly. "Here I am, living to such an ancient age, my friends dying and leaving me behind . . ." She smiled suddenly, and her eyes, which had clouded over, cleared. "Ah, but there are always new friends to make."

She took my hand. Surprisingly, I welcomed her dry,

wrinkled palm, and felt somehow comforted, as I hadn't in a long time. Her touch said so much more than words. I felt a brush of sadness, but I didn't want to cry. I wanted this grandmotherly soul to tell me everything she knew about my mother; but first, I had to tell her about myself.

I told her I was here visiting my uncle for part of the summer and that I'd been living with my mother in California when she died. While I talked, I wondered how well this woman had known my mother. Apparently well enough to remember her and recognize her in me, even after twenty years. She probably knew more about her than I did, or at least the part of her life that she had spent as Tiffany Hutch.

"Your mother and I were good friends," she explained, "and it didn't matter that I was thirty years older. She needed someone, you know, after her parents died. She had her brother, of course, and he did everything he could for her—dropped out of college to come home and look after her—but every girl needs a mother, in one way or another. I like to think that I helped fill that role for Tiffany.

"She was delightful, so energetic and ambitious." The woman chuckled. "All you had to do to get her to do something was tell her it couldn't be done. She loved a challenge. But she didn't always think before she acted, and that got her into trouble more than a couple of times." She shook her head, still smiling. "Oh, where the time goes . . . It seems like only yesterday she was in here, chattering on about her graduation and plans for the future." The woman's smile flickered. It was obvious what she was remembering, and I knew it hurt her—it hurt me, too—but I needed her to go on.

"Can you—can you tell me about it?" I attempted. "About what happened at—the mansion? I know some of the story, but . . ."

"Poor child." I wasn't sure whether she was referring to me or to Tiffany. I could feel the woman reading my eyes, sensing the longing that was there, the longing for all I did not know, and I knew she wanted to help me. Maybe—maybe even as a favor for Tiffany.

"It was such a sad thing to happen," the woman began. But when she told the story, it was as I'd already heard it . . . from my uncle, from the newspaper articles . . . and I wasn't satisfied. Because everyone thought they knew what had happened. But they didn't. Not really. Because they hadn't been there.

If indeed my mother's fall had been an accident, then yes, it was a terrible thing. But was it a reason to leave home? To never come back and never make contact with family or friends left behind? No. There had to be something more. Was I the only one who saw it this way?

"Did you ever see her again? After the accident, I mean?"

"Oh, yes. Of course. I saw her in the hospital as soon as they let me. Poor girl. She was never the same after it happened. Oh, her memory came back—most of it, at least—but the fall and the shock combined left some sort of scar—on the inside, I mean." The woman shook her head. "Psychological or emotional, they call it. And it takes a long time for something like that to heal, if ever."

An emotional scar. How awful it sounded.

"Tiffany was right, I suppose, when she said the best thing was to get away. She was so anxious to get away, it almost seemed as if—but of course that is the best way when something like that happens. Start over. A new town, a new life."

I wanted the woman to back up to the "as if"—it was the "if"s I was after.

The woman sighed. I wished I could reach inside her mind and pull out every strand of memory that had anything to do with my mother, anything that might trigger something else and give me answers instead of more questions. My only hope was to keep her talking.

"Did you know my father?"

The woman shook her head. "Tiffany became very closed and secretive after the accident. But she did tell me she was getting married—that was a few months after the accident. So quickly it happened! I think he was one of her doctors."

I swallowed a lump in my throat. "Yes. Dr. Robert Finley. I don't remember much about him. He—died when I was two. A car accident." I blamed it on those twisty mountain roads of Colorado. Maybe my mother did, too; maybe that was why we had moved to California. But I guess I'd never know for sure.

"So both your parents are gone?" she asked, and I nodded. "And now you're living with Peter. Odd how life turns in a circle." I agreed, and didn't bother to clarify that I was not "living" here, merely visiting.

"Poor Tiffany." The woman shook her head. "Tragedy after tragedy. She never had it easy. But perhaps now she finally has peace, God rest her soul."

I was quiet. *Please let her be at peace, dear Lord.*

But this did nothing for me, her daughter, who was still living and struggling in a very confused world. There was so much my mother had left behind, so much she'd left undone, and as her daughter, I felt bound to finish it.

"Tiffany didn't tell me where she was moving, and I didn't press her. I was glad she was getting married. What she needed was stability, a family, a husband. I only hoped she'd made the right choice." Realizing what this implied, the woman patted my hand and hurriedly added, "I didn't mean it to sound that way, my dear. Things change, and I'm sure your mother loved your father very much. It's just that it was such a surprise. She had seemed so serious about another man. Before the accident, I mean. I even suspected they were making plans to run away together." Her eyes twinkled mischievously. "Of course, Peter wouldn't have approved—but I wasn't going to tell him. Ah, young love . . ." The woman lifted her eyes skyward. "And he was such a striking young man, too. Tall and dark, such classic good looks. And she was a petite beauty. They seemed so right for each other! Tiffany confided in me, you see, and I knew she loved this young man. He worked in Hanson's Hardware store, and they were together so much those couple of months before . . ."

I was relieved when she let the sentence trail off. If I heard the word "accident" one more time, I'd probably scream.

"Tiffany had seemed so happy, so sure, before the accident"—I bit my tongue—"I don't see why her fall had to change all that. But then again, it might not have had anything to do with her change of heart. That's another thing about young love. The heart is fickle.

"Oh, but I'm rambling," the woman said, taking me by the arm and leading me between a row of low tables on which green plants tangled together. "I'm sorry. I know this isn't why you came, to hear me reminisce about the past. I'll help you find some plants now and stop taking up your time. But you were just such a surprise! I could almost believe you were Tiffany stopping in for one of our chats."

If she only knew how eager I was to hear any detail she could recall. Like a dry sponge, I'd been soaking up every drop of information. I didn't want anything to sidetrack us, least of all plants.

"This young man," I said, stopping under a hanging plant. It began dripping water on my head, but I didn't move. "You really think she was serious about him? Really, truly serious?" I waited, my muscles tense.

"As serious as an eighteen-year-old can be."

I knew that that was serious.

"And his name," I persisted, "do you remember it?" I hoped she didn't think I was becoming overly inquisitive, that my interest was stretching beyond natural, healthy curiosity. But she didn't indicate anything to suggest this.

She seemed, in fact, quite eager to continue.

"Oh, yes," and my mind spoke the name as she said it, "Christopher Renton." She looked very pleased with herself for remembering, but I made no comment, merely clenched my hands. I had known it would be him.

"I always thought they were going to marry," the woman continued. "It was only a matter of time. And when Tiffany confided she had a secret, it wouldn't have surprised me if it was that she was engaged. But that was before the accident. And she never did tell me."

A secret. I wondered what it had been. Plans to marry Christopher Renton, as this woman suspected, or . . . the discovery of a treasure map?

"Oh, dear, you're getting wet." I let the woman lead me out from under the dripping plant. I needed her to lead me out because it was as if my mind was disengaged from my body. My feet moved but my mind wasn't controlling them. It was too taken up with questions.

I let the woman load me up with plants she thought I wanted, and I nodded automatically to the gardening advice she rattled off, though I absorbed none of it. She continued to chatter as she arranged the plants in a shallow box. "For easy carrying," she explained. Then, "My goodness, I don't believe I told you my name! It's Martha Myers, but please call me Martha."

Only after promising to "come again anytime for a short little chat," was I able to leave.

I was reluctant to go, but I noticed the sky was darkening, and I didn't want to get caught in a spring storm. I promised Martha I'd be back soon, and I meant it.

Chapter Fourteen

If I had been familiar with Wisconsin weather, I would have realized I had to hurry if I wanted to reach my uncle's house before the storm struck. Unfortunately, I wasn't, and I lingered along, absorbed in my thoughts, mulling over all Martha had told me. It wasn't until the box of plants began weighing heavy in my arms, becoming almost impossible to carry because the wind kept snatching at it, did I look to the sky and panic.

A threatening mountain of clouds was rumbling in from the west, so quickly I could actually see the mass swelling and growing. Green leaves whirled by me in a cyclone and my eyes raced to the skyline in fear of sighting a tornado.

In the time it took me to cross the street, the black clouds were almost on top of me. I shivered in a gust of wind, and my bare arms prickled when I saw how deserted the street had become. I felt as if I were the last person on earth, left alone to the mercy of the storm.

The blast of a horn, then a voice, startled me. "Hey, Robin! Jump in!"

Even as I turned, I knew who it was. Justin. I wasn't stranded in the storm after all. Amazing. How did he always manage to appear at such unexpected—yet perfectly convenient—moments? I hadn't heard him pull up. Now he was idling his Jeep at the curb, holding the door open and waiting for me.

Ominous as the sky was, I hesitated, shifting the box of plants in my arms. Even in the middle of such a predicament as this, something in me—stubbornness, pride, or both—didn't want to accept his help; it battled the other part of me that wanted so strongly to run to him with no urging at all. My realization of such divided feelings scared me. While I worried, large drops of rain began firing down from the sky, sounding like a thousand bullets striking the pavement.

"Are you going to stand there all day?" I thought I saw Justin make a move as if to close the door and drive off without me, so I ran forward.

I was greatly conscious of the bulky box of plants as I maneuvered it awkwardly inside with me before slamming the door. I sat with my ears burning, waiting for Justin to make some derisive comment about me and my funny cargo.

He pulled smoothly away from the curb. "Some nice looking plants you've got there," he said, not taking his eyes off the road. "But isn't it kind of pointless to start a garden when you're going to be leaving soon?"

The rain, pouring down heavily, created a blind of liquid silver on the window. "I didn't say I was starting a garden."

"Okay. Then what do you want with all those plants?"

I was tempted to make a smart comeback. Then I wondered why I so often felt defensive when I was near Justin. Was it to hide gentler feelings? Maybe I was afraid of revealing these feelings because I wouldn't know how to handle them.

"To plant them," I replied.

Justin smiled but wisely dropped the subject.

During the silence that resulted, my eyes followed the rapid movement of the windshield wipers. No matter how viciously they thrashed the rain, they did no good. I wondered how Justin could drive. By instinct? As I sat there, a strange feeling prodded at me, like it had last night when I'd first sat in this Jeep with Justin. My eyes still following the relentless wipers, it came to me.

"Is this green Jeep yours?"

"No, I stole it. Of course it's mine." He laughed. "Why?"

I remembered days ago, the Jeep in the parking lot of Little Italy—the Jeep Philip had just missed hitting. True, I'd

155

only caught a glimpse of it, but it had been green. It could very well have been this Jeep. Justin's Jeep. I sucked in my breath. And that would mean Justin had also been at Little Italy.

"Well, are you going to answer me?" he prodded.

"I think I saw it the other night—when I was out with Philip." I watched Justin closely, waiting for a reaction; but, frustratingly, he never faced me, and his profile was not enough for me to read any change of expression.

"What—this Jeep?"

"Yes. Well?" *Reassure me*, I thought.

"You might have." His voice gave me no clue. "Or it might have been any number of other green Jeeps."

Or not, I thought, uneasiness closing like a hand around my heart. Why couldn't he deny it or give me a straight answer? I didn't recall seeing Justin at the restaurant that night, but then I hadn't been paying attention to the other diners; I'd been too absorbed in myself. He could have been hidden at one of those dim corner tables, and I'd never have known. I recalled how he had come to the park, then to the library with me, and I tried to remember if I'd mentioned where I was going that night. I was pretty sure I had. Which led to one conclusion: if Justin had been at Little Italy, it would not have been a coincidence.

Maybe I'm just being paranoid, I thought. *After all, in California I wouldn't think twice about seeing the same kind of car even three times in the same day.* Sweat broke out on my forehead. *I wouldn't be so paranoid as to keep track in the first place!*

Then again, this wasn't California. This was Lorens, Wisconsin, a small town, and how many people drove identical automobiles?

As a gigantic bolt of lightning ripped across the sky, producing a thunderous crash, I jumped in my seatbelt, almost spilling the plants. Dirt sprinkled onto my feet. I quickly acted as if I were adjusting the plants in the box. I didn't want Justin to think I was afraid.

But I was. I didn't like storms. I didn't know what to expect, and I gripped the edges of the cardboard box so tightly my knuckles hurt.

Protect me, dear Lord. Protect us.

Justin, not seeming to notice my discomfort, was rambling on about his Jeep. " . . . a bit beat up, and it sure guzzles the gas, but it's always gotten me where I want to go." He smiled. "And it comes in mighty handy for saving girls who get caught in storms. Here you go," he said, pulling to a stop. I looked up to see we were in my uncle's driveway.

Justin turned to face me. I found myself looking into his brown eyes, eyes that led to somewhere I'd never been . . . and I searched them, desperately wanting my suspicions to be wrong.

"Thanks for the lift home," I said. "I don't know what I would have done if you hadn't come along when you did."

"You'd have gotten very wet. Come on, give me that box and we'll make a dash for the door."

Gladly, I turned the box over to him, and a moment later we were standing at the front door, dripping under the shelter of the veranda. A fierce wind shrieked around us like a wild creature. Thunder reverberated so close that I thought this must be the end, and I wished I were inside, hiding under a bed.

The moment I put my hand on the doorknob, I felt a terrible chill run through me. The door was locked, and I hadn't taken a key. I knew my uncle kept one hanging inside on a rack, but I'd been so preoccupied this morning, I hadn't thought to take it. When I left, I locked the door behind me out of habit, since I'm always the last one out of the house when going to work. All this raced through my head in an instant, while Justin stood on the porch holding the box of plants, dripping patiently. What was I going to do?

Trembling, both from the cold and the fear of being stuck

out in this storm, and—worst of all—admitting my incompetence to Justin—I slipped my hand in my pocket, making as if I knew what I was doing. When my fingers touched cold metal, my heart leapt. For a second, I almost believed wishful thinking had made the key materialize; but as I drew it out, I remembered it was the one I had found just this morning down the side of the chair.

It looked as if it could be a house key. At that moment, there was nothing more I wanted it to be. With a silent prayer, I placed it in the keyhole.

It fit, and the key turned easily. Sending up a prayer of thanks, I darted a look at Justin before pushing open the door. He gave no sign of having noticed the drama I'd just gone through.

We had just stepped inside, and I was still holding the door open for Justin, when the wind tore it from my grasp and slammed it shut behind us. Instant darkness. I felt as if I'd entered a tomb. Or, at the very least, the wrong house. I flipped a light switch but nothing happened.

"Power must be out," said Justin. After crouching to set the wet plant box on the floor, he stood up.

I'll never know what he meant to do next, for I was struck with terror that he would go, leaving me alone in this creepy house in this nightmarish storm, and I clutched at his arm. "Don't go!"

It was too dark to read Justin's face. I wondered if he wore an amused smile, or if he looked as embarrassed as I felt. I quickly tried to amend my words, to make them sound like anything other than the panic-stricken plea they were. "There's no reason for you to go," I said slowly, deliberately. "You don't want to drive in that. The storm's getting worse. It's dangerous." I felt my face flushing, and for that reason I was thankful for the darkness.

"I won't go," he said, "if you don't want me to."

"You gave me a ride home. The least I can do is let you stay."

"Of course. It's only right that you should pay me back. Thanks."

The words sounded dry, and I wondered why. A great crash of thunder put an end to my speculating. I automatically reached for Justin's arm, but he grabbed mine first and pulled me away from the door.

"Let's get downstairs."

I thought I felt the house shaking.

"Go! Go!" he ordered, almost pushing me down the stairs and into the basement.

We retreated to the farthest wall. In the cool, dim concrete surroundings, I tried to catch my breath, but musty air clogged my lungs. There was no light to see by, but when I raised my eyes, I found them looking into Justin's, which almost shone in the darkness. Eyes in the dark can be a scary thing. But I wasn't scared.

"Do you have any flashlights or candles down here? Any matches?" Justin turned and began rummaging along the wooden shelves lining the wall.

"Maybe," I said, having no idea, but joining in the search among canned foods and boxes. I didn't know anything about the basement because I'd only been down here once— soon after I'd arrived—pausing on the bottom stair only long enough to know it was a basement.

"Here we go." Justin struck a match and lit a twisted gold candle. Tear-shaped drips of solidified wax clung to its sides; I wondered when it had last been lit, and what for. "That's better."

But I didn't think so. If anything, it was worse—the flame heightened the eeriness of our surroundings by bringing out the shadows. Flickering shadows. Justin moved to a corner and I followed.

I tried not to flinch at a loud thunderclap. "I don't like storms," I said between clenched teeth. The only answer I got was another crash of thunder. "I hope there aren't any tornadoes." I rubbed my cold arms and found myself saying,

"Ever since I saw *The Wizard of Oz* when I was little, I've been terrified of tornadoes." I stopped. What a dumb thing to say. I blamed it on the darkness, the storm, the basement, my crazy situation. I stole a glance at Justin. His face was shadowy, but I thought I saw a smile.

"At least I don't have to worry about tornadoes in California," I added defensively.

"No, I guess not. Instead, you worry about earthquakes."

"Very funny." I didn't give him the satisfaction of knowing I was, in fact, more afraid of earthquakes than tornadoes.

Something must have caught Justin's eye, for he returned to the shelves and started fumbling around. He came back with some kind of brown, leather-covered box. "What's that?" I asked.

He pulled up a thin antenna, a wand of silver in the candlelight. "A radio." He wiggled some dials and the radio began making crackling sounds, interspersed with high squeals. "Maybe we can pick something up on this storm."

I waited in my cold, dusty corner, watching Justin's capable hands working the dials. His long, slender brown fingers. My gaze moved up to his dark hair, which fell slightly over his forehead as he looked down, so intent on the radio in his hands. Shadows highlighted the tense muscles of his face as he concentrated, frowning slightly.

A voice suddenly broke through the static. "—severe thunderstorm warning—*crackle—crackle*—in effect until—*crackle*—thirty P.M.—*crackle*—tornado warning"—my heart stiffened—"to remain in effect until—*crackle*—advise you to seek shelter—*crackle*—a low area—*crackle*—"

Justin took one glance at me and switched the radio off.

"Darn thing's enough to give me a headache." He stared at the radio in his hands. "It's nothing we don't already know. We'll be fine."

I thought I felt the house rattle, and I backed so far into my corner I was almost climbing the wall. "My uncle's still in town, at the bookstore—"

"He'll be fine, too," Justin assured me. "Hasn't he lived here his whole life? I'm sure he's seen worse storms than this. He'll know what to do."

I began nodding my head in agreement, then froze, my eyes riveting on Justin. "How do you know he's lived here his whole life?"

Justin didn't answer right away, just stood there holding that old radio, looking at me as if he didn't quite understand the question. Finally he spoke. "You might be surprised by how much I know about you and your family."

I'd expected a denial, a joke. Not this. A finger of fear, something I'd felt too many times already in Justin's presence, touched me. An icy touch. Ever since I'd first met Justin and he'd left me with his strange words of warning, I'd felt something wasn't quite right about him. Little things, but little things add up.

"What do you mean? What do you know about my family?" My voice came out in a parched whisper.

Justin set the radio down. "I'm a reporter. I know lots of things. And what I don't know—I can find out."

"You didn't answer me." I wasn't going to let anything slip by this time, no matter how much I might not want to hear it. "What do you know about my family?"

"You don't have to make it sound like you're accusing me of something criminal. Your uncle's last name is Hutch, right? Okay. Now, if you can recall, I was planning to do a story on that old bookstore of his. So I found out who runs it and where he was from. Turns out he's lived here his whole life, except for a few years away at college." Justin spread out his hands. "It's that simple."

Sure, Justin made it sound rational enough, but I was beginning to think he had a special talent for that.

"Nowadays it's not so difficult to find out what you want to know," he continued, "as long as you know the right channels to go through."

"Doesn't a person have a right to privacy anymore? It shouldn't be that easy."

"Maybe not," Justin said, "but it is."

"And then some things that you need to find out, you can't." I looked down at my hands. "It's so frustrating."

"Things such as . . . ?"

"You know." I sighed, too tired to evade the truth. "About my mother. If I could just know what really happened up at the mansion that day she fell, or at least talk to someone who knows, who was there . . . like that Christopher Renton. He was a lead, but it didn't get me anywhere." I spoke vehemently now, forgetting the storm. "I feel like I'm up against a brick wall and there's no way to get through."

"Then maybe you should stop trying. You've done enough. Maybe it's time to leave the past alone."

I'd told myself the very same thing, but hearing Justin tell me made me all the more determined not to give up. "No, I haven't done enough! I can't just quit."

Justin sighed. "Why are you so stubborn?" He ran his hand through his hair. "Why is this so important to you?"

"Because—because the past affects the present—my present. And my future."

Justin's eyes fixed on mine. "How?"

I was struck with a sudden, deep desire to startle Justin, and in a split second, I made my choice. "We're close," I whispered, "very close to finding the treasure map. The one that Connie Ingerman supposedly hid and no one ever found."

I admit now that what I did was foolish—no, make that plain stupid—revealing such information to please a whim—but I didn't realize the danger at the time. "Someone *did* find it. My mother. And I'm going to find it next."

I was disappointed by Justin's reaction, or lack of. I saw no shock on his face, only a sort of steady, intense concentration.

162

"We're close," I continued, not knowing when to shut up, "closer than anyone." I was surprised at myself for showing such fervor. It didn't sound like me speaking. In fact, it sounded like Philip. He was the one devoted to finding the map. I hadn't even cared much about it, exciting as it sounded. What really mattered to me was learning about my mother. My eagerness about the map had come from Philip's contagious enthusiasm; but he wasn't here now, so why was I speaking like some sort of feverishly greedy, gold-struck fool?

"We?" was all Justin said.

"Philip Barnstrum and me."

"Oh, yeah. Philip Barnstrum. Sorry, I just can't seem to remember that name."

Even if there was a mocking tone to his voice, it didn't camouflage the seriousness in his eyes, and I was suddenly afraid I had said too much. Way too much.

"You won't—say anything about this to anyone, right?" I tried to disguise the worry in my voice, but failed miserably. What had I done? Had I lost my mind? I'd just revealed the story of the century to a story-hungry reporter! And if Philip ever found out how I'd betrayed him—

"Don't sound so worried—"

"I'm not. I just don't want you to go—spreading the news. For obvious reasons."

"Why did you tell me, then, if you don't trust me?"

I didn't answer. I didn't know the answer.

"Look, I use facts, not assumptions. And you haven't discovered the map yet. Have you?"

I shook my head.

"Then it's nothing concrete. I don't use rumors. So relax."

He picked up the radio and resumed fiddling with the knobs. "Of course, if you do make a big discovery, I'll be the first to know, won't I?"

I didn't answer.

"After this Barnside guy I mean, of course."
"Barnstrum," I said.
But I still didn't answer his question.

Chapter Fifteen

$\mathcal{T}$hough the storm continued to rage outside, with a fury that battered the walls and penetrated the basement, I was aware only of the silence between Justin and me.

Justin continued to play with the radio. I listened to static and squeals until I wanted to snatch the radio and throw it out a window. But I managed to control myself, mainly because I had a feeling Justin was trying to annoy me; and if he was, I certainly wasn't going to let him know he was succeeding. Also, the closest window was farther away than I was willing to go.

"Are you looking for another weather report?" I finally asked, careful to keep my voice patient.

"No."

I compressed my lips.

"Here we go!" Justin set the radio on the shelf and looked up in triumph as music began playing. I was so surprised, I smiled.

Justin smiled back. Without warning, he held his hand out to me. He even swept a bow. "May I have this dance?"

My smile faded as I hesitated. I hoped Justin couldn't see me blushing. "I—I'm not a very good dancer."

"Doesn't matter," Justin said. "I am. Just follow me; you'll get the hang of it." I caught a faint, insolent challenge in his eyes.

I lifted my chin. "All right." And I took his hand.

Then just like that, we were dancing. Carried away by the sweet strains of music, I became lost in the enchanting candlelight atmosphere. It didn't seem real that I, the school wallflower, could be dancing so easily, and yet it seemed more real than anything else. So I'd missed my prom back home. Big deal. I hadn't even had a date.

I forgot everything but the moment. No longer was the wind and rain and thunder a threat, but rather it became a piece of atmosphere to be tucked into the background along with the music.

In Justin's arms, I felt protected. Completely. I never knew being held by someone could feel like this. And now that I was convinced the storm couldn't touch me, my worries melted. In retrospect, I found it frightening that I could be so easily subdued. But the thing was, I wanted to be.

I didn't know what station Justin had found; I only knew it was perfect. Nothing too rocky, nothing so dull that it would make us fall asleep on our feet. It was just right to keep us dancing. No more did I smell the musty basement, but a mix of rainwater and leather, which was odd because Justin wasn't even wearing his jacket. The moment was magical.

Even now I can easily recall the songs we danced to. And every once in a while I catch one playing somewhere— unexpectedly—and I have to stop what I'm doing, wherever I am, and remember . . . All else vanishes and I am there again in my uncle's basement, dancing by candlelight with the strangest man I'd ever met, while a storm rages outside.

"Memories are made by moments like these . . ." There was something so soft and soothing in the rhythm of that song, and as we danced, my feet never felt the ground. " . . . but memories fade. Oh, darling, please . . . be more than a memory to me."

"I thought you said you weren't a good dancer," Justin whispered into my hair.

It was a moment before I answered. "I guess it depends who I dance with."

My head only reached Justin's shoulder, yet we danced so easily together. Being close to him made me feel small and light and, I'll admit, even beautiful. Resting my head against his chest, I could hear his heart beating. Fast.

How long did we dance? Time meant nothing to me, so I can't say. All I know is, it lasted forever yet went by too swiftly.

A song came on with a wonderful tune, and I liked it—until I heard the lyrics.

It was foolish of me, really. I'd heard "Breakfast at Tiffany's" before; I knew the song was referring to the Audrey Hepburn movie (a strange movie that I never had figured out). But at that moment, when I was very susceptible to emotion, "Tiffany" was all I heard, and it brought thoughts of my mother rushing back to me. My throat tightened and my eyes blurred.

I stumbled. Almost stepped on Justin's foot. "Please, let's stop," I said.

The spell was broken. Justin let go of me and, as if he knew why I could no longer dance, walked over to the radio and turned it off.

I couldn't look at him, didn't want him to see my eyes for fear of what he might read there. The only sound was the sound of breathing. I held my breath a moment and listened to Justin's deep breathing, convinced I had ruined everything. All the beauty that we had just shared was destroyed like a beautiful painting splashed with black paint. I wondered if he regretted his offer to dance with me, an offer that had surely been made on impulse. Was he ashamed? *Please, don't be,* I pleaded silently. *I know I must look like a fool, but if you have any compassion, you'll understand.* I wanted so much for him to understand.

"Listen—the storm's stopped."

"You're right!" I cried with too much enthusiasm. I wondered how long the storm had been over. We hadn't noticed. Neither of us. This cheered me slightly, to know I hadn't been the only one seduced by the atmosphere.

Justin blew out the candle and we climbed the stairs,

emerging just in time to see my uncle enter the house.

I was standing slightly behind Justin, and I had to gather my courage to step out into full view. My uncle stood in the doorway, streaming rainwater and staring at me, making me feel as if I'd done something terrible. I half expected his mouth to drop open.

Justin spoke first. "Hello, sir. I hope you don't mind, but I gave your niece a ride home. She got caught in the storm—"

"We went downstairs to be safe," I cut in. "There was a tornado warning—"

"I know," my uncle interrupted. "It was a false alarm. The tornado didn't come within three miles of us." His eyes fixed on Justin and would not move. My eyes darted back and forth between the two men. Like the first time they'd met, I felt they were in some sort of silent battle.

"I was just leaving, sir," Justin said, as if refusing to fight the battle. He gave me a nod as he went to the door. "Take care, Robin."

"Thanks again for the ride," I called after him. He was almost to his Jeep when he stopped in a puddle and turned around. "No problem," he called back.

I closed the door and leaned against it, confused. Confused about everything. Philip, Justin, my uncle . . . I looked at my uncle, who still stood dripping in his rumpled coat. His wet hair looked thinner than ever, plastered to his head. I realized I had forgotten to return Justin's jacket and that it still hung draped over the desk chair in my bedroom. I would have run out the door to stop Justin so I could return it, if my uncle weren't here.

"What were you doing out in the storm?" he asked, slowly taking off his coat and shaking it so that water droplets hit me.

"Getting some plants. The storm took me by surprise. It came up so suddenly, I—"

"You should be more careful in the future." His voice

was grave. "You don't want to have to accept rides from strangers."

It was like a slap in the face. "Justin's no stranger. You met him before, and he was nice enough to give me a ride. The least you could have done was show some appreciation." I narrowed my eyes. Back when Justin had wanted to write that story, I'd sensed my uncle's hostility toward him. I hadn't understood it then and I didn't understand it now. Yet I'd felt that the resentment had nothing to do with the story. Now I was convinced. "What do you have against Justin?"

"I assume you mean Mr. Landers." My uncle ambled into the kitchen, and I followed. "What makes you think I have something against him?"

"It just seems like every time you see him, you get—I don't know—defensive, and—and rude."

"Every time I see him? I've only seen him twice. Should it be more?"

"You looked like you wanted to throw him out."

"Was there a reason for him to stay? The storm is over."

"That's beside the point. You're not hearing what I'm saying. I'm talking about the bigger picture. What do you have against Justin?"

My uncle turned to face me. "Truthfully, I don't trust him." He looked at me, and I could see his eyes behind his glasses, gazing so strongly into mine that my eyes wavered. "And I'm concerned his intentions aren't what you think."

"Oh, so now you can read minds."

My uncle opened the refrigerator door and stood looking into it. "No, I don't claim that. But it's my responsibility to look out for you. I think you should be careful whom you choose for your friends."

I straightened to my full five feet two inches. Not that it mattered; my uncle wasn't even looking. "I should have known. It's a control thing. You don't want me to have friends. You just want me to—" my eyes shot around the clean kitchen—"to wait on you. Having friends would be asking too much. I've already lost everything I used to have —why should I even try to have a life?" I wanted him to say something to fuel my anger, but he remained silent, apparently fascinated by the interior of the fridge. Maybe because it was stocked for a change, thanks to me.

"It's a control thing," I repeated. "But guess what? Here's a news flash for you: I can take care of myself. And I certainly don't need you telling me what friends to have or not have." I threw up my arms. "You're just like my mother! Overprotective. Suspicious of everyone and everything!" I turned on my heels so hard that the rubber soles of my sandals squeaked on the linoleum floor.

Feeling the pressure of tears, I raced up the stairs two at a time and shut myself in my room by slamming the door. Pictures rattled on the walls. In some distant part of my brain, I realized that I should apologize to my uncle for my disrespectful outburst, but my horrible pride wouldn't let me. Not yet.

Toppling onto the bed, I let the tears fall. I cried till I wore myself out. Then I lay with my tear-stained face, staring up at the ceiling, not really seeing it. I could feel the tears evaporating, leaving dry salt trails on my face.

I kept picturing my uncle standing before the fridge, deaf to my words, contemplating what to eat when all he'd end up eating anyway was pizza. That was how much I mattered.

My anger gave way to a dull, aching sorrow. I held it inside me, nursing it so it wouldn't die, until I suddenly became disgusted with myself. Self-pity would not help me solve my problems.

I propped myself up on one elbow. Maybe my accusations against my uncle had been somewhat exaggerated and unjust, but his own accusations had been harsh. I remembered what he'd said about Justin, how he'd called him a stranger and warned me not to trust him. I screwed up my face. *What he means is I should beware,* I thought sarcastically. *He might be an escaped convict or a psycho or something.* My eyes fell on Justin's jacket draped over the desk chair, and I remembered how soft and warm it had felt.

I sighed and sank back down. *Justin's just a normal guy. Like Philip, and my uncle doesn't make a big deal about him.* I stared up at the white ceiling. *How awful to be my uncle or my mother, always worrying, never having a moment's peace.* A person couldn't live like that—it would drive them insane.

I yanked the pillow out from under the quilt and buried my head, fearing that already this obsessive mistrust was infecting me. Hadn't I had similar suspicions about Justin? Was it in my blood, this suspicious nature? Was it in my genes? Had I been born with it? Or had I caught it, like a disease? Would it grow until it consumed me?

I jumped up from the bed. Why wouldn't my mind just shut up? As I looked for something to throw in frustration, my eyes landed on the Victoria Holt novel I'd been reading recently, the one my mother had received from Christopher Renton. I grabbed the book, but instead of throwing it, I dropped myself onto the window seat and, tucking my legs up under me, determined to finish it.

I certainly had no difficulty keeping that resolution. Almost instantly, I was pulled back into the story. The characters came alive in my mind, and I became the heroine. I felt her feelings, her desperation and terror, and for a little while, forgot my own problems.

When I finished reading, I sat holding the closed book in my hands, savoring the suspense. It was all very fine in a book, where it belonged, and as long as it was happening to someone else.

Eventually, I tilted my head back, letting my gaze trail along the titles of the books packed tightly in the shelves above the desk. I stood, eager to look through the collection of Victoria Holt novels and choose my next read. I stepped up on the desk chair, enjoying the thrill that knowing I now owned these books gave me. The Victoria Holt novels were lined up neatly. *Probably in order,* I thought, seeing that *Mistress of Mellyn* was first in line.

It fascinated me to think that these books had stood packed exactly like this, collecting dust for twenty years. My mother had been the last to touch them, to open them.

I was about to pull out a promising title, when I paused, noticing the book below. It was identical to the one I had just finished reading and still held in my hand. Curious as to why my mother had two copies of the same book, I pulled it from the shelf.

When I opened it, I almost choked on the dust that flew from the pages. A stale odor assaulted my nose, but that wasn't what made me catch my breath. The pages were filled with cursive writing. I recognized that writing. Thumbing through the coarse yellow pages, I realized what I was holding. Not a printed novel, but a hand-penned account of my mother's life.

My mother's diary.

A passage into her past.

I almost fell off the chair. My mother had kept a diary! I never would have guessed it. Yet here it was, in my quivering hands.

I let the paper jacket flutter to the floor. Fleetingly, I assumed my mother must have used the novel jacket to camouflage her diary. How well it had worked. All these years it had sat here, waiting for me. Now that I had this diary, would the pieces of the past that I had been pondering over finally come together? I gripped the book tightly. It had to hold the answers to my questions, the questions I wanted to ask my mother but could not. Tiffany could answer them.

Feeling giddy, I stepped down from the chair and carried the diary to the window seat. It was time to do some serious reading.

I opened the cover and read an inscription: *This very*

secret diary belongs to Tiffany Hutch. Then I turned to the first page.

April 1, 1974

No, it isn't a joke. (Please note the date.) I really am starting a diary! It's amazing that I never started one sooner, because I like to write. I'm always writing stories, and maybe writing about my own life will make it more exciting.

Some girls buy those dinky little books with the even dinkier locks that are easier to open than keep locked, but I decided if I'm going to go to the trouble of keeping a diary, I want to do it right. And who wants to have a million little diaries, one for each year, cluttering up their room? Not me. So I bought this big fat blank book. It should last me a really long time. Unless, of course, something exciting happens and I write constantly!

Now, of course, I face the problem of keeping this diary secret. But it really isn't much of a problem. It will blend in perfectly in my bookshelf, just like any other book. Besides, who's going to look for it? There's only my brother, Peter, and he isn't a nosy person. Sometimes I almost wish he was, because that would be more fun. But he's old—23—so I guess that's why he's so serious. And he works hard, on account of it's just him and me. I wish he could learn to have more fun, but I guess you just get boring like that when you get old. I turn 13 in twelve days, but I'm always going to have fun and stay happy, no matter how old I get.

Last year was hard—to stay happy, I mean

—but time helps, I guess . . . I'll always miss my mother and I'll always love her, but that doesn't mean I have to be sad. That's what Peter told me.

I wish my mother had kept a diary. It would be the one thing I'd want to keep of hers if I had to choose one thing. Because it would be like a part of her.

Oh well, at least someday my daughter will have this diary. Then again, maybe I'll never get married! Most boys are so annoying. When they're with their friends they either ignore you or tease you, and when they're alone they either act really stupid and think they're groovy, or else they're too shy to talk.

Tears trickled into the corners of my smile as I continued reading. A number of short entries followed, just little accounts of day-to-day happenings. Nothing exciting.

I guess my mother thought so too, because the entries became less frequent, and it was obvious her interest was waning.

Keeping a diary is becoming boring. It's not that I don't like writing, but nothing ever happens in this monotenous (did I spell that right?) little town, and I can't write about nothing.

When I found the next page blank, my heart skipped a beat; I was afraid that was all there was. I turned the page before I could get too disappointed, and when I discovered another entry, relief flooded through me.

The handwriting looked more mature on this page, smaller and more uniform. The date above the entry confirmed my guess that this entry had been written quite some time later.

June 6, 1978

Here you are, still waiting to be filled after all these years. I'd almost forgotten about you, but not quite. Today I remembered because I actually have something worth writing about!

It came about in the most unlikely way. Today Peter finally decided to fix the dripping kitchen faucet. Then of course when it was all apart and he had his hands full, he needed me to go pick up some washers for it. As if I know anything about that sort of thing.

I went anyway, to Hanson's Hardware. It's just off Main Street, and although I've seen it a trillion times, I've never actually been inside.

If I'd only known what I was missing!

You see, I needed help finding what Peter needed, and this guy who works there helped me. He was stocking shelves when I came in, and when the bells rang he turned and smiled at me. That smile . . . from the moment our eyes met, I knew.

With his help, it only took a minute to find what I needed, but I stayed much longer. (And it turned out Peter didn't need the washers anyway—what we need is a completely new faucet.) Somehow, like magic, we were talking, and we got to know each other so that I feel like I've known him forever. Yet there's something about him, something that makes my heart pound when I'm near him, that makes me want to know him more.

I've always thought it corny when I heard or read about "love at first sight." And it is corny

175

—unless it happens to you. Then it's real. Very real. And not the least bit corny.

Oh, how easy it's going to be to fill this diary now! Suddenly, my life looks thrilling, so full of promise, and all because I met this guy. He asked if he could see me again, and I said yes. His name is Christopher Renton, and oh, I know he's going to change my life.

Chapter Sixteen

I t was as if I'd begun some awful drama, one that I knew ended in tragedy; yet because I'd begun, I had to follow through to the end. But where would it end, and did I even want to know?

I made a solemn promise to read the entries in order. No matter how tempted, I would not skip to the end. If I didn't read the entries this way, I might miss something important. At the same time, I was repelled by the thought of actually reaching the final page. I didn't think I would be able to face the finality of it, what the last entry might—or might not— reveal.

No. I would not skip to the end. I would reach it soon enough.

So I sat in that window seat for what must have been hours, turning pages almost feverishly, the paper rough beneath my fingers, reading how Tiffany's friendship with Christopher grew. Through her written words, I could almost see the relationship playing out before me. I might have laughed at how it reminded me of a sappy soap opera, only the laughter choked itself off long before it reached my throat.

August 1, 1978

Christopher and I spent the whole day together. He is so wonderful. I've never known anyone like him. I can sit and talk with him for hours and not be bored—it's amazing. I never tire of focusing on his face as he speaks, never tire of

Past Suspicion

the unique way he smiles, the intense, vivacious sparkle of his eyes, or hearing the sound of his voice—

Pen ink streaked across the page.

Oh no! I just caught sight of my wrist, the one on which I always wear my special silver bracelet—from my brother on my sixteenth birthday—and it's bare! The catch hasn't been closing right lately and the bracelet must have fallen off somewhere today. Why wasn't I more careful?

But I'll try not to panic. Think. Think where I might have lost it. Let's see. I spent the day with Christopher. Most likely the bracelet dropped off in his car or at his duplex. I'll have to ask him to keep an eye out for it. Hopefully I didn't lose it when we went walking through the park. I couldn't bear the thought of some old lady finding it and using it for a cat collar or something equally disrespectful. If I ever find it I'll make sure not to wear it until the catch is fixed. Oh, how could I have been so careless? What a rotten ending to a wonderful day.

I looked down at the silver bracelet on my own wrist, thinking, *This must be that bracelet.* But didn't she lose it in the mansion? She must have found it, only to lose it again, I reasoned, and touched the clasp. I'd have to be more careful than her, because I'd be devastated if I ever lost it.

Absently fondling the bracelet, I returned to the diary. Excitement and expectancy beat in my heart as I read more about Christopher Renton. My mother had been so close to him. Now, in these pages, I could finally learn what he was really like.

178

Or could I? My mother analyzed him, praised him, gushed over how perfect he was . . . how could I be sure my mother's perception of him was true? Even the clearest vision could be blurred by love, couldn't it?

My contemplation was shattered by the rude ringing of a telephone. I sprang to my feet in a daze, hardly knowing where I was, I had been so absorbed in the diary. My head swelled with a rush of dizziness and I almost lost my balance. I forced myself to take several deep breaths, filling my lungs to capacity, then exhaling slowly, purposely. This cleared my head and my vision. But by this time, the phone was silent.

I was just turning back to the diary when I heard a knock on my door.

"Robin," I tensed at my uncle's voice, "telephone for you."

I waited five long seconds before answering, "All right. I'll get it in the hall."

I listened at my door, and when I heard the creak of my uncle's steps as he retreated downstairs, I left my room and picked up the hall phone. I said hello, then heard a click as my uncle hung up the other phone.

"Hi, beautiful. How goes the treasure hunting?" It was Philip's voice, eager on the other line.

"Oh." I rubbed my forehead, still feeling slightly disoriented. It took me a moment to remember our morning meeting and my promise; the morning seemed like such a long time ago. "I mean, I'm doing what I can—"

"Good, good." He rushed on. "Look, I just wanted to know how things were going, and let you know I won't be able to see you tomorrow. I'll be out of town the whole day. Some relative I've gotta visit, you know how it is. Anyway, I'll see you again as soon as I can."

"All right." A pause.

"So you haven't found anything?" I sensed his hope and tension—so intense I almost felt it searing through the line as he awaited my answer. Suddenly, I was irritated. I wasn't sure why, only I knew I wanted something more from him than these questions.

"What did you think I would find?" I asked. "A sign in my mother's room with an arrow pointing to her closet saying, 'The treasure map's in here'?"

"Well, not something quite that obvious . . ."

"Philip," I said, exasperated.

He laughed. "Just keep your eyes open and your mind alert." His voice lowered. "You'll find it. I know you will."

I wish I had as much confidence in me. I began winding the phone cord around my finger, thinking, *I should tell him about the diary.* But something held me back. Perhaps I was being selfish, but I didn't want to share the diary. Not yet, anyway—it was too intimate a thing to share with anyone—not until I'd had a chance to read it through by myself.

"I'll try," was all I said.

"You do that." He gave an elaborate sigh. "Even a day seems too long to be away from you, Robin. I wish you could come with me tomorrow, but it wouldn't be any fun for you. We'll have to wait until we find what we're after. Then we can go anywhere we want—together."

I caught my breath. He was hinting again, which meant he hadn't forgotten what he'd told me this morning. He was serious. Immediately my heart began to beat faster and my feelings softened. I didn't want Philip to leave town, not even for a day. I was relenting, deciding I should tell Philip about the diary after all, when he said, "So do your best, and maybe you'll have something to show me when I get back."

"I think I might be getting close."

"Wonderful." He didn't give me a chance to continue. "I have confidence in you, Robin, all you need is confidence in yourself. And then you can do anything. Remember that, and I'll see you soon."

This was my opportunity to jump in and tell him about the diary, but I didn't. "Bye."

"I'll miss you." He hung up, and my chance was over.

Returning to my room, I didn't regret my hesitation; in fact, I began to feel glad that I hadn't told him. *It would have been silly,* I reasoned. *The diary isn't important to anyone but me. Besides, it would be embarrassing to have Philip read it.* This was what I told myself, but deep down I think I knew, and feared, that if I told Philip he *would* think it was a big deal, and insist upon reading the diary himself. This thought was enough to fill me with panic.

I settled down to continue reading, but it wasn't long before the strain of the long, eventful day began to take its toll. My eyes kept falling shut and my neck would not support my head, which felt absurdly heavy. Evening draped its dusky veil over my window and the words in the diary became too dim to read.

It took all my willpower to close the diary. I didn't get up right away, but stayed sitting at the window, clasping the book against my chest and leaning my forehead against the cool glass. I watched the stars prick through the blackness of night. I was so tired that the tune came to me unconsciously, and I began to hum, "Memories are made by moments like these . . ."

When I became aware of the song I was humming, I stopped. I slapped the diary down on the window seat and got ready for bed. For once, I intended to get a good night's sleep.

When I awoke the next morning after a night of deep dreamlessness, I was famished. I blinked my eyes groggily but made no move to get up. Until I remembered the diary.

Then I scrambled out of bed, so eager to get to it that I became ensnared in the sheets and almost fell over in my enthusiasm. Once at the window seat, I paused to open my window, because with my bedroom door closed all night, my room had become unbearably stuffy.

The sound of church bells floated in on the morning air. I glanced at the time and saw it was eight o'clock. I'd missed seven-thirty Mass. Great, I'd gotten a good night's sleep, but at the expense of missing early Mass. Which meant I would have to go to the nine o'clock one. With my uncle, whom I still owed an apology.

You planned this, didn't You, Lord?

I opened my bedroom door and emerged to hear my uncle just beginning to move about downstairs. I lingered uneasily on the landing. The memory came back to me of peaceful Sunday mornings at church with my mother, sunlight beaming through stained glass windows, warming us as we prayed side by side. I think Sunday was my mother's favorite day. We had never missed Mass. *And I'm not about to begin now, dear Lord, I promise.*

So at eight-thirty I appeared downstairs wearing a soft blue floral skirt and a white blouse. My hair was brushed lightly from my face and held back with a clasp. I couldn't have looked more respectable.

My uncle, who didn't seem surprised to see me waiting for him, gave me a small nod, as if of approval, and smiled.

Swallowing, I returned the smile awkwardly. My tongue felt stuck to the roof of my mouth. *Why is this so hard for me?* I realized I wasn't well-practiced in making apologies. In fact, there were probably many things I should have apologized to my mother for, and never had. *I'm sorry, Mom.*

"I'm sorry," I said aloud, "for the way I acted last night and the things I said—"

My uncle held up his hand. "That's all right, Robin. It's over and done with. How about we get going?"

Really? I thought. *That wasn't so hard.*

We set off down the sidewalk and the sun was shining, making the sidewalk look paper-white. Almost with a start, I realized that not only was today Sunday, it was the thirtieth of May. Tomorrow was Memorial Day, and the day after that was the first of June—my eighteenth birthday. A tremor of anticipation ran through me. Only two more days till freedom. I hugged this realization to myself and glanced at my uncle, doubting he even knew when my birthday was.

The quaint white church was perched on a hill. Nestled in morning light, it made a charming scene, like something on a picture-postcard or in a calendar, with its old bell tower and ancient graveyard stretching over the hill. Rising from the hillcrest, headstones reached for the morning sky. My fingers practically itched to draw the scene, and I had to fold them together to control them.

"Beautiful, isn't it?" my uncle asked. "Your mother used to dream of getting married in this church."

I felt an incredible sadness at his words.

We walked up the stone steps, through the massive wooden doors of St. Catherine's, and were immediately engulfed in a hushed, holy atmosphere. My shoes tapped startlingly loudly on the wooden floor as I followed my uncle to a pew.

I felt people staring at me. Maybe it was just my imagination, but when I'd come to early Mass last week by myself, I hadn't felt this way. Probably because there had not been very many people. That was the way I liked it. I had slipped into a back pew, then left soon after Mass was over. I hadn't wanted to talk to anyone and risk having to answer questions.

Now I sat rigidly.

But when Mass began, I forgot the people. Sunlight streamed through the stained glass windows like translucent gold and dappled us with colors. Everything was so familiar, but I didn't fight the memories that came; they were pleasant. My one problem was trying to ignore my growling stomach.

Filing out of the pew after Mass and the "Ave Maria," I found myself at the end of a line. Oops. Confession line. Not where I wanted to be.

Why not? demanded my conscience.

The problem with being a critical person was that

judgment often boomeranged right back to me. *Okay, Lord, it's time.*

I stayed in line.

When it was my turn, I stepped inside the little booth, closed the door, and knelt. "Bless me, Father, for I have sinned. It has been a month since my last confession."

It seemed a lot longer.

"Since then, I've gotten angry—well—more times than I can count. I've been selfish, ungrateful, disrespectful, proud . . ." The list kept growing until I suddenly thought, and actually said, "Wow. I'm a bad person."

I heard the priest shift position behind the screen. "How old are you?"

"Seventeen."

"You're not a bad person. Just a teenager."

"But sometimes . . . I feel angry . . . at God." *Where did that come from?* The truth of my words came crashing down on me like a wave.

"Do you know why you feel this way?" asked the priest.

I thought a moment. "He took my father. He took my mother. He took me away from my home."

"But have you considered all He has given you? God's ways are not always our own. In fact, most often they're not. He usually has a greater plan in store for us than we could conceive for ourselves. Have faith. It will give you hope and direction."

Sure, this sounded nice, but I had to be honest: I wasn't convinced. "I don't think I'm headed in any direction. I feel like I'm floating. My past is a mess . . . why should my future be any different?"

"The surest way to a bright future is to live well in the present."

"But I don't even want to live here. It's not my home."

"As long as God is in your soul, anywhere can be home. Peace can be found in accepting His will. Pray for guidance. Prayer will be your most powerful tool."

I wanted to say I'd prayed for my mother, and that hadn't stopped her from dying.

After praying my penance before the Blessed Sacrament, I stepped out into the dizzying sunlit morning, feeling refreshed, though very hungry, and ready to make a clean start.

Maybe my uncle felt somewhat the same way toward me, because on the lawn he turned to me and said, "About last night, Robin—I don't want you to get the wrong impression." He put his hand lightly on my shoulder. "I want you to be happy, to have friends, and I think you're old enough to decide for yourself who they are. I'm only asking that you be careful whom you choose. I don't want you to jump into anything. And I want you to know that you can talk to me anytime, that I'm here for you, if ever you want to ask my advice." He led me away from the front steps, where other parishioners were gathering to chatter, and under the shade of a giant tree. My eyes observed the new leaves. Maple.

"But you don't need to fight me. I'm not going to stop you from seeing whom you want to see. It wouldn't do any good. It's up to you to make your own choices. Only," he paused, looking me straight in the eye, "don't disregard me. I have my reasons for saying this. Perhaps you think them strange. Nonetheless, I'm asking you to trust me, and when I offer you advice, at least consider it."

This was quite a long speech for my uncle. I wondered how long he'd had all this on his mind. Ever since we first met? It wouldn't surprise me.

"Okay, I appreciate that. I really do."

"So be careful whom you choose for your friends." His voice lowered. "There's something not quite right about that young man."

"You mean Justin?" Of course I knew he did.

"What I mean is, you don't know him—"

"We've been through all this," I cut in, struggling for

patience. "If you have a reason for my not seeing him, please tell me. But if you don't, then don't lecture me."

I waited, but when my uncle just repeated, "Be careful," I blew a strand of hair out of my eyes, nodded, and walked away from behind the tree trunk before saying words I would regret. I felt a sudden impact as I collided into something solid. With a gasp, I looked up to see that that something was Justin.

At first, he looked as startled as me; but he recovered faster and smiled—apparently finding something amusing in the situation—while I, still flustered, managed only a mumbled, "Sorry."

"Apology accepted," he said, bowing down graciously before me. I glanced around quickly, hoping no one was watching the odd performance.

"What are you doing here?" I asked.

"Here? You mean at church?" He lifted an eyebrow. "It's Sunday. Is it so strange to go to church on Sunday? You may not believe it, but I'm a God-fearing man."

My uncle's warning fresh in my mind, I eyed him distrustfully.

Still smiling, Justin reached up and pulled at his collar. "Need another reason? All right. Let's just say I thought today would be a nice day to go to church and get knocked over by a pretty girl who, unfortunately, seems less than happy to see me."

"I am. I mean, I'm not." I wondered why I bothered defending Justin to my uncle. Why didn't I simply forget him and satisfy everyone? It would make life so much easier.

The expression on Justin's face suddenly changed, became more subdued, and I realized he'd only just caught sight of my uncle hidden by the tree. I'd forgotten about him, and was almost as surprised as Justin to realize he was standing near, listening. Yet I found a strange satisfaction at the thought of Justin being taken off guard. Already I could sense the tension rising like smoke between them.

I was almost beginning to enjoy the awkwardness of the situation, wondering who would win this battle, when I realized we weren't going to be alone long enough to find out.

The other parishioners decided to interrupt the drama by wandering in our direction. It didn't take me long to figure out why; they were eager to meet the newcomer. Me. I wished I could shrink into the bark of the maple tree. Doing the next best thing, I retreated into the shade.

They came anyway, and all I could do was put on a smooth face and smile my way through the introductions. I knew I'd never be able to remember all the names, so I stuck to a safe, "Hello, nice to meet you," and it worked surprisingly well.

My mind had wandered to concocting ways to escape the crowd, when a name caught my ear and I snapped back to attention.

"Did you say Mr. Hanson?"

A large, smiling man nodded and held out a calloused hand. "That's right."

"Hello, nice to meet you." I shook his hand and smiled. "Do you own a hardware store?"

I could have bitten my tongue off. What a question! Even standing in the cool shade, I felt my face grow warm.

The man raised thick eyebrows. "Why, yes, I do—"

"You see, I thought I remembered seeing a Hanson's Hardware in town—and I just thought maybe—" having already embarrassed myself by interrupting, I hurried on and made things worse—"I just thought maybe you owned it."

It was a lame explanation. What girl goes around making connections like that? The man looked amused, but appeared flattered that I'd noticed his store. "That's right. Hanson's Hardware's been in the family for years."

I began calculating. This man could be thirty-five, maybe forty—certainly not old enough to be the Mr. Hanson who had employed Christopher Renton. "So did your father run it

187

before you?"

"Sure did. But Dad doesn't get around very much anymore. Bad back, you see."

"Oh," I said slowly. My mind wasn't working fast enough to come up with any clever ways of finding out what I wanted to know. Maybe because I was so hungry. My stomach growled.

"As a matter of fact, I guess we'd better be getting back to him." Mr. Hanson turned to a wiry woman standing beside him, who I supposed was his wife, and said, as if my noisy stomach had reminded him, "Dad'll be wanting his blueberry pancakes. We'd better be going." He took her arm and they began to move away. Thank goodness, because my stomach growled again.

"So long," Mr. Hanson turned to call back over his shoulder, loud enough for everyone—even the dead in their graves—to hear. "Come visit the store anytime. Nice to meet a young lady who's interested in hardware!"

I flushed. This was a good time to leave.

Quickly, before others could introduce themselves, I turned to my uncle, who seemed quite content, cleverly avoiding the crowd by leaning against the other side of the tree. "Let's go," I whispered urgently.

"Why? Don't you want to make some more friends? It's kind of nice here in this shade. Cool and relaxing, don't you think?"

Before I could answer, another voice piped up. "Did I hear right?" I turned and saw a girl about my age, with a smooth, unfreckled complexion and shiny black hair, standing near me. I thought of Snow White. "Are you really interested in hardware?" She laughed, showing even white teeth. I couldn't imagine her ever having to wear braces; I bet her teeth just grew in perfectly straight like that. She didn't wait for an answer. "What a weird thing for Mr. Hanson to say. Anyway, my name's Anna, Anna Larkwood."

"Robin Finley. Nice to meet you." And she did seem pleasant, but I was so hungry and weary of smalltalk. As soon as I could, I turned back to my uncle, my long skirt swirling dramatically around my ankles, and entreated him with the first thing that jumped to mind. "I'll make blueberry pancakes if we leave *right now*."

We left.

Walking away, I suddenly remembered Justin, and for some reason I turned my head. My eyes searched through the few straggling people, and I saw Anna had moved off to the shade of a pine tree and was now talking to a tall, dark-haired young man. Justin. Though I was too far away to hear what they were saying, I could imagine them talking about "rude Robin Finley." I told myself I didn't care, but I felt a slight pang anyway. At that moment, Justin looked up and caught me watching him. I swung my eyes away.

"Wait a second, Robin!" I heard footsteps running to catch up to me, and my heartbeat quickened to match their pace. "What are you doing today?"

"Um—I don't know—I don't have any plans, but—" My mind floundered for some excuse, because suddenly I remembered I *did* have plans, important ones: the diary. But I couldn't tell him that.

"Good. How about we meet at the park?" He glanced at the sun. "Say one o'clock?"

"Really, I—"

"Come on, Robin." He smiled. "I think the ducks miss us."

He really wants me to, I thought. *He's asking me even with my uncle right here.* I couldn't help feeling pleased. Well, the diary could wait. An afternoon in the park wouldn't take all day, and it sounded, well, kind of fun. Relaxing. And with the weather so nice, I'd like to spend time outside.

But I sensed my uncle tense beside me. I hesitated, then thought, *I'm not going to be put off by his paranoid concerns. Because that's all they are.* Then for some reason, I thought of Anna. My eyes darted to her slender form and I saw her watching us. "Okay," I agreed.

Apparently satisfied, Justin left, and he didn't head in Anna's direction. My uncle and I continued up the sidewalk in silence until we were almost to the house. Then he spoke, as if it had taken him that long to find the words. "So you are going to see that young man, after all?"

"Is there any reason why I shouldn't?" *See, I'm being reasonable,* I thought. *Now let's see if you can give me a reasonable answer.*

"I'd feel better if you stayed away."

"That's not a reason."

"Is there some reason you have to see him?"

"Why do I need a reason? He's a friend. You said yourself you wanted me to have friends."

"I do."

"Okay," I stopped walking, "I get it. You want me to have friends, but you don't want me to have friends. That makes a lot of sense."

"I want you to have the right friends." We were at the mailbox now, and my uncle pulled out the Sunday paper. "How about Anna? She was trying to be friendly, but you brushed her off."

When he put it that way, I felt bad. I hadn't meant to be rude. "But we're talking about Justin right now," I insisted. "There's nothing wrong with him. He's Catholic, too, so what can you possibly have against him?"

"I'm only warning you to be careful—"

"Careful?" I flung up my arms. "Careful of what, for goodness' sake?"

"Calm down, Robin." My uncle tucked the paper under his arm and headed for the front door. The fact that he didn't get easily worked up was a characteristic I suddenly found irritating.

"All I'm saying is don't let him fool you. You haven't

known him very long." My uncle unlocked the door. "Think about it. Don't you find it somewhat . . . odd, the way this Mr. Landers keeps showing up? Don't think I haven't noticed. You're smarter than this, Robin, and you've noticed, too. Don't fall for it."

"Fall for what?"

"His charm."

I could have laughed if I weren't so distraught. Charm? Philip had charm, not Justin. Justin and his blunt comments. Then I began to wonder, was my uncle afraid I might be falling for Justin . . . romantically? No. That was absurd. He knew I was dating Philip.

"Oh, come on," I said, because suddenly I needed to convince myself as much as my uncle that this was nonsense, for he had planted a dangerous doubt. "So I see him sometimes—that doesn't mean anything. Maybe he likes me. Is that so unbelievable?"

Suddenly I wanted to cry—with fear, loneliness, pure frustration, and every other emotion that existed. The only thing stopping me was that I knew I'd never forgive myself if I broke down in front of my uncle. "Anyway," I managed to say, "it's easy to run into the same people often. This is a small town."

"Not that small," my uncle said.

Chapter Seventeen

Thank you very much, Mr. Hanson, I thought. It was because of him that I had made my impulsive offer. After reaching the house, not only did I have to search fifteen minutes before finding a blueberry pancake recipe, but I also discovered we had no blueberries.

"Well, you did promise *blueberry* pancakes," my uncle said, not glancing up from the Sunday paper when I informed him.

So, rather than go back on my word, I set my teeth and ran to the nearest store. I wanted to run. It gave me a chance to work off some tension.

Now here I stood, in a green apron over a spattering frying pan, attempting to flip blueberry pancakes without breaking them into an oozing mess. I wasn't doing very well.

But although they were shaped more like lily pads than pancakes, they did taste good. Especially to me, because I was famished.

Later, rinsing the dishes, I began to regret my rash promise to meet Justin. I wanted to get back to the diary. Every time I remembered it, sitting up in my room, waiting for me, my yearning for it became stronger . . . almost as if I could hear it calling me. I shuddered and turned off the faucet. Maybe it was a good thing I was going out.

Except for one thing. Though I would never admit it, what my uncle had said set me worrying again. Because I knew there was truth in it. Justin *had* turned up "conveniently" a suspicious number of times. I wasn't sure what to make of it, but I decided I couldn't let it get to me. I'd promised to meet Justin at the park and I wasn't going to back out now. Besides, this was my chance to finally return his jacket. Maybe even sever contact with him once and for all. Not that I would, but the possibility helped me justify my going. And I could always use the time in the park to draw. Thinking this, I grabbed his jacket and my pencil and sketchpad before leaving the house.

The sun shone brilliantly, sending down golden rays to saturate my skin; this and a refreshing breeze helped me relax. I inhaled deeply as I walked, trying to absorb and savor each scent of spring. If I paused to listen, I could hear bees humming as they collected nectar. I waved to a little girl blowing bubbles in her front yard, and she giggled and waved back.

I was surprised to hear laughter and screaming as I approached the park. I'd taken for granted that it would be as peaceful as last time. But of course it wouldn't be because this was the weekend. Not just any weekend, but Memorial Day weekend, a holiday made for being outside. Children and adults alike would be taking advantage of the gorgeous weather and time off of school and work to have fun and picnics in the park.

With mixed feelings, I searched nervously through the unfamiliar people, searching for Justin, and I wondered why I was nervous. The moment I spotted his tall figure standing beside the pond, he turned. His eyes found me almost instantly.

"Noisy today, isn't it?" he called.

I nodded, then cut right to my concerns. "I was surprised to see you at church this morning." Joining him, I held out the jacket.

He took it, draped it over his shoulder. "Yeah, well, I'm full of surprises, so don't be surprised . . . if I surprise you sometimes."

I laughed, thinking, *You say the oddest things.* I looked down at our reflections, dim in the water, his so tall, mine so short. If only I could clear this apprehension that was shrouding me, maybe I could enjoy Justin's company. I'd gladly continue defending him to my uncle if I had some support. He had to help me. All I wanted was some justification for his strange behavior. Thinking this, I decided to casually swing the conversation in the direction of Justin's supposedly coincidental arrivals.

"I wanted to thank you again for bringing me home yesterday. I was lucky you came by just when you did—"

"You're welcome."

"I don't know how you happened to come by at *just* the right moment—"

"I think we had this conversation already." Was he starting to sound irritated? "I just happened to be driving by and was happy to give you a lift."

He'd just happened to be driving by. Okay . . . why did I have to be suspicious of that? Because my uncle wouldn't believe it. Did I believe it? But where was the sense in thinking Justin was shadowing me, as my uncle had implied? My uncle was going to think what he wanted no matter what I told him. So why bother? Justin had done nothing wrong. So he'd given me a ride and taken me home. So we'd waited out the storm in the basement. Nothing had happened.

"Yes . . . well, thank you."

"Hey, what's with all this thankfulness, anyway? Once is enough." Justin's voice turned gruff. "As long as it's sincere."

"It is."

Justin peered out over the water. "I guess our ducks aren't going to visit us today. Ungrateful little things." I glanced at him, wondering at his change to "our" ducks from what had previously been "my."

"Want to go for a walk?" he asked.

"Sure." Was this why he had asked me here? To walk? I didn't know if it was Justin's intention or not, but he seemed to make everything into a mystery. Then I shrugged, not wanting to worry anymore.

With each step, I tried to kick my doubts away. There was nothing to be afraid of. At least not here when we were out in the open surrounded by people. My head hurt from constant over-analyzing. I sighed, thinking, *Maybe I need to get my head examined.*

"Something wrong?" Justin asked.

"No." I waited for him to prod, but he didn't. So after a respectable pause—during which we passed a young couple sitting on a blanket on the grass, oblivious to everyone but each other—I went on. "Life can be so frustrating."

"Tell me something I don't know." I was surprised by the cynical edge to Justin's voice.

This time when we crossed the bridge, I was careful to act normal. I focused on a tree on the opposite bank and didn't let my expression change. I hoped Justin noticed, as he was probably remembering my reaction from last time, and I wanted him to know I had overcome that, that I was stronger than my emotions.

Not far from the bridge I spotted a water fountain. Feeling thirsty, I walked over for a drink.

"No, not a water fountain," Justin insisted when he heard me refer to it as such. "It's called a bubbler."

Weird Wisconsinites, I thought, taking long, gulping swallows. I closed my eyes as the water bubbled up cold and refreshing into my mouth.

I was still carrying my drawing things tucked under one arm. I wondered if I'd get a chance to use them, or if Justin and I would simply continue walking all afternoon long. I wouldn't care if we did. It was pleasant, walking and not talking, yet not feeling uncomfortable in the silence. I wondered how we could walk so easily together, Justin's legs being so much longer than mine, but our pace was perfect.

"You know," Justin spoke up when we reached the far side of the pond, "I get the feeling your uncle doesn't like me much."

A smile cracked my face. "Really? Whatever gave you that idea?" My voice hardened. "He judges people without knowing them."

"Don't blame him," Justin said, and he leaned down to pick up a stone. I watched him rub his thumb over its smooth black surface. "Maybe he's just watching out for you." He whipped back his arm and let the stone fly. I watched it skip over the water's surface, counting five times before it disappeared. "That isn't so bad, you know, having someone who cares enough to watch out for you."

Whose side are you on, anyway? I wondered, picking up my own stone. "I can take care of myself." I threw my stone. Without skipping once, it plunked to the bottom of the pond.

"I noticed."

Not funny, I thought. But I didn't say anything out loud.

We loitered along until we came to a soft grassy bank bordered by large bushes that hid everyone else from our view. But for the raucous laughter and yelling, I could almost forget the people and think we were alone. "I fish here sometimes," Justin said, "but not as often as I'd like. I'm usually so busy."

"Chasing hot stories?" I couldn't resist asking.

"That's right." Justin grinned and stretched out on the bank, looking up at the sky. "This crazy town keeps me on my toes."

Still standing, I looked down at him lying so relaxed in the grass, and suddenly I saw him in a different way. Surrounded by delicate purple clover and dappled in shadow, he looked gentle, even vulnerable.

"Do you catch much?" I asked, not really knowing why. "Fishing, I mean." I sat beside him on the bank and began weaving my fingers into the thickly matted clover and grass.

"Not usually, but some days I have good luck."

I wondered why he hadn't gone fishing today. It would have been a perfect chance. I decided to ask.

"Today? Oh, I guess I didn't really think of it." He

propped himself up on one elbow and stared at me, his brown eyes the color of maple syrup. "That, or I thought of something else I'd rather do."

I plucked a few pieces of grass and examined them, pretending not to have heard him. The question returned. Why had he wanted to see me so urgently today? In my fingers, the grass mashed to a pulp, wetting my fingertips with green liquid. The pungent plant smell rose to my nostrils.

"Besides, tomorrow's Memorial Day. I'll get a chance to go fishing then, maybe. After the parade and everything. Hey," he sat up suddenly, "you've never seen how this little town celebrates Memorial Day, have you?" I shook my head. "You're going to watch the parade tomorrow, aren't you?"

"I—hadn't really thought about it." My mind grappled for excuses.

"You should." He gave a lopsided smile. "It would be unpatriotic not to."

He lay back down, and again I looked at him lying so at ease among the grass, the pond stretching out behind him and his dark hair ruffling in the breeze, his tan face and strong features, that distinctive nose. A slight smile came to my lips. I thought of how I was almost eighteen, and how I was planning to go back to California; and I realized there were some things I'd miss about Wisconsin, about Lorens.

I recognized this as a warning signal. The sooner I left, the better.

But the smile remained, lingering on my lips. I couldn't leave without having anything to remember Justin by. Not that I would ever forget him.

"What are you thinking?" Justin asked.

I met his eyes. "I was thinking . . . that I'd like to draw your portrait." I looked down and fumbled to open my sketchpad. "I'd like the practice, if you don't mind sitting, that is. I'll try not to take too long."

"Go ahead." He stretched his arms. "Take as long as you

want. I don't mind. In fact, I'm flattered."

I only half heard him as I took up my pencil and began sketching. In shades of gray, a face took shape and features formed, slowly coming to resemble Justin. I was so deep in concentration that when he spoke, it was as if his words came piercing through a dream.

"What?" I asked absently.

"I said, have you made any progress in your search?"

I frowned, both because my concentration had been broken and because Justin had brought up the disturbing subject that, for a while, I had managed to forget.

"Maybe," I answered, not looking up. Justin's nose was giving me trouble.

"What does that mean?" He paused, then went on when he received no answer. "Robin, I want you to trust me. I thought you did—but if you don't—if you don't want to talk about it—"

"Don't move," I ordered, pretending to be engrossed in my drawing.

"Whatever you say," and he fell back into silence.

But the damage was done. Justin had started my mind working and I couldn't turn it off. What progress was I making? None. And Philip would be back tomorrow, demanding results . . .

Frustration returned. My pencil strokes grew darker under the increased pressure. I wanted desperately to break through this mystery. Only then could I be free. Because it was like Justin had warned me: I'd started this, and I couldn't stop until I found answers, or I'd always be wondering, never at rest . . .

A plan began to form in my mind. Slowly at first, then bursting into existence like a firecracker. Mr. Hanson, the one who had employed Christopher Renton, still lived in Lorens. He had a bad back, but he was alive. I would find a way to meet the man, talk to him, and ask about Christopher. Even though I wasn't sure how I would go about asking the questions, I wanted to try. Surely Mr. Hanson could tell me something I didn't know. It was such a simple plan. Why hadn't I thought of it sooner?

I laid down my pencil and studied my drawing critically. Though it was a fairly good likeness of Justin, it didn't satisfy me. It wasn't what I'd been striving for. I'd failed to capture his heart, his soul, his essence. But then maybe that just wasn't possible.

"Very good, but you made me look better than I really do," Justin said when I showed it to him.

As we retraced our steps around the pond, I wondered whether I should mention my plan. Justin might be able to give me some helpful suggestions on how to go about interviewing Mr. Hanson. Three times, the words to ask him were almost on my lips. The first two attempts, since I was unsure of how Justin would react, the words died with my courage. The third attempt, he spoke before I could.

"What made you mention Hanson's Hardware this morning?" His voice was casual, but it put me on alert. I sensed it was a shield for real interest. True, Justin had saved me the trouble of broaching the subject, but why had he? Suspicion seeped through me like poison.

"I just made the connection."

"Yeah, I heard you say that this morning."

"You sound as if you don't believe me."

"I do. But I also think there has to be a reason for making that connection, and to mention it."

"Why?"

Out of the corner of my eye, I saw him smile. "I know you. And when you ask a question, you have a reason." He shrugged. "You're not a small talker."

You know me too well, I thought.

"So tell me," he said.

Why should I? I was struck by a fist of disappointment. Justin, too, had a reason for doing things. He had asked me to meet him at the park for a specific reason—to interrogate me—and I detested him for it and for luring me here in such a sneaky way. "Tell you what?" I asked, brushing away a butterfly that flew too near my face.

"Why you're interested in Hanson's Hardware."

I'm not sure why I answered, maybe because I didn't know what else to do. "Christopher Renton once worked there."

"I figured it was probably something like that." Justin's voice was so low, it sounded almost as if he were talking to himself.

"I want to visit old Mr. Hanson . . . see if he can tell me anything—"

"You're not going to let this go, are you?" Justin broke in. "You're just going to keep digging and digging and digging—"

"So?" I asked indignantly, to cover my confusion. *One moment you're helping me, the next you're against me. Make up your mind.* "It's my business. I have every right to dig if I want."

"Persistence can be a good thing—up to a certain point," I saw Justin clenching and unclenching his hands, veins protruding over the muscles in his arms, "but you have to know when to let things rest. The past is finished. Stop looking back."

I rolled my eyes, just waiting for him to start quoting something at me.

"You don't know what you're getting yourself into—"

"I'm just going to talk to an old man. Where's the harm in that?"

Justin grabbed my arm and stopped walking, so that I stumbled and almost fell. Justin didn't seem to notice. "You're doing this for that guy, aren't you? Because you think you have to, to make him like you." His eyes held mine. "He can't make you, Robin. Tell him no. Don't let him get you involved—"

"Involved?" I yanked my arm away. "I am involved. This

is my mother I'm talking about. How dare you! I'm not doing this for anyone else. I'm only trying to find out about her past. Is that too much to want?" I fought the trembling in my voice and my body. "I thought you understood."

To make him like you. The words burned in my heart. Was that the way Justin saw me? As such a pitiful person, no one would like me unless I served them, trying to earn a puppy-dog loyalty? How pathetic. I stalked away, my only thought being to put as much distance as possible between me and Justin.

"Robin!" He was at my side again, but I refused to turn and face him. "I'm not finished." His tone was startlingly severe. "Listen to me." I turned, almost afraid he'd grab me again if I didn't, and glowered at him.

"All I'm saying is, don't get in over your head. Don't do this for the wrong reasons. He's only in this for the map. What do you know about this Philip guy, anyway? How do you know you can trust him?"

"Oh, listen to yourself!" My laugh sounded almost hysterical. "How can you stand there and say that? You're no better—I know at least as much about Philip as I know about you—and you think I should trust you. I don't care if you are a reporter. That doesn't give you special privileges or the right to do anything you want." My knees were shaking, making it hard to stand, but the words kept coming. "You can't tell me what to do. I'm not your responsibility—I'm no one's responsibility—I can take care of myself!"

To make him like you. My mind would not let it go. "And if you think I'm so worthless that I have to buy friendship, then why do you keep bothering me? I don't need you in my life. I don't want to see you again. Ever. So leave me alone."

Justin's voice dropped to a cold, quiet level. "I can't."

The reply was so unexpected, so contrary to how a normal person would react, that I backed away, sickly confused. Turning, I broke into a run.

I can't. Those words beat in my head, driving my

muscles.

I can't. As much as those two words shook me up, it was the way he had said them that unnerved me the most. So icy that they froze my heart.

I can't.

Half an hour later, lying on my bed, my head still racing, I tormented myself over the meaning of those words. He *couldn't* leave me alone? Maybe my uncle was closer to the truth than even he realized. What kind of person was Justin? I'd thought I was finally beginning to know him, but now I had to admit I wasn't even close. He was frighteningly unpredictable, a contradiction within himself.

In my head, I gathered incidents against him. Our first meeting. He had been waiting for me outside the bookstore; I was sure of it now. And all those questions he'd asked me. His parting words. And he'd turned up again and again: at the park, at Christopher Renton's old place, during the storm, and today, at church. These meetings couldn't be coincidences.

Or was I just overreacting, analyzing a crude statement made on impulse? Had he really meant those words, or had he said them simply because he wanted to shock me, knew how to provoke me, knew where my sensitivities lay and was taking advantage of them? Why was he torturing me like this?

I jumped up and grabbed my hairbrush from the dressing table. I pulled the brush fiercely through my hair, making it fluff out as wildly as a lion's mane. Wryly, I thought how it matched my mood. I wasn't going to let Justin or anyone else tell me what to do. I'd already made up my mind.

My uncle was napping in the living room, a newspaper over his face, when I crept downstairs and into the den where I located a telephone book and looked up "Hanson." For that name, only one address in Lorens was listed: 203 Willow Street.

It was time for me to take a walk.

Chapter Eighteen

My heart was beating in my throat as I approached the clapboard house. *There's no reason to feel nervous,* I reassured myself, *I'm just making a neighborly call.* And I decided the house, painted light gray and trimmed with dark green shutters, looked friendly. Delicate, lacy white flowers bordered the sidewalk. *Yes, definitely friendly. Inviting, even.*

I stepped onto the porch and pressed the doorbell, creating an interval of time that seemed to last forever, and yet it was over too quickly. Glancing at the windows, I thought I saw a movement at the drawn curtains, giving me the uneasy feeling I was being watched.

I clutched the brown paper bag in my hands. It was filled with chocolate chip cookies, because if I had learned anything from my last experience—stopping in uninvited to see a stranger—it was not to start out without a plan. Or in this case, an excuse. So before leaving I'd filled this bag with homemade cookies, ones I had baked for Philip and me to snack on when he came over to go through my mother's papers, but in the excitement I'd forgotten—

The door opened, jerking me back to the present.

"Hello." A thin woman, whom I recognized as Mrs. Hanson, spoke before I could. Her face puckered into a questioning look. I smiled what I hoped was a bright smile, and gathered my words.

"Hello, I hope I'm not disturbing you," I began, growing nervous when she didn't assure me I wasn't. I forced myself to continue. "I met you and your husband this morning, at church. My name's Robin Finley—"

"Yes, I remember." She waited, staying behind the

partially open door as if protecting herself.

"Anyway," I said, still smiling painfully, "I—was just taking a walk . . . I thought I'd stop in and say hello. Actually, I was wondering if I could talk to Mr. Hanson, your father-in-law. I—have something for him." I held up the paper bag. "Is he home?"

Mrs. Hanson didn't answer right away, just stood there eyeing me distrustfully. No wonder. My performance hadn't been the smoothest. First I'd claimed I was taking a walk, then I'd admitted I'd planned this visit. I knew I wasn't being the most polite by dropping in unexpectedly, and I knew I wouldn't trust myself if I were in this woman's place, but I waited, heart pounding, hoping for the best. Finally the woman shrugged—probably not wanting to bother trying to figure me out—and stepped aside to let me in.

"He's in his room," she said, leading me down a short hall. "But don't stay too long. He's rather old."

Pushing a wooden door open without knocking, Mrs. Hanson announced, "Someone's here to see you." Then, shooting me one last quizzical look, she left.

A bent old man looked up from a chair by the window. He had about three strands of hair combed across his bald head. "What's this?" he asked sharply. "A visitor for me?" His face crinkled into a yellow-toothed smile. "Close the door, missy, and sit down. Sit down."

I was reluctant to do so. The room was stuffy with a smell that reminded me of old socks. But despite the man's small stature, there was something commanding about his voice, and I shut the door and sat down in a large leather chair. It was so large, I felt lost as I sunk into its depths. My feet dangled above the floor. I thought it would be a good chair for curling up in and relaxing. But I wasn't relaxed now. I moistened my lips. "I hope I'm not disturbing you," I began.

"No need for the formalities," he said, waving my words aside. "I'd tell you if you were disturbing me. Can't you see all I'm doing is sitting here? I think I know why you came—you're Tiffany's girl, aren't you?" Reading the answer in my startled face, he continued. "I heard you were in town. I've been wanting to catch a glimpse of you, to see if it's true what they say, that you look so much like your mother. Yep, it's true." He chuckled with boyish glee, and I gathered that he had been the one spying through the curtains at me.

"Mr. Hanson," I leaned forward, trying to summon a businesslike air (as well as escape the odor leaking from the chair), "the reason I came to see you is that I understand you had a man named Christopher Renton working for you at one time. Do you remember him?"

"'Course I remember," he answered, jerking his head defensively. "Just because a body gets old doesn't mean he loses his memory, unlike some folks assume. Age ripens the mind. I have an excellent memory." He tapped a sinewy finger to his head. "Christopher Renton. Why do you ask?"

"I—think he was a friend of my mother's," I said, as if that were an explanation.

"He was your mother's boyfriend."

I nodded, and I saw the old man's eyes alight on the paper bag still clutched in my hand. He thrust his stubbly chin in its direction. "What do you got in there?"

The paper made a crinkling noise as I gripped it tighter. "First tell me about Christopher Renton."

"Oh, that's the way it is, is it?" He rubbed his chin. "Smart young lady . . . bring along some bait to catch what you want." I thought I saw a twinkle in his eyes as they met mine. "All right. What do you want to know?"

"Anything you can tell me. What was he like?"

"Christopher Renton was a scoundrel," the man declared. "Yes, he worked for me—for a time. But I was hard up for help or I never would have hired him in the first place. There was something about him I didn't like from the start. He was too proud, for one thing. But with times like they were, I hired him."

205

As he talked, I sat completely still, seizing every word, wondering at the contrast of his account to my mother's. Whose should I believe?

"He stole from me," Mr. Hanson said, "and when I found out, that was the end of him. I should have reported him, but I fired him and let it go at that. I should have reported him," he repeated, grumbling.

Even though I'd only just met him, I suspected Mr. Hanson had a softer heart than he wanted to let on.

"No offense—Robin, is it?—don't know why she named you a fool name like that—but your mother couldn't see the real scoundrel behind that boy's pretty face. Oh, he knew how to turn on the charm, he did. I watched him do it the first time Tiffany came into the store. I remember so well it disgusts me. Tiffany was so taken in by him that she left the store just walkin' on air."

I squirmed in my chair, not appreciating his making my mother sound like a fool, yet not wanting to interrupt and risk not hearing what else he could tell me. He continued talking, and the steady flow of information fed my hungry mind.

"Then there was the accident—you know about that?"

When I nodded, the old man was obviously disappointed. I sensed he would have enjoyed being the one to tell me the story for the first time.

"Well, at least something good came of it, anyway," he said. "It musta' finally knocked some sense into her head, if you know what I mean. Those two had been planning on getting hitched, so I'd heard tell, but after the accident, Tiffany didn't like the boy no more. Guess she finally saw him for what he really was—a scoundrel," Mr. Hanson finished, apparently satisfied. "Now, how about that bag?" He licked his lips in anticipation, though how he knew the bag contained something to eat, I have no idea.

"But what about Christopher Renton—how did he react? To my mother's rejecting him, I mean." If he were such a proud "scoundrel" as Mr. Hanson claimed, I wouldn't imagine he'd taken it too well. "And what happened to him after?" I waited, very tense. This was the answer no one had been able to give me so far.

"Being jilted?" he said in response to my first question. "Didn't bother him that much, I guess, missy. Next thing I heard he went and got hitched to someone else quick enough, some rich gal. Then up and left, and good riddance, I said. This town didn't need the likes of him."

"Wait." A thought struck me. "How do you know all this if he didn't work for you anymore?"

"Oh, I saw his sister around once or twice before she moved."

"Sister!" This was news to me. "He had a sister?"

"Yep. Twin sister, in fact. Now she was a nice gal. Nothing like her brother."

"Does she still live here? Do you still know her? What's her name?"

"Now hold your horses! Christine hasn't lived here for ages. All the young folk always want to get hitched and move away."

"But she used to live here in Lorens?"

"Nope. She lived in the next town over, Mentawka, with her parents, then her husband, but sometimes she came here to visit Christopher. To clean and cook for him, more likely. He went out and got his own place at sixteen." Mr. Hanson grinned. "His parents probably kicked him out."

My thoughts returning to Christopher, I asked, "Do you know anything about the girl he married? Her name?"

"All I know is she was some rich gal—"

"Do you think he married her for her money?"

"Now don't put words in my mouth, missy. I didn't say that. But it wouldn't surprise me." The man's eyes returned to the paper bag and his fingers beckoned. "Now come on, you hand over that bag. I've been waiting long enough."

He was right. I held out the bag, thankful for all he'd told me. His eyes darted to the door as he took it from me. Then he peered inside the bag and smiled. "Mighty grateful, missy. Don't get much sweets around here. They tell me it'll rot my teeth. But I tell them, 'So what? I've got as much right to rot my teeth as anyone.' More right, actually, 'cause I probably won't need mine much longer." He crammed a whole cookie into his mouth. "Mmmm . . . mighty good." I stepped back as crumbs showered from his mouth.

"Well, thank you for all the information. I'd better go now. Enjoy the cookies." I put a hand on the doorknob.

"Nice talkin' to you, missy. Come again, anytime. I like company. You'll always be welcome—" he grinned with his mouth full (*not* a pretty sight)—"so long as you bring more sweets, that is." He winked at me impishly, and I fought a smile.

I left him munching happily and found my way to the front door. I heard pans clattering in the kitchen. "Goodbye, Mrs. Hanson," I called, but I wasn't surprised when the only response was another clanging pot.

As I walked down the driveway, I felt I was being watched, and I didn't have to turn to know that the curtains of old Mr. Hanson's room were cracked open and eyes were peering at me. Yet even with his strange, brisk manner, I realized I rather liked the guy. He was a refreshingly different kind of person, and he struck me as honest. I believed what he'd told me.

All the way home, I marveled that I wasn't surprised by what I'd learned. Instead, I was satisfied. I had the feeling that this was the way things were supposed to go, that pieces were steadily accumulating, and it was just a matter of time before I would have them all and could fit them together to make a clear picture. Though slowly, I was getting somewhere, and this gave me confidence.

By late afternoon, I was curled up again with my mother's diary, eager to continue from where I'd left off. The entries almost always mentioned Christopher.

Sometimes I meet him after he's done with work, and we go out to a movie, or out to eat, or just walking. He's so wonderful . . .

Blah, blah, blah . . . I sighed. This was getting monotonous. *My mother and I might look similar,* I thought, *but in this way we're sure different. I'd never gush about a guy like this.*

But what really made me sick—and I mean a deep, causing a turning-of-my-stomach sick—was realizing how naïve my mother had been about Christopher, how easily she'd let him influence her. I'd always known my mother to be fairly sensible, but I was beginning to understand she hadn't always been that way. Not when it came to Christopher. Perhaps this was why I believed Mr. Hanson's account above my mother's. It was simply more believable. Mr. Hanson, not being blinded by love for Christopher Renton, could see him as he really was.

September 2, 1978

Today was Christopher's birthday. We've been going out for almost three months now and I wanted to get him something really special, something that would last forever. I finally decided on a watch. Not just any watch, but an expensive silver one (worth every cent). The gift of time. I had Christopher's initials engraved on the back.

I was worried maybe he wouldn't like it—or that maybe he wouldn't want to accept such an expensive gift—but when I gave it to him today, I could tell he loved it. "Great," he said, "Hanson's gonna expect me to be on time from now on." But then he kissed me, and that's how I could tell. "I love it, Tiff. I'll keep it forever."

The entries went on, and I read how Tiffany obtained a job as an intern at the newspaper and began her senior year at Lorens High.

It's just too exciting. One more year and I'll be facing my future head on. There are so many decisions to make and the responsibilities are almost frightening. I hope I make the right decisions; but if I follow my heart, how can I go wrong?

Winter came, and I read about the holidays, school exams, and problems.

I can tell Peter doesn't really like me going out with Christopher so much. I think he's afraid maybe we're getting too serious. But if this is meant to be, it's meant to be, isn't it? I can't let anyone get in the way, not even my brother. Yet although Peter's had to be responsible for me ever since our mother died, he's really not an interfering person. We have an understanding to do what we believe is right, and he knows I have to make my own decisions.

After all, I'm almost eighteen. My brother's smarter than most people realize; he'll give me advice, but he won't force me to take it.

He's still the same way, I found myself thinking as I fingered the dry page, ready to turn it. *Have I been too hard on him, Lord? Maybe—I've scared him away.*

I nibbled at my lip. *I shouldn't keep thinking he's out to control me just because my mother was. Uncle Peter has let me make my own decisions. He hasn't stopped me from doing what I want. He lets Philip visit. Sure, he has advice to give, but then he does have a responsibility . . . and it's not even one he asked for.*

I turned the page, and a new year began—1979—making my heart skip a beat. As the drama continued to unfold, I was coming closer and closer to the inevitable. Yet it was more than a drama, because this had really happened.

And 1979 was the year. I had a premonition that these pages would give me the final pieces I was searching for. Suddenly, I imagined the remaining pages as a countdown, a countdown to the fateful date of May 3, 1979. I longed to reach the last page, and yet I feared doing so because of what I might or might not discover. But I reminded myself that whether or not I would like it was not a factor. I must know the truth.

On the second day of January, my mother made her first reference to the Ingerman Mansion.

> *It's been years since I really thought about the old Ingerman Mansion. When I was little, all the kids used to dare each other to knock on the door. We thought the mansion was a real haunted house.*
>
> *But then I grew up and it became just an old house sitting on the outskirts of town, forgotten . . . until Christopher and I drove by it today and he started asking me about it. Even though he used to live only twenty miles from Lorens, I was surprised he'd never heard of the mansion before. I couldn't help feeling slightly proud, telling him about it and all the old legends. Lorens might not have much, but it does have the Ingerman Mansion to make it unique.*
>
> *The mansion hasn't changed. It looks as eerie as ever. Christopher was really interested*

in it, especially the treasure map story. He started speculating, making big plans, saying we could find it.

But we were just fooling around. Most people don't even believe the story about the map is real, or if it is, they say the map was lost or destroyed long ago, maybe even found and the money spent. How can we know?

Christopher wanted to go inside the mansion. I laughed at this, but he was serious. I finally convinced him it was impossible. Old man Ingerman still owns the place, and he doesn't let anyone inside. He keeps it locked, and from what I've heard, he's a real recluse— almost a hermit—and we'd have a better chance of breaking in than getting permission.

But sitting out there in the crisp New Year's night, anything seemed possible. And for a moment, I think both Christopher and I believed we could find the map. Even now it makes me shiver.

It made me shiver, too. This sounded too familiar for comfort. Uncanny. As if it were happening all over again . . . this time to me.

As if controlled by a spell, I resumed reading. The next couple of entries were less interesting and more difficult to keep my attention on because I was in suspense, waiting for the mansion to be mentioned again.

At one point, I suddenly realized rain was pelting my window, and I looked up to see droplets slithering down the glass like tiny silver snakes. I wondered how long it had been raining. I'd been so absorbed in this other world that I hadn't noticed when it started. I got up and switched on the bedroom light because it had become too dark to read without "ruining my eyes," as my mother would say. The wind began rattling the house, and I detected a rumble of thunder far in the distance. Telling myself to ignore it, I returned to the diary.

> *Christopher won't forget the mansion. Neither can I now, though . . . I almost want to. Ever since that night we drove past and I told him about it, he's become . . . preoccupied with it. His interest in it is almost like a hobby, I guess. Kind of.*
>
> *I'm being silly, I know. But the mansion makes me uneasy.*

I wanted more of an explanation, something less vague than these evasive sentences. But my mother became wrapped up in school and work again, and there was no more mention of the mansion. Until one day in late February . . .

> *Big news: I'm going to write a feature story for the newspaper—on the Ingerman Mansion! It's such an opportunity, and I never would have thought of it if it weren't for Christopher and his intense interest in the mansion. Mr. Stafford —chief editor of the paper and my boss—was intrigued by the idea. Amazingly, this story has never been done, only passed from generation to generation among the townspeople by word of mouth.*
>
> *Mr. Stafford knows how hard I work and agreed to run the story on the condition it is up to standards. "I'll consider it on spec," he said. "I'm not going to give you any special treatment, understand?" He likes to act gruff, but he's a good guy. Fair. And I'm not asking for any special treatment—just a chance to prove what I can do.*

Christopher was thrilled when I told him. "This is just the opportunity we've been waiting for," he said. "Who knows what possibilities this might open up?" Now I'm eager to begin. I was being foolish before, letting my childish fear of the mansion get in the way of rational thinking. I plan to make the most of this and I'm going to work my hardest—harder than I ever have before. I'm going to find out everything there is to know about the Ingerman Mansion.

And you did, didn't you? I thought, allowing myself a moment to admire my mother. At least this much I recognized in her: once she set her mind to something, she did everything possible to make it happen. She was a determined person. Thinking this, I began to wonder . . . what obstacles had come her way when she was researching the mansion's history? And what had she done about them? There was so much for me to wonder as I read.

The following entries confirmed my mother's enthusiasm and devotion to her project as she began doing research.

Christopher's almost as eager as I am about this story, and if it weren't for him, it never would have occurred to me to do this story in the first place. So he deserves credit. We're a team now, Christopher and I, and yet so much more than a team.

When I came home from the library today with an armload of local history books (which I couldn't wait to read), I found I couldn't get into the house.

I realized I'd somehow lost my key between yesterday afternoon (when I also came home with an armload of books) and today.

It seems I'm always losing things lately!

Maybe because I have so much on my mind.

I remembered the key I had found lodged down the side of the chair, and I pictured Tiffany—my mother—letting herself into the house and plopping down with all her things. Eager to begin, she'd forget about her key, which probably slipped down the side of the chair . . . not to be discovered for twenty years. By me, her daughter. I knew it could happen, because I could see myself losing it in the same way.

Since Peter wasn't due to be home for at least another hour, I went over to Hanson's, and Christopher left early so we could take the books over to his place and look through them there. Of course, old Hanson put up a fuss. That man watches us like an eagle when I come in his store, and he always has some piece of candy rolling around in his mouth. Ick! I don't like that man, and he doesn't like Christopher. Luckily, Christopher doesn't care.

"He's probably gonna fire me one of these days anyway," Christopher told me. "So I don't care what he thinks. If I want to leave early, I will."

How I love Christopher. But he can be stubborn. Take his name, for example. He insists I call him Christopher, never Chris. It's some hang-up he has. Odd, because most people would have it the other way around. But not Christopher. Oh well, it's just one of the many strange things I love about him.

Still, I'm tired of writing that long name (and I sure do write it enough). From now on I'll just write Chris. So there, what Chris doesn't know won't hurt him.

Really? Contrary to what she might think, I didn't think my mother was proving anything by writing "Chris" in her diary. Not if he never knew she was doing it.

The next entry was for April 13, Tiffany's eighteenth birthday. *How strange,* I thought, feeling a shiver shoot up my spine, *that I should read this entry when my own eighteenth birthday is only a day away.* Then my whole body began shivering, as if I were afraid this was more than mere coincidence.

> *Chris came over today and gave me a Victoria Holt novel (he knows how much I like to read). It was so sweet of him that I couldn't bear to tell him I already have this title. Especially since he wrote an inscription inside. I'll treasure this book forever. As for my other copy, I had a brilliant idea. I removed the dust jacket and put it around this diary. It fits perfectly, camouflaging it so no one will ever know I have a diary. I'll donate the duplicate novel to the library.*
>
> *Then, as if the novel weren't enough of a present, Chris surprised me with a little velvet box. For a wild second I thought it might contain—but no, I won't even write it. If my intuition is right, I believe it won't be too long now, anyway . . .*

Uneasiness curdled my insides. I knew very well what my mother was implying.

> *I found a beautiful gold locket inside, with his photo in it. I couldn't imagine a lovelier gift. Now whenever I want, I can open the locket and look into Chris's deep gray eyes, even when he's not with me. I told Chris I would wear the*

locket forever, just like he wears the silver
watch I gave him.

But she hadn't worn it always. I knew that, because I had found it hidden away in the wooden chest with all the other things she had wanted to forget. After the accident she "didn't like the boy no more," Mr. Hanson had told me. Yet before the accident, she had been infatuated by him.

Why the change?

And what about the photo? There hadn't been any photo inside the locket when I found it. So she must have taken it out. How I wished she hadn't.

I don't even know what Christopher Renton looks like.

A strange thought. Should it matter what he looked like?

But I wanted to know. I wanted to be able to put a face to this person whom I had been trying to find out so much about, who had been such a significant part of my mother's life.

I stared into space, wondering how I could go about doing this.

At that moment there was a tremendous clap of thunder, followed almost instantly by a gigantic crash that reverberated through the house.

My room went black.

Chapter Nineteen

When the lightning struck, I sprang to my feet. The diary tumbled from my lap to the floor, and I forgot it as I stumbled through the inky blackness, groping for the door and blinking, feeling blind. Gradually I made my way downstairs, following the clear path that was illuminated for me by periodic lightning flashes.

Downstairs, my immediate fear of the storm faded, giving way to annoyance. "Another one?" I grumbled. "Didn't we just have a storm yesterday?"

My uncle was lighting a candle when I entered the kitchen. I watched the flame stretch and swerve on the wick as he set the candle on the counter. "So much for dinner. I was just about to put the pizza in the oven." He shook his head. "I should have known better than to replace the old stove with one of these modern electronic ones. They're supposed to be so efficient, but there's nothing efficient about an oven you can't use when the power goes out."

A great crash shook the house. I wondered if we should go down to the basement, but my uncle continued complaining about the stove as if he hadn't heard the thunder. "I should never have replaced the old one. So what if it was fifty years old? At least it would have cooked dinner."

Still frowning, my uncle opened a drawer and took out a sleek battery operated weather radio, one I'd never seen before, and tuned in to the weather report. "Thunderstorm warning . . . high winds and rain . . ." I waited tensely, but there was no mention of a tornado.

Of course I began remembering yesterday and the

contrasting static-box that Justin had turned on, the crackling songs we had danced to . . . it seemed so very odd and distant to remember it now. I began wondering where Justin was at this moment, if he was alone or not, and if he was afraid. I shook my head. No. He wouldn't be afraid.

Another, even louder, crack of thunder jolted me out of my thoughts, and I hurried to follow my uncle downstairs.

In the far corner of the basement, I heard him fumbling in the darkness. Then I heard a sizzle as he lit a candle. The pungent odor of smoke reached my nose as I watched him set the candle on a small table. This was a different candle than the one Justin had found yesterday; this one was a short vigil candle in an ornate glass holder—similar to one of the blessed candles at church. It reminded me of the one my mother always lit during prayer time.

My uncle had gone back to the shelves and was moving more clutter. Curious, I watched as he mumbled, "I think . . . somewhere . . . ah." He pulled out a shallow, bowl-shaped little basket containing an assortment of rosaries in blue, brown, black, and white. He chose a black rosary as he explained to me, "It used to be our family custom to light a blessed candle and pray for protection during storms."

His words touched me. *Our family. My family.*

"It's been a long time . . ." my uncle said. He lifted a cheap white plastic rosary and wrinkled his brow. "I think this is the one your mother used to use. Yes, I remember now. She liked this one the best because she said white looked the most holy." He gave a soft chuckle, and I had to smile as well at the childish reasoning.

My uncle held the rosary out to me. "Would you like to join me?"

Feeling a swelling in my throat, I accepted the rosary with a nod.

Then we knelt on the cold concrete floor and began, our voices blending together.

"I believe in God the Father Almighty . . . "

~

Like all storms, this one eventually passed. When we came back upstairs, the house was a maze of darkness. Sporadic thunder continued to rumble in the distance, but I liked it—it made me feel safe, hearing it so far away, knowing it had passed over and could no longer reach me. I heaved open a window and paused to drink in the delicious rainwater smell.

Eventually, I wandered back to the kitchen. "How long do you think the power will be out?" I asked, flipping a light switch uselessly.

"Depends," my uncle replied, shoving the forgotten, half-thawed pizza back into the freezer. "Might be an hour. Might be a week."

I stood eyeing the melting candle, the wax solidifying on the taper in long pearly droplets. *He has to be joking,* I thought. *No way it will be out for a week.* But even an hour was too long, I realized, because I was hungry. Now. And I wasn't going to sit around and wait for the power to come back on.

"Well," I said, tossing on the green apron I'd used that morning, "I guess I'll see what I can do about dinner." I bent down to open a cupboard and started shuffling noisily through the pots and pans. When I finally stood up and looked over my shoulder, my uncle was gone. I turned back to focus on dinner. *Anything will do,* I told myself, *as long as it's edible, and as long as it's not pizza.*

If the power stayed out for more than several hours, I knew a lot of food in the refrigerator would spoil. So I decided to be resourceful and make a big omelet, using plenty of eggs, milk, cheese, and whatever fresh vegetables were left from my last shopping trip. I found I could use the gas burners on the stove simply by igniting them with a match. I grabbed two slices of wheat bread, spread both sides with butter, and fried each side until dark golden brown, making toast to accompany the eggs.

I worked in the gloomy dimness of candlelight, and I discovered I liked it. The atmosphere was just on the border of mysterious, making it cozy. It's something you have to experience—along with butter frying, candle flame shifting, and smoke mingling with the savory smell of cooking eggs —to understand.

"We'll eat in the living room tonight," my uncle informed me, sticking his head into the kitchen just at the moment when everything was ready and I was sliding the eggs onto plates. "I've started a fire in the fireplace," he said, and I shivered in anticipation. The late May evening was definitely cool enough for a fire.

We ate in front of the crackling fire, entertained by the orange glow and leaping shadows. My eyes followed the flames, fascinated by their continuous writhing dance. Words lay absent between me and my uncle, yet nothing seemed missing. Nothing, that is, but the tension that had existed earlier. Where had it gone? Perhaps it had been dissolved by our prayers, washed away by the rain, consumed with the meal, burnt in the flames.

Warm, fluffy eggs on fried toast—I'd never had that for dinner before. And I was sure my uncle hadn't. When the meal was eaten, he hoisted himself up from his chair. "Well, we might as well finish whatever ice cream is in the freezer. It won't last long with the power out." He winked. "And we can't let it go to waste."

Digging into the half-gallon carton, we mounded two blue porcelain bowls high with French vanilla ice cream. We ate while sitting in front of the fire, the giant scoops gradually softening into creamy mounds, drowning in a lake of vanilla liquid.

"It's Memorial Day tomorrow," my uncle said after a while. "The bookstore will be closed, of course. It looks as if we have another day off."

"Mmmm," I said by way of acknowledgment. My eyes were growing heavy and my vision was wavering. There was something mesmerizing about the erratic, snapping fire. Warmth saturated my skin and soaked through my bones. Cold ice cream, hot fire—the contrast of temperatures converged in a satisfaction of senses. Sighing, I thought of how no other flavor of ice cream was quite as enjoyable as vanilla.

"They'll be celebrating in town tomorrow," my uncle continued.

For a second my vision cleared and I noticed how the fire reflected in twin flames on the lenses of his glasses.

"Every year I watch the Memorial Day parade. It's only small, starting at the high school and continuing down Main Street, but it's as patriotic as any parade you'll find. You should come along and see how a small town celebrates. Who knows? This may be your only chance . . ." The sentence faded off, unfinished. Or maybe it was finished. Though sleepy, I was conscious enough to realize what my uncle was implying. Perhaps he suspected I didn't intend to stay in Lorens much longer. Maybe he'd never expected me to.

I let my tongue run over the cold steel of my spoon, lingering on the sweet film of ice cream before I spoke. "I might . . ."

In the fireplace, a log settled, shooting embers.

We sat holding empty bowls on our laps, each thinking our own thoughts as the fire diminished into a steady orange glow. I was too relaxed to get up, too content in this comfortable interlude. Too aware that that's all it was, an interlude. In the back of my mind I knew my problems remained, tangled and waiting; but I didn't want to touch the knot tonight and provoke it into tightening. With the power out, I would not be able to return to the diary unless I wanted to read by flashlight. And I didn't. Some of me was sorry, but more of me was relieved. I wondered what part of me that was, then smiled at how I was thinking of myself as if I were a jigsaw puzzle.

"That ice cream sure hit the spot," my uncle said suddenly. "Vanilla's my favorite flavor." He smiled, then added thoughtfully, "Of course, the best way to have it is with a slice of rhubarb pie."

"I bet!" This time I had no doubt what my uncle was implying, and I had to smile.

~

The peaceful spell my uncle and I had formed in front of the fireplace dissolved during the night. I'm not sure when, maybe when the power came back on. All I know is, when I awoke the next morning, I sensed, through the haze of sleep, that something was not right. Though I knew night was over, the world hung deadly quiet.

I opened one eye and squinted to read my wristwatch, tilting it in the dimness to catch a glimpse of the golden hands. Nine-thirty. I'd slept so soundly that it was much later than I'd intended to get up. An odd sense of urgency gnawed at my heart.

With my eyes still partially closed, I stood, stumbled to my window, and snapped open the shade. Unfortunately, that's not the way to open a shade, and the whole roll disconnected and bonked me on the head. Not a good way to start the day.

Now on the brink of a bad mood, I dragged the desk chair to the window, stood on it, and spent a frustrating five minutes trying to wedge the roll back into place. Just when I was about to throw the shade out the window, it decided to stay.

I stepped off the chair. When I looked out into the dull morning, hot and annoyed, I finally remembered today was Memorial Day. The outside world was draped in mist. Below my window, the weedy, overgrown garden caught my eye. It looked forlorn, waiting to be turned over, enriched with fertilizer, and planted with cheerful, blossoming, sun-thirsty plants. And though this wait was not my fault, I felt guilty.

I heaved the window open for my morning dose of fresh air and heard a car rumble past, then fade into silence. Such silence . . . not even interrupted by a single bird. *Sing!* I wanted to yell.

I closed the window on the depressing quiet and hurried to switch on the bedside clock radio, only halfheartedly realizing, when I saw the blinking 12:00, that the power had returned sometime during the night.

"Monday mornings make me miss you . . ." floated drearily from the radio. *Spare me,* I thought, switching the radio off.

I felt worse when I entered the kitchen, only to be greeted by the large, ticking clock. My uncle had already gone into town. Why hadn't he woken me? Oh, yeah, I'd never actually promised to go with him . . .

I might as well join him, I thought. *I have nothing better to do, and I guess it's where everyone else is.* That must be why everything felt so lonely, why when I looked out the front window past the long lawn to the road, all that I could see and hear of the world was deserted and silent.

But I do have something I need to do, I remembered. *The diary.* And I felt a sudden sense of responsibility fall on my heart like a deadweight. It sat there, heavy and painful, making breathing difficult.

How could I face the diary this morning? I imagined what it would be like sitting alone in that desolate room steeped in the past. I imagined the room swelling with echoes, heard them playing off the walls, tormenting me in that room that was *not* my room. It was my mother's— Tiffany's. And it would never let me forget it. At that moment, I believed she haunted the room—if only through her diary and memories. But haunted, nonetheless.

So I escaped, to join the crowd assembled for the parade, hoping to lose myself and my thoughts in their midst.

A roadblock stood on Main Street, and the sidewalks were lined with people. People holding flags, people holding children, people holding food and drinks, people holding hands.

I walked along trying to blend into the crowd, yet feeling detached, as if I were the only real person and the others were a mirage. I wanted to reach out and touch someone, anyone, to prove to myself that they were real and I wasn't here alone. But I restrained myself. A solemn air hung over the crowd, and my heart felt no eagerness for festivities.

Not wanting to stand still, I continued up the sidewalk, taking in the patriotic decorations. Red, white, and blue streamers twined around the usually stark black lampposts and fluttered at me teasingly. From the front of almost every shop and business a flag protruded prominently, flapping noisily in the cool wind.

As I walked, I dodged children, teenagers, parents, and grandparents. Young mothers pushed babies and toddlers in strollers. Some of the strollers were decorated with ribbons.

I saw these people in as much as I realized they were there, yet I didn't really see them; their faces meant nothing to me, and mine nothing to them. Even in this crowd, I felt alone. Maybe *I* was the one who wasn't real.

When I found myself following a curving sidewalk up a gradual hill, I realized I'd left Main Street behind and was heading for the high school and the start of the parade. On my way, I passed through a residential area. With their tidy gardens, trimmed bushes, and children's toys scattered across the yards, the houses struck me as model "happy family" homes.

On a front lawn, Barbie dolls stood in what looked like a miniature parade. A bike was propped against the side of another house. Farther on, the windows of a blue house displayed childish artwork consisting of cut and pasted stars and stripes forming a construction paper flag.

My steps slowed. A smile brushed my lips, but not without a twinge of sadness. These houses represented the cheerful, normal family life that I realized I wanted—had wanted for a long time—but had never dared admit: a home with a real family, with both a mother and a father, in a house like one of these.

But a house doesn't make a home, I told myself, and left them behind.

A large cemetery swept up the hill on my right, and I walked along the metal-linked fence on my way to where a cluster of people gathered near the hilltop, awaiting the parade. I searched the crowd for my uncle's face, and when I spotted him standing off a little distance from the main group, I walked over to join him.

We waited together for the parade to begin, not saying a word. I shivered every time the wind swooped by. The sky was still cloudy, and I doubted the sun would emerge today, which would not be nice for the family picnics that I supposed many people had planned. But I had to stop thinking about other people's plans. I reminded myself I had my own plans, the diary.

A gunshot pierced my thoughts and startled me back to my surroundings. The people lining the sidewalks, noisy a moment ago, instantly hushed.

"The seven-gun salute," my uncle said quietly.

Six shots followed. Then the band began playing a sad military song. Sad, yet somehow majestic. I stood straighter. As the mournful strains of music filled the air, the band began marching down the hill. "Taps," my uncle explained. "They play that when a soldier dies, and at military funerals."

The song finished on a significant note. One, I imagined, that would stay in my head all year. Then the band struck up a blaring tune and the parade really began as a festive mood took over. An assembly of high school girls marched down the hill, twirling dazzling batons in perfect time. A sleek, dark-haired girl caught my eye, and she flashed me a bright smile of recognition. Anna Larkwood.

Boy Scouts and Girl Scouts filed by proudly, followed by

an old car with some uniformed person waving. Everyone around me waved, so I waved, too. This car was followed by an ambulance, a flashing sheriff's car, and a fire truck shrieking so loudly I had to hold my hands over my ears as it passed.

The last car scattered candy to the crowd, and I smiled as screeching children scurried forward, their tiny fingers fumbling eagerly. When a long Tootsie Roll landed at my feet, I picked it up and handed it to a little girl who held only a single lollipop. She turned big eyes and a shy smile on me, and I smiled back, feeling strangely happy inside. As if I had done something wonderful.

Finally, the last straggling children with decorated bikes and wagons rode by, and the parade left us behind as it moved on to Main Street. Many people trailed after it, others dispersed to go back to their homes or on picnics, while some chose to roam the graveyard, perhaps paying tribute to friends' and relatives' graves . . . or just wandering curiously.

Perhaps it was a morbid inclination, but I felt an urge to follow this last group. My uncle was already wandering down the sidewalk, but I turned off, passing through the open cemetery gate, and when I called to him that I'd see him later, he nodded and continued down the hill.

Some people, probably most people, consider cemeteries to be depressing, lonely places, and I'd always assumed this to be true. But as I roamed slowly through that stone garden, scattered with hundreds of unique headstones, I realized I had been wrong. Intrigued by the atmosphere, I felt my pulse quicken. The thought of how so many different people, from so many different birthplaces, had come together for their final resting place, was almost too much to handle.

I had a vague impression that I was more a ghost than a person as I flittered from headstone to headstone over the rambling, pitted land. It was a vast cemetery, trailing down the hill to meet the back of St. Catherine's.

227

As I wandered, I admired the flowers, shrubs, trees, and interestingly engraved headstones. A Blessed Virgin Mary statue stood enshrined beneath an archway of white flowers, looking gentle and loving with her hands placed together and a rosary trailing down from her fingers. Even though clouds blotted the sun, the world no longer looked so dark. I thought of my mother's white rosary and how I'd tucked it safely in the nightstand drawer with the Bible. *I need to use them both more often.*

While absorbed in my musings, I neared an immense stone at the crest of the hill, and the sudden voices startled me. They sounded deep and furious, but were coming from far enough away that I couldn't make out the words.

My curiosity made me creep closer and crouch carefully behind the large, polished marble stone. It was a monument bearing some family's last name, a name I don't remember because it wasn't important. The voices had my full attention.

They grew stronger, traveling up from the valley below. I began to hear snatches of words. I peeked slowly around the side of the stone and saw, at the base of the hill, two people absorbed in what was obviously an argument. They were so intent on each other that I had no fear of being discovered.

I stayed watching cautiously from my hiding place, straining to hear their words. Needing to hear them. Because the two people arguing were Justin and Philip.

Chapter Twenty

$\mathcal{G}$ stayed crouched behind that massive marble stone for what seemed like hours. When I developed a painful cramp in my leg, I didn't even consider moving. Something vital was taking place and I needed to know what it was.

I studied their faces. Philip was scowling, looking angrier than I'd ever seen him. In fact, I'd never seen him angry, and the expression was so unnatural it frightened me. Justin was standing sideways, so I could hardly see his face, but I could tell from the tightness of his muscles, the tenseness of his jaw, and his resolute stance, that he was angry, too.

I strained my ears to catch what they were saying, but all that reached me were stray wisps of words. Disconnected. Meaningless. Fragments of sentences I could only hear when suddenly stressed louder.

"Stay away . . ."

" . . . hurting her . . ."

" . . . warning!"

The words were spoken with such wrath, it hurt my ears to hear what little I did, but I had to stay and listen. What did this mean? I trembled in my hiding place. The very fact that these two guys—the only two guys I knew in this whole town—were together, alerted me that something was up. Hadn't both Justin and Philip told me they didn't know each other? So why were they here together? It had to concern me in some way. Uneasiness worked its way from my heart out to the tips of my fingers and toes, where it stayed throbbing like a miniature heartbeat.

Was it possible that Justin and Philip were fighting over *me*? Quick as this thought came, it was followed by a shameful rebuff. *Don't flatter yourself. Justin would never lower himself to such a level.*

Yet it was Justin's voice I heard last as Philip turned and stomped away, and it rose sharply, so I caught every word. "I won't let you. Just remember that. Leave her alone or you'll regret it!"

The forceful words resounded through the cemetery stillness. There was no answer, and with no rebuke to counter them, Justin's words took on a permanence as irrevocable as if engraved on a headstone.

I ducked behind my large stone as Justin swung around to stalk up the hill in the opposite direction Philip had taken. In my direction. I waited, my mouth dry and my heart pounding.

To this day, I wonder what gave me the strength to do what I did next. But I guess it wasn't really strength. Rather, it was one of those unexplainable impulses—an instant decision, made so fast it didn't seem like a decision at all. When I heard Justin's heavy strides and saw his long shadow stretch alongside me, I set my teeth and stepped from the shelter of my stone.

Justin, unprepared for my sudden appearance, collided into me with such power that he knocked me to the ground.

He stood looking down at me, his expression startled. This gave me courage. I picked myself up from the ground, ignoring the pain in my legs.

Still staring, Justin said, "Where did you come from?"

"Well," I said, brushing off grass and dirt and pretending our collision was his fault, "you could at least apologize."

I thought I saw a light jump into his eyes. "Very sorry," he said, and he swept me a bow.

I didn't smile. This was no time for games. There were things I needed to know, and if I stood here silently long enough, eyeing him directly, I knew it would get to him. He would wonder how long I had been here, how much I had heard, and he would have to know.

"Did you get here just now?" he asked, his voice casual. Too casual.

"No. I've been here quite awhile." I kept my eyes fixed on his, long enough so that he could read them.

"Oh," he said finally in a voice gone serious. He frowned, his dark eyebrows turning in deeply, and shoved his hands into his jeans' pockets. "I see." He glanced over his shoulder.

"Looking for Philip?"

His head snapped back to me.

"He's gone by now." I put my hands on my hips. "What was that all about? What's going on with you two? I thought you didn't even know each other. What were you arguing about? I heard you say—"

"Robin," Justin interrupted, "it's not what you think—"

"And just how do you know what I'm thinking?"

"Let me put it this way . . ."

I waited. His face lit up unexpectedly. He pulled his hand from his pocket and held it out to me, palm up, revealing a long piece of candy. "Want a Tootsie Roll?"

I pressed my lips together, fighting an absurd urge to smile. "No I do *not* want a Tootsie Roll. Stop playing games, Justin. You're only trying to sidetrack me." What did he think I was? A little kid who could be bought off with a piece of candy? "This isn't funny. Just what are you trying to pull?"

"Robin." He sighed. "First of all, calm down. I'm not trying to pull anything." He paused. "Remember I asked you yesterday if you trusted me? Well, I'm asking you again . . . to trust me." His voice lowered. "You didn't answer me yesterday. Answer me today."

I didn't know what to say. What kind of comeback was this? I suddenly recalled how he had scared me yesterday. How had I forgotten so easily, and how come I wasn't scared now? Especially when I was here alone with him—in a cemetery, of all places. *Why should I trust you?* I thought, and I saw he was still holding out that stupid candy, his eyes waiting for my answer. "Yes," I said, surprising myself, "but—"

"Then no but's. Trust doesn't work with that word. Forget what you heard, Robin. Don't ask me anymore." He held up his hand as I opened my mouth to protest. "It's important. And I promise you, I'd never do anything to hurt you. Believe me."

"The candy is supposed to be for the kids, you know."

Justin's face relaxed into a smile, and I thought hazily that giving in was worth it to see that smile. "Hey, I'm a kid at heart." He broke the Tootsie Roll and gave me half.

Chewing the warm, gummy candy gave me time to think. Was I being weak by letting the subject drop this simply? But what else could I do? It wasn't as if I could force Justin to tell me what he was determined not to. Truthfully, I didn't want to argue anymore. I remembered we were standing on consecrated ground, and this brought a prayer to mind. *May the souls of the faithful departed, through the mercy of God, rest in peace. Amen.*

Justin and I fell into step. "You see these big headstones?" I motioned to the one nearest us, which I had been hiding behind. "When I was little, I used to think people were buried *inside* the stones."

"You did?" Justin laughed. "That's a good one." After a long silence, he added, "I used to sit in the cemetery when I was a kid and read Sherlock Holmes and the Hardy Boys."

"A gloomy day like this would be just right, wouldn't it?" I tilted my head to look at the iron-colored sky. But I felt warm inside, as if sharing childhood secrets brought Justin and me closer together.

We walked carefully over the uneven land. Some headstones were so old we could no longer read their inscriptions. Some were leaning at odd angles or even partially sunken into the earth. My eyes trailed over both the readable and the unreadable inscriptions, strangely fascinated by the names of people I did not know and never would. Many of the headstones that caught my attention had small American flags poked into the ground next to them, marking those who had served in war. Veterans. And those who had died in service, some of them from as long ago as the Civil War. It made me slow my steps, thinking. I reverted to my ghostlike state, moving along lingeringly, almost as if I were looking for something, but not knowing what . . . until I saw it at my feet.

> *Steven Hutch, 1930-1966*
> *Beloved husband and father,*
> *died in Vietnam War.*

"My grandfather." I was only vaguely aware that I had spoken the words aloud, vaguely aware of the tall presence beside me, until I felt a hand come to rest on my shoulder.

"And . . . there's my grandmother's grave." I pointed to the stone beside my grandfather's.

> *Marie Hutch, 1931-1973*
> *Beloved wife and mother.*

"I—didn't know . . ." I choked on the words, feeling guilty. It made sense that my grandparents would be buried here in their church's cemetery. It should have occurred to me before now.

Nausea swept through me. My mother was buried in California—but she shouldn't be. She belonged here, in her hometown, with her family, near the ones who loved her. There was room beside the two graves. Room for my mother, my uncle . . . room for me.

"Let's go now." I clutched Justin's arm. "I've seen enough." I hadn't meant to grab his arm, and I quickly let go, though I would have liked to keep holding it. The solid muscles under the leather of his jacket made me feel safe.

How strange that at times Justin made me feel secure, while at other times he scared me.

We left the cemetery and walked down the sidewalk, eventually joining the crowd on Main Street, which had come alive now that the solemn mood of the morning had passed, leaving a day promising fun and picnics. But I wasn't really there with them. I didn't know where I was anymore, or what I was doing. I felt suspended in a dream, from which I desperately wanted to wake up. And yet I don't think I was trying hard enough, or maybe I just didn't have the strength.

"Yoo-hoo!" Somehow, that call stood out above the clamor of the crowd. When I turned in its direction, I saw Martha Myers bustling toward me, her round face beaming, her hair swept back in a bun and wound around with red, white, and blue ribbons. "How nice to see you here, my dear!"

She chattered on with great enthusiasm and I found myself relaxing as she told me how she'd enjoyed the parade and that the sky was clearing and wouldn't that be nice for all the gardens?

Then Martha noticed Justin standing beside me. She had been smiling, which by now I'd decided was her natural state, so her sudden frown surprised me. It was ever so slight, really just the fading of her smile, as if she were confused about something. But the look was so unsuited to her face that it worried me.

"This is Justin Landers," I said, making introductions. Martha continued to stare at him, her brow puckered, and I was about to question her when Justin took my arm.

"Nice meeting you," he said, giving Martha a nod. Then he turned and walked away, practically dragging me with him. All I could manage was a hasty "bye" in Martha's direction before she was swallowed by the crowd.

"I hate crowds," Justin said. "Why don't we—"

"Let go!" I pulled myself free from his grasp. "What do

you think you're doing? Couldn't you see I was talking with Martha? What's the matter with you?"

"Nothing." Justin looked at me but avoided my eyes. "I just thought maybe you were getting sick of the crowd. I know I was." He pulled at the neck of his T-shirt. "I was just about ready to suffocate. Why don't we get away from this crowd and spend the day together? We could take a picnic to the park. Do some fishing?"

"No," I said, "I can't." My irritation was fading, but the diary was tugging at the back of my mind, and I knew I had to get back to it. Today. Now. It had been waiting long enough. I felt a surge of determination, which formed into a decision. No more excuses. Today I would finish the diary.

As I hurried away, I called over my shoulder, "I don't have a fishing pole!" My heart quavered, wondering if Justin would follow me, wondering what I would do if he did.

But he didn't.

I wondered what had happened back there. Why had Justin acted so strangely? But he always acted strangely. Realizing this, it surprised me how this didn't matter—I almost enjoyed his unpredictability. I frowned. He influenced me too easily. Weird. I always realized this when he was gone, but when he was with me, it was like I didn't care. Like he had a spell over me. I knew I should stay away from him, but if I did, would he stay away from me?

With all these worries cluttering my head, my concern about Martha's odd reaction to Justin quietly slipped to the back of my mind.

~

My uncle met me at the front door. "That young Mr. Barnstrum was here looking for you. You just missed him. He said he would stop in again later today."

"Oh—all right. Thanks," I answered, edging my way past my uncle.

I ran up the stairs. I didn't feel all that eager to see Philip.

I felt relieved he'd never given me his number so I didn't feel obliged to call him. Things were too confusing for me right now, and I knew talking to him would only add to my problems; I knew he'd be asking me all about my progress in finding the map, and I couldn't deal with that right now. Any more pressure and I'd scream. Once in my room, I took a deep breath, sat down on the window seat, and picked up the diary.

April 14, 1979

It's almost startling the way things are winding down now. There's so much for us seniors to think about and prepare for. There's studying and term papers and—worst of all—exams. But then there's prom and the yearbook and graduation to look forward to.

Everything's rushing to meet me too soon! I still have so much to do before I graduate, and I've been feverishly busy on my story for the paper, trying to fit it between all my schoolwork. The mansion's history is intensely intriguing, more so than I'd ever imagined. Every time I learn something new, I jot it down, and by now I have quite a collection of notes and papers—I don't know how I'm going to make sense of them all. Yet though it's a lot of hard work, I don't regret taking up this story. Especially since it's been bringing me and Chris so close together. We talk about the mansion all the time.

April 16, 1979

It's happened—what I've been waiting for and expecting for so long, and yet it still came unexpectedly. Suddenly the whole world no longer seems real . . . nothing seems real . . . nothing but me and Chris.

Today he asked me to marry him.

My stomach flipped. *But you didn't!* I cried silently. *You didn't marry him!* How I wished that if I stopped reading the diary, I could stop these events from taking place. But the words, and my mother's past, were already written, and reading them would not change the outcome.

I think he made up his mind all of a sudden and couldn't wait. That's why he walked over to the schoolyard and asked me between my classes, outside under a beautiful tree. (Okay, I admit it was a bare and ugly tree, but everything looks beautiful to me now!) And I said yes.

We're keeping it secret, of course. There's no reason to make this difficult. I'm not telling anyone, not even Martha. They'll find out eventually. Oh—my head's spinning. There's so much to think about. So much to plan!

We're going to marry after I graduate. I mentioned St. Catherine's, where I've always envisioned I'd be married someday, but Chris wants to elope. The more I think about it, the more romantic it sounds. We'll go anywhere and everywhere; it won't matter as long as we're together. It will be an adventure.

Of course, Chris did have to choose today of all days—just before class photos were taken for the yearbook—to pop the question. I went back inside in such a euphoric daze, I bet I'll look freaky in my photo. But I really don't care, because Chris made this the happiest day of my life. The happiest so far, that is.

My mother's senior photo from the yearbook flashed before my eyes. The starry-eyed, enchanted look. I understood now what I had seen captured in her face, preserved in her smile and her eyes. Love.

Then I thought of where my mother was, just one month from this, and I felt queasy. I returned to the diary, my fingers numb on the page, but not too numb to realize that only a few pages remained.

April 20, 1979

Somehow, the days keep passing, slipping by too fast when all I want is to hold each one forever and savor each wonderful moment. Today Chris and I drove out to the mansion, and I decided to draw it; it makes such a delightfully challenging subject. Perhaps I can persuade Mr. Stafford to run my drawing alongside the story.

After drawing the mansion, I had a fabulous idea to draw Chris's portrait. He sat very patiently while I worked, content to stare at the mansion (sometimes I think it hypnotizes him). And now I have a large likeness of his captivating face to keep forever. I wonder why I never thought to draw him sooner.

Clutching the diary in a death-grip, I reread the entry, my heart pounding. Here was what I'd been waiting for, a chance to put a face to the name of Christopher Renton. I set the diary down, went over to the wooden chest, and opened it. My mother's portfolio of drawings lay inside, the ones I had never finished going through. All I could think was, *The portrait must be in here.*

I lifted the portfolio and held it on my lap, conscious of the precarious way it balanced on my knees. Slowly, I removed each page, examined each drawing . . . drawings of animals, people, and nature. I recognized the picture of the bridge over the river with the weeping willow beside it.

Near the bottom of the sheaf of papers, I found the drawing of the mansion. Holding it in my hands, I shivered, so that the paper trembled with me. Somehow, drawn all in shades of gray, the mansion looked eerier than in real life . . . more ancient and ghostly. There are phobias for so many things, I wondered if there was a phobia for fear of old mansions. If there was, I had it. And if there wasn't, I'd just invented it.

I lifted the paper, expecting to finally meet Christopher Renton in the drawing beneath, and instead came face to face with Justin Landers.

Chapter Twenty-One

$\mathcal{I}$ told myself it wasn't possible. Yet there was no denying that the face staring up at me was Justin's, no denying the angular features, cool eyes, and unique nose were his.

I shook my head. My mother could not have known Justin. Even if he had lived here when she drew this—which I seriously doubted—he would have been a baby. Right?

I realized then that I didn't know how old Justin was. I'd simply assumed he was, well . . . as old as he looked. Early twenties. Twenty-six at the oldest.

But there was my mother's name, signed unmistakably in the lower right-hand corner of the portrait, verifying that this was her work. I flipped the paper over, desperately searching for some explanation, anything that would make sense.

Chris was scrawled on the back of the drawing, and underneath it, a date: *4/20/79*. My hand steadied itself. This *was* a drawing of Christopher Renton. I let out a nervous laugh. What had I been thinking? That Justin hadn't aged, or that he was some kind of . . . ghost?

Still, I was only partially relieved, because this did not explain the resemblance. It also added a new dimension to my worries. My hands shaking again, I pulled out my sketchpad and turned to my most recent drawing, the one I had done in the park of Justin only yesterday. Comparing the two faces, the likeness was indisputable. But wait—holding the drawings side by side, I studied carefully, with an artist's eye, and saw that the jaw lines were slightly different, and not slight enough to be contributed to oversight; and the ears were a different shape. Chris's jaw was squarer than Justin's, and his ears were larger, while his nose was less prominent.

Still, these minor differences hardly reassured me. The resemblance that remained was still so mirror-like it was frightening. There was no denying a connection between Christopher and Justin . . . and as I thought this, things began to slide together in an ominous way.

Justin is related to Christopher Renton. That's the only way the likeness can be explained.

Justin could be Christopher's son. And what did this mean? I took a deep breath before allowing myself to think —aware that once I did, there could be no turning back.

It meant that my meeting Justin had been no coincidence, no matter what excuses I'd made in the past. Justin had a purpose—a sinister purpose—in wanting to know me. I recalled his visit to the bookstore. Somehow, before he'd even met me, he had known who I was and when I would arrive in Lorens.

Justin had sought me out, but for what reason?

I frowned at the drawings. The answer was here. It was something to do with Christopher Renton. And Tiffany, my mother. Something . . . being carried on from the past to the present.

Alone in my mother's old room, steeped in fears fed by imagination, my scalp prickled and my spine tingled. I glanced over my shoulder. In such an atmosphere, it was difficult to think logically, and I struggled with my thoughts.

Justin wouldn't—couldn't—leave me alone. He had told me this. I gulped, thinking my uncle was right to be suspicious of Justin. He wanted something, was after something . . . I recalled his persistent interest in my problems and concerns about the past and my mother's accident. Uneasily, I recalled how much I'd confided in him —how much I *had* trusted him. Now I knew I'd been deceived. I remembered this morning, and Martha, and suddenly I knew what I had to do to confirm my fears.

Running into the hall and grabbing a phone book from

under the telephone table, I flipped through the pages until I found Martha's name and number. After six rings, I was about to hang up, discouraged, when I heard a bright "Hello?" on the other line.

Delighted to hear from me, Martha began bubbling on eagerly about her day, but I wedged in my question. "There's something I wanted to ask you," I began, absently wrapping the phone cord around my finger. "When you met Justin Landers, that guy who was with me this morning, I thought maybe you—recognized him or something . . ." I waited.

"Oh, yes—" Martha's voice changed slightly—"that's a strange thing—did you know he looks just like your mother's old boyfriend?" She didn't give me a chance to answer. "Don't laugh," she said, and laughed herself. "I know how that sounds, but it's true! It shook me up for a moment, I must say. But then in a small town like this it's not that odd to meet relatives of people you once knew, especially when you're as old as me. But I had heard Christopher moved away . . ." She jumped subjects, and it took me a moment to realize she was now referring to Justin. "Is he a good friend of yours? The resemblance is quite interesting . . ."

Interesting. What an understatement. The phone cord, wrapped painfully tight around my finger, was cutting off circulation. I wanted to laugh, then I wanted to cry.

" . . . you should ask him about it. I never forget a face, you know, and that Mr. Landers is definitely some relation—"

Christopher's son, I thought. And I said, "Thanks, Martha, I'll do that. Bye."

But should I? I replaced the phone and freed my finger. Why should I tempt fate by letting Justin know that I knew his secret? *Doesn't he deserve a chance to explain?*

But what was there to explain? He should have already told me and he hadn't. I had been gullible enough to think he had been attracted to me, but he obviously had an ulterior motive for seeking me out. He didn't deserve a chance. If I gave it to him, he'd probably end up twisting things to make matters worse for me. No, I would be a fool to trust him.

Now I understood why my uncle had misgivings about Justin. From the very beginning, he'd recognized the resemblance to Christopher Renton. Why hadn't he told me? But what would he say, that he didn't trust Justin because he looked like someone my mother once dated? Was that a reason to avoid someone? And would I have listened to him if he had told me?

Surely my uncle was remembering Christopher's involvement with my mother. Was he afraid Justin would influence me the same way Christopher had influenced Tiffany? Did he fear, as I now did, that the past was repeating itself? Justin taking his father's part and me, my mother's? That was too crazy to contemplate.

It would mean the diary held my fate. Thinking this, I returned to it.

April 21, 1979

That old man Hanson is such a tyrant. You know what he did? He fired Chris from the store! I'm even more indignant about it than Chris, who is amazingly calm. He says he's surprised he stayed as long as he did, and he's glad to get out of there. He said he never liked working under Hanson's thumb. Of course, now he has no job. But he's not worried, so I guess I shouldn't be, either. He'll find something when he needs to.

Enough about that. There's too much happiness to write about. I've been counting down the days . . . yet time isn't dragging. I'm much too busy for that. Another reason Chris says he's glad he doesn't work at Hanson's anymore is that now he has more time to spend with me and help me with the story. It's coming along well; I hope to have it finished by June. And listen to this. I just got an incredible break, one that's sure to guarantee the story's success.

Yesterday, I finally worked up the nerve to talk to old Mr. Ingerman, and when I explained I was doing a feature story on the mansion, he was enthused about it and eager to help me—not what I expected! I so misjudged this old man. He's nice, though in an odd, eccentric sort of way, and he may even let me interview him. But the most amazing part of all is that he gave me a key to the mansion. Now I can actually go through the place whenever I want. Such a privilege is more than I could have hoped for. (The whole town will be jealous!) But it's just what I need; the story could never be complete without this firsthand research.

Mr. Ingerman even said if I'm interested, I can take any books I want from the mansion's library and look through them at home. Tomorrow, armed with a notebook and pencil, I plan to take my first tour through the mansion.

The one condition this privilege comes with is that I don't bring visitors. That's no problem; I'll just tell my friends they'll have to wait for the story to be published. And when it is, the newspapers are going to fly off the racks!

April 22, 1979

The mansion is everything I hoped and feared. And more. You step inside and are instantly transported into the past. The atmosphere, pulsating with history, is almost overwhelming.

244

So my mother had felt what I had. Back then, the atmosphere had been powerful, but I wondered if it was even stronger now. Perhaps it increased with time, grew with the tragedies.

> *I can't say I enjoy being in the mansion, for when I am, I'm filled with an unexplainable sensation of fear—almost to an overwhelming degree—and I want to turn and run as soon as I enter. It would be unbearable if I had to go through the place alone.*

My backbone stiffened. Hadn't my mother just written that she was not allowed to take anyone inside the mansion? My eyes skimmed the diary in search of answers.

> *I know Mr. Ingerman entrusted me with the key on the condition that I would be the only one to enter the mansion—no giving visits to friends, etc. . . . But this is different. This is Chris. He's a part of this just as much as I am. He's helping with the story; he doesn't count as a guest, and it wouldn't be fair to leave him out.*
>
> *Besides, Mr. Ingerman can't really expect me to go through that creepy place alone. There's no harm in Chris's coming. We keep it secret; I go in alone first, just in case anyone should see, and Chris comes a few minutes later. And let me tell you, those moments that pass before he does come feel like hours.*
>
> *Of course, I can't help feeling a bit guilty about deceiving the old man, and others like my brother and even Martha, but it can't be helped. I'm not sure I could make them understand.*

My insides felt giddy as my suspicions, the ones I'd been

plagued with ever since I'd first learned about my mother's accident, were confirmed. Things had not happened as they appeared. The simple explanation of the newspapers was wrong. Yes, Christopher had been there with Tiffany—but he hadn't come looking for her later, as he'd told the paper. My mother would not have gone upstairs and onto the balcony alone. She would have been down below waiting for Christopher to arrive.

And when he did, they would have *both* proceeded upstairs, *both* gone out onto the balcony, and then . . . ?

I swallowed. In the article, Christopher had obviously not given a truthful account. Why not? What was he hiding? I remembered how I'd thought Christopher might have taken the map after finding my mother, but now I realized that if he'd been with her before the accident, it meant something worse. It meant he had played a part in the accident.

Perhaps making it not an accident.

Maybe Christopher lied to the newspapers to hide the fact that he had attempted murder.

It was a strong accusation, but my heart, pumping strongly, believed it and sent blood gushing to my head to fuel my anxious thoughts.

I recalled Justin's aggravation at my persistence in digging up the past. I recalled certain remarks he had made, all seeming to hint that he knew something I didn't. And, if he was related to Christopher Renton, of course he would know. No wonder he hadn't wanted me searching, no wonder he'd tried to steer me clear of Christopher. He didn't want me to discover the truth, that his father had caused my mother's fall.

But there was something more. Something Justin wanted from me. Or else why—

I put a hand to my throbbing head and was startled to hear the roar of a motor. Jumping up to look out my window, I caught a flash of red as Philip's BMW sailed into the driveway and came to a whiplashing halt.

Not now! I thought. My mind was too chaotic to make intelligible conversation with anyone. But when Philip looked up and saw me at my window, I was caught. I lifted my hand in a feeble wave and I knew I had to go downstairs.

"Robin," my uncle said, meeting me at the bottom of the stairs, "there you are." As if he hadn't known I was in my room all this time. "You know," he motioned to the plants I'd left sitting by the front door, "you should get those planted."

"Yeah, I will," I said, heading for the door. (I should mention that the plants were far from qualifying as candidates for garden catalog covers; most of the leaves were curling and turning yellow.)

"There's no time like the present," my uncle said cheerily. "It's cleared up outside and the sun is shining. But that overgrown garden is going to be quite a chore. Tell you what, I'll bring out the gardening tools—I know they're around somewhere—and I'll give you a hand."

I stopped, my hand on the doorknob. "Now?"

"Now."

"But Philip just pulled up. I—"

"Good." My uncle smiled. "If he'd like to lend a hand, I'll gladly find an extra shovel."

I ran out the door, my panic multiplying. Now that I wanted to tell Philip everything, there wasn't time.

Philip had just stepped out of his car. "Hi there, Robin. Did you miss me?" He rested his hand possessively on the sparkling red hood. "How about I take you for a spin? We can—"

"Philip, I can't. Not now." I glanced back at the house. "Look, my uncle's coming out in a minute and I'll be stuck gardening, so we don't have much time. I need to talk to you —to tell you something important."

Philip immediately turned serious. "What is it?" He took my hand. "Tell me everything."

Standing in the warm spring sunshine with Philip holding

my hand, I felt safe and protected and could almost believe that everything would be all right. What a relief to finally be able to unload my fears.

"I'm glad you're back." I looked up gratefully into his eyes, so soft and understanding, and my latest worries came pouring out. I told him that I'd discovered Justin was related to Christopher Renton, that I didn't trust him and that he'd been following me. "He scares me," I whispered, savoring the comfort in Philip's arms.

"This is bad, Robin. Very bad." He, too, began to whisper. "Every time we've gone out together, I thought I noticed someone tailing us. I thought maybe it was someone your uncle had hired to keep tabs on me or you. I was concerned, but I didn't know it was this bad."

I pulled back, shocked. "Why didn't you say something?"

"I didn't want to scare you. But now . . . you need to know the truth. I did some checking up on this guy—that's what I was really doing yesterday—and I discovered he has . . . a rather disturbing background." Philip grimaced. "His father died a strange death, one I'd rather not describe, and he's got a mother in a mental home. I confronted the guy this morning, told him to stay away from you . . . You know what he's after, don't you?"

I waited, not wanting to speak.

"The map. The gold. Isn't it obvious?" Philip's jaw tensed, and his fingers pressed into my arms. "He must know about the map, and now he wants it." I sucked in my breath as Philip pulled me closer. "I'm sorry it's come to this, Robin . . . we're going to have to be very careful."

This wasn't what I wanted to hear. I pulled away just enough so I could study Philip's face. "But you don't think he's really dangerous, do you? I mean—I don't even have the map."

"Yet," said Philip, shaking his head. "Yet. But if he knows what we do—that your mother found it, and if you don't have it yet, you're the one who can find it, just like we know you will—he could be dangerous. You told him too much. Oh, it's not your fault, don't blame yourself." He pulled me closer. "You didn't know. How could you?" He smoothed my hair with his hand. "But now that you do, don't talk to him again, no matter what. Ignore him if you see him. And above all, be on your guard. He's just waiting for his chance. That's why we have to stay one step ahead of him, at all times, at all costs. You've got to find the map, Robin. Tonight."

"How?"

"Search the whole room, the whole house if you have to. Top to bottom—everything!"

My heart was pounding in my ears. "I will," I said, and I remembered the diary and that I still had those final pages yet to read. With a flash of perception, I knew those pages would give me the insight I needed. "I'll find the map tonight." I was startled by my own husky voice, but even more by my words, spoken with complete conviction.

Philip smiled, but I could see it was forced. "You find it tonight, Robin, and I promise you that tomorrow we'll be far away from this place. And you can forget this town ever existed."

Feeling slightly dizzy, I looked up into Philip's face. Had I heard right? I needed to hear it again. To be sure. "You mean that?" I asked. "Really and truly—"

"I do."

I struggled to steady myself. I searched his eyes, trying to read all that lay behind them.

Philip searched my eyes in return. "What's the matter, Robin? Don't you want to get out of here? You always said you did. And just think, you and me, we can go anywhere. But first California. You'd like that, right? We'll have the map, we'll get the gold, and when we're rich, we can do anything we want. You'll be eighteen tomorrow; no one can stop you."

Saying this, he slid the mood ring off the finger of my right hand, where I'd been wearing it since the day I found it, and slipped it onto the ring finger of my left hand. I watched without blinking.

"You know what that means, don't you?"

"Yes," I breathed. The now gold-colored stone winked at me in the sun and my eyes became mesmerized, wondering what the color symbolized. "It's just—" *I haven't even prayed about this.* My heart beat at a frantic pace, giving me the sensation that it was dancing to wild music. "It's so sudden."

"It has to be. I'm afraid for you, Robin." Philip squeezed my hand.

Oh, never let go, I thought, half closing my eyes.

I heard a low rumble as the garage door began to open behind us, and I realized my uncle was coming. I stepped back, but my eyes never left Philip's.

"I'll call tonight," he said, and reaching out, he touched his fingertip gently to my lips.

"Hello there, Philip," my uncle called as he approached, an assortment of garden rakes and shovels protruding in all directions from his arms. "We were just about to start some gardening. You're welcome to join us if you'd like."

Amusement lit Philip's eyes, which stayed on mine as he drew his finger away from my lips. "Another time, maybe." He ducked into his car, gunned the engine, and mouthed, "Tonight," before shooting out of the driveway.

I stood coughing in the exhaust, terrified to feel my confidence draining, as if it was being pulled away by Philip's car; I tried to hold onto it, but it slid from my grasp. My fears, always ready to take over, came crowding to the foreground of my mind. I had a whole day to get through before I would be safe. How would I ever stand it? Suddenly the sunlight was no longer comforting, and I felt hot and cold all at once.

Why did Philip have to go off and leave me? I wondered,

taking a shovel from my uncle's pile. *He could have stayed to help with the gardening. At least we would have been together.* What did he have to do that was so important, him with his free life and no responsibilities? Probably nothing. Then I smiled, because I couldn't picture Philip working in a garden.

Oddly enough, I began to picture Justin, sleeves rolled up and his muscular arms shining bronze in the sunshine.

Thrusting my shovel into the earth, I banished the image.

Chapter Twenty-Two

I longed to tell my uncle how pointless starting this garden was because I wasn't going to be around to take care of it. Tomorrow I would be gone. Tomorrow at this time, I'd be flying free over the highway, heading with Philip for California. Gold country.

As I worked the ground, turning over clumpy earth and chopping it with my shovel, perspiration popped out on my forehead and dribbled down my temples. I continued thinking about all that was happening to me, and I wondered where I would be right now if I'd stayed in California. I'd be working full time and looking ahead . . . but ahead to what? I didn't know. What I did know was I'd be alone. *Thank You, dear Lord, for sending me Philip.*

It was late afternoon by the time all the plants were safely in the ground. Only when I was brushing off my dirty hands did I realize I still hadn't told Philip about the diary. *Well,* I rationalized, *I didn't get a chance.*

There had been so many more urgent matters to discuss. I recalled my promise—my firm resolution to find the map tonight—and I wondered how I could promise such a thing. How could I be sure I would find the map? Yet a vibrant, expectant sensation thrilled within me, telling me that because I had finally decided to do this, to find the map, I would. This thought drew me to return to the diary, and I started for the house.

Unfortunately, Memorial Day made my uncle ambitious not only for gardening but also for grilling out. "We can eat dinner outside, have a picnic and enjoy the spring evening," he said. To me, who only wanted to get back to the diary, this made the evening sound like eternity.

My uncle wanted to cook brats, and of course it turned out that we had no brats. For that matter, we had no brat buns. Consequently, I made a quick trip to the grocery store and ended up buying as many groceries as I could carry, enough to stock us up so I wouldn't have to keep running back and forth to the store. If my uncle suddenly decided we needed maraschino cherries, we would have them.

But, while paying for everything, I realized with a jolt that stocking up on groceries should no longer concern me. After tomorrow, I wouldn't be living here, and my uncle would probably eat pizza every night for the rest of his life.

As soon as I left the store, an uncomfortable feeling started bubbling in the pit of my stomach. At first I told myself it was hunger, but the feeling spread until it affected more than my stomach. As I walked along the sidewalk, I kept glancing behind me. I didn't see anyone, but as soon as I faced forward, I felt the feeling again, stronger. A feeling that told me someone was watching me . . . following me. I quickened my pace while the paper grocery bag became a boulder in my arms.

After all I'd discovered about Justin, it had been a mistake for me to come into town. The paranoid feeling grew until I felt like a balloon swelled to the bursting point. A balloon painted with a target. Ludicrous as it sounds, I was convinced that at any moment a figure would appear beside me or a green would Jeep roar up and kidnap me.

Reaching the house seemed like a miracle. I ran inside, aching to deposit my load. My stiff fingers would hardly loosen their hold on the grocery bag. When they did, my hands were so unsteady that it took me a full two minutes to unpack. Even then, I almost dropped the jar of maraschino cherries.

And after all that, I still wasn't free to return to the diary. My uncle managed to think up all kinds of odd jobs for me to do—locating a bag of charcoal, helping him drag the picnic table out from storage, setting our places—so that I didn't have a spare second. When my uncle suggested that pasta salad would be an ideal addition to our picnic dinner, I automatically began boiling a pot of water just to get it over with. All the while, my thoughts spun in high gear, my mind revolving on the map. I had to find it. Everything depended on it. Especially Philip.

Realizing this, I felt a twinge of apprehension. The map, the map—that seemed to be all Philip cared about. Rinsing the cooked pasta in a colander in the sink, I asked myself, *Would Philip still want me if it weren't for the map?*

I gave the colander a vicious shake. Of course he would. I knew he would. I didn't have to reassure myself. Philip cared about me. He hadn't even known about my mother and the map until I told him, unlike Justin, who had known all along, probably his whole life. I dumped the pasta into the creamy dressing, mixing fiercely with a big spoon.

My uncle and I ate crisp brats and warm pasta salad in the backyard at the picnic table to the accompaniment of chirping crickets. Eating heartily, my uncle looked as if he didn't have a care in the world. I wondered what it would be like to feel so content. True, I appreciated the peacefulness of the spring evening, the gentle breeze and the twittering birds . . . but there was such a sad, temporary air lingering over it all, making me acutely aware that this was my last night, my last dinner with my uncle, so that I suddenly found my food difficult to swallow. I surveyed the yard, thinking I never would have believed I could feel reluctant to leave this behind. I had let myself get used to life here, to the point of almost caring for it.

But I've made my decision, I thought, chewing rapidly. *I'm not going to waste my life in this small town, and I can't let sentiment displace rational thinking. By this time tomorrow I'll have begun a completely new life, the life I want to lead, and I'll leave this one behind forever.*

"I've enjoyed this weekend off," my uncle was saying,

oblivious to the thoughts grinding through my head, "but it will be nice to get back to the store tomorrow, don't you think?"

I looked up from my plate, confused. It hadn't occurred to me that I would be working tomorrow. I'd just assumed . . . well, that tomorrow would be *different.* It was my birthday, after all, and I would be leaving. But of course my uncle didn't know this. I'd had three days off already, and he expected me to work tomorrow. "I guess," I said. My mind began struggling to overcome this new obstacle. I'd have to get off early, complain I had a headache or something, so Philip and I could get a head start. *Just a little white lie,* I rationalized. *Forgive me, Lord.*

Darkness had fallen by the time I climbed the stairs to my room. I switched on the light before settling into the window seat, but not before seeing the starry masterpiece framed by my window. The sky looked like a sheet of tar on which someone had thrown a handful of glitter, and I was awed by God's artistry.

Thinking this, I felt called to read the Bible, to dip into the sacred pages for some guidance, but I couldn't resist the stronger temptation to return to the diary. It seemed as if I'd been away from the diary forever, yet the instant I picked it up, I was transported so swiftly to the past, it was as if I'd never left it.

May 1, 1979

I'm so excited by my discovery that I've already scribbled a short piece for my article. Now to analyze it in my diary. As it is, I can hardly control my fingers enough to write this. I found an old letter in one of the books from the mansion. It's a letter written by Connie Ingerman, and in it, she mentions the map. More than that, she hints at its hiding place!

255

I'd almost given up hope of turning up anything significant among the assortment of books in the mansion's library, but tonight when I was paging through an old novel, I unexpectedly came across an envelope tucked between the pages. It's addressed to a Stephanie Barrington. From what I could make out, she was a friend of Connie's who lived back east in Philadelphia.

But the letter was never sent. Why? Did Connie forget to send it, or did she simply decide not to? Or perhaps she never got the chance, had meant to send it, but . . . there's no way of knowing for sure, I guess, but these are the sort of things I plan to analyze for my article.

Tonight it's late, too late to call Chris, but I'll bring the book with the letter back to the mansion to show him tomorrow. He'll be as thrilled as I am.

The letter, written by this heartbroken girl longing for her love, brought tears to my eyes. Being in love myself, I can understand how she must have felt—as if she'd lost everything— everything that meant anything. Because all gold really is is a cold metal, and it cannot replace a living, loving person.

The letter was long and depressing. It's no wonder they say Connie committed suicide.

And yet, I wonder . . . it might not have been suicide. I mean, they found her dead and assumed this, but they could not know for sure. What if by simply accepting it was suicide, they were blind to the possibility that it might have been an accident?

I remembered my dream. The feeling of sadness, then freedom as I leaned against the balcony, and finally, fear, as I realized I was falling. *It could have happened like that,* I thought. Then I shook my head, reminding myself to focus. It was my mother's, not Connie's, mystery I was trying to solve. But it comforted me somehow to think that my mother had asked the same questions I had, and hadn't simply accepted everyone else's conclusion about Connie.

I suppose I'm an optimist. I don't want to believe that anyone would really take her own life, even for a broken heart. Losing love is a sad thing, surely . . . but not a reason to kill yourself.

Why didn't Connie mail the letter? It's dated the day before her death. Wouldn't she have mailed the letter first, if she was planning to commit suicide? But of course she might not have planned it. Maybe she did it on impulse. Or maybe she never had the chance (every angle has been playing through my mind, as it should if I want to make a good reporter), maybe there was foul play—maybe she was threatened by someone who wanted the map. She wouldn't tell them—and then . . . murder. A motive? The map, of course. The map and the lure of gold.

Or maybe my imagination is overactive. I don't know. What I do know is, the letter holds the answer to finding the map. Realizing this, did Connie perhaps decide not to send it? (There I go again, I can't seem to stop speculating.) Because there is a part in the letter that makes it sound as if Connie hid the map under the floor. She said it is close, so I'm thinking in her room, and she has thick carpet . . . I wonder if she hid it under there? Tomorrow, I intend to find out.

With icy fingers, I turned the page to May 2, 1979—the day before my mother's fall.

My life has taken such a twisted turn in such a short time that it is all I can do to comprehend it. I only hope that writing this out will help me clear my mind and think things through.

I was right about the map. Yet I feel no elation in writing this, no triumph. All that has drained from me. Today, my eyes were finally opened and I have seen Chris for who he really is. I'm no longer blinded by infatuation; instead, I'm choking on disappointment. All my high expectations are crumbling to dust, being blown away by the wind . . . but I'm getting ahead of myself.

The map was there, under the carpet as I suspected. Ridiculous how easy it was to find. The carpet near the door wasn't fastened down (like my carpet), and I simply lifted the edge and slipped my hand under it and over the rough wood. My fingers brushed paper, and it was the map, lying flat on the floor.

That's when a shadow fell over me from behind. For half a second, I think I feared it was Connie's ghost come to guard the map. But it was only Chris. He'd arrived as usual. I'd been so eager to see if the map was there that I'd actually braved going up to the room alone. I thought Chris would be proud of me.

When I found the map, I was ecstatic that it was real—that it was there in my hands—but when I looked up to show Chris, I felt a terrible chill. The look on his face produced a feeling far worse than any ghostly presence could have. I think he was angry that I hadn't waited for him, that I'd found the map on my own. It was his eyes that gave him away. I was about to explain, when he tried to grab the map from me. Instinctively, I pulled back. Fragile as the map was, I warned him not to touch it. But what I wanted didn't seem to matter anymore (and now, I wonder, did it ever?). Chris snatched the map from me. I never even got a chance to show him the letter I found yesterday.

I'm beginning to suspect the truth of our relationship, how it's been all along—or at least ever since that accursed night when Chris first saw the mansion and I told him Connie's story. I think that's when he latched onto the thought of finding the gold, and now he can't let go. It's become an obsession. Ever since that night, I guess this day of reality has been coming.

Chris said the map is complicated. "We'll need time to study it." I didn't say anything. Chris says to think of what this map means for us: a new beginning . . . a new life. The thing is, I don't see it his way; I don't see the map as rightfully ours, to take and use to find the gold. We can't keep this secret. It has to be revealed to old Mr. Ingerman. I tried to explain this to Chris—that the Ingerman fortune has dwindled and that old Mr. Ingerman needs the money, that he could use it to preserve the mansion— but Chris wouldn't listen, and there wasn't time for arguing. It was getting late, and I had to get home because I'd promised Peter I'd make dinner. Chris softened suddenly (in a last attempt, I think, to win me to his way of thinking) and tried reasoning with me, saying no one will ever know if we take the map. But the thing is, we will know. And God will know. I'd have the heaviest burden of all, because I was the one trusted. Maybe that doesn't matter to Chris, but it does to me.

I told Chris I needed time to think. So that's what I'm doing now. But I already know what I have to do. Maybe tonight will give Chris a chance to cool down and realize we have to act responsibly with this discovery. No matter how tempting it may be, we can't just disappear with the map as he wants to. At least I managed to take the map back from him, after agreeing not to breathe a word of this find to anyone, and to meet him at the mansion tomorrow to come to a decision. Even so, "Don't you trust me with the map?" Chris asked in an injured tone.

"I can keep it safely hidden."

"Bring it with you tomorrow," he told me.

It's obvious Chris resents that I am the one who found the map. Immature, I know, but I can read it in his eyes.

Which brings me to my main concern. I don't want to believe it, but Chris is not the man I thought he was. The sad thing is, I don't think it was a sudden change of character on his part, but rather a sudden realization of his true character on mine. Now when I look into his eyes, all I see is greed. It hurts me, after all I thought I'd found in him, but I think maybe . . . I only saw what I wanted to see. I hope by tomorrow he'll have gotten some sense into his head. That he'll be different, not the stranger he was today.

It's awful to have this happen when everything was going so smoothly. But then maybe it was going too smoothly, and no matter what, it would not have lasted. Better to find out now than later. Things change, people get older, wiser . . . I feel decades older today than I did yesterday . . . and I'm thinking maybe I was too hasty, agreeing to everything Chris wanted. I'm thinking many things . . .

But tomorrow will provide the verdict. I hope Chris will be reasonable, but if not, well, I'm prepared to do what it takes. I'm not backing down. I have the map hidden in my room, and here it will stay until I can figure out how to proceed, how to reveal this find to the right people. I won't let Chris get his hands on the map again until I know I can trust him, though now I'm afraid this may never be. I'm terribly disappointed in Chris. You think you know someone—completely and utterly—then they shatter your beautiful picture of them, and you realize it was an illusion all along.

But then maybe I'm jumping to conclusions. I hope so. Tomorrow I'll know for sure. Tonight, however, with this terrible weight on me, I wish I'd never found the map. Indeed, I almost think it is cursed.

I turned the page, but it was blank.

There was nothing left to read.

I closed my eyes, finding slight comfort under the dark pressure of my eyelids. My head was thumping heavily, as if I'd been reading a terrible suspense story. *That's what my mother's diary is,* I thought grimly. *Only worse . . . because it's true.*

I felt empty, let down that there was no more. Then I

realized I didn't need more. It became suddenly clear to me what had happened that fateful May day. My mother had returned to the mansion, alone, to meet Chris, and he was waiting for her. And for the map.

Anger shot through me. How could my mother be so foolish? So naïve, so trusting? She'd walked right into a trap. No one knew that Chris was at the mansion, that he had been there other times, too. She'd kept it secret, so if anything should happen—an "accident," for instance—no one would realize Chris was involved. Everyone assumed she was there alone; they had no reason to believe otherwise.

I thought of my uncle. Even if he suspected what had really happened, he had no way to prove it. No wonder he had reacted the way he had to seeing Justin. No wonder he was suspicious of him.

True, I had no way of knowing exactly what had happened that day—whether Chris had planned to hurt my mother or simply acted in passionate anger—it didn't make much difference to me because the outcome was the same. He had been there with her, and I knew somehow he was the one responsible for her fall. I knew it. And at that moment, I hated Christopher Renton with every fiber of my being.

Amid this hate, I managed to turn my bitter mind to the map, determined to find it. But where should I begin? Philip had said to look everywhere. But I didn't need to, I realized. My mother had said it was in her room. This room.

My eyes shifted from the framed pictures to the nightstand, dresser, bed, desk, and bookshelf. Then to the window, door, and closet. I'd already been through the closet, but I might have missed something. Then there were all those books—the map could be tucked between any of those thousands of pages. There might be a hidden compartment or secret drawer in the dresser or nightstand.

The thought of tackling every possibility no longer seemed simple. It could take me all night and I still might not turn up anything. As the possible hiding places multiplied, the room didn't seem small and tidy anymore, but large and messy. What chance did I have of locating one thin piece of paper among all this?

I realized then how much I had been counting on the diary to tell me where to search—at least give me some clue —but my mother had not even hinted at her hiding place. In her room, yes, but the big question was, where?

Concentrate, I thought, setting down the diary. *Where would I hide it?*

No—not where would I hide it—where would Tiffany hide it? I tried to put myself in her place, and suddenly I felt myself almost disconnecting from where I was and slipping, slipping backward through the years . . . into the past.

I wasn't alarmed.

My head felt light, but not empty. It felt clear, refreshed . . . relieved and no longer cluttered. I closed my eyes and took a deep breath, and when I opened them, their gaze drifted to the doorway. I walked to the door and stood facing the room, thinking, *This is where the room begins.*

My gaze fell to my feet, where the edge of the carpet met the hall. I got down on my hands and knees and tugged the carpet up. It lifted, but not very far because just inside the door, to the right, the nightstand was pinning it down.

I dragged the nightstand away and peeled up a length of faded carpet, revealing a rough, musty-smelling wooden floor. And there, about two feet to the right of the door and a few inches from the heat register, lay a yellow envelope.

Chapter Twenty-Three

$\mathcal{M}$y first thought was, *Of course—why not hide it under the carpet?* It had worked for Connie, why not my mother? I would have laughed at the simplicity of it if my throat wasn't so tight.

The phone sprang to life, jarring me to my feet. Envelope clutched in hand, I dashed to the hall phone, calling to my uncle, "I've got it!" because I knew it would be Philip. And I was eager to talk to him.

"Hello?" I breathed into the phone.

"Robin?" Yes, it was Philip. "You sound—excited—" The excitement in his own voice was obvious.

"I found it," I gasped, and I rushed on incoherently about how I'd only just discovered the map and about the carpet and the way it wasn't fastened down—

But I don't think Philip heard anything I said after the part about finding the map. His voice sounded as if he were speaking from very far away. "It was meant to be, Robin. It's ours now. Nothing can stop us." I could almost hear the plans racing like a train through his head. "We'll take it and get away from here. We'll start our new life together on an adventure." A pause. "Robin? Marry me."

I caught my breath. Even though I'd known it was coming, had been aware ever since he'd slipped the ring onto my left finger, hearing it spoken still came as a shock. But wait—the way he'd said it—so sure of himself. It wasn't even a question.

"Robin?" He had probably expected me to leap at the proposal. I let him repeat my name a couple of times before I spoke.

"Why do you want me to marry you?"

A strange laugh on the other end. "What kind of question is that?"

"Just answer it."

"All right." I heard him clear his throat. "I love you. I love you and that's why I want to marry you."

It was what I had been waiting to hear, but I stayed silent, fingering the yellow envelope.

"Robin? Are you there?"

I shook myself. "Yes." I walked into my room, stretching the phone cord as far as possible before closing the door. Then I moistened my lips and said, "We need to make plans."

This is the answer, I assured myself. *Get away and start a new life.* Suddenly I thought of my mother and how she had felt obliged to turn the map over to Anthony Ingerman. But he had been the last Ingerman, and now that he was dead, so was the obligation. Things were different now than they had been for my mother, and I told myself it was okay for Philip and me to take the map. We were not bound to reveal our discovery. Yet every so often, as Philip and I planned our getaway in urgent, hushed tones, I became hesitant. Eventually, Philip detected my uncertainty.

"Robin, don't worry. Are you afraid I only want to marry you for money? No, I know you didn't say it but I know it's what you're thinking. Listen, I want you. The map is only a bonus. For both of us. You know I need to be free. I would never tie myself down to someone unless I had to. And I do have to, because I love you." Philip put such feeling into those last three words, my heart melted.

"We have to trust each other," he went on. "It's great that you were able to find the map tonight, but that's not why I'm asking you now to marry me. It's because tomorrow's your birthday—tomorrow you can come with me and no one can stop us. We don't have to wait." I could picture him smiling his perfect smile as he said, "Come on, where's your sense of adventure?"

His earnest reassurances smoothed away my worries. We resumed making plans, and whenever pin-needle doubts pricked me, I ignored them. Because this was right. I could feel the thrill return, the thrill Philip never failed to ignite in me. Clearly we were meant to be together; I needed Philip to complete my life. *And that's love,* my heart whispered.

When I explained that I had to work tomorrow, we decided I should go to the bookstore as if everything was normal, thus raising no suspicions. Evening would be better for travel anyway, Philip said. We could make a late disappearance and drive all night before my uncle even realized I was gone. Not that I thought my uncle would make any trouble. But I told Philip that if I could manage, I would get off early and get my things ready so we could leave at the first opportunity.

"I don't know how I'll ever be able to wait for tomorrow," Philip complained. "I wish we could leave right now."

"Just be patient," I jumped in, startled that now the idea had sprung to mind, Philip would consider it seriously. "Tomorrow is time enough. Oh, and Philip," I scrambled through the nightstand drawer for pencil and paper, "give me your number so I can get ahold of you."

After jotting down the number, I picked up the envelope, turning it over speculatively in my hands. I hadn't even gotten a chance to glimpse inside it yet. Now I couldn't resist. I ran my finger under the flap as Philip said goodbye. "I can't wait to see you tomorrow—and the map." The last part he said jokingly, but the words rang uncomfortably in my ear.

"Philip," I said, "you would feel the same way about me, even if the map never existed, right?"

"We've just been through all that, Robin. Of course I would. You and I were meant for each other. Never forget that. But you did find the map, didn't you?"

"Yes, I found it."

"Of course you did. Take good care of it now, and I'll see you tomorrow."

I didn't move for at least a full minute after I hung up the phone. I kept playing his words over and over in my head. He did love me; he'd told me so. The map made no difference . . . *Remember that,* I commanded myself.

But my fingers were numb as I carried the envelope containing the map back to my room. After finally hiding it away inside a desk drawer, I prepared for bed.

My night prayers were brief and disturbed by distracting thoughts.

I lay in bed for a long time, staring up at the blank cavern of the ceiling, telling myself everything was going to be all right, that I was doing the right thing . . . but I didn't have a very restful night.

When my uncle knocked on my door the next morning, I grunted that I was getting up, then dropped out of bed and trudged to my window to pull open the shade.

Sunlight streamed through my window like clear gold, cascading over me and filling my room. My soul swelled with the sudden warmth, and I felt good about mastering the art of opening the window shade so that it didn't come crashing down on me.

The rays of sunlight felt like God's grace shining on me, brightening my mood and altering my outlook. I had assumed I would feel nothing special on my birthday, thought I'd outgrown being excited, but I guess I was wrong.

I was eighteen, and it felt wonderful. I thought of Philip and our plans for today, and my skin tingled with anticipation as I splashed cold water on my face.

I was ready to leave for work extra early, eager to be off and get the day moving. My uncle was ready to go when I came downstairs. With a smile on his face, he suggested we leave right away so we'd have time to stop at a café for breakfast. "To celebrate your eighteenth birthday."

My surprise showed. "You didn't think I'd forget, did you?" my uncle asked. "The first of June . . ." His voice drifted off. "I remember when your mother turned eighteen."

I wondered how he could talk about her. But maybe remembering the good things, the happy times, helped him forget the pain. Walking down the sidewalk, he continued talking about her. "She had a mind of her own and she liked to use it. And I let her. When she made mistakes, she learned from them. She knew if she wanted to make her own decisions, she'd have to live with the consequences."

Why are you telling me this? I wondered. Pink and white petals from crabapple trees lay sprinkled in our path, and more petals fluttered down like soft confetti dancing on a breeze.

"We all have to make choices in our lives," my uncle went on. "We can't depend on others to make them for us." I didn't say anything. "Well, I hope you enjoy your day, Robin. You certainly don't have to work at the bookstore—unless you want to, of course. Take the day off, enjoy yourself."

I was tempted to accept the offer, but only for a moment. Remembering what Philip and I had discussed, I didn't want to act too eager. My uncle might suspect something. The way he'd been talking about my mother made me particularly uneasy.

"That's all right," I answered slowly. "After having three days off, I really don't mind coming in today." I could tell by his quiet agreement that my uncle was pleased.

Maybe he gets lonely in that old store, working by himself. This thought had never occurred to me before. *Maybe this is part of being an adult. Understanding people, relating to them.* I suddenly felt wise and mature, particularly under the influence of realizing I was soon to be a married woman.

We turned down a street that we passed every morning. We approached a quaint little café that, with its white siding and sky blue shutters, I could easily have mistaken for a house. Only the small, ornately carved wooden sign standing in the front yard beside a trellis-arch gave away the building's true identity. A mug of steaming coffee surrounded by smiling pansies was painted on the sign.

Before following my uncle inside, I made the mistake of glancing across the street. I caught sight of a low, stone-front building with the words "Lorens Daily Journal" lettered across it in black. My stomach tightened. *Lorens Daily Journal* meant only one thing to me: Justin. The last person I wanted to think about. *If I can avoid him for today,* I told myself, *I'll never have to see him again.*

While my uncle ordered breakfast, I worried about running into Justin. And I was afraid, because I knew now what he was after. What would he do if he knew I had found the map? How much was it worth to him?

But he doesn't *know I found it,* I reassured myself, my fingers tightening on the smooth porcelain handle of my coffee cup. *And I'm certainly not going to tell him.*

"Come now," my uncle said, "the coffee's not that bad." He offered me vanilla creamer. "Add a little of this and it will be the best you've ever tasted."

Turning my attention back to my uncle, I discovered he could be almost charming, even when dunking donuts. After living here for two weeks, I was amazed at how little I knew him; and it was with a slight twinge of guilt that I accepted the delectable (translation: expensive) breakfast of sweet pastries and rich coffee. What would he think of me if he knew what I was plotting?

To ease my conscience, I tried to make the most of the time we had left together. Sitting at the blue-checkered table, I attempted a meaningful conversation. Strange thing was, I soon forgot that I was making a purposeful effort, and after that it came naturally.

My uncle and I had been sitting near the back of the café, so it wasn't until we were ready to leave that I turned and noticed Justin sitting at a small table near the front, looking for all the world as if he was absorbed in reading the newspaper in his hands. Only I knew better.

He's spying on me. As if to confirm this, Justin's eyes shifted up from the paper and caught mine. I could not resist narrowing my eyes and giving him what I hoped was a withering look as I approached the door.

It was the wrong thing to do. Justin's eyes held mine and somehow pulled me nearer to his table so that I could hear him when he spoke. "Gold."

"What?" I asked in an alarmed whisper.

"I said, 'gold.' Look at your mood ring." He pointed. "Gold means you're feeling nervous. What's the matter?"

I swung away from his table to follow my uncle out the door, chastising myself for even having acknowledged Justin's presence.

My uncle, in front of me, had apparently missed the interchange. My knees felt like marshmallows as we left the café behind. I fingered the smooth round stone of my ring. Justin thought he was so smart.

Thank you, Justin, I thought. *You have already succeeded in spoiling my day.* I glanced at my watch. *Eight-thirty. Congratulations. This must be a new record for you.*

The encounter, though outwardly insignificant, disturbed me greatly, and all through the morning I counted the hours to noon, for this was the time I decided to take my uncle up on his offer. In the meantime, I found some distraction in making cardboard signs for the bookshelves, in order to categorize the books according to genre. On the "Romance" sign I painted a rose; on "Horror," a dagger dripping blood; on "Mystery," a magnifying glass, and on "Religious," a white lily.

"You're quite an artist," my uncle said admiringly. I mumbled a thank you. I couldn't tell him that the signs would make it easier for customers to find books when I was no longer here to show them where to look.

By noon I had all the signs hung. "I *would* like to get out and enjoy some of the day," I admitted, my eyes on the clock, knowing I couldn't bear the combination of the quiet bookstore and my loud thoughts one minute longer, "maybe even work in the garden . . ." Immediately, I felt guilty, hinting at such a thing when I had no intention whatsoever of gardening. But my uncle was only too willing to let me off early.

"Go ahead," he said. "I'll see you later."

I didn't answer. I was too conscious of opening the door, conscious that this was the last time I'd hear these jingling bells, and that I would *not* see him later. I paused with the door open, turning to sweep one last look through the store's familiar interior, seeing the tall shelves, the new signs, the rows of books, and finally, my uncle sitting at his desk, absorbed in paperwork.

Without warning, he looked up and his eyes met mine. Questioningly.

I let go of the door, and it banged shut behind me. I prayed my uncle hadn't seen anything in my lingering gaze that would give me away.

That final slamming of the door proclaimed the end of my interlude in Lorens. Now I could look ahead. I was on the brink of living my own life—with Philip. My heart beat faster with the prospect, increasing my excitement as the blood coursed through my veins. I sprinted up the sidewalk, inhaling deeply, enjoying the feel of the clean air filling my lungs to capacity. *This is it,* I thought, *the first step in leaving the past behind.*

I thought of Philip's smile and of his handsome face, his lively spirit, his lovely words, and I knew this was the right choice. We would get married and go to California. Of course that was the right choice. I'd have to be crazy to think otherwise. How many girls only dreamed of having a chance like this?

When I entered the house, it felt solemnly empty. The

271

rooms radiated loneliness. I never had liked being in this house alone; it had too much of its own character, which seemed determined to take over when no one else was around. I ate a quick lunch, but I have no idea what I ate. I do remember it was tasteless and took forever to chew.

I couldn't free myself from the house's atmosphere, from the brooding desolation, the pensive listening, waiting and watching. I opened the windows, but the outside sounds were too soft to cover the monotonous ticking of the clock.

Upstairs, I pulled out a suitcase and busied myself with packing. But I couldn't rid myself of the jittery feeling that kept compelling me to look over my shoulder. Finally I switched on the radio, wondering why I hadn't thought to do so sooner, and tuned in to a station that was playing an upbeat song. Taking advantage of the fact that no one was around to protest the noise, I cranked the volume up full blast. *Because that's what normal teenagers do.*

It didn't take me long to finish throwing my things together. Just basic things because I reminded myself I was starting a new life, and this was the time to discard the past and begin anew. Besides essentials, I packed drawing materials and a few books.

I hesitated at my mother's diary. I wanted to take it, for all it contained and for all it stood for. It was my one link to my mother's past and to the part of her I had never known.

But I do know her now, I realized.

I didn't need to take the diary. I had read it once, and that was enough; I would not forget. Besides, I did not think I could read it again. I shoved the diary back into its camouflaged place in the bookshelf, wondering wryly when it would next be discovered—if ever.

With dramatic finality, I snapped the clasps of my suitcase shut. Just as I was about to heave the suitcase off the bed, I happened to glance out the window. I thought I saw a figure walking down the driveway. Leaving my suitcase, I moved to the window.

My vision focused on Justin Landers.

"No," I whispered, gripping the curtain. I pulled it partially around myself, but the gauzy material couldn't hide me. Before vanishing from view, Justin glanced up, and I knew he saw me.

Panic seized me. Here I was alone and unprotected, and Justin was coming to the door.

The door. I realized I hadn't locked it behind me. I tore down the stairs, my feet keeping pace with my racing heart. The last thing that would stop Justin was an unlocked door. I had to reach it before he did.

My hand fumbled at the lock, expecting the door to be thrown open at any moment.

Miraculously, it stayed shut. Just when I got it locked, there was a loud knock. I tried to calm my palpitating heart, telling myself I was safe now. I collapsed with my back leaning against the door and took a deep, drawn-out breath.

"Robin?"

I jumped at the sound of his voice, so close it was like he was standing next to me. It took me a moment to realize he was standing at a nearby open window.

"Robin? Come on, open up. I know you're in there."

That's right, I am in here, and I'm alone, I thought. *You know that. And that's why I won't open the door.*

Why was Justin here? I searched my mind frantically. I hadn't told him anything to give me away, had I? He couldn't know I'd found the map. Perspiration broke out on my forehead as I recounted our meeting this morning. The only word I had said to him was "What?" How could that get me in trouble?

A flimsy window screen was the only thing separating us. And that wouldn't stop anyone. Even if Justin hadn't seen me, the music—which was still blaring loudly—gave me away. Apparently I had done just about everything wrong that I possibly could: left the door unlocked, the window open, and the music advertising my presence.

"Go away," I said finally, though I knew it would do no good. I stayed pressed against the door, finding a strange, though false, sense of security from the solid support against my back. I didn't want to move and risk seeing Justin's face peering in through the black mesh of the screen.

"Robin, we need to talk. It's important."

For some reason, I smiled at his words, even though I wanted to cry.

"Please, Robin. Give me a chance."

But that was what I could not do. I could not give him the chance to influence me in any way, as he always managed to do, taking me unawares—winning me over—and I never realized until it was too late. He would start off slowly, unraveling my doubts, then—*bang!* He'd get me.

"Robin?"

I squeezed my eyes shut till they hurt. *Please, Lord, make him go away.*

"Robin?" Justin persisted.

Fine, I thought, gathering all my courage, *but I'm keeping my distance—and the door locked—no matter what.*

Warning myself to be on guard so as not to fall for his shrewd tactics, I moved to face Justin at the front window. Dark as the screen made his face, I could tell he needed a shave. He'd probably been up all night plotting against me.

"What do you want?" I asked in a stony voice. Not a hint of fear leaked through, and I was almost encouraged by how in control I sounded.

"For starters, I'd like to know why you're hiding from me. I thought we were friends."

I almost laughed. So that's what he thought, did he? He had a lot to learn. I chose my words carefully. "Friends trust each other, and I have no reason to trust you. You've been using me, lying to me. You—"

"Hold it right there." Justin paused, as if catching himself, then lowered his voice before asking, "What are you talking about?"

"Lots of things." Gradually gaining confidence, I squared my shoulders, thinking, *I can use the phone to call for help if I need to.*

Except a call would take time . . . and even more time for help to arrive.

"Like saying you wanted to do a story on my uncle's bookstore. That was just your way of getting to me. You had no intention of writing that story. I bet you're not even a reporter. That's a facade, too." My face grew hot as my mind ran off with accusations. "You said you didn't find anything out about Christopher Renton, but you really know everything. You just didn't want me to know because—" I stopped, causing a terrible hush as I tottered on the brink of revealing everything. Unable to bear the silence, I lost my balance and rushed on—"because you know he's responsible for what happened to my mother—you know because you're related to him!" This last accusation hung like a knife between us.

"You're right," Justin finally said, so quietly I almost didn't hear. "I wanted to tell you, but I didn't know how you'd take it. I'm sorry if I misled you. But I didn't lie—"

"You acted as if you knew nothing. Played innocent. That's just as bad. I bet your name isn't even Justin Landers—"

"Wrong," he broke in, "it is."

That took a moment to digest, but for some reason I believed him. "So you're not Christopher's son?" This was even harder to believe. "But you *are* related . . ." My confidence in dealing with this situation was rapidly draining.

"That's right. I'm Christopher Renton's nephew. And I know, I look just like him." Behind the screen, his face looked black. "Does that mean I'm his twin?" he asked bitterly. "Or that I'm the same person? Is it my fault he did the things he did?"

It was as if he was reading my mind, shooting down my

275

accusations before I could hurl them. "I'm not Christopher Renton any more than you are Tiffany Hutch."

I shook my head. "What is it you want? You've been after something ever since we met. I know you've been following me . . ." I was weakening, giving him a chance to explain. Desperately, from the core of my heart, I wanted him to give me an answer that would banish my doubts and fears once and for all.

"Maybe there's a reason for that . . . Look," he raised his arm, and for the first time I noticed the long rod in his hand, "I got you something for your birthday. A fishing pole. You said you didn't have one."

I could not believe this. This was not what I wanted to hear.

"Happy birthday."

I felt sick. "I don't need a fishing pole. I don't even know how to fish—I've never fished before—" This was beside the point, but I kept going, fabricating excuses and not knowing why.

"Then I'll teach you. Come on—right now. I didn't expect anyone to be home. I just wanted to drop this off. But then I heard the music and saw you—" he interrupted himself—"but don't you think this is kind of lame—talking through a screen? Why don't you open the door—"

I took a stumbling step backward, shaking my head.

He sighed and held up his hands in defeat. "You still don't trust me. Okay. I understand." His words rattled with the emptiness of a burned-out light bulb. "But take the pole anyway. I'll leave it by the door."

"I told you—I don't want it—I don't *need* it—I won't even be here to use—" I stopped. "I'm sure I don't like fishing."

"But you said yourself you've never tried it. You won't know until you do."

My head halted in mid-shake when I became aware of familiar music playing in the background, ". . . memories are made by moments like these . . ."

"They're playing our song," Justin said softly, and my mind flashed back to that afternoon of the storm when he had danced with me in the basement and I'd felt safe in his arms. *Oh!* He was doing it again! Squeezing my heart for every drop of emotion it held.

"Go away, Justin." It came out more as a plea than an order.

I couldn't be sure because his head was lowered, but I think he smiled when he said, gently, "You don't really like that Barn guy, do you? You don't really want to spend the rest of your life with him."

I opened my mouth, but the words took a moment to come, and when they did, they were spoken on a highly cynical note. "Can't you even call him by his real name?"

Justin lifted his head and squinted at me, hard, through the screen. "I could, but—"

"Just go away. And take your fishing pole with you."

"Sorry, Robin, I can't do that." His voice sounded strained. "It's not mine. I already have one. I wanted you to have it, but if you really don't want it . . . well, give it to your uncle. Maybe he'll use it. Happy Birthday."

Justin lifted his hand as if to wave. It reached halfway, then, as if it was too much effort, he let it drop.

He disappeared from behind the screen, and when I saw him again he was walking up the driveway. He didn't look back.

As soon as he was out of sight, instead of feeling relieved, I felt foolish cowering inside the locked house like a frightened child.

Behind my thoughts, the song continued, " . . . but memories fade. Oh, darling, please . . . be more than a memory to me . . ."

I unlocked the front door, opened it, and stepped onto the porch. The fishing pole leaned against the house, looking shiny and new. I stared at it for a moment, then shook my head and picked it up.

"Thank you," I whispered.

Chapter Twenty-Four

$\mathcal{I}$ took the fishing rod inside, hesitated near the stairs, then ran up to my room. I waited till the song ended, then turned off the radio.

The tune lingered in my mind as I stood fingering the smooth length of the rod, the translucent line, the peppermint-striped bobber. Something like a smile came to my lips. For a moment, I forgot my plans with Philip. I was picturing myself with Justin. We were fishing together, talking, arguing, laughing—

It was then that I caught a glimpse of my face in the dresser mirror, and it made my heart drop. The starry-eyed, enchanted look vanished, but not quick enough to convince me it hadn't been there. My mother's yearbook picture flashed into my mind, her own face captured with that look. Her photo had been taken right after Christopher proposed to her. *That's how you look when you're in love,* I thought. Then, fiercely, *I am in love—but with Philip—not Justin!*

Anguish and anger pressed at my heart. I couldn't love Justin—didn't want to love him. He was not worth loving. All he wanted was the map, and he would do anything to get it, including stealing my heart. *He's bewitched me, like Christopher Renton bewitched my mother. And no wonder,* I thought, *it must run in his blood.*

Well, I'd just have to be stronger than the Renton spell. I shoved the fishing pole into the back of the closet, near the chest—as if that would make it disappear—slammed the door, and yanked my suitcase from the bed.

But putting troubles behind me mentally wasn't as easy as doing so physically.

Justin's visit had stirred my feelings into a tornado. How could I marry Philip when I felt like this, so torn between myself that I didn't know what I wanted? My ears roared with blood rushing through my head. I ran to the window for fresh air.

There's the mail, I thought stupidly as the little white mail truck puttered past. I turned and walked downstairs and outside, welcoming any excuse as a diversion to my problems. Walking outside was a perfectly normal act, yet I felt as if I was moving in a trance.

At the mailbox, I was further diverted and surprised to find an envelope for me among the bills. At least, *Happy Birthday* was typed on the front, so I assumed it was for me. Nothing else identified the plain white envelope, no return address, no stamp.

Wait a minute. This couldn't have been delivered in the mail. Someone put it in the mailbox. Isn't that illegal? I thought as I tore open the envelope and pulled out a white, rectangular card. On the front were typed the words: *You know what I want. Get it, or . . .*

I opened the card too quickly to be frightened. Taped inside was a photo of two familiar graves. I recognized them as the graves belonging to my grandparents, the ones I had seen for the first time yesterday. On the grassy plot beside them, three letters were printed boldly in permanent marker: RIP.

Now I was frightened.

The sinister implication of those letters was all too clear. My fingers trembled, almost dropping the card as I stood spotlighted in the sun beside the mailbox. I glanced about, half expecting someone to leap out from the surrounding shadows. Every bush, every tree, was a threat. I raced for the house.

Cowering inside, I realized that this was worse than I could have imagined. I was not blowing things out of proportion. Someone was after me, and he wanted the map desperately enough to kill me for it.

I let out a low whimper. Every creak of the house made my heart flinch. How come I'd never heard these noises before? My head spun as I thought, *I have to do something. Something to escape this feeling of being trapped on a spinning roulette wheel. It keeps spinning faster and faster. Will it ever stop?* I wondered giddily. *And if it does—what then?—where will I end up?* All I'd ever wanted was to have control of my life . . . but I'd never had less control than now.

I ran upstairs and scrambled to locate the piece of paper with Philip's number on it, thankful that I had thought to ask him for it, then dialed the phone with as steady a hand as I could manage.

"If you'd like to make a call . . ."

I slammed down the phone.

Taking a deep breath, I picked it up and dialed again.

Philip answered almost immediately. I don't remember what I said, only that my words came out in a panicked jumble. But hearing Philip's voice helped calm me. He told me to hang on and he'd be right over. "Be ready to leave when I get there."

Oh, I will be, I thought, hanging up and wishing I didn't have to break the connection. Being alone in the house made the moments of silence that followed, torture. My numb mind began to thaw, to think. Terrible thoughts.

Justin had left me this threat. I didn't want to believe it, but I couldn't deny it. He had just been here, and he had said himself that he hadn't expected anyone to be home. He had come here for a reason. To give me a birthday present. Was this it? This horrible card in my hand?

I went downstairs and sat at the window, waiting tensely for Philip. The moment I saw his car pull in, I ran out to meet him, almost insane with relief.

"Are you ready?" Philip's voice was earnest, his arms around me only a moment before pulling me into the house.

"I'm ready. Philip—" I ran to catch up to him, for he'd headed straight for my room as if he knew my suitcase was waiting there—and I thrust the photo into his face. I wanted to be reassured, protected . . . I wanted him to make everything all right.

"Oh, Robin . . ." He took one look at the photo and clutched me against him. "My poor Robin. That guy's really serious. He must be crazy. But don't worry." He held me so tightly I could hardly breathe. "I'll take you away from here." Philip released me, and while I struggled for air, he said, "Let's go. Get your stuff."

This is it, I thought. *No more time to think.* But I didn't need more time. I'd made my decision. I handed Philip my suitcase.

"You have the map?" he asked.

"The map?" Then, quickly, "Oh, yes." I grabbed the envelope from the desk drawer and shoved it into my jeans' pocket. "I've got it."

I didn't even have time for one last look around the room —the room where, in a way, I'd come closer to my mother than I'd ever come before. Here I'd discovered her past. She'd left this room behind, and now it was my turn.

I galloped down the stairs at Philip's heels. Philip, so capable. I was in his hands now, and glad to be. I was safe, and this was what I wanted. He would take me away. I would escape all this turmoil. Escape, run away . . . I slowed. Was that what I was doing? Running away, as my mother had?

No, I told myself slowly. *This is different. My mother was running from the past. I've discovered all I can. My work here in Lorens is done. Now I'm running for my safety.*

I was almost to the door when the phone rang. Philip was already outside, tossing my suitcase into the back of his car. I hesitated. "I'll be there in a second!" I called, turning. I dashed to the hall phone, grabbed it and let out a winded "Hello?"

"Robin?" The voice belonged to my uncle. My hand tightened on the receiver. *Oh, why did I answer the phone?* I lamented silently. *I'm in no condition to carry on a conversation. If I had any sense at all, I'd have let it ring. I don't live here anymore.*

I strove to keep my voice sounding normal as a thousand thoughts surged through my mind. I heard my uncle saying that he would be home a little later than usual this evening, that he had some errands to run after work . . . I was only half listening.

This is it, I thought as my eyes swept the pictures on the walls, the annoying old clock, the roses wilting beside the Virgin Mary statue, the faded wallpaper . . . I realized how much I had taken for granted during my stay. Two weeks—such a short time, really. I hadn't taken advantage of the time to get to know this house, my uncle, or the town. But it was too late now. Through the open door, I saw Philip striding toward me.

My uncle, however, was in no hurry. "So what have you been doing so far? Keeping busy?"

"Yes . . . Actually—I was just heading out the door." Philip was almost to the front porch. My heart pounded faster as I became increasingly conscious of what had previously been stirrings of uneasiness, turning into a torrent; and pricks of regret, into stabs. "Philip is taking me to see the Ingerman Mansion. We—we're going to spend the afternoon there."

"The Ingerman Mansion?" My uncle's voice lifted with notable concern.

"Yes." I waited expectantly, not sure why I had said that. Philip came to stand beside me. Possessively, I thought. I had a sudden hope that maybe by telling my uncle that I was going to the mansion, he would forbid me—maybe even say he was coming home to prevent me.

Of course, he didn't. I knew it was a long shot. My uncle had already made it clear that he thought I should make and be responsible for my own choices. "Well, just be careful," was all he said now. "And happy birthday. I'll see you later."

No, you won't, I thought.

I said, "Goodbye." The word sounded so final. And as I replaced the phone, with Philip standing impatiently beside me, I knew that was because it was.

"That was my uncle," I said.

Philip swore, shocking me. "Why did you answer it?"

"I had to," I defended myself. "He knew I was home, and if I didn't answer he would wonder where I was. Besides, now I know he isn't going to be home until at least five-thirty. So we're in the clear—we'll be well on our way by the time he gets home."

Slowly, Philip nodded. "Good thinking."

But I was wondering what my uncle would think when he finally got home. It didn't seem right to just take off and leave him forever wondering what had happened to me; he must have gone through enough worry with my mother. Maybe I should leave a note.

Suggesting this to Philip, he said, "Let the old geezer figure it out for himself."

"Don't call him a geezer."

But Philip only grabbed my arm and pulled me out the door to his car. I tried not to resist him. *Of course he's tense and worried,* I reasoned, *because of what we're doing. I'm nervous, too.*

But as we drove off, I kept throwing Philip sideways glances, uneasiness swelling inside me. His lips were set in a thin, firm line, and he hardly seemed to realize I was here. This was not the way I would ever have expected our elopement to be. This was supposed to be an exciting, romantic escape. So why didn't I feel free? Why did I feel more like I'd just become a prisoner?

In subconscious distress, I began twisting the metal bracelet around my wrist. I looked down at my mother's engraved initials, and strangely, this calmed me. I could almost feel my mother near me, understanding what I was feeling.

Most likely the bracelet dropped off in his car or at his duplex . . . This line from the diary flashed into my head. I never had figured out how the bracelet had been found in the mansion, since my mother had written these words before discovering the map. I'd merely assumed she must have found the bracelet and then lost it again, for how else could Philip have found it under the carpet? But she had never mentioned finding it, and I remembered she had also written that if she ever did, she would make sure not to wear it until the catch was fixed.

Now I examined the catch. It was secure—had to be, because I'd been wearing the bracelet since Saturday and it hadn't come off. But if the catch was fixed, how had my mother lost it again?

"Where are you, Robin?" I looked up to see Philip—the old Philip—smiling at me, one hand barely on the wheel, the other hand reaching over to me. Cruising at his customary racing speed must have helped him to regain his confidence.

"You look a million miles away . . ." His fingers brushed my hair and ran lightly down the curve of my face. Such soft fingers. I closed my eyes, savoring the caress, and forgot the bracelet.

"Dreaming about the future? California? I bet you can't wait to get back there. I know I can't. The beaches, the sun—there's just no other place quite like it, you know?"

I settled back against the seat, smiled at Philip's handsome face, and found myself relaxing. My misgivings had been only natural, but now that we were on our way it was time to leave them behind.

No more doubts, I ordered myself. *Philip and I are so right together.* I closed my eyes again, envisioning the new life we would begin in California, perhaps near the ocean in a little trailer by the sea . . . I wouldn't care, as long as we were together and we had love. Money didn't matter.

I no longer felt afraid to tell Philip, as I had over the phone last night. This was the right time; holding secrets between one another was no way to start married life.

"Phil," I began.

"I'd prefer Philip, if you don't mind."

I began to shrug and say, "All right," when the words froze on my lips. I glanced at him and saw he was still smiling, but the rigid way he held his jaw told me his words were not a request. This jarred something from my memory. Again, it was the diary . . .

"What were you saying?" Philip prompted.

"Nothing." My voice came out in a husky whisper. Christopher Renton had refused to be called Chris. An odd demand. How strange that Philip should feel the same way about his own name.

"Why?" I asked, turning and focusing on Philip's face.

"Why what?"

"Why 'Philip,' but not 'Phil'? It's just a shortened version of your name. Does it really matter?"

He shrugged, but the motion looked forced. "I guess not. Personal preference, that's all. It's what I'm used to. It's what my dad always called me."

"Oh." I was still concentrating on his face. This was the first time I'd ever heard him mention his dad. *What would you look like,* I wondered, *with dark hair? And without that mustache? And you have gray eyes, don't you?*

"Something wrong?"

I looked quickly, innocently away. "No. Nothing." But my mind was working, remembering, piecing together madly. "What were you saying about California?"

"I was saying what an awesome place it is." Philip's voice grew eager. "This time of year especially—it's really alive—but of course you know that already."

I was squinting steadily ahead of me, at the sun-glared stretch of road. "Yes . . . but how do you know?" I took a deep breath. "I thought you said you'd never been to

California."

"Me? Never been to California?" A pause. "You must be mistaken. I never said that."

"But you did," I insisted. "I'm sure of it . . . back that first day I met you in the store, you said—"

"I don't think so," Philip cut in. "You must have heard wrong." I noticed how both his hands tightened on the wheel.

"Must have," I said.

But I knew I hadn't.

There was silence between us . . . if you could really call it silence. The air was crammed with sounds: the roaring motor, the rushing wind, and my screaming brain.

I've been wrong about you, Philip, so very wrong. You've played me for a fool, I thought, squeezing my fists. *And I fell for it.* I had been too caught up in being suspicious of Justin to stop and realize how suspicious Philip's own behavior was.

I shot a glance at Philip. He sat so confident and cool that it repulsed me. I edged a little away from him, as much as I dared to without his noticing. But I was still trapped, sitting in his car, letting him drive me farther away from Lorens with each passing second. The wind whipped my hair and grabbed the cold sweat from my body.

I wanted to say something, but the right words wouldn't come. Maybe there were no right words. What had started out as an exciting adventure had turned into a frightening mistake. Somehow, I had to fix it. I told myself I would, when the moment was right. But when would that be? And how would I do it?

God, help me.

Despite the prayer, a chilling fear took hold of me, breaking out in small bumps over my skin and creeping up the back of my neck.

Certain things became clear. Justin wasn't the one who had put the threat in the mailbox. He didn't know I had found the map, and even if he had suspected, why make the threat? He'd had an ideal chance to get what he wanted today. He'd had me alone a number of times, in fact, but he had never threatened me. And yet I'd come to distrust and fear him.

Who had spurred this fear? Philip. Always Philip. I'd accused Justin of seeking me out, of pursuing me. Until now, I'd been too blind to see that this applied to Philip, too.

Philip had sent me the threat. He was the only one who knew I'd found the map. He was the one who would benefit from scaring me because it would throw all suspicion off himself by putting it on Justin, and make me scared enough to run away.

I sat up straighter. I could admit to myself now that deep down I'd never truly intended to go through with this elopement. Philip must have sensed this and used the threat to push me over the edge, make me feel as if I had to run just to be safe.

Now I realized what I should have from the start: Philip wanted the map—he was the one who would stop at nothing to get it—not even promising to marry me.

I can't marry Philip. This realization didn't hurt as much as I thought it would have—or should have. And I knew why. I didn't love him. Simple as that. I just had to realize it, and when I did, I understood what had happened. I'd been blinded by Philip's charm. I'd been lonely, wanting to fall in love so much that I'd let myself believe I'd found it in Philip, simply because he'd made me feel wanted.

But if all Philip wanted was the map, he couldn't be serious about marrying me. I swallowed hard. Philip's own words—"You know I need to be free"—flashed through my mind. He'd told me he would never tie himself down to someone unless he loved her. I knew he didn't love me; all he wanted was the map.

So what did he intend to do with me . . . ? What was I to him but an anchor weighing him down?

"So where do you want to get married?" Philip asked as casually as if debating wallpaper patterns.

"In church, of course. You know I'm Catholic."

"Thought Catholics weren't supposed to elope," Philip said.

I should have thought of that earlier and saved myself a lot of trouble. "They're not supposed to marry non-Catholics, either," I said, "and you're not Catholic, are you?"

"What gave me away?" Philip laughed.

I didn't join in.

"Don't tell me you've suddenly decided that matters to you."

"A little late now, isn't it?" *Lord, help me. What have I done?*

"Yes, it is. I don't need God. Neither do you. The only way to get what you want out of life is to make it happen yourself."

His words hit me hard. So disrespectful, so wrong. And yet, that's how I'd been living my life—it was all about getting what I wanted, with seldom a thought for God.

The sudden bumping of the car over a rutted dirt road jarred me into becoming aware of my surroundings. "This isn't the main road. Where are we going?" I couldn't hide the rise of alarm in my voice.

Philip's eyes crinkled at the corners as he smiled, one of the things I'd imagined I loved about him. "Just thought we'd take a little detour before leaving Lorens completely . . . see the mansion one last time. It's the place that started it all, you know."

It sure did, I thought. *Years and years and years ago.* I gripped my seat tightly. Like Connie Ingerman and my mother before me, I found myself wishing the map had never existed.

"Besides, you said yourself there's no hurry. I figure we've got just about all the time in the world. No one suspects a thing, and by the time they do—well, everything will be taken care of, won't it?"

I smiled and nodded unhappily, feeling sick to my soul. How could things turn out so wrong? Barely eighteen, and what a mess I'd made of my life.

Lord, how could this happen? Hadn't I prayed for guidance? Suddenly, I realized the truth. Yes, I'd prayed, but it had been sporadic and, for the most part, shallow. I hadn't consulted God about the truly important things. Deep down, I think I'd been afraid of His answers. So I'd done my own will, every time.

Suddenly, I thought of my mother's Bible and rosary, sitting forgotten in my nightstand drawer. Longing for them, I had an inspiration.

"Philip, if there's no hurry," I attempted, "I have a favor to ask you. I forgot to pack something really important—irreplaceable—can you just turn around and—"

"Too late," he cut in, "we're here."

We rounded a bend of trees and the mansion appeared before us, a forbiddingly massive form with its solid walls, flaking paint, and dark windows looking like thick, black slabs of ice.

Philip cut the engine and dead silence followed. Even the birds did not sing. I thought this was a bad sign, and tried to remember if I'd heard birds singing the last time I was here. I couldn't recall. Why didn't they sing? Did they sense something wrong?

I knew I did. Danger.

But wait—get a grip, I ordered myself. *Think. This could be a good thing.* After all, what opportunity for escape did I have while Philip was driving? This might be my chance to get away.

Only thing was, I knew I was balanced on the brink of something treacherous; I'd have to be very careful, because I had no way of knowing what was going on in Philip's mind or what he was planning.

Above all, I could not let him know that things had

changed between us, that I knew who he really was. Because that just might send him—and me—over the edge.

Chapter Twenty-Five

$\mathcal{P}$hilip's eyes fixed on the mansion. In a grossly hungry way, I thought. "Come on," he said, hardly glancing at me as he took my arm.

And my legs walked. They let Philip lead me to the mansion, that fearsome place that I had promised myself I would never again enter. His grip was strong as we waded through itchy grass, stumbled over clumps of weeds, and struggled through the window. And I didn't fight him because I was afraid of what he might do.

Use your head, I directed myself. *Now's not the time to run.*

But when would be?

Then there I was inside the mansion, alone with Philip. Philip Barnstrum. *Barnstrum!* For the first time, I heard how ridiculous the name sounded, and I had to bite my tongue to keep from laughing. I recalled the remarks Justin had made about Philip's name. Justin knew—he knew Barnstrum was not Philip's real name. Why hadn't he told me?

Simple, I thought miserably. I hadn't trusted Justin, and he knew it. I wouldn't have believed him even if he had told me. I would have made excuses, as I had all along, seeing only what I wanted to see. *And what name,* I asked myself, *should Philip have any reason to keep from me?* Of course, I knew the answer: Renton.

"Upstairs," Philip ordered.

I lifted my head to give him a defiant glare, but it was lost in the shadows. I wanted to tell him I wasn't a stupid lovesick kid ready to fall for his every command, but the words stuck in my throat. I mounted the stairs, which creaked and groaned in protest. I'd never felt more alone.

But I'm not alone. Dear Lord, be with me. Guardian angels, protect me.

As I passed the beautiful young woman's portrait, the portrait of Connie Ingerman, her eyes reached out to mine, and for a moment it was as if she'd come to life. Now, more than ever, I needed her to speak, to tell me how to escape—

"Let's not take all day," Philip's voice prodded from behind.

You just said we have all the time in the world. I thought this, but I said nothing.

For some reason, Philip led me to the rose room. Connie's room. He was smiling strangely, as if he knew something I didn't, and I found myself swallowing rapidly as he headed for the glass doors of the balcony. He pushed them open and sunlight streamed in, falling on the faded carpet and bleaching it white.

Philip turned around, transformed into a silhouette against the brightness, and motioned me to his side.

My feet walked and my eyes widened in horror, for at that moment it was easy to believe that I was being drawn out onto the balcony to meet my fate, the fate of both Connie and my mother before me.

Why did Philip bring me here? This question hammered at my skull, but it never reached my lips. Probably because I didn't want to hear the answer.

"Look at this beautiful view, Robin." Philip clutched my hands, and his palms felt disgustingly warm. I looked down and saw, strapped to his wrist, a silver watch glinting in the sunlight, telling me something . . .

With a sharp intake of breath, I knew what it was. Though I'd never seen the watch before, I recognized it. I didn't need to see the underside to know that the initials *C.R.* were engraved there.

"Your hands are cold, Robin. They feel like ice." He began massaging them. "Why?"

I tried to shrug his words aside, even managed a smile. "They're always cold." I prayed he didn't guess the truth, that I was scared to death. My mouth, dry as cotton, tasted sour.

"No, they're not, Robin. Something's wrong." Philip squeezed my hands. "Tell me what it is." His voice became tender and he moved closer. His face neared mine, and in that instant I realized he was about to kiss me.

My heart constricted inside my chest. Everything about Philip repulsed me. I struggled in horror as his face leaned toward mine. More than anything, I wanted my lips never to touch his and to bear their stain forever. Using both hands, I pushed him away. He wasn't expecting that, and he staggered back.

He caught his balance, then seemed to freeze. During the chilling silence I could tell he was evaluating me, coolly calculating, and I saw the true Philip emerge. A nerve on his face twitched, making one side of his mustache convulse. His jaw muscles tightened. His eyes locked on mine.

"Good. The game's over, Robin." His voice was calm. "No more fooling around. You know what I want. Give me the map." As he held out his hand, his watch flashed in the sun.

Anger that I didn't know I could feel ignited inside me. I hated Philip for what he'd done to me, how he'd deceived and used me. I hated him for who he was.

"Your name's not Barnstrum—it's Renton!" I was wearing Tiffany's bracelet because I was her daughter. Philip was wearing Christopher's watch because—"You're his son. You're Christopher Renton's son!"

"Congratulations, you win the prize," Philip sneered. "Figured it out a little too late though, didn't you?"

How I detested the smugness in his voice and on his face. It gave me the strength to retort, "It's not too late. At least I didn't marry you—" Philip moved threateningly near, and I tried to shove him away again. But this time he was ready.

Grabbing my wrists, he yanked me toward him and to the edge of the balcony. My courage gone, I cried, "How could I have been so blind?"

All because I was so concerned with controlling my own life. I'd forgotten to turn to the only One Who is in control of us all.

God is in control, not me. And not Philip. God, forgive me. I trust in You.

"I'm sorry things had to turn out this way." Philip smiled his flawless smile, showing he was anything but sorry. "I wouldn't have minded marrying you, you know. Someone to take care of the food and the kids." Almost as an afterthought he added, "I wanted a son someday, Robin."

"Why, *Phil?* So you could poison him the way your father poisoned you?"

Philip's nostrils flared, and his mustache contorted, making him look sinister. "I said don't call me that!" He drew his hand back as if to slap me. I braced myself, but he dropped his arm and spoke with composure. "My father was smart. If it weren't for him, the map never would have been found. He had a right to that gold. It was your mother who was stupid, for holding out on him."

"What are you talking about? She had amnesia—she didn't remember the map!"

"Sure, that's what she claimed. But she was lying. My father told me all about it. Your mother just wanted it for herself—"

"That's not true!"

"She took off and cheated my father out of what was rightfully his."

"No! You're wrong—my mother never—"

Philip ignored me. "Your mother thought she was so smart." Philip's grip tightened on my wrist. And those eyes, those eyes that for so long I had thought of as gentle gray, turned into cold steel. "Like you think you are, just because you figured out Christopher Renton was my father. But

295

you're not. You're stupid."

Philip ran his fingers up my arm, making my flesh crawl as if a centipede was racing up it. "See this?" he asked.

I blinked. My scar—the scar my mother had told me I'd gotten from a broken glass vase—

"You know what that's from? How you got that? Bet your mother never told you about the accident, did she?" Philip regarded me smugly. "Stupid. She should have told you—then you could have watched out . . . for me."

It began to make sense why my mother had been afraid to let me out of her sight. Who wouldn't be, with a lunatic like this on the loose?

"By the way," Philip said, "how did she like the flowers I sent her in the hospital? A nice reminder of my father?"

The lilacs. Philip had sent them.

He smiled. "It's what he would have wanted me to do, to let her know she hadn't won. She thought she'd gotten the best of my father after her fall. When she got out of the hospital she thought she would just go on without him, forgetting that if it weren't for him, she never would have found the map. But he didn't let her forget. He did things to remind her, like sending her meaningful gifts, climbing up the oak tree to her window at midnight and tapping on the glass; but she still wouldn't give him the map or tell him where she'd stashed it—"

"Because she didn't know! She—"

"Then she ran off, thinking she could escape." A wicked smile crossed Philip's face, freezing my words. "But my father followed her, made life hell for her. He haunted her, from Wisconsin to Colorado to California. I know, because my father told me everything." He sounded proud. "You know how kids get bedtime stories? That was my bedtime story—night after night—"

"That's sick."

"I loved it. And the best part about it was it was all true. My father promised me he would take me with him when he found her, and we'd get the map back together. It took him a while to trace her, but he finally located her living with her husband and you, hiding in a shack in the Colorado mountains. He made a plan. Had it all figured out. He waited till one evening when your mother was alone with you. Then he came—"

"Stop it! Why are you telling me this?"

"You're the one who wanted to know—who kept digging up the past." Philip shook me. "Well, now you're gonna know. Everything."

My ears roared, but it didn't block the sound of Philip's voice. "See, my father was smart. He knew how to get what he wanted. Kidnapping you for ransom of the map would have worked, too, if your fool father hadn't interfered. He went after my father—chased him on those mountain roads." Philip's face twisted. "There was a crash. That's how you got that scar."

The roaring in my ears grew louder. I'd known my father had been killed in a crash, but I hadn't known the circumstances. I could almost hear it now, the screeching tires, the breaking glass—I'd been there! I'd been in that car crash—and survived. How?

Philip, who knew me too well, read my thoughts. "Oh, you came out of it all right—only a few cuts." He sounded disappointed. "You were thrown from the car. So was I. I wasn't as lucky as you, but I won't go into that. I wanted to be there. I wouldn't have missed it for anything."

I blinked, stunned.

"That's right, my father took me along."

"He must have been crazy," I whispered.

"My father wasn't lucky like yours was, either—"

"My father was killed!"

"That's right. He had it easy." Philip's eyes smoldered. Thank goodness he wasn't looking at me or they could have burnt a hole through me. "My father suffered for years from that accident. And it never should have happened." The hatred in Philip's voice intensified. His fingers bit into my arm. "It wouldn't have happened, if your father hadn't interfered."

What warped logic. Philip was actually blaming this on my father, on my mother—and now, I realized, on me.

"I healed, but I watched my father suffer until he died. But I swore to him," Philip's eyes swung back to mine, "I swore to him that I would find your mother and make her pay—" He let go of me to smack his fist into his hand.

Seizing my chance, I bolted for the door.

"You can run, but you can't hide!" Philip laughed. "I'll find you wherever you go!"

My heart pounded like a frantic war drum. In the rose room, I searched madly for something to defend myself with. Anything hard. Anything heavy. Anything sharp.

The fireplace poker.

But Philip was at my side before I could take hold of it. I let out a cry as he grabbed me and pulled me back onto the balcony. My sandals skidded on the wooden planks as I tried to resist, but he dragged me to the edge and held me pressed against the rail. My head swam. Philip knew I couldn't take this, but still he rambled on.

"By the time I finally tracked your mother down, she was already dying. Death—" the word came out sounding like a hiss—"the only way she could escape . . ." Philip turned his glinting eyes on me, and his voice dropped. "Now you're the only one left. I'm sorry, Robin," and I almost thought I heard real regret in his voice. Maybe it was my imagination, but I reached out to it. It was the only hope I had.

"Why are you doing this to me?"

"I can't help it. I told you, I made a promise . . . I promised my father I'd get the map. And I have!" Triumph blazed in his eyes. "And now it's mine!" His face was so near that his foul breath flooded my nostrils.

I grasped at the rail, desperately trying to avoid Philip's face, to avoid looking down—both were unbearable. My mother's written words raced through my mind. *You think you know someone . . .*

Oh, Mother! We were both so deceived! I wondered if this was how it had happened with her and Christopher. Was I going to fall from the balcony, too, in an "accident"? No, I wouldn't let it happen!

But it's not in my control. Trust in the Lord.

"Don't fight it, Robin. You have no choice. You know what I want. Give me the map." Philip's voice turned bitter. "You owe me that much at least. After all these years of searching, and it ends up being in your mother's old house, after all—"

"But don't you see? That proves she wasn't holding out on you or your father. She really didn't know where the map was."

But it was as if Philip hadn't even heard me. He wedged me up against the rail—the unsteady rail. Did I hear a creak? I tried to push my weight back on Philip.

"If I give it to you—what then—what about me?" I gasped.

"I can't take you with me now, can I? You've gone and ruined that plan. But I've got other plans." To my great surprise, Philip hauled me off the balcony and into the rose room.

He yanked a heavy braided cord from the drapes and seemed to contemplate it. "This should hold you for a while," he muttered. I thought he was going to tie me up in the bedroom—that I could have borne—but instead he heaved me back out onto the balcony, and I realized the horrible truth. He's going to tie me to the railing.

My heart continued shooting pleas to heaven. Through the confusion, I thought I heard something like the sound of a motor. I strained to listen, but my heart was beating so loudly that I couldn't trust my ears. When I no longer heard the sound, I was afraid my desperation had made me imagine it. Philip certainly hadn't heard anything; he was too intent on tying my hands to notice anything else.

"There now, aren't I considerate?" He yanked the rope one last time before standing. "Now you can enjoy the beautiful view."

With all my strength, I tugged, trying to pull my hands from their bindings. When they came free, I was so surprised that it took me a moment to scramble to my feet.

Philip cursed and jerked me so roughly that for a second I was airborne and I thought he was going to throw me over the balcony.

"You think you can get rid of me like this?" I gasped. "Just—force me over—another victim for the mansion? And no one will ever know?"

"You shouldn't give me such dangerous ideas. I might take you seriously . . . not a bad idea. A little messy, maybe, but—"

"It worked for your father, didn't it?" I dared to say. "He pushed my mother over!"

Philip straightened and the rope dropped to the floor with a thud, but his grip remained tight on my wrists. "That was an accident," he said sullenly. "He never meant for her to go over. But she wouldn't listen to him, wouldn't listen to reason. She was stupid, like you. She struggled with him and the railing broke—"

I shook my head at what hadn't occurred to me till now. "Then this isn't the same balcony." Even in this desperate situation, my mind strove for logic. "The railing would be broken."

Philip lifted one eyebrow suggestively. "Unless someone repaired it."

In preparation for a replay.

"Philip," I pleaded, pausing in my struggle. "Think. You don't want to do this to me." I was trying to reach out to the gentler part of his heart that must exist, somewhere. "You don't owe revenge to your father. How can you think like that?"

His eyes hesitated, and for a wild second, I believed I was getting through to him.

"My uncle knows I'm here with you—I told him on the phone!" It was the wrong thing to say. Philip's eyes sparked into flames and I lost him.

"You shouldn't have done that, Robin." Philip shook his head. "You know what I do to people who double-cross me?"

"If you do anything to me—if they find me—they'll know—"

"I'll be long gone by then." Philip kicked the rope over the edge. "And so will you."

"Here. Here's the map!" I yanked the crushed envelope from my pocket. "You can have it! I don't want it—and how can you even think my mother wanted this thing? Enough to risk her life and her family? She didn't!"

I was almost sobbing. "She just didn't remember where it was. If she had, she would have given it up long ago—just to be free of the curse of you Rentons. Of—of being *hunted* all her life!"

And I knew it was true. In that moment, I understood completely the torment my poor mother had suffered. Alone. Because she hadn't wanted to scare me. That had been her sacrifice.

The least I could do was forgive her. I did, and my soul cried to her for forgiveness for not understanding sooner.

Like an animal, Philip snatched the envelope from my hand. For a split second, he forgot me. And that was all I needed.

I broke free with a frantic burst of energy and raced through the doors into the rose room. This time I didn't hesitate, but ran through the room, into the hall, and onto the landing.

Heart in my throat, I was about to race down the stairs when, aghast, I heard footsteps pounding up them in my direction. But how? Philip was behind me.

Then I saw who it was coming up those stairs, and I wanted to fall into his arms. Because it was Justin, and I knew I was finally safe.

Thank You, God!

Then I felt the arm around my throat.

Chapter Twenty-Six

$\mathcal{G}$ et your hands off her, Philip! Have you gone crazy?"
Yes! I wanted to scream. *Yes!* But the arm around my
throat would hardly let me breathe, let alone scream.

"Back off, Justin," Philip ordered, yanking me away
from the stairs. My eyes flew to Justin's, pleading. He had
halted on the steps, yet stood with every muscle tensed and
ready.

As if in rewind motion, Philip dragged me back, back
through the rose room, back through the glass doors, back
onto the balcony. I tasted the salt first, and when I felt the
wetness on my cheeks, I realized tears were sliding from my
eyes. I blinked fiercely, trying to keep my vision clear. If
ever there was a time I needed to stay focused, this was it.

Over my shoulder, I saw a flick of motion. Justin, like a
shadow, was following us. Steadily, cautiously, as if he knew
what he was doing. This gave me hope, and my brain began
to function rationally. *Justin is here. That makes two against
one. Philip might be winning now, but if Justin and I play
this right, we can beat him.*

I didn't ask how or why Justin was here. It didn't matter.
All that mattered was that he was here, here to put an end to
this nightmare. *Be with him, Lord.*

"Philip," Justin's voice was low, sounding so grim it
would have scared me if I wasn't already petrified. "You've
got what you want . . . now let her go."

"Ha!" Philip pinned me with his side against the rail
while he held the map clutched in his hand. My eyes went to
it. "Don't think I don't know what you're after, Justin. We're
cousins, after all."

"Whether we like it or not."

"The game's over, Justin. I've got your queen."

"This isn't chess."

"You're right." Philip's voice hardened. "It's treasure hunt. You want the map, too. You've been after it all along. Pretending you're looking out for the girl—*Spht!*" I flinched as Philip spat his contempt, just missing my foot. "Drop the hero act! You don't have me fooled. I know you want it as much as I do."

Justin didn't reply. His mouth stayed in a straight, hard line while his eyes went to mine. Like they had once before, the first time we met. It was as if I was hearing them ask, *Do you trust me?*

And this time I answered, *Yes.*

Justin stood poised and waiting. Like a panther ready to pounce.

I felt Philip's own body tense against mine. "Well, you can't have it. The map's mine. Mine by birthright—so just back off!" Philip motioned violently with his right hand. The hand with the map. "I'm warning you—one step closer and—"

I don't know how I did it, but I reached forward, snatched the map, and flung my arm over the balcony.

Philip whirled around, fire in his eyes. "Give me that!"

Everything happened at once: Philip's eyes saw only the map, and Justin, taking advantage of the moment, lunged for Philip. In the same second Philip grabbed for the map, I jerked my hand away. Bodies collided against the rail, and the weight was too much for the wood. There was a terrible splintering sound and I felt the rail giving way. All sense of balance disappeared, and my stomach lurched.

I started falling with Philip beside me.

Then suddenly, before I even had a chance to scream, I was being pulled in the opposite direction, back to the glass doors and back to safety . . . as Philip disappeared over the edge with a horrible cry.

~

The silence that followed was painful to my ears. It was a thick silence, hanging in the air like a smothering blanket, too heavy to throw off.

Relief had not yet registered in my mind. I was trembling, weak and exhausted, and my legs wanted to crumple beneath me. The only thing stopping them was Justin, holding me so tightly in his arms that I could hardly breathe.

And all I could think was, *Hold me tighter, and never let me go.*

His stubbly chin pressed against my cheek, and I welcomed the prickly feel of his unshaven face. Slowly, he released me, but he stayed near.

As if by an unspoken understanding, we moved back onto the balcony. I didn't want to look over the edge, through the jagged remains of wood and the gaping space where the rails had been, to what waited below, but I knew I had to.

Far below, Philip lay deathly still among the grass, flowers and rocks, his body twisted in an unnatural way. Was he alive? I closed my eyes and turned away, and Justin led me back to the glass doors. As he did so, I managed to speak. "We'll have to go down—"

Maybe it was hearing my voice that made Justin find his own. "I'm so sorry." When I looked up and saw the pallor of his face, my heart reacted with a strange pang. He rushed on, trying to explain, and all I could do was stand in the doorway staring at him. "I never wanted this to happen! You have to believe me. Philip was the one after the map—"

"I know," but it came out as a whisper, too soft to hear.

"—when I heard he'd left Lake City, I was afraid he'd gone after it. He always said he would. When I found out there was a daughter, that you were coming to Lorens, I knew I had to get to you before he did—do something—do my best to warn you. I don't know, at least keep an eye on you—" He ran his hands through his thick hair. A short pencil dropped from behind his ear and I watched it roll over the wooden planks of the balcony and disappear over the edge. I almost giggled.

Justin, still rambling, never noticed. "—I didn't want to scare you. If I'd only known how serious he was. Oh, Robin. I never thought he'd take it this far, but I shouldn't have taken the chance. I swear—"

"Don't," I interrupted.

For the first time since Philip's fall, Justin looked directly at me. His face went blank. "Don't what?"

"Don't swear." I laughed a nervous laugh, breaking the tension.

"So you're really all right?"

"Yes."

"Thank God."

Yes, thank God. Then I saw the envelope, still crushed in my grasp, and I lifted it. Justin's eyes went to it, and his sudden change of expression alarmed me. "Justin?" I asked cautiously. "What about the map?"

I shouldn't have asked.

"The map—" Justin snatched the envelope from my hands—"is what caused all this trouble. Don't think I wanted it—I never did—I still don't!" he said fiercely. And before I could interject, he was tearing the map to shreds, not even taking it out of the envelope first. I watched the pieces sail off the balcony and scatter into the air . . . hundreds of irretrievable scraps sailing away on the wind.

A spark lit inside me. But it wasn't a spark of anger. It was nothing like anger. It was relief, gratitude, and so much more. I felt as if I could fly right off the balcony. Only I didn't want to. Because I wanted to stay right where I was. With Justin.

I followed Justin when he turned to go inside. Together, we made our way through the rose room, down the curving staircase, out the window, and around to the rear of the mansion. All this in silence, but it didn't feel like silence. Too much was going on inside my head.

Stepping out back was like entering another land. An air of survival hung over the garden, simply because it had been thriving for years without human interference. These strange thoughts deserted my mind when I reached the rock garden below the balcony. Seeing the blood-spattered, crushed grass, I let out a strangled cry. Philip was nowhere in sight.

Tearing back through the tangled grass, I reached the front of the mansion. I halted, stunned. Philip's red BMW was gone.

"No!" I stumbled forward, my thoughts turned wild with disbelief. We couldn't let Philip escape. I spotted Justin's Jeep. "We have to go after him! We have to catch—"

"Come on!" Justin grabbed my arm as he ran by. With slamming doors and spinning wheels, we zoomed out of the clearing and onto the dirt road, dust flying.

~

Neither of us said a word as we raced the roads in pursuit of Philip, our eyes scanning for a glimpse of red. We covered roads and recovered them, drove for what seemed like hours, didn't want to admit defeat.

"We won't stop searching," Justin said finally. "Not unless you say. It's your call."

I didn't answer right away. All this driving had given me time to think, and I was thinking about Philip. Philip speeding at ninety miles an hour. Even if nothing else Philip had told me was true, I believed what he'd said about being free. He had to be free.

"You can stop," I said. "We'll never find him."

Justin made a U-turn. A minute later, he pulled off the highway and into a gas station. When he got out to fill the tank, I leaned over to the driver's side and saw that the needle of the gas gauge was on empty. I shook my head and leaned back in my seat.

"You're right, you know," Justin said as he climbed back into the Jeep, then started it up. "We'll never find him."

The terror was embedded so deeply in my heart, I could hardly get the words out. But I had to ask. "What if he comes back? What if he still wants revenge—what if . . . ?" Justin's hand left the wheel and went to mine, and my words faded as our fingers twined together.

"He won't be back," Justin said quietly, but with conviction. "He knows what would happen if he did. He knows he's lost, and he can't face it—can't face being wrong. He never could. He's the kind who'll tip over the chessboard rather than lose." Justin squeezed my hand. "Don't worry anymore, Robin. It's over. All over."

Over. I repeated that word in my mind like a prayer.

It's over. But after these past two intense weeks, I found that incredibly hard to believe. Maybe I was in some kind of state of shock—and I told myself I certainly should be—but I felt lost in an anticlimax, let down, as if things were over too suddenly. I expected something more. Something more than this silent drive back to my uncle's.

I looked at Justin, wondering what he was feeling. But, as if to make up for his previous flood of words while on the balcony, he remained silent. Finally, I could stand it no longer.

"What are you going to do now?" I wasn't even sure what I meant by the question, but I knew the answer I got wasn't the one I wanted.

"It's still a nice day." Justin attempted a smile. "I'm going fishing." He pulled into my uncle's driveway and left the engine running, obviously waiting for me to get out. I opened my door but paused before stepping down.

"Thank you, Justin."

"Don't thank me, Robin." He didn't even turn his head to look at me. "I didn't do anything . . . more than I had to."

Both my feet were on the driveway now. I looked up at

the house, still empty, so large and waiting, and I thought, *It's going to be a long afternoon here, alone.*

Justin started pulling away when I turned back to him. "Wait!" I lifted my arm to get his attention. He stopped. Then, without further explanation—just trusting he would wait—I dashed to the house and up the stairs to my room. I pulled the Bible and rosary out of the drawer and set them on the nightstand where I'd be sure to see them later. Then I rummaged through the closet, pulled my fishing rod from the back corner, and ran outside to join Justin.

~

That afternoon I discovered I liked fishing. The peaceful quiet of the park, the sun warm on my skin, the lucid water . . . and Justin there beside me. I liked to look down at our ripply reflections as we stood together on the bank. A couple of times, I think I caught Justin doing the same, and this reassured me.

Because there was still something not quite right, something hanging in the air between us so that we were together, and yet apart; even when he stood close and guided my arms to show me how to cast, the distance remained.

I wanted to speak, and yet I felt hesitant, waiting for Justin. *He must sense it, too,* I thought, and I told myself he would speak in his own good time.

After what we'd been through, I couldn't blame him for his silence. If only I didn't still have so many questions.

"Lake City," I said, recalling Justin's words on the balcony. "Is that where Philip lives?"

"Used to. With me and my mom."

"But isn't—" I hesitated, embarrassed to say it—"isn't your mom—sick?"

"Sick?" Justin repeated.

"I mean—isn't she in a mental hospital?"

Silence. Then Justin let out a low whistle. "Did Philip tell you that?"

I nodded, and Justin shook his head. "It's his mother who's in the mental hospital. And no wonder. His father drove her to it. Soon after Philip was born."

For the first time, I realized how young Philip must be. Twenty at the oldest. I imagined him without his cocky attitude, without his mustache, and he looked . . . like a kid.

"Philip never needed that gold," Justin said, his voice sounding raw. "He's got plenty of money. It was all about the challenge, all about winning."

Justin knows a lot about Philip, I thought, *and no wonder. They're cousins.* When he told me that his mom had taken care of Christopher and Philip after the car accident, I suddenly made the connection that Justin's mother was Christine. *That's why Justin looks so much like Christopher. His mother is Christopher's twin.*

"Since they lived with us for a while," Justin said, referring to Christopher and Philip, "I used to overhear stories . . . crazy stories. And Philip liked to brag. I never did think he was quite right in the head. As I got older, I asked too many questions, dug into the past a little too much—like someone I know." He glanced at me, his lips making a partial smile. "That's when I discovered some family history I wasn't too proud of. But I've always liked asking questions. Maybe that's why I became a reporter."

I smiled. "All those strange questions you asked me when we first met . . ."

"I needed to find out how much you knew."

"And you found out I didn't know anything . . ." My words faded and I focused on my bouncing bobber.

"How did you know to come to the mansion?" I asked finally.

"I knew something was wrong when I heard you were headed there."

I shook my head. "But how did you know I was going there?"

Justin recast his line before answering. "I went to the

310

bookstore. To talk to your uncle. After seeing you this morning, I decided it was time to explain everything to him —why I'm here, why I've been following you, who Philip is, and what he was after. I didn't know what else to do. I couldn't get through to Philip, and I couldn't take this anymore, couldn't sit by and watch things get worse—"

"You knew I was planning to leave, didn't you?" I asked quietly.

"I don't blame you for wanting to get away."

There was silence for a moment while I watched the sun glimmering in golden ribbons on the water. "So what did my uncle say?"

"I never talked to him."

"But you just said—"

"I went into the bookstore, but I never got the chance to talk to him. He was on the phone—to you. And when I heard him mention the mansion, I knew something was wrong, that you'd never go there by choice. I left the store before he even saw me—Hey! You've got a bite!"

I caught two big fish that afternoon, and Justin caught one. "Beginner's luck," he scoffed, almost like his old self. And yet—not quite. Something was missing from his voice.

It was enough to keep me wondering, enough so that I couldn't let him go until I knew. Something was bothering him, but it was separate from the terror we had gone through. I needed to know what it was, because anything that bothered him bothered me, too. When Justin took me home, I persuaded him to stay for dinner.

"Your uncle won't want me," he protested.

"Just let me talk to him."

When my uncle arrived home that evening, I waylaid him on the front steps and asked if Justin could stay. "I know why you don't like him," I said. I took a deep breath and met my uncle's eyes. "He told me who he is. I know about my mother and Christopher Renton. I know you didn't like Christopher, but don't hold that against Justin. Give him a chance and get to know him. Please." My uncle frowned. "If you do, I'll bake a rhubarb pie tomorrow."

Behind his glasses, I caught a twinkle in my uncle's eyes. Justin stayed.

My uncle had brought home two boxes, and this was why he had been late getting home. Out of one of them, he lifted a beautiful bakery birthday cake. It was decorated with roses tinted in pink, and I'd never seen my name look as beautiful as it did in those curly frosting letters.

"So where's Philip?" my uncle asked during the delicious dinner of grilled fish and corn on the cob.

At my uncle's question, I stopped chewing. I couldn't help making eye contact with Justin. "He's gone," I said, "and I don't think he's coming back."

My uncle lifted his own eyes and gave me a strange look, a look that I somehow deciphered as: "At least you had the sense not to go with him." And I wondered how much I'd misjudged my uncle, how much he'd suspected, how much he'd known all along. Maybe someday I'd ask him.

What really pleased me was that when my uncle and Justin got to talking, they discovered they had a common interest, fishing. And that was enough to begin fanning away the hostile barrier between them.

"He's not at all like his uncle," my uncle confided to me when we were in the kitchen getting plates and forks for the cake. "I think I could learn to like him. As long as he likes rhubarb pie, that is."

I smiled, thinking, *Maybe I'll ask him over for dinner again tomorrow night and we can find out.* I took a carton of vanilla ice cream from the freezer, the jar of maraschino cherries from the cupboard, and returned with them to the kitchen, feeling a flutter of worry and hope inside me as I looked at Justin.

His eyes avoided mine.

The remaining box was wrapped in funny pink paper, a purple ribbon perched on top. I had no idea what was inside;

I certainly hadn't expected presents. This birthday had already given me enough surprises.

The box contained a diary, a fat blue leather book gilded in gold. I flipped through the blank pages, and instantly I knew what I would use the book for.

"I wasn't sure what to get you, Robin," my uncle said, picking up the torn wrapping paper. "I hope you like it. Your mother never kept a diary, but I often thought it was too bad she didn't . . . for your sake." He crumpled the paper into a pink wad. "Anyway, happy birthday."

I couldn't speak, but it didn't matter. I reached over and hugged my uncle shyly, and I knew that from now on, things were going to get better between us.

While my uncle lit the candles on my cake, I glanced at Justin from beneath my lashes. He saw me looking, and I blushed. I could feel him watching me while I made my wish and blew out my candles. All eighteen of them.

So my wish should come true.

That evening, after the cake and ice cream was eaten and the dishes cleared, I asked Justin to take me for a ride in his Jeep.

"It's such a nice evening," I said longingly.

Justin took me, and it was very different from those wild joy rides with Philip. Much to my relief.

The sun was sinking in a pink watercolor-washed sky. While gazing out the window, trying to catch a view of the skyline, I had a sudden idea. Before I could lose my nerve, I turned to Justin.

"Remember how you said the best place to watch a sunset is from the mansion's balcony? Let's go there now. Let's see the sunset."

Justin raised his eyebrows but kept his eyes on the road. "Are you serious?"

I knew he was thinking of how I hated and feared the mansion. And after what had happened there today still so fresh in our minds, I must be crazy to want to go back.

313

Yet it was suddenly important for me to do just that—go back and face my fear and overcome it. I took a deep breath.

"Yes. Very serious."

Chapter Twenty-Seven

As we approached the mansion, I felt my heart skipping beats. The mansion had never looked more foreboding, wound as it was now in the wispy gray shadows of evening, but I continued walking because Justin was behind me. I didn't even have to turn to reassure myself he was there. I just knew.

Inside the mansion, the white furniture forms heightened the gloomy atmosphere, but I didn't give them a second glance. Justin took my hand and guided me past them and up the stairs. I saw Connie Ingerman's portrait, her sad eyes, her lips that were about to speak . . . and I knew now what she would tell me if she could: the only true treasure on this earth is love.

Yes, I know that now, and I left the portrait behind.

I passed through the etched glass doors, with Justin right behind me, and walked out onto the balcony. The instant I saw the horizon, all impending fear departed. The sky was smeared in brilliant pink, blending into golden orange before bursting into a fiery fringe around the sun. A few puffy clouds were stained pink, like cotton balls that had been dipped in bright dye.

I don't know how long I stood there, silently gazing at the beauty, the colors surging through my soul, my soul praising the Lord.

Eventually, Justin spoke in a low, gentle voice. "I'm glad we came."

Reaching for his hand, I said, "So am I." I no longer felt weighed down by the tragedies that had taken place here, but lifted up by hope.

When Justin said no more, I turned to look at him and caught him staring down at a yellow scrap of paper near our feet. He saw that I saw it. "I'm sorry—" he made a sound deep in his throat, like he was fighting to get the words out —"I'm sorry I destroyed the map."

My heart constricted inside me. *No,* I thought, *don't say that!*

"It was yours. If anyone had a right to it, you did . . . You found it. I shouldn't have destroyed it—I had no right—"

"You had every right. Do you really think I wanted it?" I asked, incredulous. At the same time, I wondered if this was what had been bothering him all afternoon. "After the pain it's caused so many people? I'm glad it's gone."

There was a pause. "I'm glad you're glad." He smiled. "Man, it felt good tearing that thing to pieces . . ."

I returned the smile, but when his smile faded and his eyes slid away from mine, I knew something was still wrong.

"I bet I know what you wished for tonight," Justin said.

"Oh?" I made my voice sound indignant, hoping to challenge him into a witty response. "Do you think you can read my mind or something?"

"No." Justin raked his hand through his hair and gave a strange laugh. "Don't think I'd ever be able to do that."

I had a feeling he was making fun of me, but I didn't mind. In fact, it encouraged me. I was thinking up another clever reply when Justin suddenly turned and walked away.

"Justin . . . wait. Where are you going?"

He stopped, but he didn't turn. Staring at his stiff back, I couldn't take this any longer. "Something's bothering you. What is it? What's the matter? You won't talk to me, you won't look at me, you—"

Justin swung around. "I'll tell you what's wrong—it's you. You and your words and your thoughts . . . and this sunset. How much am I supposed to take? I've gotten to like you, and this wasn't supposed to happen." All the anger dropped from his voice. "I wasn't supposed to fall for you."

His brows furrowed. "You've changed my life, and now I have to say goodbye."

"What do you mean, say goodbye?"

For a panicky second, I thought he meant he was leaving Lorens. Then I realized he meant me. My birthday wish—California. Suddenly it became clear. Justin thought I still planned to go back to California.

And he didn't want me to go.

Something caught in my throat—a laugh or a cry—it never came out, so I don't know. Temporarily unable to speak, I shook my head.

His eyes downcast, Justin said, "I prayed for you. Even before I met you, I prayed for you. I just want you to know— I'll keep on praying for you—even after you leave."

I swallowed hard and the corners of my mouth quivered. *He's a good man, Lord.*

"Justin," I finally managed to say, "I'm not leaving."

He looked up. "You're not?" He took a tentative step and then returned to my side. "Even after all that's happened? I'd think you'd want to get away."

I considered his words as I turned to the sunset.

What Justin was saying meant running away . . . to escape bad memories. But I didn't want that. I wanted to stay right here and face them. *With the Lord's help.* And in my heart, I felt a gentle stirring, an ethereal whisper, and I knew without a doubt, that this was right.

"How could I leave?" I asked softly. "Where else would I be able to see a sunset like this?"

"Nowhere this side of heaven," Justin assured me.

Absently, I fingered my bracelet. I knew now that my mother hadn't been careless with it. She'd never found it. Christopher must have had it all along, then passed it on to Philip. That would be just like him. Philip hadn't found it under the carpet; he'd just said that to pull me deeper into his warped plot.

Justin touched the bracelet and said, as if he didn't want

to, yet had to, "You know, I'm still related to Christopher . . . and Philip. Nothing's ever going to change that."

"I know. And it's funny. I thought it mattered; I hated them so much. I think about what Christopher did—leaving my mother lying on the ground all that time alone and in pain because he needed an alibi—but now, I only feel sorry for him and Philip. Imagine the kind of life they had." I shivered, and Justin moved closer. He put his arm around me so lightly I would not have known it was there except for the rush of emotion that filled me.

"So you aren't afraid I might have 'bad blood' in me or something?"

He'd said the words half-jokingly, but I answered seriously. "No, Justin. I'm not afraid. Besides," I said, my voice lowering, "do you remember what you told me today, this morning? About who we are?" I took a deep breath. "It's true. You're not your uncle and I'm not my mother . . . We're ourselves. God gave us our own lives to live."

My eyes focused on the setting sun, which was balancing just above the horizon like a shimmering golden ball. "That's why I'm staying in Lorens. Remember I once told you, 'home is a place where you live—a place you love'?"

"Yes?"

"Well, I've found that place."

Justin drew me near, looked deep into my eyes, and whispered, "Well said."

Then he kissed me, very gently.

And I thought, *This is the kiss I've been waiting eighteen years for.*

It was worth the wait.

Epilogue

Once in a while, I wonder about Philip. I like to think he finally saw the truth that day he fell, and couldn't take it, and that's why he ran.

Perhaps he went off to seek his fortune in another country. I hope so, because I like to think he's far away. But there's always the possibility that someday down the road he, or some descendant, may return . . . and I'm not taking any chances.

So I have filled this diary with my story, because this is how it happened and how it must be remembered. I know I couldn't have put this book to a better use.

Now this is recorded, I can leave the bad memories behind without fear that the past will come back to hurt other unsuspecting people.

Someday, if I'm blessed with children of my own, the account will be here so they will know the truth. And can be ready. Just in case a mysterious stranger does show up someday, searching for something.

I'm finally grateful my mother sent me here to Lorens, though I still sometimes wonder why she did. She couldn't have known what would happen. She would never have knowingly put me in danger. I guess she sent me here because she really had no other choice. But I like to think it's also because she wanted to finally make her peace, through me, with her brother, her hometown . . . and her past. She'd left so much undone, and she didn't want to leave it like that forever.

There are some questions I may never have the answers to. But that's okay. My life, my future—they're in God's hands. Right where they've always been.

My mother is still in my memory—she always will be—but I remember her now in pleasant things. Like in my room, which no longer feels haunted; when I look at the thriving garden; and every time I bake or eat a rhubarb pie; and, of course, when I lift my thoughts to heaven.

As for the map, I think my uncle used too much water when he shampooed the carpet. Whatever the reason—be it a combination of the water, the heat from the register, or simply time taking its toll on the delicate paper—while on the phone talking to Philip that night, I discovered the map was faded and completely unreadable.

But that doesn't matter. What matters is that Justin destroyed the map when he believed it led to a fortune. He did it for my sake. And that's worth more to me than all the gold in the world.

Though I've put the past behind me, one thing remains undone. On the crest of a hill in the little town of Lorens stands a picture-postcard church that never held the wedding of Tiffany Hutch. But tomorrow when her daughter walks down the aisle, with a simple white rosary entwined in her bridal bouquet, I know my mother and father will be watching with happy hearts . . . and praying for my future.

About the Author

Therese Heckenkamp, eighteen when she completed the first draft of *Past Suspicion*, has been writing stories since before she could spell. A homeschooled student, she won numerous writing awards while growing up.

Therese lives in Wisconsin with her husband and two children and is currently working on more novels. Her second book, *Frozen Footprints*, is a Christian suspense thriller for readers 16 and up.

Learn more at www.frozen-footprints.com

Therese always welcomes reader feedback and comments.

Visit her online:

Therese's website: www.thereseheckenkamp.com

Facebook: www.facebook.com/therese.heckenkamp

Twitter: www.twitter.com/THeckenkamp

45035654R00181

Made in the USA
San Bernardino, CA
30 January 2017